ϕ/R8

1√ 4/97

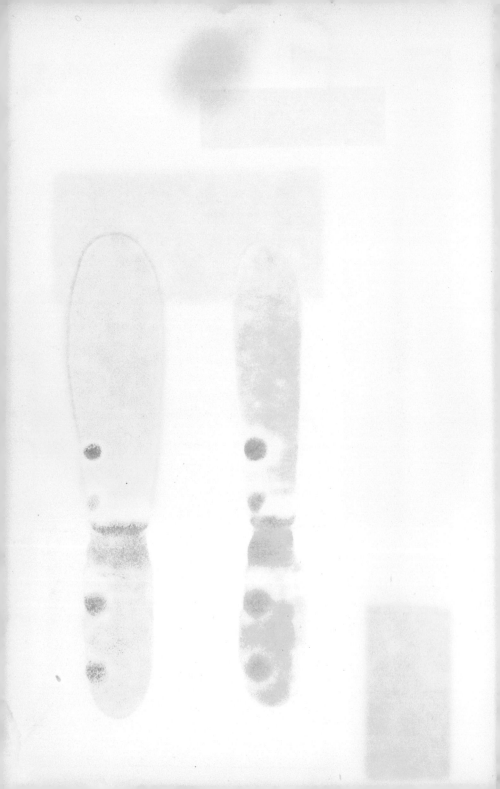

Bright Young Things

Bright Young Things

JOSEPHINE EDGAR

St. Martin's Press
New York

BRIGHT YOUNG THINGS. Copyright © 1986 by Josephine Edgar.
All rights reserved. Printed in the United States of America.
No part of this book may be used or reproduced in any manner
whatsoever without written permission except in the case of
brief quotations embodied in critical articles or reviews. For
information, address St. Martin's Press, 175 Fifth Avenue,
New York, N.Y. 10010.

Library of Congress Cataloging in Publication Data

Edgar, Josephine, 1907-
    Bright young things.

    I. Title.
PR6015.0857B75   1986   823'.912   86-3973
ISBN 0-312-09627-5

First published in Great Britain by Judy Piatkus (Publishers)
Ltd.

First U.S. Edition

10 9 8 7 6 5 4 3 2 1

Dedication

For my sister Ann Hunt and for the beautiful Blossom Law who married Len Harvey, the great British boxing champion, and all the other bright young things who may still be with us to remember that unique and long-ago world, this book is gratefully dedicated.

Bright Young Things

Chapter 1

SPRING 1928

'What is Sir James Peak like?' Helen Redmaine asked her mother over the breakfast table.

She was twenty-three, a tall girl with a coltish grace and simplicity, a touch of the Redmaine arrogance in her sensitive face.

On this March morning she was going up to London to an interview for a job in the studio of the firm of James Peak (Publicity) Ltd.

Her father, the Honourable Alexander Redmaine, had been a brilliant commercial artist, and an associate of Sir James before the war. He had been killed in France on the Somme in 1917, when Helen had been eleven years old. She could just remember her father. He had held a commission as an official war artist, and his grimly humorous and tragic drawings of the men in the hell of the lines had depicted the true nature of the war. It had been an accident. An ammunition truck had skidded into the car in which he had been travelling, killing all the occupants.

Apart from this terrible loss the war had not touched either Helen or her brother Duncan to any great extent. But at twenty-three, she knew money was tight now, and she would have to earn her own living.

She had just completed her course at the local art school. She knew it would be hard to live up to her father's brilliant success. She had never had an interview for a job before. Her mother, remembering the work Sandy had done for James Peak during the war, for which his knighthood had been a

1

recognition, had written to him, and had received an affable but vague reply. It was on the strength of this that Helen had sent in her application. But she did not want her mother to know how very nervous she was.

'James Peak?' Mavis frowned vaguely, buttering the hot slices of toast and piling them on to an old blue Nankin plate. Her husband had once said that everything she touched turned into a still-life, and it was true. The kitchens looked like a sunlit picture by Vermeer, with beautiful china, and the bunch of yellow tulips in a green glass jug. 'Oh, I hardly knew him. He wasn't our sort at all. I suppose he must be well over fifty. A bit vulgar. Very bouncy – gift of the gab.'

Her son Duncan raised his sandy eyebrows and winked at his sister.

'Talks a lot, but doesn't actually say much – Dads found him most amusing. A wily old bugger, Dads used to say.' Mavis had an airy habit of repeating other people's bad language as though she had no idea what it meant. 'Savile Row suits and engraved Christmas cards.'

Duncan shuddered exaggeratedly. 'How low can a man sink?' he cried. He adored his mother and thought her beautiful and slightly nutty. He was twenty-one and very like his father.

'He cheated Dads,' went on Mavis, not vindictively. 'He never paid him for the last commission. It wasn't used until after Dads was killed. So he must have been a wily old . . . what Dads said.'

'Ladies don't say bugger,' Duncan said priggishly.

'Who says?'

'I do. I was told at my prep school. I said my mother did and she's an Hon. and that put them in their place.'

'You were a snobbish little brute,' Mavis said affectionately, 'and *I* didn't say it. It was what Dads said.'

'He's pulling your leg, darling,' Helen said gently.

Duncan rose, unfolding his thin, whippy height. His fair-skinned face was still almost beardless, his curly hair brushed fiercely in an effort to subdue it to a fashionable polish. He would be a very handsome man one day.

He put his arm round his mother's shoulder and she saw the long, bony boy's wrist below the sleeve of his outgrown sports jacket, and sighed.

2

'The day's dole, please,' he said.

She gave him five shillings. 'Where are you going?' she asked anxiously. 'You're not hanging about that film studio again? Dunky darling, you know Uncle Royston would be furious if he knew . . .'

'Well, don't tell him.'

'But we're going there to dinner tonight.'

'What's that got to do with it?' He kissed her, playing the affectionate baby to get his own way. 'Look, I'm meeting Barry Goldman, whose Dad practically owns Greenstreet Studios, they're casting today for *The Fury and the Flame*. It's all about the French Revolution. He said I could watch the screen tests and see the rushes afterwards. It'll be wildly exciting. They might discover a new Garbo. I'll run Helen to the station now, and then I'll get back in time to meet her off the four-thirty and get into my mildewed dinner jacket to be all sweetness and light to Uncle Roy. I won't mention the studio – hope to die! Hurry up, Nell! I'll go and get her started.'

He went out, whistling like a blackbird, and in a few minutes there was the roar of a motor bike engine and the alarmed flutter of white wings from the dovecote outside.

Five shillings was a pittance for a boy of twenty-one who would be Lord Breterton one day – barring accidents and miracles. Mavis's brother-in-law, Royston, the present Lord Breterton, Sandy's elder brother, paid Duncan's university fees and gave him a small allowance during term time. He had paid, grudgingly, for both the children's education. He went on a great deal about the folly of marrying outside one's own class. Duncan and Helen resented this oblique slur on their mother and said so. Mavis did not seem to mind.

Duncan was film mad and his friendship with Barry Goldman had gained him an entry into the Greenstreet Studios, not twenty miles away as the crow flies. Not half an hour away as a motor bike goes. He spent nearly every day of the vacations there and almost every evening at the cinema. His conversation was entirely about camera angles, directors, stars and the advent of sound which he said had certainly come to stay. His dream was to become a director. His room was a library of movie information; he talked movies as other

3

boys talked cricket or girls. He was not a film fan like any normal teenager. The stars were not gods and goddesses of glamour to him. They were the materials the director used to tell his story. His gods were Griffith, de Mille, Lubitsch, Rex Ingram and Chaplin.

Helen came back into the kitchen, wearing a light blue suit, the hem shortened to the fashionable new length, and an emerald green beret on her wavy bobbed light brown hair.

'Duncan needs clothes,' her mother said worriedly. 'And they're expensive. I was going to ask Uncle Roy for an advance. He can be very generous – when he's in a good temper.'

Helen gave a scornful little snort, torn by the anxiety in her mother's beautiful eyes. Uncle Royston was a monster.

'I don't know what I should do if Roy did not help me,' Mavis added worriedly. 'And – film people always seem such riff-raff. You read such frightful things about them. Drugs and divorce, and those awful Hollywood parties.'

'But Greenstreet is not in Hollywood. It's only a few miles away. Dunky's all right, Mums, don't worry.'

'I wouldn't like Uncle Roy to hear about it.'

'Well,' said Helen exactly as Duncan had, 'don't tell him.'

Mavis felt guilty and envious. Duncan and Helen were Sandy's children – Redmaines of the grandiloquent strain, totally unaware of their own charming arrogance. Nothing hidden, no tact. They had not been born into an ordinary family. She worried sick about whether she was doing the best thing for them. Sandy – like Duncan – had loathed the idea that he might one day inherit the title and Ayling Place. He considered the prefix 'Honourable' ridiculous and never used it. During their marriage they had lived a happy successful life among interesting people, rarely visiting Ayling Place or seeing Lord Breterton. The two brothers were worlds apart. Breterton was a childless widower of nearly sixty. It seemed to him that all his brother's disasters had started when he had met and fallen in love with Mavis, then a student at the art school where he had taught painting.

Mavis knew perfectly well that Duncan's allowance would vanish as Helen's had done if it were discovered that he spent all his university vacations at Greenstreet Studios. Correct behaviour, county life, and the right kind of friends were what Uncle Royston expected from his nephew and niece.

Mavis would try to reassure herself. 'I had a lovely marriage; I have wonderful memories; I saw so much of the world. I knew such exciting, creative, famous, talented people. No two people were ever as happy as Sandy and me, and I have two splendid children.'

She told herself this – first thing on waking, in the grey hour of doubts and apprehensions, but sometimes it sounded very hollow. She still wept for her husband, for his sanity and laughter. But Sandy was a handful of smashed bones somewhere in France and she was a woman unused to standing on her own.

An impatient hooting from the front of the house told them Duncan was waiting. Helen tied a scarf over her emerald green beret, and looked doubtfully at her blue suit.

'Do I *look* all right?'

'Oh my darling,' said Mavis rising, 'I am so sorry.'

'What for?'

'That you have to go after this potty job instead of doing all the things Dads and I planned for you.'

'Oh, stuff!'

'He was going to send you to Paris and Rome.'

'Mummy, *please* forget all that.'

'Maybe there's something we could sell.' Mavis glanced round the kitchen hopefully.

'If we sell anything else we'll be eating on the floor!'

The hooting became imperative. Helen picked up her portfolio.

'Don't you worry about Duncan, Mums. *Or* about me.' She kissed her mother as though she were kissing an anxious child. 'And *don't* look like that, I *won't* reconsider Uncle Roy's offer.' Lord Breterton had offered to finance a 'season' complete with presentation at Court and inexpensive ball. Helen had refused. 'If he wasn't such a reactionary old skinflint he'd give me the money anyway. Remember Dads used to say, "Never put strings on a gift". 'Bye now, darling.'

She went shooting off through the sunlit hall, swift and graceful as a swallow, and climbed into the sidecar of the secondhand motor bike, the pride of Duncan's heart, bought

5

with saving and sacrifice and a host of menial holiday jobs. Scarved and goggled, a leather helmet pulled down over his ears, he was waiting impatiently. Mavis, shading her eyes from the low morning sunlight, waved to them until they were out of sight.

The garden looked beautiful, glittering with last night's rain, the mill-stream wound away beneath the tall railway viaduct across which Helen's train would chug on its way to London. Daffodils were everywhere in the grass.

Sandy had loved the viaduct. It was one of the reasons why they had bought the house. She remembered all the pictures he had done of it, striding across the valley, sending long arched shadows across the garden at sunset. He had painted so many fine pictures of it, and they had been bought by galleries across the world. That had been before the war.

An old De Dion Bouton came trundling out of the stable gate on to the gravel forecourt, reminding her that it was a working day. Lady Millicent Dermott, a spinster cousin of Sandy's, her partner in the wool shop, and her tenant, occupying a flat over the garage in what had once been the coach-house, was at the wheel.

She was a square, middle-aged lady wearing a large, battered felt hat and an ancient Burberry raincoat, always prepared for the worst of the English weather. She was surrounded by baskets and bags stuffed with wools and wool samples and knitting patterns. She was the manufacturing half of the business; Mavis, who had trained in fashion design, was the designer and saleswoman. Beside wool and silks and general craft supplies, they also sold beautiful woollen garments. The shop at the gates of Ayling Place was only open in the tourist season, Easter to the end of September. They designed and knitted for next season during the winter with the aid of one or two local home workers. They were preparing for their spring opening.

'Aren't you ready?' Cousin Millicent called impatiently. She adored Mavis – and she had also adored Sandy. The children were, in a way, her children too. 'Hurry up, hurry up,' she called. 'We've travellers coming this morning.'

'Coming, coming!' Mavis hurried into the house and presently came out again, wearing a long, warm cardigan with a cosy scarf collar in pale coral coloured wool. Her hat was crocheted in white and trimmed with one coral coloured rose. Millicent sighed at her perfection – but Mavis, she thought, would have looked beautiful in a potato sack.

She locked the door and climbed into the car. It had large carriage lamps, and everything on it seemed to be made of brass including a brake shaft like a signalman's handle. It steamed merrily up hills, but was so heavy it needed a strong hand going down. Millicent drove it with great bravura and kept it gleamingly polished. It was painted green and gold and reminded one of a tin of golden syrup.

'Heard the kids go off on that damned motor bike,' said Millicent, negotiating the turn into the lane, and stopping while Mavis nipped out and shut the garden gate. 'Where were they off to?'

'Well, Nell's off to town after a job.'

'Job?'

'Yes. In Sir James Peak's firm. She wrote to him. In the studio.'

'The war advertising chap Sandy worked for?'

'Yes.'

'She turned down Royston's offer of a season, then?'

'I'm afraid she did,' Mavis began doubtfully.

'Good for her. Told old Roy to put his money where the monkey puts the nuts, I hope,' said Millicent with pleasure. 'Where's young Dunky going then?'

'He's dropping Helen at the station. Then – he's going to see a friend.' She did not tell Millicent about the Greenstreet Studios and Barry Goldman.

'Keeping out of mischief, eh? Good lad. He's getting nearly as good-looking as his dear father,' said Millicent, implying that no one could possibly be that. 'Will he earn anything?'

'Well, I hope so,' Mavis said doubtfully.

They drove through the lane to Ayling which was a large market town, or a small cathedral city – or one might say a small town with a large and venerable minster, which had been of considerable religious importance back in the dim mists of history, but now, apart from a station and its weekly cattle market and a cinema called The Grand Biograph containing about two hundred seats, Ayling held little interest to

7

the general public. Duncan had caught the cinema fever there from the Saturday children's matinées. And there was, of course, Ayling Place.

Ayling Place was some five miles outside Ayling. It was open to the public in the summer and its grounds were popular with picnickers, for it was only an hour's run from Marylebone.

The shop owned by the cousins was just outside the ornate wrought iron gates of the great house. *Millicent et Mavis.* There was a snob appeal locally in buying one's woollies from Lord Breterton's cousin and sister-in-law – like eating Sandringham lamb.

Millicent squeezed the De Dion through a narrow carriage entrance at the side of the shop, oak beamed and picturesque and very inconvenient, produced a medieval looking iron key and unlocked the side door.

'Nell will have to find digs in London,' she said. 'It's not economical to travel up every day.'

'Oh no!' Mavis cried in horror. 'Nell's so young. I *can't* let her live alone in London!'

'My dear girl,' said Millicent, with all the confidence of a woman who has never been a temptation to any man, 'she's twenty-three. Don't be ridiculous. There are hundreds of young gels living alone in London. Find her a good hostel.'

Driving to the station, Duncan was saying to Helen, 'You'll have to live in London during the week if you get this job! Have you thought about that?'

'Not yet.'

'You don't want to get into one of those young ladies' hostels with no gentlemen friends and the front door locked at ten-thirty. Might as well be in reform school.'

'I don't want to, but digs are difficult. You don't have to worry about that at Oxford.'

He did not reply.

'You're not thinking of flunking out?' she said in alarm.

'I'm just thinking,' he said mysteriously.

The train could be heard a quarter of a mile away. She took her portfolio out of the sidecar, and Duncan revved up the bike, calling over the sound of the engine, 'The best of British luck, old thing!' and roared off in the direction of Green-street. Helen bought her return ticket and went thoughtfully on to the platform. He *wouldn't,* she thought. Then, well, he *might*! There was no knowing what Duncan might do.

Captain William Hyde-Seymour, known as 'Willy', ran down the steps of the cheap lodging house behind Waterloo Station – a bleak, clean place, for single men only. His beautifully tailored suit was brushed and pressed, his shoes gleamed with a military shine, his regimental tie was perfectly knotted, his bowler was at the correct Guards Officer angle, although in fact he had been in the infantry, O. C. Transport.

He went across Hungerford Bridge at a smart pace. When he had first been demobilised he had been surprised and happy just to be alive, but now he had become used to it. He was thirty-one, good-looking and totally untrained for any-thing except soldiering – he had gone straight into the army from school.

He had invested part of his gratuity in good clothes and for a short while had enjoyed himself in the hectic gaiety of post-war London. He had been an extra in films, a car salesman until he had borrowed a showroom model once too often, a dancing partner, a brush salesman, and now he was running a street band. It was made up of ex-service men and they were waiting for him under the arches of Villiers Street, a neat, shabby-smart group, blowing short riffs and phrases on their instruments, locked even at this chilly morning hour, in the intimacy of sound that only musicians know. He noticed one of them was missing – the clarinettist. As the jazz epi-demic spread through the night clubs the boys who played the new music were getting jobs. If one more went they wouldn't have a band. Willy was the organiser – he was tone deaf.

'Good morning, boys. Where's Tom?'

'Got a job,' the drummer said. 'Night club. Two quid a week and free beer.'

'Good luck to him,' Willy said. He envied the musicians. They were all so sure of what they wanted to do. 'Right, we'd better get started – where's the box?'

One of them handed him a wooden collecting box painted in red-white-and-blue, and the words 'Ex-Servicemen' in large letters, and they went up Villiers Street to the Strand. A couple of policemen stood at the corner and one of them winked as Willy gave them a courteous good-morning, and said, 'Watch it, Captain.' They could not touch them so long as they kept moving.

'Right,' said Willy. 'Straight up as far as the Aldwych, then come back to Trafalgar Square and through the West End before lunch. Piccadilly and Park Lane.' He found the rich were always generous at meal times. 'Let's get started before those Welsh buggers arrive.'

The London busking scene was being invaded by choirs of out-of-work miners from the Welsh pits. They sang like angels and, white-faced and shabby, stirred the conscience of prosperous London. Ex-servicemen had lost their novelty.

They set off towards the City, marching along the gutter, blasting gaily into Colonel Bogey, breaking it up into a swinging jazz rhythm. They marched in single file. It was hell on boots. Willy went slightly ahead, rattling his box. Office girls, beguiled by his frank blue eyes, delved into their handbags. Men mostly ignored him, and one said rudely, 'Isn't it about time you got a proper job?' To which Willy replied, 'Have you one you can offer me then, sir?' The men who spoke like this were always too old to have been in the trenches.

Last year the band had done extremely well. Armistice Day they had taken twenty-five pounds. But now depression was beginning to bite and people were sick of the war.

Willy wanted a chance to get in somewhere where he could screw a future out of life, and he had only one thing to sell – his own personality. He was already past thirty – he sometimes got into a sweat about that.

He saw Sir James Peak walking jauntily along towards Kingsway. He recognised him because Sir James was adept at getting his face into newspapers. It was one of Willy's tricks to recognise celebrities by name, it was a sure touch.

He set off after the rather corpulent, superbly tailored figure in the pearl grey suit, a grey Homburg set at an angle on his thick, waving silver-grey hair. Sir James had a strutting, very confident walk. William drew alongside, saluted, rattled

10

his box, bade him good morning. 'Remember the ex-service chaps, Sir James?'

Peak stopped, his dark, protuberant eyes glared suspiciously. 'Congratulations on your knighthood, sir. I read about it in *The Times*.'

Peak was surprised and pleased. He liked recognition. The medal ribbons did not impress him – he was besieged by ex-officers wanting jobs. Friends of friends, sons of friends – none of them any use to him. But it was smart of the chap to recognise him. He acknowledged a fellow opportunist and put half-a-crown in the collecting box.

'Can't you find anything better than this, heh?' he demanded.

He took a cigar from a heavy leather case, clipped it and Willy instantly had a light ready for him, his blue eyes searching the heavy jowled face. Peak had a slight American accent and he smoked cigars like an American – Willy noticed with faint disgust the set brown gob he discarded in the gutter.

'The band has been a good thing,' he said, airily, 'and,' he grinned, '*no* taxes.' Sir James's eyes twinkled appreciatively. He was drawn to the young ex-officer – something buccaneering about him. 'But it's finished now. I'm looking for something else.'

'As what?'

'That's it, sir. All I know is soldiering.'

Sir James restrained himself from questioning. He had a weakness for taking a chance with people – the trouble was getting rid of them if they proved useless.

'Well, good luck to you,' he said turning away.

'Thank you, sir. I am lucky. I was lucky to get out of France in one piece.' He tagged alongside Sir James. How to crack him? Sentiment? Conscience? 'A lot of better chaps ended up on the wire.'

It hit home – it usually did. James Peak had made money and a successful business while a generation of younger men were being slaughtered. He had no sons. It did not keep him awake at nights – but it sometimes caused him unease.

'Give me a ring some time,' he said rashly, immediately wishing he had kept his mouth shut, 'I may hear of something.'

11

'William Hyde-Seymour,' said Willy quickly, producing a card. 'It's extremely good of you, sir. I'll take you up on that.'

He crossed the road and rejoined the band as they marched off westward tearing away at the swinging *paso doble* rhythm of *Valencia*. Land of orange groves and bloody sweet content. Wearing his feet out on the London pavements in all weathers. De-dum-de-dum-de-dum! He was sick of the whole thing. He would certainly telephone Sir James Peak.

Matthew Wilson, Sir James's studio manager stood on the traffic refuge in the Strand at the junction with Wellington Street. He saw Sir James's jaunty back ahead and hung back, for Sir James was a stickler for time-keeping and Matt was in no mood to listen to him going on about punctuality. He noticed Helen Redmaine running up the Aldwych towards Kingsway with her portfolio beneath her arm, and her long-limbed grace gave him a pang of delight as though a beautiful bird or a swift young deer had crossed his vision and his dark, sardonic face lit for a moment with sheer pleasure. Sir James was safely out of sight now, so he crossed to the pavement and went on towards the office.

The studio at Peak's was a long light room on the first floor of the building, level with the tops of the plane trees that grew along Kingsway. His own office was a glass-partitioned rabbit hutch at the far end – he could keep an eye on the studio and its staff of two experienced commercial artists and four juniors.

He took off his jacket and put on his overall, rolled up his sleeves and looked morosely at the drawing he had left on the board the night before.

It showed a house taken from the hideous photographs Medway had supplied of buildings roofed with their tiles. They seemed to be used only for the dreariest type of cheap semi-detached which were now being ribbon-built in the outer suburbs of London. The front garden fence was made up of white elongated letters reading, MEDWAY TILES – KEEP THE HOME DRY AND THE FAMILY HAPPY. This was the brain-child of Mr Thomas Medway, the Advertising Manager of the company. It looked ridiculous, but he had insisted that the idea was used. There also had to be a HAPPY FAMILY of at least four people worked in somewhere. Mother, father, two children, one of each sex, gazing at the house with expressions of astonished rapture.

He drew in a girl running up the path, flicked in the light brown hair, the emerald green beret, the blue suit, the long exquisite legs, ankles fine as an antelope's, and smiled.

Did you not see my lady
    Go down the garden singing?

He ran the path to vanishing point, and with a brush of rose colour and green indicated a distant garden heavy with bloom.

Where'er you walk,
    Cool gales shall fan the glade.
Trees, where you sit,
    Shall crowd into a shade.

He drew in a tree casting a heavy shade in bright sunlight.

He scratched the tip of his nose and grinned, unpinned the drawing and put it aside, and on a new sheet traced out the ugly house again, drew in the goggle-eyed Medway family gazing at their scarlet roof. But as he worked he glanced occasionally at the running girl. She had been so swift and lovely and young.

Helen was waiting in Reception to be summoned to Sir James's office. She looked through the magazine laid out on the table showing examples of Peak's advertising, and found them uninspiring. Few luxury products. No women's advertising. No furs, or famous soaps or perfumes. None of the goods advertised with beautiful paintings by people like Kirchener or Edmund Dulac or Baribal. The sort of high-class work her father had excelled in. She wondered why.

After a few minutes another girl came in and sat down opposite her. She was so incredibly smart and beautiful that Helen decided she must be an actress or a model. Not very tall

13

but exquisitely proportioned. When she swung one silk-clad leg over the other and raised her chin to examine her make-up in the tiny mirror of her gold compact every movement was deliciously and deliberately provocative. Her big eyes were an incredible colour, like aquamarines, like sea-water, and they were fringed by long expertly mascaraed lashes.

The flat waves of hair beneath her chic scarlet hat were pale gold. Her mouth was like a cupid's bow, the lower lip full, soft and tempting, was as vividly red as her hat. She wore a black and white check suit with a long jacket and a very short skirt and a red carnation in her lapel. On one wrist she wore a small diamond and platinum watch, and on the other a moiré strap with the words BOOTS in diamonds and platinum. She looked up, met Helen's fascinated eyes, and asked coolly, 'Got a smut on me nose, then?'

'I'm so sorry,' the colour flushed up Helen's cheeks, 'I didn't mean to be rude.' Then frankly envious, she said, 'That is *the* most beautiful suit!'

The girl snapped her compact shut and put it away, apparently mollified. 'Well, ta very much,' she said, 'at six quid it should be. I got it secondhand at a posh slop-shop in Sloane Street.'

Helen felt her blue suit and crocheted beret unutterably dowdy by comparison.

'My name's Helen Redmaine. I've come after a job.' She held out her hand. The other girl looked surprised, then put hers into it. It was absurd but Helen felt it was momentous.

'Me too,' said the girl in the red hat. 'My name's Lillian Skinner. But everyone calls me Boots.' She waited, then explained, 'It's a joke, see?'

'Boots? Oh,' light dawned, 'Lilley & Skinner? The shoe shops?'

'Yeah. Silly, isn't it?' She thrust out the slender wrist with the moiré strap and the word 'Boots' in diamonds. 'My chief boyfriend gave me this. Well, it breaks the ice. Makes people laugh. Stuck to me since my first job.'

'Were you on the stage?'

'No,' said Boots with a touch of resentment. 'I wanted to – but it's no good without training, and it costs money to train. My dad said he'd have the hide off me and all stage girls are

14

tarts. Much he knows about anything but beer and dog-racing, and he doesn't know much about that, the money he loses. I've left home now, so he can't say nothing.'

Helen was enthralled. Boots was like a girl out of a novel by Gilbert Frankau; looking like a photo from *The Tatler*, sounding like a girl on a market stall.

'What sort of job do you want?'

'Well, now I'm working at Benjie's Club in Swallow Yard off Bond Street. Hostess. Not bad. Five bob a week for clothes and a percentage on the drinks. Tips from dance partners. *And* you get the day off. No future in it, of course. My chief boyfriend doesn't like me working there.'

'Why not?'

'He's mad jealous. I mean, he picked me up there, so he thinks I might find another chap.' She opened her eyes with a kitten stare of innocence, and added, 'Well a girl has to look out for herself.'

Helen had never had such an intimate conversation on so slight an acquaintance. She felt laughter rising, but a warmth as well.

'You call him your *chief* boyfriend. Are there some – well, lesser ones, then?'

'Oh yes,' Boots said practically, 'of course.'

'And he doesn't know?'

'No fear. He'd have me guts for garters. Nor do they.'

Boots looked at Helen and Helen looked at Boots – cool brook green into sea-coloured pools of innocence. 'I think you're pulling my leg,' Helen said, and they both burst out laughing.

'No,' Boots said, shaking her head, a-bubble with laughter. '*Really*. It's tricky, but it works.'

'Are you in love with this chief boyfriend?'

'No! He's old – must be forty. Lots of dough. I've only to say something's pretty and he gets it for me!' She fingered her diamond watch with pleasure. 'He thinks a nice little job in an office would occupy my mind and keep me out of mischief – I ask you!' She and Helen collapsed into giggles again. 'Anyway, he's a friend of Sir James, and his name is Tommy Medway, and he's asked Sir James to find me something to do. Tommy's away a lot, selling tiles, I suppose. He's going to

15

America soon and he wants me settled in something safe before he goes. He said he can't find me a job in his own office on account of his father being Chairman.'

'Well, I suppose it might be awkward.'

'Yes. And his wife might hear about it. She's in society. Anyway, Sir James said he'd see what he could do, and Tommy's one of his best clients – so, here I am.'

'I'm jolly glad,' said Helen. 'I hope you get the job.'

'I hope you do too.' Both the girls were aware of an instant liking. Something to do with mutual independence and irreverence; something to do with starting out in a difficult but usually comic world.

'What's he like – this Peak?'

'My mother says he's sort of bouncy. She also said my father – my father was killed in the war – said he was a wily old bugger.'

'I'm sorry about your old man, if you liked him.' She looked round critically. 'It looks dead boring here to me.' She yawned, delicately like a cat. 'What kind of a job did you say you wanted?'

'In the studio – commercial artist.'

The big eyes were impressed. 'I reckon it's wonderful to be able to *do* something. Now, I can't do anything, not really.'

'Except look stunning and make people laugh.'

'Well, thanks, but that's not what I mean. Something you're born with. It's what you get out of what you're born with that counts. I don't seem to have nothing to work on . . .' She suddenly switched the subject as though it was a little painful. 'Do you live in London?'

'I'll have to if I get this job. Do you?'

'Yes. Always have. Born here!'

'Alone?'

'I've a room in this big old house in Pimlico. Use of bath. It's mostly let in single rooms. Belongs to people called Murphy, cheap – but not all that clean. Not dirty, but not clean, if you get it. I'll have a look out for you if you like.'

'Would you, that's most awfully good of you.'

'It's nothing. I'd be glad to.' Boots gave her warm endearing smile. 'You're nice, I think. Ever so posh but nice. Most posh people try to put me down.'

Helen giggled. 'I bet they don't succeed,' she said.

16

Boots produced a diary in real Morocco leather and a small gilt pencil. 'Give us your phone number – I'll give you a ring if I hear of anything.' She took down the address and telephone number and extracted an embossed card from a pocket in the diary, which read *Miss Lillian Skinner, 3, Becker Street, SW1*. 'Give me a ring if you get the job.'

'I will, and thank you. I hope you get the job.'

Boots stuck her tongue in her cheek. 'I will,' she said, 'if I want it.'

A neat woman of about thirty in navy blue with white collar and cuffs, with an air of laundered discretion, came in. She carried a notebook and pencil.

'Miss Redmaine?'

Helen stood up and picked up her portfolio.

'Sir James will see you now. Miss Skinner?' She looked at Boots with a faintly disapproving air.

Boots consulted her glittering watch.

'Will you tell Sir James that I've an appointment with Mr Medway at twelve, at the Savoy Grill. I have to get my nails done first, so I can't wait long. We're having an early lunch and going to the races.'

She snapped open her compact and examined her red lips with concentrated indifference. Her voice had been ferociously upper crust. The secretary was visibly undermined.

'I will tell Sir James at once, Miss Skinner.'

'You do that, ducky,' said Boots, and she drooped one eyelid at Helen as she passed.

The idea of working at James Peak (Publicity) Ltd had acquired unexpected dimensions of glamour and adventure. A very different life to the Mill Cottage and a provincial art school. With people like Boots Skinner about *anything* might happen.

The secretary escorted Helen to a large, expensively furnished office overlooking Kingsway, where she was asked to wait. The carpets were thick, the mahogany desk enormous. It was furnished with a spotless blotter, an elaborate cut-glass inkstand and pen tray with some highly sharpened pencils, and a large Lalique ashtray containing a cigar-butt which the secretary whisked away into a waste basket. The most positive and beautiful things in the room were the originals of her father's splendid wartime posters, all in blocks of solid colour, small captions of large letters, and strong design, each of them with an instant individual message. The last one, in grey and black and white, with the gaunt silhouettes caught in the barbed-wire against white moonlight was particularly dramatic.

On the desk there was a photograph of a handsome dark-haired woman in a glittering evening dress, the hard lines of her jaw softened by misty re-touching, one of of a dumpy girl in an unbecoming organdie dress. There was also a large bowl of fresh hothouse flowers and on the wall a bad portrait of a man in a pale grey suit, with a pearl tiepin, silvery grey hair and a pugnacious stare. The wily old bugger, she presumed, and at that moment Sir James came bounding in, cigar in one hand, exuding an air of urgent efficiency.

He carried a sheaf of advertisement pulls and, grabbing up one of the telephones on his desk, shouted, 'Come in here, Peggy!' His secretary shot into the room her face pinkly anxious.

'Clear the desk, Peggy. Take away those damned flowers. Tell Mr Crowley I want to see him about the position booked for Drayton's tyres in next week's *Express* in five minutes. Didn't we state next matter? We're paying for that and next matter it has to be.' His protuberant dark eyes rested on Helen as though he had just seen her. 'Who's this?' he demanded.

'Miss Helen Redmaine, Sir James,' said Peggy apologetically, 'about the studio position. And there's a Miss Skinner waiting to see you too.' She told him about the Savoy Grill and the race meeting.

'Skinner? Oh yes, blast it! Tommy Medway's little piece.' He had promised to find her a job and keep an eye on her while Medway was away. He must have been crazy. But Medways were important clients, and it paid him to put Tommy in a position of obligation. His old man virtually owned the company.

'Ask her not to wait. Tell her I'll phone Mr Medway at the office and perhaps they could have an early lunch with me. Twelve-thirty at the Savoy. Then get Medway on the telephone and fix it with him.'

18

When Peggy had left the room he gave Helen a surprisingly disarming smile, and held out his hand.

'Sit down, my dear. I had your letter. You're very like your father.'

Helen sat down.

'So you want a job in the studio?' The sharp dark eyes looked up from the letter. 'I thought a young lady like you would be coming out? Presented at Court, and that sort of thing? I've a girl of my own coming up to it soon.' He indicated the photograph of the dumpy girl in frilled organdie.

'Mum's family wanted me to,' said Helen, 'but I went to art school instead. It's a lot of tosh, I think.'

The girl was astonishingly like her father. He could remember Sandy Redmaine and his young wife very well. A handsome couple with an airy indifference to the conventional social round – all the things other people schemed like the devil to achieve, they seemed to find slightly hilarious. He remembered, slaving away in his first small office off Ludgate Hill, envying them, their obvious passion for each other, Sandy's brilliant talent, and their free Bohemian life.

'Dads had planned for me to study in Paris when I finished at the local art school, but we can't afford that now. I wrote to you first because he worked for you, so I knew your studio must be good.'

'You mean there's no money?'

'There's a bit. The house – and what Mum earns, and the bit of capital he had invested. He had no pension – he was an official war artist, not a combatant. But Duncan had to be seen through school – and university. And I haven't started.'

'Your mother has a job?'

'She's in business – with her cousin, Lady Millicent Dermott. They make a living out of it.'

'Your father wasn't very provident.'

'Well, he didn't expect to die at thirty-nine,' Helen said defensively. 'We always had a lovely time. He was a happy hedonist.' Sir James looked blank. 'He believed that life was meant to be enjoyed,' she explained. 'It was his philosophy.'

'Quite, quite,' Peak said testily. He hated being out of his depth. 'But it was foolhardy to go to France when there

19

was no need. He was over age. He was doing work of national importance. Things were going splendidly – for both of us.'

'Well, he didn't see it that way,' she began belligerently, and then remembered that she had come to get a job, and a future employer had to be pleased not argued with. She said quickly, 'I've brought my portfolio if you'd like to see it. I have my Diploma for painting, but I've no experience of commercial art. But of course, if you feel I'm not right for the job, I do understand . . .'

'Wait.' He had remembered, uncomfortably, that he had not paid Redmaine for the final poster of his commission, which had not been used until after his death. 'I tell you what, you go along and see my studio manager Matt Wilson. If he feels he can use you, that's OK.'

Helen flushed and her eyes brightened gratefully.

'It's awfully good of you, Sir James.'

'That's all right my dear.' He felt the pleasant glow of a good deed and rang for his secretary. 'Peggy, take Miss Redmaine through to Mr Wilson's office. Has Miss Skinner gone?'

'Yes, Sir James. I got through to Mr Medway and he said they would be delighted to meet you for lunch.'

'Right. Book me a table for three.' He shook Helen's hand. 'Remember me to your mother. Perhaps she would like to have tea with my wife one day?'

Helen gave a puzzled little nod and a murmur of thanks and followed the secretary out. Why on earth should Sir James suddenly ask Mums to tea? Was it that Hon. thing again? Or the mention of Cousin Millicent? She remembered the misty photograph of Lady Peak in her Vionnet evening dress and Cousin Millicent in her ancient Burberry and weather-stained floppy hat, and tried to imagine them hob-nobbing over tea. It was not easy.

The telephone rang in Matt Wilson's office.

'Oh, Wilson,' said Sir James, 'I'm sending in a kid called Helen Redmaine. Sandy Redmaine's daughter – I think you knew him?'

'Yes, indeed.'

'I'd like to help her – I think they're hard-up, well you know

20

what the Honourable Sandy was with money. We could take her on as a junior in the studio. If she's any good. Two pounds a week? OK. I'll leave it to you.'

He rang off and Matt threw down his brush. It had taken him three cups of coffee and several cigarettes to get going on the Medway project. The sketch looked like a particularly unattractive fire station. He did not want another studio junior, especially a girl. And he particularly did not want to stop his work to interview her.

Sir James was always taking on young women who were completely untrained. Usually girlfriends, poor relations or ex-mistresses of business friends. It was a temporary measure to keep them out of mischief. He supposed this one was another pipsqueak of a sub-deb – though he remembered Sandy Redmaine as a fine artist and a nice man. Then he saw that the girl who was following Peggy Prior through the studio was the one he had seen in the Aldwych, the one with the emerald green beret and long, delectable legs.

He was disconcerted. She had been a glimpse of spring beauty never to be seen again, and it was as though an almond blossom tree had sprung up through the linoleum on the office floor.

Peggy Prior made a brief introduction and left. Helen saw a tall dark, unsmiling man with a slightly receding hairline, remote grey eyes and an expression of acute irritation.

'I'm sorry,' she faltered, 'if it's inconvenient.'

'Every interruption of work is inconvenient,' he snapped. 'Sir James has no idea that creative work takes time.'

Whoops – a prig! Careful. Remember you need a job. Be tactful. She fixed a grave glance on the roughed out advertisement on his drawing board, and he managed not to laugh at her expression.

'What do you think of that?' he challenged.

'Oh, well, er . . .' she flushed an exquisite pink.

'Go on. Say what you think.'

'The roof's too red. Or the wrong red.'

'Looks like a fire station?'

'Yes. And who wants to live in a fire station?'

'Quite.' He sounded just as irritable as he looked. 'The whole point of these abysmally hideous tiles is that they never

21

fade or lose colour with wear.' He took one out of a box on the table, and handed it to her. 'So how would you make them attractive? How would you depict this product in an advertisement which would make it irresistible to the prospective customer?'

He did not laugh. He made her feel as though she was back at art school.

She said cautiously, 'Put in a sunset light. Red sky at night. So it looks like an after-glow?'

She caught an unexpected gleam of hilarity, but the voice sounded just as edgy.

'Very devious. How about having a volcanic eruption in the front garden? Sit down, sit down. Put that thing down.'

He whipped the portfolio away from her and put it on the table. She felt the threat of angry tears. Matt saw the colour rise again in her cheeks. He supposed most men would see a tall streak of a girl, with a clear upper crust voice, reddish brown hair, and a delicious high-bridged little nose. Like a well-bred, snooty, golden eaglet. Nice but shabby clothes. He found her utterly beautiful. He thought of Bonnard endlessly painting his wife. There were some women who, every time they moved, challenged the imagination. Something he had learned to be wary of. He sat on the edge of the table and scowled at her.

'You've no experience?'

'No.'

'Training?'

'I was at art school until recently. I took my Diploma.'

'In what?'

'Painting.'

'Not commercial art?'

'No.'

'Oh.'

What a pure, broad forehead she had. What a full, soft mouth. And the colouring glintingly fair. To paint a face like that would be sheer delight. She was sitting on the edge of the hard office chair, tense with anxiety.

'Aren't you going to bother?' she blurted out.

'Bother?'

'To look at my work?'

22

'Oh. Oh that!' Helen's cheeks were red with repressed temper and disappointed tears. 'Oh yes, of course.' He turned with relief to the portfolio, undid the strings, and began to turn the drawings and water-colours over rapidly. It was typical art school stuff, unsophisticated but basically very good. She had it in her to be a good painter one day. Particularly the line drawings and pen and ink washes, full of contrast and movement.

'It's good,' he said brusquely, 'but not much use to us here. A good knowledge of lettering would be a more useful asset.'

'Couldn't I learn that?'

'Aye, you could.' He turned and caught what he thought was a burst of nervous laughter, quickly suppressed. 'Have I said something amusing?'

'You're scaring the hell out of me,' she said, and he realised she was on the verge of tears. 'I don't know whether you expect me to laugh or cry.'

'For Christ's sake don't cry,' he said in alarm. He glanced apprehensively out into the studio, 'They'll think I'm making indecent suggestions.'

She gave an eruptive sound, laughter and tears struggling for supremacy. 'I've never applied for a job before. I can't help it if Sir James knew my father and is doing me a favour. I *need* favours. I need this job. I expect to learn here . . .' She looked down at the house with the scarlet roof, and added, 'Well, I hope to learn *something* . . .'

He began to laugh, and his face, crinkled with amusement, was so charming that she wondered why he had been so horrid. She smiled tentatively in return, as though she was offering a titbit to a tiger, afraid of the defensive snap and snarl. He looked appreciatively at the drawing on the board.

'It's awful, isn't it?' Before she could reply he showed her some photographs of dreary looking houses with Medway roofs. 'This is what they send us. This is what we have to make look irresistible. We have to put in the fence of white lettering – Mr Thomas Medway insists upon it. The slogan was his brain child.' Helen guessed this Mr Medway must be Boots's number one boyfriend. 'The admiring family has to be worked in – all four of them. All blond and British. And there has to be room for the copy.'

23

'Copy?'

'That's the most important thing of all. Telling the world what a wonderful thing it is to have your roof made with Medway tiles. Whatever you design is only to illustrate the copy. Here the copywriter is King. The artist is just around to support him.'

She thought this over.

'But Dad's work wasn't like that. In those war posters there was only a line of copy, and he thought that up himself.'

'Ah *but* . . .' Matt pointed a challenging forefinger at her. '*He* wasn't working for James Peak. Only *through* him. He was working for the Ministry. And everyone knew he was the best in the business. They conferred directly with him. No longer. The war is over. The client confers with Jimmy Peak, and he confers with his copywriters and what we have to draw in this benighted studio is what those illiterate apes choose to tell us!'

'Dad said that the war posters were telling people the truth but that advertising was selling dreams.'

'Yes.' He picked up a proof from the table, a small advertisement for a ceramic firm, depicting a water closet. 'Well, young lady, what kind of a dream could you make of this?'

Her chin came out rebelliously. 'I could make a better drawing,' she said, 'that wouldn't be difficult.' The silence lengthened. 'Look, you don't have to take me on if you don't want to.'

'The youngster who did that left last month. So far he has not been replaced. That's what you'd do here at first. The small, boring, regular, mildly profitable accounts. Your work is charming and imaginative. Why do you want to work here?'

'I just want to earn some money.'

'You won't earn much. You *could* get a post-graduate course. At a decent college.'

Her cheeks burned with the difficulty of making him understand. 'I've got to start living my life and that means earning money. I'm just twenty-three and all I've ever known is home, school and Ayling Arts and Crafts School. I've got to help. I can't afford just to study. I hope that one day I'll exhibit and sell pictures. Dads wasn't ashamed of being commercial. Are you?'

24

He gave her a long, angry look and then, unexpectedly, smiled – a sweet pained smile, as though it hurt him.

'Not really. I need the money too. Forget what I've said. Can you start next month? That'll be . . . mm . . . on the twelfth?' He consulted a wall calendar. 'Sir James said two pounds a week. That's more than he usually pays for a beginner.'

'Oh, yes, thank you.' Her eyes lit gratefully.

'I'd see about taking some extra classes in lettering. You'll learn tracing and layout here.'

'Thank you,' she said again. Her heart was racing. She had actually got a job. Confidence flowed back into her and she glowed.

'Well, that's it,' he said briskly.

She gathered her drawings into her portfolio and fastened it, and in doing so knocked the original sketch of the Medway drawing on the floor. The same aggressively tiled roof, the same slogan worked into the white garden fence, but running joyously up the path, flicked in with assured brilliance, the long-legged, running girl in the emerald green beret.

'Why, that's me,' she exclaimed, and realised he was stiff with embarrassment. 'Well, it looks like me.'

'I sometimes jot down impressions. I happened to see you running up the Aldwych. I'd no idea, of course . . .'

'That I was coming for the job? Of course.' He relaxed. 'It's awfully good,' she said wistfully. 'Are you going to use it?'

'No. The instructions are a typically English family. Pa, Ma, and two kids. One of each sex. No dryads.'

The bosky-green eyes looked up at him, startled, and the colour rushed up her cheeks at the expression in his eyes. Was he trying to flirt with her? A man so old? At least thirty-five. Her excitement increased. He picked up the sketch from the floor and regarded it morosely.

'I'll bet Dad would have made use of it,' she said, 'It's so beautiful.' She flushed. 'The picture, I mean, not me.'

The harsh face swung towards her, warm with amusement. 'Why not? You are a beautiful child.' Her nose went up, she tried to freeze him out, but her eyes glinted with mischief. 'Would you like the sketch?'

'Really?'

25

'Of course – if you want it.'

'I'd love it. Thank you.'

'Well, I'll see you on the twelfth – goodbye, Miss Redmaine.'

'Goodbye and thanks again.' She picked up her portfolio and escaped. More seemed to have happened in the past two hours than had happened in her entire life. She had met a gorgeous, funny, and perhaps immoral girl. She supposed Boots was what people called a gold digger. But what fun she *was*! She had talked to the great and bouncy and wily Sir James Peak, who had given her a job, and Mr Matthew Wilson, studio manager to Peak, had told her she was beautiful. Out in the sunshine of Kingsway she gave a little skip of triumph before flying down towards the Strand.

There were one or two things that she would not tell her mother – about Boots, for instance and her offer to find her a room. Or the look in Mr Wilson's dark eyes when he had stopped being horrid and had been so very sweet.

Matt Wilson watched her from his office window and laughed at her triumphant skip. She would be bored out of her young mind within a month. Or she would slog away at it and it would destroy any spontaneity her present work possessed. But – she wanted the job.

They all wanted something – the girls who came to work in the office these days – before the war they had been different. It was as though the war had blown open a cage of predatory butterflies.

If it had not happened Helen Redmaine would still be a sheltered young lady comfortably provided for by a very successful father. But over nine hundred thousand fathers and prospective husbands had been killed.

So the girls put their wares in the window, shortened their skirts, rouged their lips, shingled their hair and searched for their opportunities with bright and eager eyes. He knew how to deal with most of them, the flappers – the bright young things.

But this young dryad with the pure, wide brow and eyes the colour of burn water, with her absurd, colt-like innocence, and utter lack of pretension, was a greater temptation than any easy little piece out for a good time. He wished heartily that he had told Sir James she was hopeless and that her work would not do at all.

When Helen got out of the train at Ayling, Duncan was waiting for her on the platform, pacing up and down with his hands clasped behind his back like Felix the Cat. She wondered why everything he did seemed to relate to the cinema.

She stopped him at the end of one of the pacings and he looked at her blankly, and said, 'Oh, hello, Nell. Had a good day?'

'I got the job,' she told him.

His eyes lit up. 'Good-oh. So did I.'

'You didn't tell me you were trying to get a job.'

Outside the station he stopped, his eyes shining like one who has experienced a revelation. Helen was used to this.

She put her portfolio in the sidecar, tied the scarf round her head and got in.

'What is this job?'

'Clapper boy!'

'What on earth's that?'

He explained. 'When a scene is shot it has to be named and numbered so you can find it when you want it. So they have a chap with a wooden clapper board with the name of the film, and the number of the take, and when they start rolling . . .'

'Rolling?'

'The camera starts working, he snaps this, and it gets photographed, like a chapter heading.' She was silent, and he said, 'A film's like a book. Just following on. Suppose you had several scenes in this station – you would take them all in one day. They might be at the beginning and the middle and the end of the story. So they have to be labelled so you know where they fit in.'

'The penny has dropped.'

'Well, Barry's father, Mr Goldman, says I can work through the summer hols.'

'Uncle Royston will explode if he finds out, and pop will go your allowance.'

'He won't find out. No one will. Barry and I will work it. Barry's only hanging on to please his old man – he's going to take cinematography soon. You can get a course at the London Poly. Oh, don't you start worriting like Mums. Listen. Rudi Strauss started shooting today.'

He waited, but as no recognition dawned in his sister's eyes, exclaimed, '*Rudi Strauss*. The Great German director!'

'Never heard of him.'

'You must have.' He rattled off the names of Strauss's most famous films and then said, 'You're hopeless. But the general public never remember the director. Only the stars. Well, he liked me . . . and told Mr Greenstreet he would like me to be on the set – sort of general floor boy and interpreter. He said it all begins with enthusiasm, and enthusiasm was infectious. Eleana Dolek is the star, and she's his wife, but they were testing about four actresses for a small part. Afterwards I saw the rushes – that's the developed film – and Strauss asked me what I thought about them. So I told him.'

'I'll bet you did!'

'Strauss asked me to say which girl I thought the best, and they gave the one I picked the job. She had beautiful bones.' He waited for a second, then added, 'And they're paying me three pounds a week.'

'What?' Helen cried.' That's a working man's wage! Just for banging two pieces of wood together?'

'They pay good money in the film business.'

'So it seems. Well, we'd better get home.'

He got into the saddle, kicked the starter, and they sped off through the town towards the Mill Cottage where they found Mavis and Cousin Millicent already changed for dinner at Ayling Place, and getting anxious in case they were late. Lord Breterton was sending the car and it always came on the dot. Duncan sailed in to the attack.

'I've got a job for the vac – this one *and* the long vac too. And Peak's have taken Nell on in the studio.' He kissed his mother in a congratulatory manner. '*Both* your children are now earners, launched on their careers.'

'Oh dear,' said Mavis doubtfully. 'Well, hurry up and change. I've put a clean evening shirt for you Duncan. And, darlings, don't say anything about the film studio to your uncle . . .'

'All right, all right . . .' Duncan fled away from the room

only too willing not to talk about his activities.

'At your age I hadn't to think about a job,' Mavis said to Helen. 'I was already married and a mother. I never had to battle with the world, thank goodness, at least not while Dads was alive.'

'And a proper little softy he made you,' said Cousin Millicent tenderly.

'All these people he'll meet, whom I won't even know. It worries me. How do I know what they are?'

'But you used to like interesting people.'

'Well, don't say anything to Royston about it,' implored Mavis, 'you know how he goes on. We don't want a good dinner spoiled. Let's just keep it to ourselves?'

'I see your point,' Lady Millicent agreed. 'Righty-ho. Oh, Helen my dear, I have the address of a hostel in Bloomsbury for young ladies. A student I met at the Royal Needlework Society lives there. She says it is clean and comfortable, very reasonable and quiet. They vet every gel most carefully. Only gels from good families. No riff-raff. Not even old Roy could object.'

'Good-oh,' said Helen thoughtfully.

'Do hurry up and change, darling. The car will be here at six-thirty and West has to get back to wait at table.'

'Don't fuss, Mums.' Helen went out, carefully shutting the door. Then she went very quietly along the hall into the study where the telephone was kept, and called the exchange and gave the London number that Boots had given her.

A superior female voice answered.

'This is Miss Lillian Skinner's residence.'

'Please say it is Miss Helen Redmaine. We met at Peak's this morning. She'll remember.'

'Oh,' said Boots in her natural voice, 'Hello, ducks. Did you get the job?'

'Yes.'

'So did I. Only two quid a week, but Tommy'll have to make it up to me. We had a good day at the races.'

'Did you win?'

'Well, he did. I don't risk my own money on horses.'

'Will you look out for a room for me?'

'There's one here. Semi-basement – a bit dark but not bad.

29

It's even got its own lav, because it's the only decent room down there, and there was this washplace for the servants – when it was a big house. Fifteen bob a week.'

'Tell them I'll take it,' said Helen recklessly.

Chapter 2

When Sir James arrived home that evening he found that his wife, Charlotte, and his daughter, June, were already changed and waiting for him in the drawing room. Charlotte was his second wife, a smart American from New York. They had lived together for some years, marrying after June's mother, his first wife, had died. She had refused to divorce him, and there were no grounds on which he could divorce her. Since her death June had lived with them. She was eighteen.

Sir James was very proud of the new house in Ebor Place, a large, terraced early Victorian mansion, which Charlotte had had expensively 'done over' by a fashionable interior decorator. It glistened with new soft furnishings, fine carpets, antiques and rather bad paintings. She employed a florist to come every other day to 'do' the flowers, just as she employed a man to come round and wind the clocks and another to tune the piano.

Now they were married she was a dedicated social climber. She was by no means where she wanted to be but she was certainly in the swim. She wished James had been landed gentry, but at least his profession assured her attention in the society columns and magazines. The press needed advertising revenue and Sir James represented big advertising. His friends were all in the press, business or advertising. But he admired Charlotte and could now afford to let her have her head.

She was looking very splendid tonight in an orchid satin dress by Molyneaux with a skirt cut in panels embroidered with crystal beads. When she walked the panels swung open showing the brief, tight under-skirt and a glimpse of her fine, strong legs in their pale flesh coloured stockings. They were dining at home, then going to the theatre with friends.

June was very like her father, and his looks did not transmute very happily. She was short and solid with large dark eyes in a round, sallow young face. Her expression was that of an apprehensive child. Charlotte and Ebor Place had been a traumatic change in her life.

During the long years she had lived with her mother in Putney she had rarely seen her father. She knew he would have liked a pretty daughter to show off, and that she was a disappointment to him. But he kissed her affectionately, saying, 'How's my girlie, then?' And she was grateful.

Charlotte poured him a cocktail from a large silver shaker, brought it to him and proferred a kiss.

'You *must* hurry, darling. Just one little drink, and then off upstairs to change.'

He noticed that the fine wrinkles round her eyes were clogged with face powder, and that the well corseted bracing of her sturdy figure was hard to the touch. She was forty-three. He remembered the hilarious luncheon he had had at midday with that fool Tommy Medway and his enchanting new girl, and how when he had casually put his arm round her she had felt both soft and strong, like a kitten. What a little stunner she was!

'I don't want this stuff,' he said tetchily. 'Tell what's-his-name to bring me a Scotch and soda up to my room.'

Tying his white tie, brushing his thick silver hair, he thought he was not such a bad-looking man for his age. He could not get that girl of Tommy Medway's out of his mind. She was mouth-watering. Like a piece of delicious fruit, ripe for the picking. He rubbed his full sensual lips, ruefully. The Medway account was coming up for re-scheduling soon and he was pressing them to increase the national press advertising. He had to keep in with Medway, and that was why he had promised to give young Boots a job and keep an eye on her while Tommy was away. He would be a fool to paddle in that pond. But he had been a fool to make the offer. That kid was gaol-bait if ever he saw it. He sighed, checked his note and cigar case, and went down to dinner.

The food was excellent – beautifully cooked and served. He relaxed.

'Funny thing,' he said. 'A kid called Helen Redmaine came in today about a job in the studio. Her father did some work for me during the war. Brilliant chap. He did those arty war posters the Ministry put out. I was all set for a follow-up campaign, but then he went off to France as a War Artist and got himself killed. Accidentally. Silly beggar. Quite unnecessary. Left a wife and two kids.'

'That's awful, honey,' said Charlotte absently.

After the theatre she had arranged to meet friends at the Kit-Kat for supper and dancing. James did not care for dancing.

'Her mother,' James went on, 'keeps a knitting shop now. Thought you might care to ask them to tea – or something? One weekend, down at Whitelands. They live at Ayling.'

Charlotte frowned. 'My list for Whitelands is pretty full this summer.'

'Sandy's brother is Lord Breterton now – they're pretty upper crust. Sandy met her at the art school where he was teaching.'

Charlotte was all attention. 'You say she runs a shop?'

'Yes. At the gates of Ayling Place. With a cousin, Lady Millicent Dermott.'

'Of course, I'd be delighted,' Charlotte smiled. 'When we go to Whitelands for the summer, perhaps? Why didn't you tell me you knew them?'

'I don't. Not my sort. Not yours either, Charlie. Not smart. Old country family, pretty hard up. Out of the top drawer of course. Not Sandy – he was a real Bohemian.'

He really was too exasperating. He would fill the house with sales directors and advertising men and their boring wives and never even mention he knew titled people. 'I'll certainly get in touch with Mrs Redmaine.' She rose briskly. 'No time for coffee. Is the car round, Fletcher?'

'I'm afraid not, madam. Hawkins is indisposed again. I have telephoned Godfrey Davis.'

'God damn it!' roared Sir James. 'I pay a man to drive and then have to go to a hire firm!' June cowered. His rages always frightened her as they had her mother. 'What the devil's the matter with the fellow?'

'I expect he's drunk again,' Charlotte said indifferently. 'I told you that we would have to get rid of him. Come along, June honey, let's get our wraps.'

A month later William Hyde-Seymour telephoned Sir James to remind him of his half-promise about a job. Sir James had forgotten about the encounter in the Strand.

'I've nothing in the office,' he said discouragingly, 'I need a chauffeur, but of course that's not what you're looking for.' He thought this would choke Willy off.

'Why not?'

'Well, public school, ex-officer, too upper crust.'

'How much?'

Sir James grinned. There was something about Willy that appealed to him.

'It's for a single man.'

'Well, I'm single. How much?'

'Two pounds a week. Uniform found. One weekend in each month free and one evening a week. No overtime. A few pickings. Guests tip. Take me to the office, fetch me back. I use taxis in the day. Then you run Lady Peak and my daughter about. Evening duty – often late – theatres and such. Small flat over the mews behind the house. Rent-free. That's a perk.'

'I'll take it.'

'Can you drive and service a Rolls?'

'I was O. C. Transport. I can drive and service anything.'

'Right. I'm sick of hiring cars. You don't drink, do you?'

'Not on duty.'

'I'll get you put through to my secretary. She'll give you the address and make an appointment for Lady Peak to see you. If she thinks you're OK you can start right away.'

'Thank you, sir. Oh, Sir James?'

'Yes?'

'Maybe later on, if something turns up in the office? Any-thing. You'll give me a chance?'

'We'll see,' Sir James said impatiently. 'Just now I'm only

interested in getting a chauffeur.'

Willy drew in a relieved breath. It would tide him over. The band had finally broken up. He had lost a packet of money at a gambling club a week ago, and he would have to pawn his watch to pay the landlady and get his clothes. It wasn't much of a wage but rent-free rooms in Belgravia weren't to be sniffed at. He might even have some cards printed – who was to know it was not one of those smart mews properties?

He spoke to the secretary and made an appointment to see Lady Peak at Ebor Place the following morning. He wondered what she was like, but had no doubts at all about getting the job if a woman had to decide. He went off to the pawnbrokers whistling Colonel Bogey.

For her first months at Peak's Helen felt that she was destined to spend her life in a dismal half-lit world.

She was assigned a drawing table in an L-shaped corner at the back of the studio where she needed the light on over her drawing board every minute of the day. The front of the studio, near the large windows, was assigned to the senior artists. She could see them in silhouette from her dismal cubbyhole, consulting with Matt Wilson or working hard with the permanent stoop that surgeons, dentists and commercial artists all seem to acquire.

The senior artists were both middle-aged and married. They arrived on time and left on time to catch their trains to the suburbs, unlike Matt Wilson who seemed to surge in and out at all times, bringing a curious gust of vitality with him, and once he was at his board doing four times the work of anyone else.

All the work that came her way seemed to be concerned with plumbing or patent medicines. Because she was young and nice they gave her good advice about spacing and the size of captions, and the names of various types, and adopted her as a sort of quiet, intelligent pet who was surprisingly clever and well-trained. They sent her on errands to the stationery supplies, gave her humbugs to suck and allowed her to sharpen her pencils on the machine each one had clamped to his drawing board.

The other juniors were younger than herself, youths who had had brief art courses at night school and polytechnics. The most senior, a callow boy called Alfred Wykes, she liked very much. He was a weak draughtsman but his lettering was impeccable, and he had a good knowledge of types. He was generous and helpful. He fell in love with Boots when she appeared as receptionist in the space buying department. She was sweet to him – as indeed she was to everyone – but he knew it was hopeless, so he switched his attentions to Helen.

Alfred, named after Lord Tennyson, was a mixed-up boy. He wrote her Pre-raphaelite poetry and took her to the Tate Gallery to see the Rosettis. When she said all the women had incipient goitres and she preferred the Impressionists anyway, he was very hurt. They remained friends but she was glad when the poetry stopped because she thought it awful tosh.

She went out to lunch almost every day with Boots, Alfred and Lily the telephone girl, and other juniors from the office. They lunched at the nearest ABC on glasses of milk, poached eggs, rolls and butter, office scandal and Boots's exploits with her admirers.

Compared to Matt Wilson, Helen found all the men at the office very young, or middle-aged and conventional, or middle-aged and lecherous. She soon learned which ones it was a good idea not to get in the lift with.

Matt Wilson had a saturnine and rather piratical look. He only spoke to her about work, and nearly always delegated it through one of the seniors. But he left her a note recommending a local evening school with an introduction to the teacher, where she could enrol for lettering and lay-out, which she did. He also lent her two fine books on lettering, and when she plucked up courage to thank him, he merely said, 'That's all right – don't spill ink on them.'

She found herself thinking about him quite a lot.

She moved into the basement front at 3, Becker Street the week before she started at Peak's after a battle royal with her mother and Cousin Millicent, who – surprisingly for a passionate advocate of feminine emancipation – declared her in moral danger.

'You might meet *any* type of person in such a place,' she proclaimed.

Noticing the rather shop-worn ladies hanging round the back of Victoria Station on her way home, Helen decided she was quite right.

The floor was already covered with a stained and dismal drugget, and the furnishings consisted of a single divan, a chair, a table and an enormous Victorian wardrobe. For the sum of five shillings Mr Murphy painted the walls with white distemper, and she spent most of Sunday scrubbing the drugget with carpet shampoo.

'It smells like an 'orspital,' said Boots. She pointed to the big angled drawing board, 'What's that, then!'

'That's my drawing board. My father left it to me. And the bench with drawers for paintings and paper. And his palette and easels and paints and brushes. And the picture. He wrote to Mums and said if anything happened I was to have them. The picture is one of the best he ever did. Mums could sell it for five hundred pounds – maybe more. He said there were no strings attached – I can sell it if I want to – but I won't.'

'You loved him didn't you?'

'Yes,' she answered briefly, then, 'Give me a hand with it.'

Between them they lifted the large oil painting and hung it on the hook Helen had already driven into the wall, then both girls stood back and looked at it.

It was the garden at Mill Cottage in full summer bloom, the viaduct striding across the valley, a field of corn spiked with poppies beyond, and two small, sandy-haired, naked children splashing in the mill-stream. In the dark semi-basement it was like a window opening on to a glorious summer day – it filled the mind and heart with joy.

'Where's that then?' asked Boots.

'It's our garden at home. That's my brother Duncan, and me – when we were kids. That building is the old wheel house where the big millstones for grinding the corn used to be housed. Dad had it converted into a studio. Someday I shall work there.'

'You're nuts about that picture, aren't you?'

'Yes,' Helen said fervently. 'It reminds me that life can be perfect now and then. I hope I never, never have to sell it. It would be like amputation. Losing a bit of me. But I have one more picture to go up.' She produced Matt Wilson's sketch of her running up a garden path, flying hair under the green beret, flying deer's legs. She had had it framed.

'That's a Medway sketch.'

'Yes. Mr Wilson said I could have it. He didn't think Sir James would want it.'

'You go for him, don't you?' Boots said curiously.

Helen pulled a face, 'Not really. Sometimes he's very helpful, and sometimes he pulls my leg, and sometimes he's sarky. He can be *very* sarky.'

'Sometimes he flirts,' said Boots. 'Lilly tells me lots of girls ring him.'

Helen thought about this. 'Yes, so I can imagine.' She thought silently for a long minute, then shrugged Matt Wilson away. 'Well, anyway, he can draw like an angel.'

'Let's get up to my room and make some tea.'

Boots had a large room on the first floor, more expensive than Helen's. They travelled to work together on the top of a number eleven bus. But Boots seemed to have engagements every evening, not with the jealous Mr Medway, who was back from America but had to take his family to Antibes on holiday. He brought her a dozen pairs of superfine silk stockings and a silver fox fur from New York. He sent her almost daily postcards from the South of France. She promptly sold the fox, saying it was only for women over thirty, and took Helen out to the Empire Cinema and to a delectable dinner in Soho. Helen realised that Boots's idea of food was not confined to glasses of milk and ABC rolls and butter.

She had unexpectedly proved an asset in the Space Reception. She had to greet the advertising reps from newspapers and periodicals, and take their cards in to the chief space buyer, Miss Klein, and if she did not wish to see them, turn them down pleasantly, at which she was adept. She learned which were the important men who were always seen, and who represented the small and unimportant publications and were never seen. When a campaign was underway and the space schedule made up, the department was under siege; Boots managed the importuning reps with tact, sweetness and humour. Sir James was delighted with her.

The window of Helen's room looked out on to the front area steps leading up to Becker Street. Through the railings

38

there was always a shifting scene of passing legs and feet. Working at her lettering she came to know some as regulars. The split worn leather and bunions of the old match-seller, the polished boots of troops from Chelsea Barracks off for the evening, and Boots's lovely legs and exquisite shoes flying across the pavement to a taxi. It was always a joy to get back home each weekend, even if she had to face her mother's anxious eyes.

'You must do what you like, my darling,' Mavis said. 'Of course you must. But it doesn't stop me worrying. It's my privilege to do so.'

The most startling thing that happened at home was the arrival of a cheque for one hundred pounds from Sir James Peak in payment for the final war poster Sandy Redmaine had done for him eleven years ago. He apologised – the finished work had been received after Sandy's death and had not been invoiced. There was also an affable suggestion that they should go to Whitelands to tea with Lady Peak, at some date convenient to themselves. Sir James and Lady Peak would be in residence at Whitelands later in the summer. His wife would telephone and arrange a date.

'What on earth for? I hardly remember him,' said Mavis, then brightened, 'but it was decent of him to pay up after all this time. Perhaps he is not as wily as I thought.'

'Or maybe – more,' said Cousin Millicent, who quickly forgave Helen for turning down the hostel with the well-vetted 'gels'. Uncle Royston had been told that she and Duncan had taken 'Holiday Jobs' but not about Becker Street or Greenstreet Studio.

Mavis wrote and thanked Sir James but suggested that they put the visit to Whitelands off until September as both she and Lady Millicent were busy with the shop. 'Perhaps,' she said hopefully, 'They'll have forgotten all about it then.'

On a showery grey day Helen and Boots ran from the bus into the marble entrance hall of Dominion House, their stockings splashed, shaking their umbrellas. They went up the marble stairs round the lift shaft to the first floor where Peak's offices occupied the best premises in the building, Boots turning left into the Space Department, and Helen right to the front of the building and her shadowy corner at the rear of the studio. The two senior men looked up and bade her good morning, and Alfred said, 'Hello, Nell.' She hung up mackintosh and umbrella, put on her overall and sat down. As yet there was no work on her desk.

This evening she was meeting Duncan who was bringing her ten pounds, her share of Sir James's cheque. Duncan said they should spend it on clothes, and she certainly needed some. Most of her clothes were her mother's cut down – the fluffy blue suit still the major item.

She pinned a sheet of paper to her board. The sun came out and, as though she had switched it on, Boots came in on a waft of expensive scent, carrying a small piece of paper and wearing a look of urgent busyness. Every man in the room immediately stopped work and smiled as she crossed to Helen's side. She put the paper down on the drawing board.

'There's nothing on it,' said Helen.

'Pretend there is,' said Boots, and Helen obediently picked it up and gazed at the blank white square with concentrated interest. 'It's better to carry a bit of paper about and look important if you want to wander round the office – no one ever asks what you're doing.'

'What a good idea. You are Machiavellian, Boots.'

'Is that catching?'

'Oh, come off it. What do you want?'

'I want to know if you can come out with me? Next Wednesday?'

'I think so. Where to?'

'Out to dine and dance – then maybe night-clubbing.'

'By ourselves?' said Helen, startled.

'Come off it, ducks. 'Course not. A fellow I know just asked me. But I said I couldn't, on account of Tommy,' she pulled a mocking face, 'not on my own. So he said to bring a girlfriend, and he'd bring another fellow.'

'Is that what they call a blind date? Like in the movies?' Helen asked delightedly.

'Yes, that's right.'

Helen had felt sure that knowing Boots would be exciting. She seemed to originate adventure. In the forbidden gossip sessions in the telephone room the other girls would listen to her open-mouthed – they all wanted to do what she did, and some of the more sophisticated ones did. Even at school every one had longed to be grown-up and be taken to a night club.

The gossip columns reeled off the glamorous names competing in the social scene. The Ruthven twins, the Beaton sisters, Margaret Whigham, Barbara Hutton. If Uncle Royston had had his way Helen would now be moving in this world. She could not imagine it. It was as excitingly foreign to her as darkest Africa.

Most of the films they saw had at least one night-club set where exquisitely dressed extras sat around a dance floor; jazz music, corsages of orchids, white waistcoats and champagne. No one ever ate anything. Duncan said they were 'dress' extras, which made her think of clothes. Oh, heavens – clothes!

'I haven't the right sort of dress,' she said.

'I'll lend you one of mine,' Boots said magniloquently, 'we're about the same size.'

Across the studio Matt Wilson's office door opened and his tall long-legged figure, reminding Helen of the herons in the mill-stream at home, came stalking out bearing straight towards her.

'Hey, Boots, scram!' she hissed. 'Mr Wilson's coming over.'

'Who cares?' said Boots, but as he came in earshot she added, 'Righty-oh. I'll tell Miss Klein it's OK.'

Matt raised his eyebrows, picked up the blank piece of paper and gave it to her. 'Don't forget your important message, Miss Skinner.'

She squeaked with laughter and the saturnine face relaxed and grinned, and Matt gently patted her round little seat as she walked off across the room, the eyes of the studio following her wistfully. Matt watched her too with amused, appreciative eyes. Helen was conscious of a vague, inexplicable sadness. He looked down and caught her expression.

'Are you all right?' he said concernedly.

'Of course.' Helen stood up – she was a tall girl, but even so she had to look up at him.

'You looked a bit sad.' Before she could deny it, he said irritably, 'Don't say you've got a pain? That's why I don't like girls working for me. They're always up and down. Menstru-

41

ation – it's always coming on or going off.'

Helen was profoundly shocked. Her cheeks blazed and she wondered what her Uncle Royston would think of this impossible man, so blatantly mentioning the unmentionable.

'I am not menstruating,' she said icily.

'We are not amused,' he said, scanning her outraged face. She knew that if she wasn't, he was – very amused. He was teasing her. The foul *brute*. He said, unexpectedly humble, 'Forgive me, Nell. I can be a pig at times.'

'Yes,' Helen said unrelentingly, 'you can. And my name is Miss Redmaine – I am only Nell to my friends.' She looked at the sheaf of layouts he was holding and said, in the same frozen tones, 'More lavatories?'

'No.' He was watching her like a fighter, waiting for her to drop her guard, but she would not look away. 'No, it's much more exciting. Liver pills. We get down to the basics of life at Peak's. Especially in the small ads.' He put on a pair of horn-rimmed glasses and read the caption in his hand, '*WHEN LIFE HAS ITS TENSIONS IT IS WORTH TAKING* FRIENDLY *ADVICE*, in caps. Lower case, *Friendly's Liver Pills are a reliable tonic and help to relieve Constipation. They clear the system gently and relaxingly and assure* (caps) *REGULAR HEALTH*.' He looked at her with gentle query and she burst out laughing.

'That's better,' he said with relief.

'Are you trying to drive me away with this awful stuff? I know you say you don't like girls, but this is ridiculous.'

'I didn't say I don't like girls,' he said sweetly. 'I adore girls. I just don't like working with them. It's too unnerving.' Then, brusquely, 'Well, someone has to do it. This wants a new sketch, a life sketch. You haven't been given one before. Can you do it?'

Her face lit up. A life sketch! 'Oh *yes*,' she said confidently, 'of course I can. I'll have a look at Friendly's guard book and see what they're doing.'

He grinned at the way she was picking up the jargon. As she bent over her board, her hair, so close to his lips, curled slightly, individual hairs glinting red or gold under the desk light, and smelling of lemon soap. All of her smelled delectably of well-washed youth, sharp and clean, like a nice schoolgirl. She looked up at him, twisting her neck, startled to find his face so near. He stood back hastily and saw her shoulders relax.

'I've brought you the last two ads,' he said, and put two advertisement pulls on her drawing board. They both showed a haggard woman sitting at a table with her head propped on her hand, hollow cheeked, her mouth drooping, her forehead wrinkled with agony.

'Jumping Jesus!' exclaimed Helen. 'That would put me off taking the things *for ever*. They ought to show the result – what she feels like *after* all this regularity.'

'You've got a point,' he agreed. 'What do you suggest?'

'Someone busting with health and vitality. Full of life and devilry. Someone like Boots.'

'Boots? Oh, *yes*. The girl in Space who is driving all the men up the wall? She a friend of yours?'

'Yes.'

'I should not have thought she was your type at all.'

'Why not? Because she sounds common?'

'Maybe.'

'You're crazy,' said Helen loftily. 'She's the most *uncommon* girl I've ever met.' She gave a small frown and said wonderingly, 'She believes absolutely in herself. Absolutely.'

'And you don't?'

'No. I know I can draw. I know I'm not ugly. But I'm not sure about *me*. Boots seems to know where she is in life. I don't know at all.'

There was a brief silence, then he said brusquely, 'Well, I'll leave the idea to you. If you do an attractive sketch I'll submit it. They might have to rewrite the copy and *they* won't like that. If they turn it down you'll have to do another misery picture. I want it ready to show J. P. on Monday, and get down to the block-makers next week. I'll give it to one of the boys if you like.'

'Certainly not! I *want* to do it,' she said indignantly.

He nodded briefly, and went back to his office. She sat down at her table and pinned the two miserable ads up on the board and squared up her new paper to start. She seemed to miss him when he was out of her sight. It must be because he knew so much she wanted to know.

43

She worked very hard, not going out to lunch, eating a sandwich Alfred brought back for her and a cup of weak office tea brewed up in the telephone room, which housed cups and a gas-ring. She roughed in a typewriter on a desk, and on a rack on the wall behind a tennis racquet and a net of tennis balls, and sitting at the desk a sketch of Boots in tennis kit, glowing with health and vigour. She finished it late in the afternoon and on a separate slip wrote, '*FEEL YOUR BEST AT WORK OR PLAY, THE FRIENDLY WAY*'. Then she set her layout side-on with the original dejected woman, and pasted them up into a double page spread with another caption – '*WHY NOT FEEL WELL ALL THE TIME?*'

It would be much better, she thought, if the artist wrote the copy – of the two, it seemed to her copy-writing was a piece of cake.

She waited until she saw Matt leave the office, his shoulders hunched, a portfolio under his arm, the dark felt hat crammed down over his forehead, and then she slipped in to his office and put her lay-out for Friendly's Liver Pills on his table where he would see it when he arrived in the morning.

The room seemed bleak without his lean, offhand, vital presence. On his drawing board carefully covered with a transparency was his finished advertisement for Medway Tiles. In colour, containing all the stipulated items. The glaring red roof, the white lettered slogan making up the fence, the beaming family group, blond and British, glowing with pride of ownership. It was wonderfully efficient, well done, the drawing spot on, the use of the space masterly. Why then did it make her feel so sad?

Was it the little sketch of herself which she had had framed and which was now on her wall at Becker Street? When he could draw like that how could he be content with this slick rubbish?

She hoped he would not be angry at her two-page spread. It really was cheek. Artists did not suggest copy – it was not considered their province. But she could not see why.

She and Boots walked along the Strand to the Corner House at Charing Cross, and went up to the first floor. The lushly carpeted restaurant had a large circular opening guarded by a balustrade, where one could look down on the

44

ground floor restaurant below. The band played a selection from *The Vagabond King* and then broke into *Valencia*. It made Helen think of the bouncy way Sir James came through the office when things were going well. Helen loved the Corner House. It seemed to her such good value – the waitresses in their black and white, like dream parlourmaids, the amber lights, the entwined bronze of the balcony rails.

Helen warned Boots that she was meeting Duncan, and Boots said interestedly, 'You mean you have a real brother? I haven't seen mine for years.'

'Why not?'

'One's in Australia, one's in the navy, and the other was missing in France. He was the eldest.'

'And you never see them?'

'Never. We all left home the minute we could. The one in Australia and the one in the navy send Mum money sometimes, and write. They were older than me. I was a late mistake.'

'Would you like to see them?'

'Never thought of it.' She looked round appreciatively. 'It's cosy here – I've been to all the snooty places. But it's nicer here. No one is scared of the waiters. Everyone knows exactly what they will have to pay. No one is showing off or spending more money than they can afford. I like it.' Her beautiful eyes were looking over Helen's shoulder towards the door, and she said, 'Look what the cat's brought in. Where d'you think he's parked his ruddy 'orse?'

Helen turned round and saw a familiar figure approaching. 'It's my brother, Duncan,' she said. 'I'll order for three. Tea and fruit buns.'

Duncan made a dashing if slightly eccentric figure. He wore his breeches and riding jacket and boots, all very good quality and paid for by his uncle, who considered riding essential for his heir apparent. Duncan rarely rode but he enjoyed wearing the kit. With it he wore a very new and beautiful yellow polo neck sweater, bought with Sir James's unexpected bonus and a wide brimmed black hat of soft luxurious felt, pulled down dashingly over his eyes. Helen was seized with the giggles.

His handsome eyes searched the room for them, as he adopted what he hoped was the super arrogant attitude of

45

Rudi Strauss. He would have worn a monocle if he had dared, but knew that would make Helen die laughing. He located her, waving hilariously, sitting with a girl wearing a black and white costume and a black hat with a large yellow flower.

He went over to them with what he hoped was the authentic Strauss stride, and it was not until he was quite near that he totally forgot the impact of his new image struck by her extraordinary beauty. He hesitated, took off the dashing felt hat, colour running boyishly up his cheeks, and sank slowly down into a vacant chair at the table.

'Are you with my sister?' he asked.

Boots looked at Helen, screwed the tip of her finger into her forehead to indicate mental derangement, and said, to nobody in particular, 'This one's nuts – you *sure* he's your brother, Nell?'

'As ever was! Dunky, stop playing the great director. Boots, this *is* my brother, Duncan. Duncan, this is Boots Skinner who works at Peak's and who got me the room in Becker Street.' She poured his tea. 'Duncan's in films.'

'Oh, that explains everything,' said Boots. 'Have a bun, love.'

'Thank's very much.' He took a large buttered bun, and bit into it. Boots watched him with interest. She was not used to young companions. In her experience, young men had no money and were a waste of time. Helen was the first young person with whom she had ever made friends. She found Duncan weird but nice. Like his sister . . . *really* nice.

'I like the pullover,' said Helen, 'and the hat. Is it a Borsolino?'

'Yes. Burlington Arcade.'

'I might have known. Only the best for Duncan. Have you brought me my loot?'

'Yes, here it is.' He took out two crisp white five pound notes. 'Mums went to the bank this morning.'

Helen kissed them and put them away in her bag. 'Thank you, Sir James Peak. Part of some money he owed my father,' she explained to Boots, 'for a painting. One of the posters he did before he was killed.'

'And Peaky's only just paid up?' They nodded. 'The wily old bugger – as your mum said. What on earth made him pay up now?'

46

'Because he wants Mums to meet his wife who wants to get into Society.'

'She doesn't know, poor lady,' explained Duncan, 'that we're not *in* Society. We haven't a brass farthing. And my uncle – who is Lord Breterton – is a mean old stodge who does nothing but hunt and wonder if the umpteen miles of roof on his damned great house will last another winter.' He pushed his chair back, made a square frame with his forefingers and thumbs, and squinted at Boots through it as though he were looking through a camera lens. 'Gorgeous. Now look up.' Boots caught on, and rolled her aquamarine eyes ceilingwards. 'Right. Now down. My God – your eyelashes make shadows like Garbo's – they do that with lighting, of course, and her lashes are false. Now turn your head, slowly raise your eyelids and look seductively over there.' Boots did this towards a young man at a nearby table, who promptly dropped an eclair into his tea. Duncan leaned back. '*You're perfect.* You haven't a bad angle. A wrong feature. Have you never had a film test? Or thought of going into films?'

'Who hasn't? Thought of it, I mean. And lots of gentlemen have asked me that.'

'I'll bet – it's a corny old line.'

'You're kidding,' Boots said indulgently, and he flushed again with his unexpected, attractive boyishness.

'Don't pull my leg,' he protested. 'I *am* working in films. And I *am* serious. You *ought* to have a test.'

'I've done a bit of modelling. But – it's too late for me. It's going to be all talkies. I don't talk right, do I?'

'You could learn all that,' he said impatiently. 'Lot's of actresses do. Gertrude Lawrence, Jessie Matthews . . .'

'*Not* Jessie Matthews?' breathed Boots. Jessie Matthews was a personal idol.

'Yes. She came from Berwick Street. You can get over all that if you really want to.'

Boots considered him. 'You really mean it, don't you?' she said incredulously.

'Of course. Why shouldn't I? Tell me, what do you mean to do with your life?'

Boots grinned. 'Get some rich bloke to marry me. Or if he

won't marry me, keep me, and settle enough on me to be all right when he moves on.'

Duncan considered it as a serious proposition.

'You mean exploit your beauty as an upper-class whore?'

Boots blinked – at a loss. She wasn't used to being taken seriously. She had expected a shocked protest.

'Well,' she hedged, 'I hadn't really thought of it like that.'

'Well, how had you thought of it?'

'Don't you lecture me!' she said angrily. 'All girls do it. That's what they're all after really – even posh girls. It's not as though I can really *do* anything. Not like Nell. I've no training – and no brains.'

'Oh, don't tell such feeble lies,' Helen said angrily, 'you can make rings round most of the people at Peak's. It's just that you're so damned pretty you've never had to think about anything else.'

'Ah,' crowed Duncan, 'Nell has it, spot on. Now, if you're serious about this particular career, and I presume you are, you'd do better in films than in an advertising office.'

'I would?' Boots was completely at a loss.

'Of course. You'd meet much wealthier men, so you'd do better as a gold-digger, and you'd do better when you decided to sell.'

'Sell?'

'Your virginity. That's what you plan, surely?' Boots blinked. 'You *ought* to take speech training. You'd get a better class of opportunity. Rich men like girls who sound as well as look right. You'd be surprised at the number of debs on this game. Come to think of it being a deb is the same business, but strictly legal.' He rose, and offered his hand, ineffably courteous, all his father's charm and the Redmaine breeding in evidence. When she put her hand into his he looked down on it with intense pleasure and turned to Helen, 'Look Nell, at this hand. Do you know there are lots of beautiful women who have awful hands. We have girls on the casting books just for close-ups of hands *and* feet and legs, for when the star has thick ankles. You could do that, for a start. You'd earn as much as you do at Peak's while you take speech-training.'

'Hey,' said Boots derisively, 'you'll have me in Hollywood in no time.'

'Why not?' His sincerity was infectious. 'You live in the same house as Nell, don't you? Same telephone number? I'll be in touch. Why don't you bring Miss Skinner down to Ayling for the weekend, Nell?'

Helen wondered about the effect upon Uncle Royston if he happened to call, but she said staunchly, 'Of course. But it'll have to be later on – after August. Mums won't have time until then.'

'Oh yes, I forgot,' he explained to Boots. 'Mums and Aunt Millicent have this wool shop – it's open in the summer when people come to visit the house.'

'What house?'

'Ayling Place.' Her beautiful face was slightly puzzled. 'That's the name of the house. The busy time – for the shop – is in the summer when people come to look at it.'

'What do they want to look at it for?'

There was a pause – Helen and Duncan were touched. She just had no knowledge of a house like their uncle's. Her question was direct and innocent. Why should people come to look at a house?

'It's very old and full of interesting things,' explained Helen. 'People like to look at them.'

'They pay? Like the Tower of London? Or the zoo?'

Duncan's face collapsed, thinking of his massively important Uncle, and Aunt Millicent in her old hats, surrounded by knitting and the rainbow hues of fine wools.

'More like the zoo,' he said. 'We'll take you to see it. Well – goodbye, Miss Skinner. Goodbye Nell.' He paused, then repeated thoughtfully, 'Skinner? That won't do. There's Otis Skinner. But he's an American poet. I don't like Boots, either. Wouldn't look good on the credits. I'll think that over. You don't mind changing your name?'

'I hadn't thought . . .'

'Well, *do* think. See if you can come up with something. Something romantic!'

They watched the tall, thin young figure weave adroitly through the tables and out through the glass door, jamming the new Borsolino rakishly over one eye.

'Is he always like that?'

'It's growing on him. Since he met Strauss.'

'He was pulling my leg?'

'Oh *no*. He was perfectly serious. The family doesn't realise just how serious. He's a Jaberwocky person.'

'"For he was very stiff and proud and said you needn't shout so loud",' Boots quoted unexpectedly, and in answer to Helen's quick, surprised glance, added, 'Had it at school. *Alice Through the Looking Glass*. Good, isn't it?'

'Yes.'

Helen picked up the bill and Boots opened her purse and said, 'Come on, how much? Halves.'

'Mine's more. Duncan's not too stiff and proud to let me pay for his bun.'

'Keep it halves,' said Boots with her sudden devastating, sweet bright smile. 'It was worth it for the laugh. First time I've paid for a fella in my life. I reckon it was cheap at twopence ha'penny.'

It was a fine evening and they rode to Victoria on the top of a number eleven bus. Boots was unusually silent. When they got to 3, Becker Street she asked Helen up to choose a dress.

Her room was large and high ceilinged, the front drawing room of the old house. But there was a collection of night-club dolls and souvenirs, some bright cushions on the divan, and a large bunch of red roses in a big jam jar. It was very clean, smelling fragrantly. On the large modern dressing table with a huge circular mirror, the only piece of furniture that actually belonged to her, was a collection of expensive scent and spray bottles and containers for fashionable cosmetics. That and the gramophone. There were no books or pictures.

Boots opened a wardrobe – one half was full of evening dresses. Helen goggled. She had only ever possessed one and that had been cut down from a flowered taffeta of her mother's.

'I got them when I was hostessing – at Benjie's. You had to have a good many, because some of the chaps came every night. Some are secondhand models, like my check suit. I got some in Berwick Street. Five quid, most of them. Some of them in sales.'

She took out a floating chiffon in pale green over a silvery underslip. 'How about this? Eau-de-nil.'

50

'It's lovely. Are you sure?'

''Course I am. It looks like you. It needs a bean-pole type. I'm a bit short for it.'

'Well, thank you. I'll try it on.'

'Take it in if you want. I don't wear it much.'

'Thanks awfully. Oh, by the way. Who is this friend of yours? The one we're going out with?'

'Oh, didn't I say?' said Boots offhandedly. 'It's old Peaky. He stopped me in the office and asked me.'

'Sir James?' Helen was shocked. *Sir James! Important!* The boss. An old man. Married. Her concern showed.

'Well, he promised he'd keep an eye on me,' Boots said airily, 'and I went out with one of the reps, and Lily – ' (Lily the telephonist was a storehouse of inter-office scandal) ' – told Peggy Prior, who told the Old Man. He had me into his office for a ticking off. Well, I said a girl can't stay in every bloody night just because her number one fellow is away. So he said he would take me out somewhere really nice, if I promised to behave until Tommy came back.'

'And will you?'

'Nah,' Boots said scornfully. 'I'm ditching Tommy anyhow. When he comes back. I can't stand blokes that breathe down my neck. I'll lay off until the Old Man gets the Medway contract signed – well, that's why he's keeping off the grass, isn't it? Then maybe I'll leave.'

'Boots – tell me.' Helen drew in a determined breath. 'D'you sleep with any of these men?'

'What difference would it make to you if I did? It ain't your business.'

'It wouldn't make any difference. Not about being friends – or inviting you to Ayling. But about next week, going out with you and Sir James and some chap I've never met. If you sleep with men, that's your business – but I wouldn't like them to think I would. I'd feel a fool if they did.'

'Well, don't worry. Actually, I don't. They all hope I will. No harm in them hoping. I think men are a lot of rubbish, anyway.'

'Then – how do you get out of it?'

'That's dead easy. Start talking about getting married. Or engaged. Or say I'm worried about his poor wife and that a

51

girl has to look to her own future, and what a strict old devil my dad is and how he'd take the skin off anyone he caught messing me about, and that he once did eight rounds with Billy Wells.'

'Did he?'

'No, of course he didn't. Drunken old bum couldn't push a paper bag in. But it makes them sheer off. There's always another – leastways there always has been so far.'

'You are a terrible girl,' Helen said admiringly. 'A sort of professional virgin.'

'You insulting me?'

'No, I wish I had your nerve.'

'You don't have to worry what blokes think of you, love,' Boots said with her warm, endearing smile. 'No one could think anything wrong of you. 'You're the real McCoy. Real nice. You and that barmy brother of yours. Real *posh*, but ever so nice.'

Telling Duncan about it at home at Ayling that weekend, Helen said, 'It gave me quite a turn. She's only eighteen yet she made me feel as old as the hills. I'm an absolute innocent compared to her, and yet in a way she's a child compared to me. I mean, even if she was what she pretends to be, she'd still be a child . . .'

'Like Clara Bow,' he said. His comparisons were all cinematic.

'Yes, yes. Oh, by the way, she says she'd be glad if you would find someone to teach her to speak posh.'

Duncan's face lit eagerly.

'*Really*? That's marvellous! I'll find out.'

He had had a wonderful week. Strauss had been cutting the opening sequences of the film and had let him sit in and watch, and shown him how to select and discard. He was enthralled. He knew that this was the heart of the whole thing.

'It's like a great jig-saw puzzle,' he explained. 'The bits come up on this little projector, and you recognise which are very good, which tell the story, how they'll look run together and what will make the effect you want. You stop the projector, and select the bits and work them together. It's a very important thing to learn. Strauss let me try – he said I've a camera eye.'

'This Strauss,' said Helen, 'he's not one of those Oscar Wilde men that Mums warned you of?'

Duncan looked at her scornfully. In spite of his sophistication he still had the faintly callow look of a schoolboy, the pure carved cheeks and mouth.

'Don't be ridiculous, Nell. He's crazy about Eleana Dolek, his wife. In Hollywood you have to get married if you're a star – I mean you can't live together. You'd lose your ratings.'

'Because they're shocked?'

'Oh no. Because they think the public might be. Stars have to be perfect. But really at Greenstreet we're all too busy for lechery. We've got to finish this film on schedule because Strauss and Eleana have to go to Hollywood, and then he may make a film in Germany again. And he says that if this Hitler gets into power Eleana won't go back because she's Jewish, and then he would want to leave Germany too. It's horrid for them because they both love Germany.'

'I thought Hitler was a squib?'

'Strauss doesn't think so. He says he's biding his time. He says if the Allies press for the war debt then the mark would collapse, and there'll be terrible unemployment, and that's when they'll have to look out for Hitler, because he promises to cure all their troubles.'

Things had changed since they had been working – they had changed. They did not tell each other everything, and neither of them told their mother everything. Helen supposed that was part of living one's own life. She was not sure that she liked it. But it was certainly exciting. Sometimes alone in the bleak room in Becker Street she thought – 'No one knows what I'm up to. I could do anything.' She supposed Duncan felt the same. New people, unknown situations, feeling, so often, a little out of depth, not letting anyone see it . . . like falling in love and not saying anything about it. Not to Duncan, or Boots, not to Mavis or Cousin Millicent . . . not even to herself.

Chapter 3

June Peak had a small but charming bedroom on the third floor of the house at Ebor Place. After the small terraced house where she had lived with her mother, everything here seemed on a very grand scale. It was a young girl's bedroom out of a glossy magazine, all shell-pink carpets and rosy chintz.

June thought it was lovely, but felt it had been decorated for quite a different girl. Someone very pretty; an achiever, popular – in fact the sort of stepdaughter Charlotte would have gloried in, and the sort of daughter Sir James would have adored.

She admired, but was in awe of her stepmother. It seemed that having done over the house, Charlotte was now trying to 'do over' her, and she wished she had the courage to tell her she was wasting her time.

She must hurry. This morning she was going out with Charlotte who did not like to be kept waiting. She put on a rose-beige marocain with a short skirt of fine pleats and a smart little jacket, which did nothing for her short, plump figure. She tried hard with her hair which, naturally, springy, took a great deal of setting to reduce it to the fashionable smooth and regular waves. She made up her face very carefully – she had had lessons on how to do that at a Bond Street beauty parlour. The bill was staggering and June could not see that she looked all that different.

She went down to Charlotte's small sitting room – 'my office' Charlotte called it. The rooms on this floor were higher and more spacious. It was walled and carpeted in off-white with brocaded and gilded Louis Quintz furniture, and hangings in lilac and rose. There was a bedroom and bathroom attached, like a little flat, and Sir James had similar accommodation across the landing.

June wondered, in an embarrassed way, about their love life. She remembered her mother had referred to Charlotte as 'his American whore'. One night, she had glimpsed her father, in an elegant dressing-gown, crossing the landing, knocking gently, and being admitted into his wife's kingdom. She could not guess at what time he returned. She thought it an odd way of being married.

It was from here that Charlotte ran the house and her own and James's social life – and, as an after-thought, June's as well. She had a secretary who worked in a small dark disused pantry in the basement.

Charlotte was at her breakfast table, drinking coffee and going through her post. She wore a negligée of rose-coloured chiffon and a cap of écru lace trimmed with satin rose buds. The coy little boudoir cap was ill-suited to her large-featured face and black shingled hair. She lifted a cheek for June's token kiss and lit a Russian cigarette which she smoked through a long, shagreen holder.

June sat down and the maid served her breakfast. She was ravenously hungry but was only allowed grapefruit juice and one piece of dry toast with a scraping of marmalade. Charlotte was firm about keeping her weight down.

'Have you your schedule here with you, Junie?'

'Yes, Charlotte.' June opened a large diary – every morning she and Charlotte coincided their diaries. Charlotte's was usually full – every hour accounted for. June's was not. It irked Charlotte a little. She should be immersed in the pre-deb social round. A girl of eighteen should have her own dates – and friends.

'Now, this morning?'

'Well, we drive you to Ardens, then Williams takes me on to the dentist, and then we pick you up, and we go to Poirets for your fitting, and then we get back here in time to change for your luncheon party. Then tonight you and Daddy will be out to dinner.'

'Ye-es,' Charlotte frowned slightly. 'I think maybe you'd

better skip the lunch, honey. Have yours in the morning room. All the folk who are coming are too old for you. I feel real bad, Junie – I know so few young people for you.'

'It doesn't matter.'

'It does matter,' said Charlotte firmly. 'We planned to bring you out next year – and this pre-season year is important. I'd hoped you'd made friends at school. What will you do this afternoon?'

'Well, I was going to the cinema. Locally, to the Metropole.'

'Alone?'

'Well, I could take Ruby.' Ruby was a young housemaid, promoted to 'maid' June when she needed it. Charlotte herself had an autocratic Frenchwoman of whom everyone was slightly in awe.

'You certainly can't go alone. But don't let her be familiar.'

She had had no idea when she had agreed to take on James's motherless daughter that it would be such an uphill task. She had twenty much publicised guests from the theatre, arts and aristocracy to luncheon and June would be a skeleton at the feast. A plump, brown-eyed little skeleton, but still an embarrassment.

'Very well, then. But we mustn't make a habit of it.' She rose. 'I'll go and get dressed. Will you ring down and say we'll want the car in half an hour?'

'Yes, of course.'

'Oh, say, honey – what do you think of Williams?'

'Williams?'

'Yes. The new chauffeur.'

'*Oh*! I think he's very good.' She hesitated. Williams had been with them for two months now. He had proved efficient and reliable. She did not know what to make of him – and neither did Charlotte.

'Yes. I'm very pleased,' Charlotte said thoughtfully. 'Such a change from that drunken Hawkins.'

June burst out suddenly, 'I am sorry I'm so awkward, Charlotte.'

'My dear,' Charlotte said kindly enough, 'don't talk such nonsense. You're young. I want you to be a success because that's what Daddy wants for you. He's worked so hard to give us everything and it's right that he should enjoy it all. And so

56

should you. You've a position to live up to now he is *Sir* James Peak. You must learn to be proud of it.'

'Oh, I am.'

'Well then. Order the car and put on your hat.'

June went back to her room to put on a straw cloche hat trimmed with pink daisies and to collect her gloves and handbag. She barely glanced at herself in the mirror, always thinking she looked as though she had been crushed in some sort of press, forcing her neck down into her shoulders, her bust down into her hips, and swelling her legs out below her short fashionable skirt.

Charlotte was already waiting for her in the drawing room, standing at one of the tall windows looking down into the street. Outside there was sunshine, and beyond the corner by the church, the trees in the square were in full summer leaf.

'Is the car here? I told them before I went up to my room,' asked June anxiously.

Charlotte started and turned. She was in navy, with touches of white, with pearls and a white hat with a dipping brim. She moved in an invisible auro of Chypre. 'It's OK,' she said, 'Williams is waiting outside.'

Willy Hyde-Seymour was uniformed in grey to match the Rolls. He opened the rear door and saluted with military precision. If his manner was perfect, his glinting blue eyes told the woman of forty-three and the girl of eighteen that the deference was skin deep and he knew all about women. June felt a queer weakness in her knees which she had never experienced before. Charlotte nodded briefly.

'Good morning, madam,' said Willy.

'My lady,' corrected Charlotte sharply.

'My lady,' he repeated, with a slightly incredulous air which immediately made Charlotte wonder if she was right.

It was she who had insisted on calling him Williams. Hyde-Seymour was ridiculous for a servant. She knew that he had applied for work in Sir James's office, but there had been no opening. She had told him at their initial interview that familiarity was something she would not tolerate from the staff, and he had replied gravely that he would try to give satisfaction, but followed the remark with his bold and bonny smile. Fine, white, regular teeth, red lips below cropped fair moustache.

She was beginning to find him a little disturbing.

She stooped to get into the car, saying over her shoulder, 'Take me to Ardens in Bond Street.'

Willy regarded her posterior view and wondered what she would do if he pinched it – he would bet it was armour-plated with corsetry and not rewarding. If he put out a hand to assist her she would think he was old-ladying her. Tricky. He waited until she was seated and June stepped forward. He winked good-naturedly and saw the colour run up under her smooth olive skin. A small round peach, he thought, closed the door and walked round to the driver's seat.

He could just see June in the driving mirror. Like a currant bun now. Round, pale, two fine dark eyes. He drove very efficiently, stopped outside Ardens, ran smartly round and opened the door.

'At what time will you require the car, my lady?'

Charlotte was holding the side of the door to lever herself out, and he offered an assisting arm. She hesitated, put her hand on the grey-coated sleeve and felt the muscle beneath as he gently eased her forward on to her feet. He looked at her mouth and, beneath the navy gaberdine, her full, rigidly supported breasts, and smiled. Erect, Charlotte removed her hand, found her breath quicken and hoped she was not going to blush. Was the impudent young brute trying to flirt? She looked sharply into laughing blue eyes.

'In about an hour and a half.'

'I'll be here, my lady.'

'You don't have to say it every time you open your mouth,' she snapped. 'Take Miss June to Wimpole Street. And don't keep me waiting.'

She went into the calming atmosphere of scent, humming hair-dryers and the acrid smell of permanent waving fluid, and pink-overalled ministrants, and relaxed gratefully into a chair. After a few minutes she thought again, 'The impudent young brute', but this time, indulgently, a little amused.

Willy, meanwhile, drove June to the dentist. His respectful manner had vanished. After a minute he picked up the speaking tube, and whistled a summons through it. June stared like a fascinated rabbit before lifting it gingerly off the hook. 'Yes?'

'How long will you be in the dentist, miss?'

'Not very long.'

'We'll have time to kill?'

'Yes. I suppose so.'

'So what d'you want to do?'

'Do?' she repeated foolishly.

'How about Regent's Park? Stretch our legs.'

'If you think it will be all right.'

'Who's to know?' Willy said airily, and hung up.

In the dental chair her cheeks were hot and her heart was beating fast. The dentist was concerned.

'Do you feel quite well, Miss Peak?'

'Oh yes,' she said hurriedly, 'I often go hot like this – and I did rush up the stairs.'

'At your age!' he said reproachfully. 'You *must* tell Lady Peak. Maybe you ought to have a check-up on your heart.'

'It's nothing – just such a rush. Please get on with it, I have to meet my stepmother in an hour.'

Twenty minutes later she ran down into the sunshine. Willy opened the door without rising. 'Want to sit in the front?'

'I – I don't mind.'

They sailed into the park, and he stopped the car near the lake.

They strolled across the rustic bridge – or rather, Willy strolled, while June trotted at his elbow in a bemused trance. The trees were greener than any she had seen before. The sky was an intenser blue. She had a peculiar feeling at the bottom of her abdomen, as though something hot was melting there and running up into her breasts and down the nerves to her legs. A sensation of pleasure that was akin to pain.

She had never been out with a man – ever. Not even with a boy. She knew quite well a servant should not behave as Williams was behaving, and that she should put him in his place, but she had no idea how to.

'I don't think Lady Peak would like me being in the park with you,' she ventured.

'Well, don't tell her.' Willy lit a cigarette and offered one to June. She shook her head vigorously.

'I think we ought to go back.'

Willy looked at his watch. It was, she noticed, gold, thin

and rectangular, and as expensive as her father's. He took off his cap and wiped the red weal it had pressed into his forehead. His thick, crinkly hair grew low. She could smell the new cloth of his uniform, and what she had come to think of as Daddy's smell. Tobacco, whisky, good toilet soap – but this was different. It was a young smell, making her think of a clean young animal.

'There's ages yet. No one will see us here. It's only kids and nannies, and nannies only gossip to other nannies.'

'I didn't have a nanny.'

'Nor me. I was born in India. I had an ayah. She was all right. Brown. With big brown eyes. Like you, and,' his eyes slid down, 'nice big tits.'

And once again the slow smile that seemed an invitation to unknown mischief. Her cheeks burned scarlet. She felt suffocated.

Two squirrels bobbed, bright-eyed, near their feet. Willy took a bar of nut chocolate from his pocket, broke off two squares and threw them to the squirrels, who sat up, holding the gift between their paws, nibbling delicately.

He laughed. 'Funny little beggars, aren't they? A bit like you.' He put a piece of chocolate in his mouth and offered her the rest. She shook her head again vehemently.

'You don't like it?'

'I'm not allowed it. I'm on a diet.'

'Righty-ho.' He ate all the chocolate and tossed the silver wrapping on the ground. June restrained herself from picking it up and finding a waste-basket. He unlocked the car. 'Better sit in the back now – we don't want anyone in Bond Street seeing you in front. Not with the blasted chauffeur, what?' He burst out laughing, and she got into the rear of the car her gloved hands twisting, her scared, excited eyes gazing at the strong column of his neck.

They sped down Portman Place.

'Big splash at lunchtime today?' he asked. 'All the nobs?'

'Yes. I won't be there.'

'Why not?'

'Oh, they're all very smart and famous. I'll have lunch upstairs. Then I'm going to the Metropole.'

'Alone?'

'I might ask Ruby.'

'The upstairs maid? You might as well ask me. I'm a much better class companion. *And* I'm off duty.'

For a moment she thought she would stop breathing. Then she managed a reproachful smile, and said, 'Please don't tease me.'

'All right. Go into the circle and sit in the back row. The half-crown seats. Right? Forget Ruby.'

She knew she should either not go to the cinema, or if she did, take Ruby and sit downstairs. But she did not. She had one awful moment when Charlotte, beautifully waved and made-up, changed into flowered chiffon, took her in to the drawing room, introduced her to some of the guests, and actually gave her a sherry. They all talked loudly to each other, but never seemed to listen. Supposing Charlotte decided to have her at the luncheon after all?

She hardly breathed until Charlotte said, 'Now run along, Junie. Lunch is about to be served. She's going to the movies – you know what kids are for the movies.'

At two o'clock she was sitting in the end seat of the back row of the circle. At the exact moment when the lights began to fade Williams appeared, changed into a lounge suit, and said, smiling, 'Move up, Squirrel.' Which she did.

He dropped into the seat beside her and his arm moved along the back of the seat. Presently it dropped round her shoulders and his left hand slid expertly down the front of her dress. All the new sensations surged up in an overwhelming wave. She was floating on the verge of unconsciousness. His other hand turned her face up to his and his lips began a gentle probing into hers. Five minutes reduced her to yielding, mindless, responsive desire. Then, just as expertly, Willy stopped, putting her gently away from him, bewildered, ashamed, guilty, yet longing for something more. No point, he thought, in taking it too far. She was under age, it was a little risky. Nice little thing. He took her hand between his, casually. She was trembling. He was surprised by her capacity for passion. But then he guessed the Old Man was, or had been pretty hot stuff in his time.

*   *   *

61

'You're really thrilled, aren't you?' said Boots as they finished dressing in her room.

'Well, aren't you?'

'Nah,' said Boots indifferently. 'I would've been two years ago. Before I left home. I've been everywhere. Ciro's, the Savoy – that's the best, the bands are great. The Kit-Kat, the Café de Paris – all the Soho ones. The Gargoyle and the Hambone, and Benjie's where I worked for a bit. The Embassy . . . posh or scruffy, I know them all. It's what chaps start with when they're out to get you. A night out. I suppose they think it softens you up. Me, *I* think – *watch it Bootsy.* Flowers, theatre, dinner, dancing. Sometimes you just wish they'd think of something else.'

She sighed with such a blasé and dispirited air that Helen giggled. Boots always made her laugh. It was a sort of gift. She said quite ordinary things that everyone was always saying, but the way she said them made you laugh.

Both girls looked perfectly lovely and it had been a hectic day. They had rushed up to Jack Jacobus in Shaftesbury Avenue in the lunch-hour to buy Helen a pair of silver dance shoes.

She found it difficult to concentrate on her work afterwards. The Friendly Liver Pill idea which she had produced had gone down well with the clients and she had learned today that they had agreed to take a whole page spread in the *Daily Sketch*. The thin, miserable woman, and Helen's radiant office girl facing each other. Matt had given her the whole new layout to do. She had been surprised by the reaction in the studio. Some of the juniors were so jealous they could hardly speak to her, and even the two seniors regarded her suspiciously from their supposedly unassailable position.

'I've been here eighteen months and never had a chance like that,' said one boy.

'Well, you can't draw for nuts,' declared loyal Alfred. 'Not like Helen.'

'It won't do her any good. Old Wilson won't let on to the Old Man that it's her idea. He'll think Wilson thought it up.'

'Oh yes he will,' cried Alfred shrilly. 'Mr Wilson always gives credit where credit's due.'

One of the seniors, Mr Meakin, who had come over to

inspect, lit his pipe and puffed avuncular clouds of smoke round her cubbyhole. 'You're very good, young woman. Like your father. I knew him well in Peak's early days. Sad loss. Peak never knew he had a genius working for him!'

'Thank you, Mr Meakin.'

It gave Helen a glow of delight. She must remember every word to tell her mother at the weekend. But at three o'clock Matt Wilson came storming across to her.

'Don't let success go to your head.' He slapped down the pull of the half-page spread. FRIENDLY is the name of this benighted firm, not FRINDLY. There is an "E" in it.'

'Oh! I'm sorry.'

'Well, put it right in the rough, and get it back to the block-makers. Get them on the phone and explain. They haven't had the final OK on it. J.P. wants it on his desk first thing.'

As soon as Matt Wilson had gone, Alfred came over and helped her paste out the offending word and put in a new run of letters.

'You're all thumbs.'

'I'm going out tonight. I want to leave early to get my hair done.'

'Somewhere nice?'

'Frascati's.'

'La Vie Bohême! Who with?'

'I don't know.'

'Blind date? *De*-licious! What are you wearing?'

'Green chiffon. Boots has lent it to me.'

Alfred's eyes widened ecstatically. Boots's clothes, looks and Cockney self-assurance were already a legend in the office. Most of the men were in pursuit of her – dallying around Space Reception like nectar-intoxicated bees. Laughter followed her innocent impudence.

'I'll bet you have a fantastic time,' said Alfred. 'Don't do anything I wouldn't do. Here, get this into Wilson and then get off. I'll clear up for you.'

'Alfred, you're a sweetheart,' she said gratefully.

Boots was waiting for her in the main entrance hall at five o'clock. She hailed a taxi and they whisked up to her hairdresser in Shaftesbury Avenue. It had a theatrical clientele, not the cloistered luxury of Bond Street, but it was large and efficient, it's silvered walls decorated with enlarged photographs of musical comedy stars and some minor film actresses.

Boots's straight golden hair was shampooed and marcelled into shining regular waves, with two perfect curls, like horizontal questions-marks flat against the pure line of her cheekbones. Helen's thick auburn mop was cut expertly, finger-waved and tamed into springy curls. Their fingernails were dipped into warm soapy water, scraped and filed, the cuticles pressed down with orange sticks. Boots had hers lacquered bright red. Helen had hers buffed till they shone. These ministrations cost her two pounds. They went back on a bus to Becker Street to dress, Helen feeling luxurious and guiltily extravagant, for she had never had a professional manicure or hair set before.

At the house there were two florist's boxes waiting for them, each containing a single orchid wired into fronds of maidenhair fern. One was pale pink and purple, the other white and pale green. There was a card from Sir James, reading, 'To dear little Boots and her friend, looking forward to a happy evening.'

'First step to seduction?' enquired Helen.

'Don't make me laugh! Any girl who falls for an orchid must be barmy. But old J.P. seems to be going to town. I wonder who he's bringing along? I hope he's over forty and loaded.'

'Do you really like older men?'

'I like them better than young men,' Boots explained ingenuously, ''cos they've got more money and they're easier to manage. I reckon I don't like men at all. But how else can you get a good time?'

'Does J.P. know you're bringing me?'

'No. I just said I would bring a girlfriend.'

Helen looked at her suspiciously.

'Well, I mean that keeping on eye on me for Tommy is all a lot of old rope. But with you there he'll behave.'

'Oh dear,' Helen was aghast. 'D'you mean I've no sex-appeal. Am I too stuffy?'

'You're a lady. It's like a hallmark, stamped all over you.

64

He fancies me, and he thinks I'm a little bit of skirt. I'm not, but he's not to know. But with you there it will be quite different.'

'Poor man. He'll feel cheated.'

She felt rather let-down. Somewhere during the evening her virtue might have been threatened. It was a bit boring to think it was perfectly safe. She looked at the flowers doubtfully. 'I don't know that I care for these great orchids.'

Boots took the purple and pink one and fastened it into the centre of the large black tulle bow on her hip.

'It looks stupendous on black,' said Helen. She unwrapped the silver paper and wire on the white one and fastened it into her hair just behind her ear.

Boots clapped her hands. 'But you haven't an evening coat. Try this.' It was a large Spanish shawl of white silk covered with embroidered blossoms. Helen wound it round her. 'That's marvellous! You look like a million dollars. I always felt like a grand piano in it myself.'

They were all keyed up. Full of laughter and excitement, posing before the mirror.

'The vestal virgins,' said Helen, 'gowned and garlanded for the sacrifice.'

'What's the time?' said Boots, and looked at her diamond watch. 'Cripes, it's after nine. That's OK, we want to keep them waiting. We'll get a taxi!' They stopped one going west, sharing the cost. Like comrades in arms, Helen thought. Like buccaneers . . . It *was* exciting. She hoped that Sir James's friend would not be too old, too rich, and at least moderate fun.

Sir James was waiting in the entrance foyer of the restaurant beside an impressive bank of expensive cold foods against a background of potted palms. Beyond large glass partitions they could see the interior of the restaurant, and hear the sound of music. With Sir James was Matt Wilson.

His face lit up with surprise and delight when he saw Helen. She had no idea that her own face was smiling and shining with pleasure and relief.

'My God,' Sir James said despondently, 'she's brought the Redmaine girl. We'll have to watch our step.'

Matt tried not to laugh. It just had to be her and not some

little pusher out for what she could get. How utterly lovely and ridiculously young she was. He ought to get out of the evening somehow. But he did not. He took her hand, and smiled into her shining eyes and said, 'Helen! How lovely!'

The foursome at Frascati's was not much of a success so far as Boots was concerned. The food and the wine were delicious, the dance band excellent, and Sir James was all attention. But Boots was not interested in food or drink, or Sir James's importuning hand beneath the tablecloth. She wanted to dance, she danced beautifully and Sir James did not care to dance. Matt Wilson dutifully danced with each girl in turn.

When it was her turn Boots chatted and laughed, and when she said something funny he laughed too, but she was aware that his eyes were watching Helen sitting at the table with Sir James, and that Matt was smiling at Helen over her head, and that Helen was not listening to a word Sir James said, and that so far as Matt was concerned she might not have been there.

It made her feel queer. Sad. Not jealous. As though she was invisible. She was not used to being overlooked. She had thought Helen deserved some fun, and it had been a bit of a lark, this blind date turning out to be the aloof and saturnine studio chief. But they seemed to be falling in love before her eyes. She could not believe it.

Helen and Matt Wilson danced in a dream. Everything was dreamlike. Insubstantial. The lights were lowered almost to darkness, and from somewhere a dim rosy glow touched the heads of the dancers as they moved slowly round to the music, the rhythmical sound of sliding feet like the slow sound of pebbles being shifted by a gently lapping tide.

Matt did not dance with the dedicated expertise of Helen's generation, but his body felt the music of the plaintive slow waltz and he guided her with authority, his lips resting on her hair. The maidenhair fern attached to the white orchid tickled his nose, making him want to laugh and to sneeze and to love her until he died.

66

All alone, I'm so all alone,
   There is no one else but you.
All alone, by the telephone,
   Waiting for a ring, a ting-a-ling.

I'm all alone – every evening,
   All alone, feeling blue,
Wondering where you are – and how you are,
   And if you are, all alone too?

Her head drooped against his shoulder. He looked down at
her half-closed eyes, and the pale rosy lips just parted, so near
to his that the surge of his desire became unbearable and he
stopped dancing. Helen sighed, and her heavy white lids and
long lashes lifted, and a hitherto unnoticed dimple twinkled in
her cheek.
   'You're good enough to eat,' he said.
   'Please – eat me!'
   'I really want to kiss you.'
   'Then why don't you?'
   'You wouldn't mind?'
   'I was beginning to think you never would!'
   He bent his head in the rosy dusk and put his lips on hers,
gently, sweetly, sensuously and felt the slim, fine-boned body
shiver with delight.
   'Oh God!' he said.
   'What's He got to do with it?' Helen murmured drowsily.
   A little owl. A little pissed white owl. Big, blinking eyes,
small imperious nose, soft to touch as downy feathers.
   'Shall we get out of this? Get off somewhere on our own?'
   'Oh *please!*'
   'We'd better tell them.'
   'You tell them.'
   They drifted back to the table, hand in hand.
   Boots was sitting disconsolately with a small pile of useless
acquisitions before her. A spray of red roses, a gilded box of
Abdullah cigarettes, a pretty paper fan. A box of chocolates
and a box of Turkish Delight. A Kewpi doll dressed in pink
feathers. A flask of scent. Placatory offerings? Because Sir
James was sixty and did not care to dance? They looked up in

67

bewilderment at Helen's face drunk with happiness for any-one to see.

'If you don't mind,' Matt said politely, 'we'd like to leave. Helen has never been to a nightclub – it's a lifelong ambition. Would you care to come along?'

Sir James shook his head so that his jowls quivered.

'I have to get home,' he said. 'We're going into the country tomorrow and my wife likes to make an early start. How about you, my dear?'

Boots looked at Helen and Matt and knew that anyone accompanying them would be a gooseberry.

'No thanks. Sir James will take me home.' She made a warning little grimace at Helen, who smiled back uncon-cernedly.

'I'll bring her safely home,' Matt assured her.

'You'd better.'

'I won't be late, Boots.'

'Come in with the milk if you like,' Boots snapped. 'I'm not your mum, thank God.'

Matt and Helen took a taxi to Piccadilly and kissed each other all the way there.

They stopped at the entrance to the narrow court leading to the Hambone Club. People were leaving and arriving. A young man in immaculate evening clothes was leaning against a wall vomiting, watched by a slim, elegant girl who said petulantly, 'Oh Ralph, *really*! You are *too* sick making!'

There was a door framed with coloured bulbs and a neon light with the name of the club above a door leading into a narrow corridor packed with people trying to get in past a large, uniformed bouncer. The beat of jazz came up from the cellar with an overwhelming stench of cigarette smoke, alco-hol, scent and the sweat of packed bodies. Helen went pale.

'I don't want to go in,' she said faintly.

'I don't blame you.' He put his arm round her shoulder and they went down Windmill Street into the Circus. In spite of the lights and the traffic it seemed emptier and more spacious than in the day. A few flower-women were still at their baskets, hoping to catch late romantics, and the morning's newspapers were being sold on the corners. He bought her a bunch of Parma violets, ghost flowers, grey in the street lights and scentless – part of the dream.

'Oh look,' she said, 'it's a full moon. Let's walk.'

'Why not?'

They walked down through St James's into the Mall, where Helen took off her shoes. 'They're hurting me,' she said.

He put one into each pocket, and his arm round her shoulder again. Her arm went confidently about his waist. It had rained while they were in Frascati's.

'It's lovely and cold and squidgy,' she said, as they walked along the gravelled pavement. Under the trees they stopped and kissed again, long slow kisses, not yet of passion, but of the sweet and tender preliminaries to passion. He put his hands on her waist and lifted her until her breasts were level with his lips, and found and kissed the nipples through the tight green bodice; she collapsed against him, sliding down into his supporting arms.

He held her close, saying, 'Wait . . . my love, wait for me, my love . . .' and they stood beneath the trees for a long while, until she sighed and straightened her tall slim body, and he said abruptly, 'I'm married, you know.'

'Oh!' She pulled the folds of the Spanish shawl protectively round her breasts. 'I suppose your wife would not like this at all.'

'She won't know.'

'You won't tell her?'

'I never see her. I haven't for years – seven to be exact. We are separated.'

'In that case,' she said seriously, 'you might just as well kiss me again.'

He laughed as he did so, but this time, he was more restrained. 'I must get you home. You go to my head – more than my head. Do you want to be raped in the Mall?'

'It couldn't be rape – to be raped the girl has to be unwilling. I'm ever so willing, and I think it would be lovely.'

'You mean – it's the first time you've felt like this?'

'Oh, yes.'

He sighed, straightened up. He could just see her face in the lamplight, her curly hair blown about her face, its once neat finger waves ruffled into maenad ringlets, the now crushed white orchid hanging rakishly over one ear. Her silk

69

stockinged feet were stained with sand and mud. He wanted to laugh at her, the little scarecrow, and he wanted to cry, but most of all he wanted to take her into his bed and love her through the night.

'Oh, child!' He shook his head. 'I guess you must still be a virgin.'

'You'd be right. What difference does that make?'

'Well, I wouldn't . . . I mean I wouldn't take advantage of you.'

'Advantage?' Helen repeated in astounded tones. 'What *do* you mean?'

Matt thrust his hands into his pockets and stalked slowly towards Buckingham Palace, his white scarf hanging from his neck, his sparse, curly hair on end. A long shadow marched, elongated before him, switching behind as he passed beneath the lamp standards. Helen ran after him and caught his arm, winding her arms about him.

'Well,' he said awkwardly, feeling as foolish as though he was trying to explain the facts of life to an innocent but turbulent niece, 'it's something I can't give you back if I take it away from you.'

'It's not a pound of tea,' she said reprovingly. 'My father once told me that when your daughter is seventeen you are terrified of her losing her virginity, but when she is twenty-five you are terrified she never will.' He laughed grimly. 'I was nine at the time. He was a very sensible man.'

'He sounds it,' Matt said drily. 'And you're twenty?'

'Twenty-three now,' she said smugly. 'Age of consent. Do what I like.'

'Not always good for little girls. I'm thirty-eight. That's supposed to be the age of discretion.'

'Discretion is no use to us. We shall just have to cram as much love as we can into life, seeing you're already so old.'

He said, 'Oh, heaven bless the child!' and lifted her up in his arms and kissed her until she was faint with love and limp with desire.

'Oh, Mr Matt Wilson,' she sighed, 'I do adore you so. To think that until recently I thought of you as a bad-tempered man.'

70

'So I am,' he said. 'Very bad tempered, and I have to get you home. Is it far?'

'Quite, thank goodness,' she said. 'Look at the moon. Everything is silver. Look at the lake!' The full moon had sailed into the water. 'Let's go slowly. Eke out the time until we meet again tomorrow.'

He did not answer. Her arm was about his waist, his lying across her shoulders. Every now and then she put her lips down on his hand, then she pulled it down beneath the Spanish shawl until it rested on her left breast. Such a neat, small girl's breast. A dryad. He could feel her heart beating steadily beneath the silk of her dress and was scared of her calmness and his own wild feelings, walking together along this dangerous precipice of love.

They went over Ebury Bridge into Pimlico. There were fewer lights and the great plane trees in the squares made black moving shadows on the paving stones. An occasional policeman passed on his beat, the moonlight catching the glinting buttons on his tunic. A taxi passed, heading back west, with late lovers, entwined like themselves; the occasional stumbling drunk. It was too late for the whores. They had gone home to their lairs around Gillingham Street. The city seemed very clean, washed silver and white by the great full moon.

'I knew your father fairly well,' he said. 'He was a remarkable man. Always said what he meant. He taught me a lot – I was working for Peak at the outbreak of war. He had a studio in Salisbury Square. He used to let me work there with him in the evenings. He never told me what to do – he said that was what I had to find out for myself.' Helen nodded – she could hear her father saying it.

'Yes. He said mistakes were all part of experience. He said if you never made a mistake you never learned anything. I didn't know he'd been killed until I got back to Peak's after the war – I couldn't believe it. I was in the line and came out alive, and he was a war artist and got killed. Peak was so angry, you'd have thought Sandy had done it deliberately. Your father was the only man I knew who could impose his ideas on Peak – no one does any more. The firm lives on the Old Man's personality, not on its quality of work.'

71

'*You could.* You could if you'd be bothered.'

'You're a perceptive little beggar.'

'Why aren't you interested in your work any more?'

'Let's stop talking about me. Your father was an aristocrat – or so Sir James says.'

'Yes. My grandfather was Lord Breterton, and my Uncle Royston is now. Unless he marries again and has children, poor old Dunky will get the title. That's my brother.'

'Why *poor* old Dunky?'

'It's not much cop.' He grinned, recognising Boots's phraseology. 'That enormous great house and a comparatively low income. The Redmaines are very bad at marrying money. Look at Dads – and now Duncan's fallen for Boots. And it looks as though I'll never be married at all.'

'Shut up,' he said, glanced down and, in the silver moonlight, saw her lips tremble. 'Oh don't my baby!' He turned her face up and kissed her again, and in a minute the sadness had gone and she was smiling, and nestling into him like a kitten, warm and softly sensuous.

They were outside Number 3 Becker Street. There was a light showing through the fanlight and they could hear a woman's voice. 'Someone's telephoning,' she said. He looked up at the tall, gaunt house.

'Which is your room?'

'Down there,' she pointed to the basement. 'You could sneak down, wrapped in a cloak like Don Giovanni. Except, of course, you could never be like him – he was a cold seducer.'

'You know nothing about me.'

She went up the steps, turned and stretched out her hand to him. He hesitated, then took it.

'I love you,' she said. 'Love me too.'

He drew her down into his arms and kissed her, then put her away from him.

'Goodnight,' he said, and then, 'Goodbye, my baby.'

He walked away, hands thrust into his pockets, a long black shadow following him. A taxi came round the corner and he whistled, and when it stopped got in and drove away without glancing round.

*   *   *

72

Shortly after midnight Sir James paid the bill and summoned his car. Conversation had petered out as they drove westward towards Belgravia, Boots sitting in silent abstraction. She regarded Sir James with a certain sympathy. Poor old thing – it had been as boring for him as it had for her. She felt his left arm go round her shoulders and his right hand come to rest on her knee.

'Isn't this cosy?' he said tentatively.

Boots glanced up at him with a sweep of her fabulous lashes and down at the large fleshy hand on her knee and took a cigarette out of her case and lit it without replying.

'Didn't you enjoy yourself?'

She lifted an indifferent shoulder.

'Don't you like Frascati's?'

'It's OK I suppose. One place is much like another, 'in't it?'

Sir James was chagrined. 'Where does Tommy Medway take you?'

'Oh, usually the Savoy, and then we go on to Ciro's, or the Embassy. Or sometimes somewhere like the Gargoyle. You know, Bohemian like. Or sometimes in the summer we go up the river. It all depends.'

'On what?'

'On whether he's flush or not. If he wins, well, we go on the spree and he buys me somepin' nice. Like this watch here.' It glittered in the dim interior of the car. 'Sometimes he plays Roulette – I like that. He gives me twenty quid to gamble with.' She didn't add that she never gambled.

It was all very well for Medway, who had a rich and accommodating wife who asked no questions so long as he asked none of her. Sir James had chosen Frascati's because he knew that it would be most unlikely for Charlotte to go there. Boots was getting underneath his skin. He always wanted things that were apparently unattainable. Like the big office in Kingsway, the Rolls, the house in Ebor Place, and the title. He did not particularly enjoy them – he had just wanted them. His podgy hand tightened on the silken knee, creeping round inside her thigh.

''Ere!' said Boots, 'Lay off!'

He glanced at Willy Hyde-Seymour's back beyond the glass partition, and hurriedly withdrew his hand.

'You can be a real little tease, can't you?' he said.

'I can be anything I want to be,' she said enigmatically. 'I wonder where they went to – Helen and Matt Wilson.'

She had watched them go, watched the tender way Matt had wrapped the Spanish shawl about Helen, and the weird feeling of having missed out on something important swept over her again. Sloppy. Wet. Ridiculous. She was afraid for Helen, and yet envied her. She sighed, and said again, 'I *wonder* where they went?'

The car was held up in the traffic at Hyde Park Corner, the taxis, late buses, and pleasure-going limousines jamming as they tried to infiltrate into the outward bound streams.

'Not anywhere very smart,' said Sir James. 'Matt Wilson hasn't the money for high-life. I mean he has a decent job with me, but it's nothing spectacular – and he has that wife to keep.'

'Wife?' She was alert, big-eyed, a suspicious young animal scenting danger for her friend.

'Yes. They're separated, but he still has to keep her. He left her and he's got no evidence against her. Boy and girl thing, after the war. Cold little bitch by all accounts.'

'Oh.'

'I've been thinking,' he said. 'You're not getting a very big wage.'

'Two pounds a week!'

'Well, that's fair. For a beginning. But now you know your way around. You might move over to my side of the office. Do my personal reception and filing. Help Peggy Prior out.'

'I can't type or do shorthand.'

'You can type. I've seen you.'

'Two fingers. I've taught myself while I've been at Peak's.'

'You could learn. I'll pay for lessons.'

'How much? How much would you pay?'

'Well, whatever it costs.' He knew the fees were not very high.

She smiled, and kissed the side of his jowled face, feeling the bristle uncomfortably on her lips, turning aside when he would have taken more.

'You're a sweet old thing,' she said. 'I'm thinking of chucking Tommy Medway when he gets back. I'm fed up with it.

74

Sometimes he's skint and sometimes he splashes money about like he's got three arms, and he's jealous as hell. A girl likes to know where she is.'

'You won't until the new contract's signed?' he said in alarm, and she looked at him with innocent eyes.

'*Not* if you're going to be nice enough to pay for typing lessons.'

The traffic eased and the beautiful car slid forward; Boots looked around her . . . the great bulk of St George's Hospital; dimly lit ward windows, rows and rows of beds. She shivered.

'Are you cold?'

'No, I'm tired. You live round here, don't you?'

'Ebor Place.'

'Well, why don't you go home and let what's-his name – Williams – take me home.'

'I was hoping you'd ask me in. There's a bottle of champagne in the boot.'

'Not a chance.' She drew away from him, pulling up the ruched collar of her black evening coat round her ears. 'Remember, you're only keeping an eye on me while Tommy's away. Or until I ditch him. Or until I think of something else, and right now I'm thinking of B-H-E-D, bed.'

He thought so too. He was tired. He told Williams to drive to Ebor Place.

'Drop me on the corner,' he said. 'Don't draw up before the house.'

Williams stopped the car at the corner of the Square where Ebor Place began its L-shaped turn towards Victoria and the less fashionable streets of Pimlico. She allowed Sir James to kiss her cheek, adroitly avoiding any further contact. The car moved smoothly forward. She leaned back and pretended it was her car.

'Where to, madam?' a voice said, nearly in her ear. She picked up the speaking tube and said in her telephone voice, 'Number 3 Becker Street, Pimlico!'

'Real tart's area you live in,' said Willy. 'What are you up to with the Old Man, baby? Playing hard to get?'

She had not seen him before. He waited down in the street for Sir James, the hall porter telephoning up to the office when he arrived. She was curious about his crude familiarity and his smooth, upper-class voice.

'You sound like a funny sort of chauffeur.'

'You sound like a predatory little bitch.'

'Hark at him,' Boots said indifferently. 'You bin listenin' all this time?' She bent down and took off her high-heeled black satin shoes. 'My feet are killing me.'

'You think you can look after yourself?'

'It's not been difficult so far.'

She hung up the speaking tube, plugging the stopper in.

The car drew up outside Number 3. Willy jumped out, and opened the door as she bent to put on her shoes. He saw a white shoulder and sleek golden hair. When she looked up and the yellow light from a street lamp illuminated her face he drew in a sharp breath. He had not expected anything quite so lovely.

'Allow me,' he said, and knelt down and took the shoes from her hand. She swung one arched foot out and he slipped a shoe on and his warm, strong hands slid up to her knee and under her skirt.

'It's not difficult with soft old men. How about me?'

She looked steadily into his handsome face, quite aware of his strength and youth and virility; his gentleman's voice and his seducer's manner.

'Shove off, handsome,' she said, and gave him a small push with her foot so that he just went off balance and had to put his hand on the pavement to steady himself.

She brought her heel down smartly on to the back of his hand. He yelped, cursed, lost his balance and sat down on the dirty pavement. Boots slipped on her other shoe and went swaying up the steps to the door with a rustle of silk and a breath of L'Heure Bleu, saying in her very best voice, 'Thanks for the buggy-ride, old boy.'

He heard the door close behind her, and drove away. His bruised hand was already swelling. He had thought she would be quite easy.

He put the car away and went up to the tiny flat above the garage. Outside the door was a basket containing a slice of game pie from Fortnum's, a small tin of *foie gras*, two ripe peaches and a half-bottle of Chablis. He grinned – a love

76

offering from little Junie. But it was Boots he thought about as he opened the bottle and poured the wine, and took a bite of the delicious pie. He had experienced an uprising of desire that alarmed him it was so uncontrollable.

The irate voice of the landlord yelled from the darkness at the back of the hall as Boots went in and switched on the lights. The telephone was ringing.

'Will ye answer that bloody contraption, for the love of God, miss. It's some bugger been afther you the whole blessed evening.'

'Sorry Mr Murphy!' She hurriedly removed the receiver, and said, 'Miss Skinner here.'

It was Duncan.

'I've been trying to get you for hours,' he said crossly.

'It's one o'clock in the morning. This telephone is a public one in the hall. You're waking the ruddy house. Is it a fire, or what?'

'I've found you a voice teacher. I telephoned today and made an appointment. Where the hell have you been?'

'I do go out.'

'With one of your old men, I suppose,' he said disgustedly. 'Listen, I've talked to a lot of people I know, and they all say that May Rampton is the best person for voice production.'

'That old actress!'

'She was very famous. And she's great. I know her. I told her you hadn't much money. She charges a pound an hour, and if she has to correct a bad regional accent it will mean at least two lessons a week. She says if you're hopeless she'll tell you right away. She has a studio in Endell Street.'

'Couldn't you have rung in the morning?'

'I said you wanted to do films, and she turned her nose up. But I said you were the most beautiful girl I had ever seen and totally photogenic like Garbo. Then she laughed – I don't know why.'

'Oh Dunky, you are mad!'

'But do you want to do it? That's what I want to know. I've made a date and I said I'd ring her tomorrow if you did, and confirm. She takes evening students. Will you do it?'

77

'I dunno,' she hesitated, 'I've done all right as I am.'

'I can't see that you have,' he exploded. 'All you've got is a few gee-gaws and a few mean old chaps hanging about you. You must be bored silly half the time. I wouldn't have bothered, but you are unique. You've got a face to launch a thousand ships and burn the topless towers of Illium.'

'Come again?'

'Don't you *want* to do something different? You can't just take things off other people all your life. You've got to try to make something of yourself. To be beautiful – like you – is special. *It's a talent.* Every day here we have girls with no talent and not a patch of your looks trying to get a test. *I'll* get you a test. I swear I will. If I ask Strauss he'll give you a test. But you've got to lose that accent. Talkies are coming – even looks like yours won't be enough.'

The absurdity of it all filled her with joy. The emptiness of the evening with Sir James lifted. Both Duncan and Helen had this effect upon her. They were both so sure that they could make life give them what they wanted – not just success or money, although that was part of it – but interest and achievement and fun and love along the way. She was younger than both of them but she felt older. She wanted all their brave dreams to come true.

'OK,' she said recklessly, 'I'll have a go.'

'Spiffing! Meet me outside the office on Monday evening at five o'clock, and I'll take you along. I've made an appointment for you at six. Can you manage the money? Two lessons a week, a pound a lesson? I could help – well, a bit . . .'

'No,' she said quickly, 'I'll manage it.'

'Right. Five o'clock on Monday.' She waited for him to say something else, something personal, but all he said was, 'I asked Mums if we could bring you down one weekend. She said wait until the end of the stately home season, and then she'd love it. Will you come?'

'Yes. If you're sure.'

'Of course I'm sure. We've got to think of a new name for you . . . Lillian is OK but *not* before Skinner. How about Lillian Lang. Lillian is euphonious – and it has a feeling of white and gold. Lily-like. Imagine films in colour! They will be, of course, one day. I don't think Boots is glamorous enough.'

'Oh *Dunky!*' she burst out laughing.

'What's so funny?'

'You are!'

'I don't see it. Well, goodnight.'

'Goodnight.'

She put down the receiver, thinking of his gawky good looks and height, like a yearling colt or baby giraffe. Lillian Lang? Euphonious! Cripes! White and gold and lily-like? She began to giggle shakily, when she heard footsteps stop in the street outside and the low murmur of voices. There was a long silence. She sat down on the stairs, as though her knees were weak. She knew it was Matt and Helen outside, and that Helen was being kissed as she, who had been kissed so many times, had never been kissed, and the heavy emptiness came back. The feeling of being left out, of missing out.

Then the heavier footsteps walked slowly away, and she heard Helen's key in the doorway. She came in wrapped in the Spanish shawl, her curly hair on end, the white orchid brown and crushed, hanging precariously by a bobby-clip. She was carrying her new silver shoes. She stared at Boots in a bemused way, and smiled dreamily.

'Duncan just rang.'

'At this hour? Did he want me?'

'No. He wanted to tell me he's found a voice trainer for me.'

'Oh good! That's splendid, Boots.'

'Nell, he's *barmy!* About this film thing. He says he can get me a test. Is he serious?'

'He's always serious. Well, people are when they really want something. He's very practical. You could do with some speech improvement anyway.'

If anyone else had said it she would have blown with indignation, but she knew Helen was not being snobbish or sarcastic but simply telling the truth.

'He says to tell you that your mother will give you a date about asking me for the weekend later – when the season's over.'

'Good.'

'Nell, are you sure you want me to come? I mean – wasn't Duncan just showing off?'

'You are a funny girl,' Helen said, puzzled. 'Why on earth should he do that? You seem to think everyone has an ulterior motive.'

'What's that mean?'

'Well, pretending to be nice to get something out of you.'

'Like sweet-talking and sending orchids when all they want is to lay you?'

'Quite.'

'Well, most of them do – all men, anyway.'

'Oh, Jumping Jesus, Boots, you've got a beastly suspicious mind.'

A door at the back of the house opened and a weary voice shouted, 'For the love of God will you young women go to bed and not stand jawing all the blessed night keeping people awake.'

'Sorry, Mr Murphy!' they chorused.

'Coffee?' whispered Boots. They crept upstairs, switching off the hall lights. In her room she lit the gas ring and put out cups.

'Did you go to a nightclub?'

'We went to the Hambone but we didn't go in. It looked awful. Jam-packed and everybody sloshed.'

'Yeah. No class.'

'So we walked back.'

'All the way from Piccadilly? In your stocking feet? Aren't they sore?'

'Yes, but it was lovely. Moonlight.'

Boots made Camp Coffee, hot and sweet and handed Helen a cup. 'You're nuts about Matt Wilson, aren't you?'

'Yes.'

'He's married, you know.' She spoke painfully; not wanting to hurt and shock, yet wanting to warn her friend.

'Yes. He told me. What's that got to do with it?' She yawned into Boots's uncomprehending face. 'I'm dead. See you in the morning.' She crept downstairs into her basement room and was asleep in five minutes.

Boots undressed, set her hair in flat, pinned curls, and secured it in a pale pink net. She carefully creamed off her make-up before she got into bed to lie awake, watching the beams of the car headlights flashing over the high ceiling.

She had spent her girlhood cheating, charming and cajoling her way into good times and pretty things certain that ultimately it would lead to security, to a wealthy life, like the girls in the movies, like Joan Crawford, and Leatrice Joy, all dancing and parties and wonderful clothes and fantastic houses. She wondered now if she really enjoyed all this. It was always the same, like the repeating pattern on the shabby wallpaper. It seemed to her she had never had any real girlhood at all. The vegetable lorries were trundling past towards Covent Garden before she fell asleep.

Chapter 4

Next day both girls felt a trifle hung-over when they went to the ABC tea shop for lunch.

'What are you eating?' asked Boots.

'Poached egg and baked beans.'

'Ugh! After champagne! Fair gives me the horrors! I'll have a cup of coffee and a bun.' When it came she buttered the bun with fierce concentration, and demanded, 'This old girl Dunky's taking me to meet. D'you know her?'

'I've seen her on the stage.'

'What's she like?'

'I don't know. She's a very good actress, but she's an old woman now. She was very beautiful. Dads knew her in his salad days. Look Boots, no one's making you do it. If you don't want to, tell Dunky to go to hell.'

'It's just that I don't know what he's getting me into. But he's the only bloke I've ever met who thinks I'm worth a couple of ha'pennies, really. D'you know, I'm scared of your brother?' Helen nearly choked into her coffee. '*Truly. Imagine* – that sniffy kid! Here, Nell, have you noticed that today chaps are either like schoolboys or really old?'

'That's the war. Even the ones that are young are old if they were in the trenches. Dunky's not so young – not in every way.'

'I don't care whether I let blokes down. They all ask for it. They're only after one thing with me. A bit of nooky. That's all they think there is to me. Except that barmy brother of yours. He *expects* something from me! I don't know quite what, but he does. *Potential*? I've got to realise my potential, he says. Never heard the bloody word until he started in on me. Honest, Nell, it takes all the stuffin' out of me. I get scared I'll let him down, then I'd be letting myself down, and you too . . .'

'Jumping Jesus, Boots, Dunky and I are nothing. You don't have to bother about us.'

They finished their lunch, ordered more coffee and Boots lit a cigarette, looking at Helen through the spiral of smoke. Helen's chin was propped on her hand, her eyes a-dream. She always looked so pure, her skin and lips so lovely, without make-up; sort of fresh, countryfied, uncontaminated.

'And how is the great romance this morning?' Boots asked with heavy sarcasm. 'Did he rush to fold you in his arms?'

'In the studio? Don't be silly. I saw him on the other side of the room, and he nodded, as he always does. He gave all the work to Mr Meakin to give out, and then he was in conference with Sir James all morning.' Her candid eyes met Boots's uncompromisingly. 'Well, for heaven's sake, Boots, we don't want the whole office to know we're in love.'

'*I'm* not silly,' said Boots, 'I don't imagine some chap's nuts about me after one slightly boozy evening. When we were coming out of the office he passed us, going out with old Brooker. He didn't even glance at you.'

'Well, he wouldn't, would he?' Helen said firmly. 'Not with old Brooker. You know he tells everything to his wife, and his wife's a friend of Miss Klein's. Of course he couldn't speak to me.'

'Well, he needn't have pretended not to see you!' Boots said, and crowed, '*What* did I tell you. They're all the same. *Men!*'

'They are not,' said Helen, 'there's no one in the world like Matt Wilson. He's in love with me.'

'Pooh. You ask Lily. She's heard him making dates with his birds over the telephone. Theatre girls he likes. Mr Cochrane's Young Ladies.'

'Well, we only met last night. Really met, I mean. I fell for him when I first saw him. I know he loves me now. No two people could have felt like we felt otherwise. I'm not jealous of his past.'

Boots gave up. 'You're crazy like your brother. Matt

Wilson is a married man – he's not even rich, not with what he has to pay his wife. There's no future in it for you.'

Boots shut up. They went back towards the office in silence. It was not a quarrel but they had nothing to say to each other. Along the Strand they saw the familiar tall figure, soft black hat crammed down on his head, striding towards Kingsway, hands in pockets, broad shoulders disconsolately hunched.

'There is Matt,' cried Helen, and started forward joyously after him.

Boots caught her arm. 'Don't. Helen, don't chase him . . . don't make yourself cheap . . .'

Helen's face flushed, her chin went up, and she looked at Boots with her withering Redmaine stare. 'Let go of my arm, please,' she said, 'and mind your own business.'

She pulled free – she could just see Matt's black hat above the crowd of lunchtime office workers, waiting to cross to the eastern end of the Aldwych, and went bounding after him with her swift gazelle speed. Boots stood still. The policeman on point duty held up the westward flowing traffic, and Matt crossed. Helen caught him on the central island. Pushed her hand through his arm.

He turned and stared blankly down at her, and it seemed seconds before recognition dawned in his eyes. He raised his hat. 'Helen?' he said politely. 'Did you want me?'

She did not believe it – she thought he was teasing her. The colour flushed up under her fair skin. 'Of course I want you,' she said mischievously. 'Didn't I make myself clear last night? Don't *you* want *me*?'

He moved away, so that her hand fell from his arm. The eastward traffic was stopped, and a large brewery dray with big plodding horses was holding up the mass of hooting automobiles. He glanced at her, smiled, said, 'It was a good evening. Although I was a bit the worse for wear towards the end. We had a good time and a nice evening. Thank you for making it so. I must go – I have an appointment just after two . . . oh, by the way. The Old Man's delighted with the Friendly Liver Pill layout . . .'

He raised his hat again, dodging off through the traffic and out of sight. Helen stood there motionless. She could not believe it. That Matt should speak to her like this – bored, flippant, a little sheepish.

She remembered his lips and hands upon her, his arms holding her close in the moonlight, the sensation of floating on a sea of delight.

Boots came up and stood beside here. Helen shook her head like a dog shakes moisture out of its fur, shaking the past few minutes out of existence.

'What did he say?'

'He said he was a bit drunk last night. Thanked me for a pleasant evening. Said the Old Man was very pleased with the Friendly Liver Pill layout.' Her colour began to return – a small frown appeared between her brows. 'Did last night really happen?'

'It happened. He's getting out of it.' Boots said furiously, 'The pig. Aren't you mad?'

'If last night happened as I remember it, I don't believe him – he was pretending. Why should he pretend it meant nothing to him?'

They walked slowly, side by side, up the Aldwych and into the office. Stopped on the first floor. Boots looked at Helen's pure, puzzled face, and said, uncomfortably, 'Well, maybe you're right, and he doesn't want anyone to know. I mean there are fifty people in this office and any of them might have seen you with him, and you know what a lot of natter-mouths they are.'

Helen said gravely, 'You don't believe that, do you?'

'No.' Boots could not bear to see Helen look like this – defeated. People like Duncan and Helen could not be defeated. 'I believe he's giving y ou the brush off. Don't take on about it.' She gave a shaky smile. 'Oh, come on, Nell, you're worth three of that half-baked artist.'

'I think you're wrong, Boots. I think that is what he wanted me to think. The trouble is – I don't know why.' Surprisingly she put her arms round Boots and hugged her. 'Good luck with the voice training, Bootsy.'

Boots was shaken by this spontaneous affection.

'Friends?' Helen asked.

'Mates,' Boots replied. They smiled at each other with love and relief.

'Don't let Dunky bully you, Boots. He's nuts about you really.'

'Is he? He's a funny way of showing it. But I suppose it takes all sorts.'

'What does?'

'I don't know. It's what my mum says when she can't understand things. Like why the Old Man spends all his money on booze and doesn't pay the gas. "Well," she says, "it takes all sorts."'

'I'll see you at Number 3 this evening. 'Bye now.'

At four o'clock Miss Klein sent one of her girls over to say that Boots was to go to Sir James's office at once.

'I'm to take over here until you get back.'

She sat down at the desk with an expression of prim disapproval and began to wind some paper into the machine. Boots took her time checking the scarlet of her lipstick and the smooth waves of her golden hair.

'Wonder what he wants?' she said airily. 'Going to offer to keep me in sin, I shouldn't wonder!' The other girl went bright red and typed furiously. It was exactly what she had been thinking. Silly cow, Boots thought, and sauntered out. She went into the secretary's room where Peggy Prior and her assistant were busy with Sir James's voluminous correspondence. They looked up with the same knowing, prim expression, and Peggy said, 'Go right in, dear.'

Sir James was alone in his office. He stretched out his pudgy, clean, beautifully manicured hand as soon as the door closed behind her, and then tapped his knee invitingly.

'Come and sit down, girlie.'

Boots kept her distance. 'Someone might come in.'

'That door,' he pointed to one on his right, leading directly into the corridor, 'is locked. And Miss Prior wouldn't dare come in – unless I rang for her.'

'Well trained secretary?'

'Oh, come on, you're not frightened of me?' She shook her head. 'I guess we all had a bit too much to drink last night. I promise I'll be a good boy. Don't you trust me?'

Boots sat down on the corner of his desk, and dangled a slim, delectable leg. She wore her yellow dress and pearl earrings and high heeled white shoes with square toes and

86

yellow straps. She ravished him – just her nearness, and the radiance of her youth. She smiled, and said, 'What did you want to see me about?'

'What we spoke about last night. You coming to work over here at the main reception desk. You'll do my personal filing, you'll make tea or coffee for any of my visitors. You'll keep my appointment books. There are two, one on my desk, one you'll have. You'll have to see they coincide. You'll greet my callers and bring them along to see me – through the corridor door – when I ring. I've noticed how you remember names over at Space Buying – that's useful. And how you can get rid of people tactfully. Miss Klein's told me. Do you think you can manage it?'

'What about the girl I'm replacing?'

'She's going to Accounts.'

'And what will *she* say?' The smooth blonde head jerked expressively towards the door of the secretary's office.

'Miss Prior? Nothing. Why should she?'

'Ah!' So Peggy Prior was used to these sudden switches. Making room for anyone who took his fancy. Dirty old devil. 'I don't want to cause no trouble. I can manage that. Anything else?'

'Well, I'd like you to take up that secretarial course – evening classes. It would be useful, and it would keep you out of mischief.' He cocked a hopeful eye at her. 'Give you an excuse not to see Medway too often. Of course, you'll have to see him occasionally, until the new contract is signed. I'll pay for the lessons.'

'What will it cost?'

'Oh, thirty bob a session, perhaps two pounds. It's a policy of the firm to pay for secretarial training – for promising girls. There's a very good secretarial school round the corner.'

She thought about the speech-training lessons with Madame Rampton. 'Hm,' she said thoughtfully.

Sir James was disconcerted. 'What were you expecting?'

'Nothing,' she said. 'But this is just swapping a job. I don't reckon it will be more interesting. At least over in Space there are lots of fellows dropping in. Some of them come in quite often,' she gave an angelic smile, guessing he had noticed that the younger men in his staff and the Fleet Street reps appeared to spend quite a lot of time leaning on the counter at Space Reception.

'Do you go out with them?' he asked jealously.

'That'd be telling. If I'm not getting more money I might just as well stay where I am.'

'My dear, I can't justify an increase in salary.'

He leaned across the desk, and turned on the compelling persuasion that had made him such a success. 'I just want you right here, close to me. When Tommy comes back we'll start to talk about the Medway contract. I've moved you now so that I can take care of you better.'

Boots stretched open one of her large blue eyes between a thumb and forefinger, tilted her face near to him, inviting examination.

'See any green in there?' she asked mildly. For a moment Sir James was nonplussed. Then he laughed.

'All right, you wicked little monkey. What do you want?'

'I want to take some lessons – speech-training. Three lessons a week, a pound a lesson. Course of twelve lessons. Six weeks.'

Sir James sighed and leaned back. He would have to tread warily. Medway was infatuated enough to take away the account if he suspected anything.

'Typing is more useful,' he said smiling, 'and I can't put speech-training through the books.'

'Who's to know it isn't for a secretarial course? You give me a chit to Accounts, and I'll find a receipt.'

'Why are you so keen on this?' he said testily. 'I think the way you speak is cute.'

Like a pet, she thought, not really thoroughbred, but ever so cute.

'It holds me back,' she said. 'Helen Redmaine doesn't talk like I do. I want to be able to go anywhere.'

He was about to say that she was a hundred times more attractive than Helen Redmaine, but met those extraordinary big, almost transparently blue eyes, and laughed again, but a little uneasily. She was a luscious little cutey and that's how he wanted her to stay.

He made out a chit to Accounts stating that Miss Lillian Skinner was to draw three pounds a week to pay for secretarial lessons, taking a six-week course. Then he took out his note-case, filled as it was every morning with spotless notes, and gave her a crisp, white fiver.

'I can't give you any more salary – but that's to buy yourself something pretty. And there may be more of those – if you're a good girl. Now say thank you nicely to Daddy.'

Boots jumped up, put her arms about his neck and kissed him, her cool mouth just missing his eager, cigar-smelling lips, and moving adroitly out of range, when he would have pulled her down on to his knees.

'Hey, you said you'd be a good boy,' she said warningly.

'Thank's *ever* so.'

She flashed away to the secretary's door, turned and said with thoughtful innocence. 'Maybe if Tommy asks what I'm up to in the evenings, we'll say it's a secretarial course, eh?' And she went out thinking, '*Be nice to Daddy*! Stupid old git!'

The door closed behind her and Sir James sat back, feeling old and exhausted. She was like quicksilver, the little devil. He rose slowly and went into Peggy Prior's office.

'I've arranged for that little Miss Skinner to work at the main reception desk from next week. Reception and filing, and she can keep my cutting book. Miss Klein says she is very promising. Show her the ropes, won't you? I'll see Matt Wilson now.'

'Promising indeed!' said Peggy Prior to her assistant when Matt Wilson had followed Sir James into his sanctum. 'He'll be lucky if he gets anything but promises out of that one.'

Soon it was all over the office that Boots Skinner was going to work in the front office for Sir James, and it went via the hall porter to Sir James's new chauffeur, Williams, who angrily rubbed a purple bruise on the back of his hand.

At five o'clock Boots ran down to the hall, and saw Duncan waiting outside on the pavement. He had added a monocle to the ensemble of riding breeches, sports jacket, polo neck, and black Borsolino; he looked pale and tense and interesting. How lovely he was – if you could call a boy lovely. But he *was* lovely and he was absurd and she melted with tender laughter at the sight of him.

Duncan eyed her with the sharp scrutiny of a trainer look-ing at a likely filly. The simple yellow crêpe dress, the black straw hat with the yellow flower under the brim. Nice touch, but a bit Ascoty for old Ma Rampton.

Boots lifted and examined the monocle.

'Goin' blind in one eye like ruddy Nelson?' she asked.

The colour rose beneath his fair, faintly freckled skin.

'No,' he said. He took the monocle and screwed it into his eye and Boots curled up and shrieked with derisive laughter. He removed the Borsolino, pulled off the monocle, chucked it in the gutter and replaced his hat.

'You're quite right,' he said sheepishly, 'Rudi Strauss wears one, and I thought it made me look older. And more interesting.'

'It makes you look a right Charlie,' she said cheerfully, 'but that's your business. Anyway, what d'you want to look like that old kraut for? You're mad enough as you are.'

He was so thin and tall and bony. Great wide bony shoulders. Long, elegant bony hands.

'You don't eat enough,' she said.

'I forget to eat. There are so many other things to think of. Like getting you a film test.'

They were walking up Kingsway, turning left towards Drury Lane and Long Acre. 'Can you keep a secret?'

'Yes.'

'We-ell, I'm not *really* back at Oxford this term.'

'What d'you mean – not *really*? I mean you are there – or you aren't.'

'You won't tell anyone? Not even Nell?'

'Oh, well, all right.'

'Well, Mr Goldman said I could stay on, if I liked, as I speak German, and Strauss likes me. I've got another pound a week and they call me Assistant to the Floor Manager, but really I'm a sort of odd job boy for Strauss.'

'Then you're not going to college?'

'Well, yes. I'll sleep there and get back in time to go to hall about twice a week. I'll manage to show up to tutorials occasionally. And Barry – that's Mr Goldman's son, my friend – well, he'll cover up for me. But Greenstreet is only half an hour from Oxford on the bike, I can get off there first thing in the morning and be back before Hall. No one will miss me. Barry told me that Strauss said I had a creative mind and acute visual perception.' Boots sniffed. He preened a little. 'Barry said his old man didn't know what Strauss was talking about, but he wants to keep him sweet because he's getting him very cheaply, and hopes to keep him for another picture. I'm a sort of go-between, between Strauss and the management and the cast. But it's a privilege to watch him work. And an education. I *can't* turn it down. It's a chance in a million.'

'Yes, but why can't you tell Nell?'

'Oh, she's got her own thing to worry about.'

Boots had to agree with that. But Duncan was off again, not really listening to her.

'Strauss wouldn't say that about me unless he meant it. He wouldn't bother. He said I had potential. That's what he's always looking for. You know what I mean?'

'Yes,' said Boots drily, 'I do now.'

He stopped at a narrow door between two fruit warehouses, shuttered in the hot summer evening.

'Here it is.'

There was an all-pervading smell of rotting oranges. On the board listing the tenants just inside the door she read, '*Madame May Rampton. Theatre School. 1st Floor. Private lessons in speech-training, elocution and deportment.*' She followed Duncan up a narrow staircase to the first floor.

'D'you really think,' she said, 'she'll make any difference to the way I talk?'

'It's up to you,' he said non-committally. 'Come on.'

He opened the door into a small untidy office where a secretary was busily typing. She looked up, smiled and said, 'Oh, Dunky! It's OK. Go in.' And they went on through another door into a large, light studio room, empty except for an elderly lady with dyed blonde hair bound by a Liberty scarf, with two equally elderly Pekinese asleep at her feet. She was smoking a cigarette. Boots waited silently. Duncan went forward and kissed Madame Rampton's hand.

May Rampton gave Duncan a sweet, weary smile. Her eyes were deep-set, haggard and still very blue. Her voice was like Black Velvet – the drink, not the material. Low and dark, with a sparkle hidden somewhere in its depths.

'So,' she said, 'Rudi Strauss's boy genius!' She looked at

Boots and said brightly, 'Well, as you said, she's certainly beautiful. It's an asset nowadays. Any brains?'

Cheeky old cow, thought Boots, and rocked her long lovely hand like the Italian women who lived around her home in Hackney.

'*Cosi-cosi!*' she said.

Madame Rampton permitted herself a frosty smile. They fixed up the lessons, and afterwards Duncan said he would take her out to dinner. The restaurant was in a basement under a French delicatessen in Old Compton Street, where the à la carte menu was two-and-six. Duncan ordered a bottle of Sauterne.

'I can afford it now,' he said, and added hastily, 'Well, occasionally.'

She told him how she had got the money to pay for the lessons and to her surprise he did not laugh.

'You don't think I should have done it?'

'It's your career I am trying to promote, Boots,' he said. 'Your private life is your own business.'

To his astonishment, and hers, for it had never happened before, her eyes filled with tears. Her long lashes became all wet and tangled, and he saw her wonderful face as in a soft focus close-up with big tears glistening, and the perfect lips trembling, and he said, 'Oh, Boots, you are so heavenly!' and kissed her.

She was startled at the rush of feeling this unexpected and inexperienced kiss gave her. He was really only a kid in spite of his Redmaine arrogance.

There were things she did that the Redmaines might laugh at, but would not dream of doing themselves. Particularly where money was concerned. To her money was something other people had and you tried to get. The Redmaines did not think like that. She decided not to tell him about the extra fiver Sir James had given her.

Willy was driving the Rolls down to a house in Wiltshire where Lady Peake and June had been spending two weeks at the end of the season with some people called Debereaux, whom Charlotte had met at a charity luncheon.

92

Sir James had declined the invitation. He could not abide country house parties and their accompanying sporting activities. He said it was quite impossible for him to leave the business.

It was a hot day and Willy found his uniform unbearable. The high military collar chafed his neck, and the leather cap lining pressed into his forehead. He took off the cap, and undid the collar. He was sick of being a servant. And he worried about June.

She was becoming a bit of a nuisance. She had discovered that it was perfectly easy to get through the mews to his flat without being seen, as the house servants always used the front area entrance. She brought him gifts, food and drink and cigarettes; small expensive presents – hogskin gloves, a cashmere scarf and pullover, pure silk ties. If he was out, she would leave them upstairs at his door. If he was in, he would let her in for an hour or so if Sir James and Lady Peak were out.

June was love-drunk. Sexually aroused and skilfully initiated, she was possessed. Her passion startled and disturbed him. To June herself it seemed as though she was only alive in his arms. She went through her stepmother's planned social round like an obedient zombi, living only for the stolen hours in Willy's rooms above the garage. A tiny living room – an even smaller bedroom – the pervading smell of petrol rising from below.

When it had started it had been no more than an automatic response to her infatuation. That kind of kid, at that age, was irresistible. There had been no particular advantage in it for him. June had plenty of pocket money, but it was the old lady, Charlotte, who had the power. But that was a game to be played very carefully and not for him to make the first move.

The Old Man had apparently forgotten the half-promise to give him a chance in the office. Somehow Willy had to remind him that the chauffeuring job was only a fill-in, that Willy was hard-working, personable and quick to learn, and only waiting for the right opportunity in life, and that the firm needed young front men with the right sort of background.

He had hoped that an opportunity to make the break with June would come while she had been away, so he could cool

93

the whole thing off. He had been very careful. He had given her the name of a discreet doctor in Wimpole Street who had fitted her up. So that was all right.

Maybe chaps like him should be paid a fee for breaking in these eager kids. He wished that Boots showed a little eagerness. If she saw him waiting with the Rolls she sailed past with her pretty nose in the air.

When he thought of her he flexed his hand angrily. It no longer hurt, but the mark was still there.

He stopped just before the entrance gates at Featherstone Hall, combed his hair, put on his cap, and fastened his collar before he drove up to the house. God above, the money some people had! It *must* be possible to get hold of some of it.

When he reached the house he was told to wait – Lady Peak was not quite ready. He sat in the car in the hot sun, the sweat gathering in the tight leather band of his uniform cap. He could hear voices behind some yew hedges where the steady plock of balls told him that tennis was being played. There was a swimming pool too, he heard splashes – he closed his eyes, thinking of cool water. A soft crunch on the gravel made him open his eyes and he saw June, dressed in a white tennis dress with a bandeau round her dark hair, coming across the large forecourt towards him.

He raised his hand to his cap respectfully but did not smile. She stopped by the open window and said, 'Willy darling, I've got to talk to you.'

'For God's sake, buzz off,' he hissed furiously. 'D'you want to get me sacked?'

But June was beyond caution.

'It's awful. She's leaving me with these people while she goes to the Riviera. They're going to take me to Scotland.'

'That'll be nice for you,' he said heartlessly. 'Get some decent shooting.' He looked up at the long Georgian façade and saw an inquisitive face bobbing above a white apron bib. 'Get away. One of the servants is watching.'

'We may not meet for ages!' she said pitifully. 'What shall I do, Willy? I can't *live* without you!'

The sweat ran down his face. No use being angry, she might throw hysterics and bust the whole thing open.

'Squirrel, be good,' he said coaxingly. 'I'll telephone you

94

here – tonight. Then we'll fix something. Look out, here they come . . .' Two man servants appeared in the porch carrying Charlotte's luggage. He said loudly, 'Thank you, Miss June. I'll just move the car up.'

He took the Rolls forward so that she had to stand back, got out and unlocked the boot for Charlotte's initialled pigskin cases to be put in. Charlotte came out of the house with her hostess. As always she had that impeccable American bandbox look – a pleated dress of black and white crêpe and a smart white, wide brimmed hat with a single black rose. She stood talking for a moment, held out her hand to June, who went to her. Charlotte kissed her, telling her to have a good time, thanked her hostess and got into the car.

'Home, madam?' Willy asked.

Charlotte gave him a little half-smile, and said enigmatically, 'Where else?'

He closed the door and walked round to the driver's seat, feeling a slight anticipatory excitement. Had she been very bored at Featherstone? Bored women were vulnerable.

The Honourable Mrs Debereaux, a distinguished nonentity of a woman, stood with her arm around June's shoulder, calling, 'Don't worry. We'll take good care of her.' June watched the car drive away, frozen with despair.

He eased the car on to the main road and into a smooth fifty miles an hour. After about ten minutes Charlotte slid back the glass panel behind the driver's seat. The usual indication that she wanted to speak to him was a shrill blast on the speaking tube.

'Is Sir James expecting you in town this evening, Williams?'

'Yes, madam. At seven o'clock. He asked me to say he would be in time for dinner at eight.'

'Ah.' She sat back, but she did not close the panel, which only opened from the inside. Willy drove on. He thought she had fallen asleep. Cautiously he moved his head so that he could see her in the driving mirror. She had moved so that she was looking at him – their eyes met and a dull colour suffused her well-powdered cheeks. Willy felt like a marksman feels when the bracken stirs and he knows his prey lies hidden, listening, quivering with fear. What would she do next? He gave her a fleeting glance of acknowledgement, but nothing else. A wrong move would be fatal. Charlotte took off her gloves and removed her white hat.

'It's so hot,' she said.

'Yes, madam.' His fair-skinned face was flushed red in the heat.

'Why don't you take off your cap? It certainly looks very uncomfortable.' It was a blatant invitation.

'That's very kind of you, madam.'

He took off the uniform cap and the red pressure mark showed lividly on his white forehead.

'You poor boy,' said Charlotte. 'Those caps must be awful in this weather.'

Willy stopped the car, undid the top button of his stiff uniform collar, and turned to face her. It was his turn to make a move.

'Lady Peak,' he said courteously, 'would you like some tea?'

'That would be just wonderful.'

'If we cut through the river towards Goring, I know a very nice quiet place. The Weirside Inn. Perhaps you would permit me to give you tea?'

'Well, I don't know . . .' She glanced doubtfully at his uniform. He smiled mischievously, got out and opened the boot, and exchanged the uniform tunic for a beautifully cut, thin tweed hacking jacket, and knotted a fine silk square in chocolate and blue round his bare throat. It was a present from June.

'Quick change,' he said. He looked down at his uniform trousers and gaiters, shrugged comically. 'They'll pass as slightly eccentric riding kit.' He produced a fine, flat gold cigarette case, opened it, and lit a cigarette for her. Charlotte burst out laughing. It was all so awful, he was so wicked and handsome, and it was very dangerous and wrong, and it made her feel twenty years younger.

The very nice, quiet place proved to be a small riverside inn, with a backwater sliding round the lawn into the main river. There were tall trees up which Virginia creeper had climbed and hung in waving fronds of reddening foliage. There were tables and chairs on the lawn, and a few couples taking tea. Willy parked the car and found a table near the river's edge – across the chuckling water there was a village, and an old flint church.

'It's lovely here,' she said. 'How clever of you to find it.'

His bold eyes teased her.

'Not so clever, it belongs to a friend of mine. He was in the army with me. Shall I be Mother?' he asked, smiling.

'Please.'

He poured expertly, passing her a cup. She looked up at him, exposed and scared, an expression he was accustomed to in women of her age. Humbled, pleading, afraid of being mocked, yet longing for the reassurance of tenderness. Longing for him.

'Have you brought other women here?' she asked.

'Charlotte,' he took her hand, 'that would be telling.'

'You're – not the sort that tells?'

'Oh, my dear,' he said reproachfully, 'I'm just so grateful that you are so kind to me.'

'You know,' she said, 'that little Junie has a crush on you?'

He laughed. 'She's just a kid – at her age girls get a crush on someone new every week.'

She smiled. 'I thought you'd better know. That's why I am sending her to Scotland with the little Debereaux girl. Mrs Debereaux and I agreed the girls need more confidence before their first real season.'

He leaned back, smiling, but did not let go of her hand.

'I just can't believe,' he said, 'that you're sitting here with me. Ever since I took the job I've watched you, hoping perhaps one day something like this would happen.'

'It's mad, of course.'

'Yes. But aren't all lovely things? And what can a fellow do when he meets a lovely lady?'

He must be very careful not to frighten her. She was an ambitious woman who had worked hard for her social position. A breath of danger and she would retreat. But he guessed he wasn't the first temptation she had yielded to since she had become Lady Peak. And yet he knew she was a woman who liked risks – at the races she would bet heavily, she liked to drive fast . . . He had a choice to make, whether to wait for the gate to open or to storm the citadel. She would be a powerful ally but a dangerous enemy.

A young man about his age came out of the inn, a typical ex-officer type, blazer, club scarf, well-brushed hair, clipped moustache. He glanced round checking the tables, spoke to the waiter and then strolled across to where a gardener was weeding and clearing the shrubbery.

'That's my friend, Jimmy Haynes.' His hands tightened on hers. 'It's only three o'clock. What time have you to be home?'

'Oh, seven-thirty will be early enough if Sir James won't be home until eight.'

'I'm fetching Sir James,' he said, smiling and lifted her hand to his lips. 'We have four hours. Four hours of paradise? My lady?'

She trembled, but did not draw her hand away.

'Did you think me a silly old snob when I asked you to call me, my lady?'

'I'm proud to call you that.' He rose. 'Just wait – I'll see to everything.'

A flicker of apprehension crossed her heavy features. He glanced round quickly, bent and kissed her.

'Don't worry – everything will be all right. Trust me. We're not children, Charlotte. I want you – you want me. No one knows. What harm can it do?' He bent to her lips again and, like Sir James, he noticed the powder in the lines about her eager mouth. He noticed her teeth were slightly discoloured with nicotine and that she had a gold crown just visible when she smiled. 'A stolen afternoon of happiness,' he murmured and, like Sir James, he thought of Boots's perfect, classical lips and flawless skin.

It was six-thirty when he came down into the reception hall and Jimmy Haynes was leaning on the desk reading a racing paper. He looked up and grinned.

'OK?'

'Yes. What won the four o'clock?'

'Danton. Good price. Did you get it?'

'No. How much? For the room?'

'Call it a fiver.' His grin widened when Willy opened his notecase and took a crisp white fiver from a wad of new bank notes. 'But you're up on the afternoon, old chap?'

'Shut up,' Willy said warningly, 'and tell Mrs Smith I'll be waiting for her at the car.'

98

Five minutes later Charlotte joined him and they drove towards London. She was burning for him, not daring yet to remember the past afternoon, and how terrible and how beautiful youth could be. She did not want to remember her crying, moaning, grateful pleasure. She wanted to gather her armour about her, like the well-fitted corselet she had just wriggled back into. She had never done anything quite so crazy in her life.

'I wish,' she said, 'that you hadn't to wear that uniform.'

'It won't be for long now,' he said easily.

'You're not leaving?' She was terrified.

He patted her knee gently. She was sitting with him in the front of the car.

'I only took the job to fill in,' he said. 'I had some debts to pay off, and couldn't afford to be out. But I've been looking around – I think I've found something. In Birmingham.'

They drove in silence for a few miles, and then she said, 'When you applied to Sir James for a job in the office, what were you thinking of?'

He let out a breath of relief and triumph. The victim had crept out of covert, and his aim had been true.

'General managership,' he said eagerly. 'I have managed one or two small businesses, and since I've worked for Sir James I've kept my eyes and ears open. I thought a trainee – under Mr Brooker – or Sir James himself. Look at it like this – Sir James's job is salesmanship really, isn't it? He doesn't write copy, or draw, or think up slogans . . . his job is to convince the client that Peak's is the best firm for the job. I could do that,' he said confidently. 'It's just learning the business. Learning what I have to sell. I know I could do it, if I had the chance. Sir James is a wonderful man – but I think he needs a younger element in the firm. The world has changed since the war ended.'

Her hand moved imploringly along his thigh, her hot cheek was against his shoulder. 'Don't leave, darling boy.'

He removed her hand, his eyes concentrating on the road ahead. She felt his withdrawal and was panic-stricken.

'Please, Willy darling. I have no influence in the business – Sir James leaves me a free hand so far as the home is concerned and June, and our social life. But the business is his world. He might be angry if I tried to interfere.'

He lit a cigarette, not offering her one, not glancing at her. Indifferent to her imploring looks and fumblings.

'When I first met him he promised he would give me a chance. He hasn't mentioned it. He seems to think I'm satisfied to be a servant all my life. Well, I'm not.'

Outside Maidenhead he stopped the car, opened the boot and changed back into his uniform. Charlotte too got out, and held her handbag mirror for him to comb his hair, brushing down his shoulders, looking imploringly into his face. She took out a small crystal spray, and would have sprayed his hot, sunburnt neck, but he knocked her hands away.

'For Christ's sake – I can't call for Sir James stinking of Chypre.'

'Willy . . .' her eyes filled with tears.

'I'm sorry. It's just so frustrating, waiting for a chance to prove oneself. Forgive me. I'll speak to him myself.'

'That would be best. And if he mentions it to me, of course I'll do my best.' She paused, and her heavy face, reddened by the heat, suddenly lit. 'I'm going to the South of France. Next week. I'm going to stay with a friend of mine who has a villa there. Why don't you ask for a holiday and come down?' He looked at her with interest again, and she pressed on, seeing him tempted, her hands patting and insinuating round the hot uniform collar, her eyes pleading. 'You don't have to worry about anything – money or anything. Just check your passport, and let me know if Sir James gives you the time off. I'd wait for you in Paris. Then we could take the Blue Train from Paris together. My friend has a beautiful place at Juan-les-Pins.'

'It might be dangerous.'

'How?' she demanded scornfully. 'Who would know? You get the time, my darling, leave the rest to me.'

It seemed to her a long while before he smiled.

'Yes, my lady.' He opened the back door of the car and as she bent to enter, gave her buttock an impudent tweak – it was as he had suspected, firmly armoured in expensive corsetry. Charlotte slapped his hand playfully and blushed, and he allowed her to pull his head down for a final kiss, eager, open-mouthed and exigent on her part, brief and condescending on his.

He drove towards London – he must not let her forget the other matter. But the chance of a few days in France, the beautiful Riviera coast, the casinos, and the money to gamble with was quite irresistible. It might be managed. A bonus indeed. He could think of his new career in Peak's when he returned.

He dropped her at Whitelands House and then went on to London to pick up Sir James.

Later, when he had put the car away, Willy opened his wallet and counted the notes. Forty pounds left. He had had to tip Jimmy to keep his mouth shut. The old girl was as eager for it as Junie but not as nice in bed. Showing signs of wear. But she was smart. She'd read the signs all right and shipped poor little Squirrel off to Scotland.

He changed into a well-cut dinner jacket. He would go out and have a decent meal and on to a club he knew, where they played baccarat. On an impulse he telephoned 3 Becker Street and asked for Boots. Maybe if he'd played it differently, thrown a bit of money about and given her a good time, he'd have had her now. But he hadn't had the money then that he had tonight.

The girl Helen Redmaine answered the telephone as though she had been waiting beside it. No, she said, Boots was not in . . . She was not back from her elocution lesson.

'Her what?'

'She's taking speech-training.'

'Christ!' he muttered.

'Who shall I say rang?'

'Forget it!' Willy said irritably and banged down the receiver.

Before he went out he rang June at Featherstone, and when she came to the telephone told her that she must be good, and that he loved her, and would see her when she returned. He cut off her tremulous protests and left his receiver off the hook. He had never mentioned the word love before, and it left June swinging in a dizzy pendulum of feeling between ecstasy and despair.

Matt seemed to spend all his time working concentratedly on

the Medway schedule, or closeted with Sir James. It was said by people passing along the corridor that voices were raised, at least Sir James's was, and that whatever it was about had put him into a very bad temper. Mr Meakin gave out all the studio work, and everyone was told to go to him with any question, and not to disturb Mr Wilson. Mr Meakin began to look mysterious and self important. Then when Helen went into the studio one Monday morning, there had been a significant change.

Through the glazed partition which separated Matt's office from the general studio she could see that Mr Meakin was sitting at Matt's drawing board. He appeared to be working there.

The second senior artist was now in Mr Meakin's place, leaving his own drawing board empty.

Slowly Helen hung up her coat and beret and sat down at her board. She had gone through two weeks of agonising uncertainty. On the rare occasions she had passed Matt in the office, he had either nodded pleasantly, or greeted her with a brief smile, never pausing for a private word. He had not telephoned Becker Street, he had left no message on her desk, or asked her to meet him. It was like her first week, when she had scarcely known him. She seized wildly on any possible explanation. Did Sir James know about them? Sir James did not like emotional entanglements amongst his staff.

She had stopped talking to Boots about him. The telephone became a monster. She stared at it but could not make herself lift the receiver. She willed it to ring, and sometimes it was for her, but it was never Matt. She longed to go running back to Mill Cottage at the weekends, hungry for the loving comfort of her home, but she could not leave Becker Street. Matt might ring. He might even call. Her mother would know at once something was wrong, and she would worry, and Helen could not tell her.

She could not believe in her heart that he did not love her. Not yet. She had worked diligently at the Friendly Liver Pill layouts, watching Matt's rare appearances through the glass panels, longing for a sign of reassurance, and receiving none. And this morning he was not there.

Mr Meakin saw her, beamed and beckoned authoritatively. Matt's name was no longer on the door. The new plate read J. K. Meakin, Studio Manager. Helen went in.

'Good morning, my dear,' Mr Meakin was alight with triumph. 'There's been a staff shake-up. You are to take Mr Mallow's place. You are a senior artist now. We're engaging a new junior, young Dykes will move into your corner and take over your accounts.

'What? All my lavatories and their cisterns at one fell swoop,' said Helen wildly.

Mr Meakin looked puzzled. He was far too full of importance to notice any kind of joke, but he did notice how bright her eyes were, and how white her cheeks.

'Now don't be too excited, Helen. It is a big promotion for you I know. But Sir James has insisted you retain the Friendly Liver Pill account – he is very pleased with your work. So will you move your stuff over into Mr Mallow's place, and then come in and have a little chat?'

'It's very sudden?'

'Not exactly. My lips were sealed until this morning. I can't wait to tell my wife.'

'I'll bet,' said Helen. Her legs felt hollow and her mouth was dry. She had to ask. 'Where is Mr Wilson?'

'He's left. Decided to freelance. Apparently Sir James has been trying to persuade him to change his mind.'

'Did he give a reason?'

'Circumstances beyond his control.' Helen flushed and paled, and a flickering ember of hope glowed within her. Mr Meakin rushed on, 'A brilliant chap, but a fish out of water here. Too artistic. Too subtle. Got bored, I think. Still, it's an ill-wind, eh, little lady.'

'I hope so,' Helen said fervently.

She went back to her corner and collected her things. She could see it all quite clearly now. He was running away, of course, for all the conventional, boring, honourable reasons. Because he was married, and because she was a virgin, and a nice girl, and a Redmaine, and he was fifteen years older than she was. He must have decided that night, as soon as he left her at Becker Street, to end it. She remembered teasing him about being like Don Giovanni – 'Except you could never be like him. He was a cold seducer.' And Matt had replied, 'You know nothing about me.' And he had kissed her again with passion, and said, 'Goodnight,' and then, 'Goodbye, my baby.'

Relinquishing her? As though she cared about any of those things. She would not even care if he had been a cold seducer – he was her beloved. But she did not believe he was. He was sweet, kind, cynical and he had fallen in love with her and she with him. They had captured everything in those few, beautiful hours, the very meaning of life and happiness. It was not like Boots had said so brutally, 'he's giving you the brush-off'. He was trying to end it because he thought it wrong, and she must not let him. Nothing so beautiful could possibly go wrong.

She moved her work and all her gear over to Mr Mallow's place, accepting the congratulations on her promotion, and later was summoned to attend a conference on the Friendly Campaign with Mr Brooker, Mr Meakin and Sir James. They were kindly, a little patronising and avuncular, but she sensed an underlying respect for her. It should have made her feel very important. Her salary was being increased by two pounds a week. She hardly listened to what they were saying. The minute she was free she went over to see Boots.

Boots took one look at her and said, 'What's up? Someone told me you'd got promotion. You look like death warmed up.'

'Matt's left.'

'I'm not going to say I told you so.'

'I've got to see him. How can I find out where he lives?'

Boots regarded her with despair. How could anyone as clever as Helen be such a fool? How could Helen, who was so proud, expose her feelings like this? Refusing to believe the obvious – that Matt was trying to ditch her.

And then, illogically, Boots was also seized with doubt. Could Helen be right? That honourable scruples held him back? Pooh – it was like something out of *Peg's Paper*. But then could Duncan really be right about his future in the cinema and her 'potential' as a great star? She thought they were both mad, and that was why she loved them. Their belief in themselves was as contagious as measles; their conviction

104

that life could be clean, bright and pure and not a lot of old rubbishy lies, a sort of grubby jungle, was almost heartbreaking. Sometimes she wished she had never met them.

'Try Posty,' she said crossly. 'She's got everyone's address.'

'Of course,' said Helen, 'thanks a million.' She fled along the corridor in search of the postal clerk.

Boots brooded at her desk. The lessons with May Rampton were beginning to grab her. She began to *want* to go. It was no sacrifice of her evenings. Watching and listening to the great old actress made her realise she knew nothing and that six weeks was useless. She envied the full-time students who could afford to study all day. Six months ago she would have said, 'What? Try for the stage? Don't pull my leg!'

And it was more than the lessons that attracted her. It was the people too. Duncan's crowd were all very young, deadly serious and keen about their work. Bit-players, film extras, camera crews, script girls, clapper boys, assistant floor and stage managers, all with their sights on stardom, trying to get in somehow, by hard work, persistence, guile and that elusive thing, luck.

Boots was fascinated by it all. Even the girls who slept around were serious – they despised the men they sought to entrap. They did what they did to get a part, a chance, a future, not a night out or a gold bracelet.

What sort of life was this? Pasting up endless cuttings. Escorting people to Sir James's office door. Dusting the cigar ash from the polished desk, making tea and coffee and serving it prettily on the special tray, putting phoney calls through to him when he wanted to get rid of them, calming others when he kept them waiting, all of which she did exceedingly well. But it was for Sir James – not for her.

She was sick of keeping two middle-aged men apart, and the price they offered had begun to seem as worthless as her job. She felt she was going nowhere. She too was restless, nervous and dissatisfied. And it was all Duncan's fault. His and Helen's.

Helen came back with Matt's address, glowing with renewed hope. Number 4 Hayman's Studio, Baron's Court. She sat on Boots's desk, and borrowed a London road map to locate it.

'Going to have a showdown?'

'Sort of.'

'So where's your pride?'

'Pride?' Helen exclaimed witheringly. 'I love him – and I know he loves me. What's pride got to do with it?'

'If I know chaps he'll run a mile when he sees you coming. But it's your funeral.' She added sourly, 'And the best of British luck.' Helen turned away, and Boots asked, 'What's holding up the Medway contract? Did you know Matt did a layout using that sketch of you running up the path to the Medway House? Tommy's crazy about it. Wants it blown into a big poster to go on all the tube stations. Calls you The Medway Girl.'

'Go on?' Helen was delighted.

'Hey, d'you think the Old Man has told Tommy that Matt has left?'

Helen stared, then said thoughtfully, 'Well, he'll have to, won't he? He'll have to get Matt to come back. Or do the work freelance if he gets the contract. Medway won't sign up without him.'

'How come you are so smart at business and so dumb about men?'

'You just say that because you think all men are alike.'

'So they are – they're all after one thing.'

'Sometimes you disgust me,' Helen snapped. She had to be angry because she was not going to let Boots know how frightened she was that her street-sharp cynicism could be true. 'Is Dunky like your Mr Medway? Or Matt like Sir James? If they behave badly to you maybe you ask for it.'

She went off to the studio with her nose in the air.

'Oh, damn!' said Boots.

She cut out a large photograph of Sir James and stuck it into the book, covering it with blotting paper and thumping it into place. Apparently nothing would make Helen believe anything against Matt. She wondered if her own mother had ever felt like that about her father, and thought cynically, 'If she did she was dead wrong – landing herself for life with that drunken old bastard.'

She hated quarrelling with Helen. She went on snipping out the pictures from the newspapers, pasting them in, neatly writing the name of the publication and the date beneath each one.

But she felt hollow with misery, and could have wept for Helen. And in some kind of bewildered way for herself.

Chapter 5

Helen worked hard through the rest of the day trying, not very successfully, to concentrate on her work, and be pleased about her promotion. But all that happened was that she watched the clock, waiting for five o'clock to come, screwing up her courage to go and find Matt. It was always best to 'have it out'. They always did at home. Cousin Millicent was a great believer in having things out. 'Otherwise people imagine unintended cruelties, and get drowned in their own resentments.' It was on the Breterton Coat of Arms. Speak the Truth Fearlessly.

It was very hot and sultry – the men were working in shirt sleeves. Then just as she was leaving, Mr Meakin came bustling up, red-faced with his new responsibilities and told her Sir James was asking for her.

'Jumping Jesus,' Helen said irritably, 'it's already five o'clock.'

'The price of promotion,' Mr Meakin said pontifically. 'As Sir James says, the job must come first. Mr Wilson used to work all hours.'

For a moment a wild hope flashed.

'Is Mr Wilson with Sir James?'

'No. Why should he be? I am head of the studio now, and I am surprised that Sir James did not let me handle this matter with you.'

Helen smiled kindly, sorry for him. Sir James's executives had to be quicker off the mark than poor Mr Meakin could ever be.

'I'll see what he wants and let you know at once.'

Sir James, already hatted and gloved, leaning on his silver headed cane, was looking at the big poster layout Matt had done for Medway, incorporating his masterly sketch of her running up towards the red-tiled house.

He looked up at her testily, and pointed to it.

'What's so special about that?' he asked.

'It's alive.'

'Alive?' He looked at the picture. 'Hmmph! You think it's good?'

'Yes.'

'I've had Medway here. He's crazy about it. Wants to base the whole of the next campaign on it. This figure . . . the Medway Girl he calls it. Thinks it will be the keystone of the whole run.' He paused. 'Why can't Meakin do something like this?'

'He's not such a good artist as Mr Wilson.'

He stared at her. It was like a voice from the past. Sandy Redmaine telling him he had no bloody taste, and if he wanted to buy talent he would have to pay for it.

'You sound exactly like your father.'

'*Really*?' Helen was delighted.

'Could you do it – something like this?'

'No. I could do something better than Mr Meakin, but not as good as Mr Wilson.' She added, 'Not in a hundred years could I draw like Matt Wilson can.'

There was a silence. Sir James looked like a large baffled baby. He cut the end of a new cigar and plugged it into his mouth like a comforter.

'You don't think much of Meakin's work?'

'He's very competent. He's a good studio manager. I have better taste, more talent and better training – I haven't got his experience. Matt has the lot. Plus.'

'You think a great deal of him?'

'Yes.' He peered at her suspiciously but her eyes were clear and guileless. 'Medway's are going to spend a great deal of money on this campaign. If you can take this on successfully I'll raise your salary.'

'Then you might as well employ Matt Wilson, now he is freelancing.'

Sir James's jowls crimsoned.

'Blasted freelancers,' he cried. 'No power over them. Too expensive.' He pounded off towards the door and suddenly wheeled back on her. 'Wilson's holding everything up. He wants to work for himself, not for me, nor for Medway. I know Medway has offered him a ridiculous salary, but he won't accept that.'

'Good for him.'

'I can't arrange the new contract until he makes up his mind. I'd treble your salary if you'd offer to do it.'

She shook her head. 'I couldn't. And I think Matt should work for himself. And I think Mr Medway won't consider the contract without him.'

Sir James snorted with anger, turned to the door, and suddenly wheeled back to her. 'You still a friend of that little Boots Skinner?'

'Yes.'

'Is she a good girl?'

Helen summoned up her ultra-Redmaine manner and gave him an astounded, frosty stare. '*Really, Sir James*! What *can* you mean?'

The crimson deepened to a reddish purple.

'No offence,' he grunted and walked out. Helen felt quite sorry for him. Boots was the ruddy limit.

She looked for a moment at the big picture of the red-tiled house and the rapturous girl running towards it straight into the arms of love. She felt her insides melt like heated caramel – to whom could she give this great upsurge of love if Matt did not want it? She could not bear to think of that.

Sir James told Willy to drop him off outside The Trocadero and to pick him up again in an hour. His meetings with Boots these days were always snatched in the early evenings, and always in places that were neither chic nor very expensive, where Charlotte would not go. He was uncomfortably aware that Boots, accustomed to the best, was not impressed. She sat waiting for him, looking a dream in a pale blue suit and a white hat with a turned back brim; she wore a long string of very good cultured pearls which he knew were a gift from Medway. He bought her a cocktail which she drank, and prattled away, eating her way steadily through the olives and salt-biscuits, and when he said he was sorry he couldn't take

110

her out to dinner, she said, 'Oh, that's a relief – what with Tommy Medway and three lessons a week with Madame Rampton, I haven't even had time to get my hair done.' He noticed, as everyone did, the marked improvement in her accent.

'How're you getting on?'

'Very well.' She looked at him with the heart-catching lift of the long silky lashes which Duncan found so photogenic. 'But I need another course. A friend of mine is getting me a film test. I need some acting lessons too – not just speech- and voice-training. I'd like to take a proper course – full-time.'

'You're not trying to get into films?' he said incredulously.

'Why not?'

'Have you got some film chap stuffing you up with a lot of lies?'

''Course not,' she said truthfully, because although she knew that Duncan could lie about many things, he would not lie about anything so serious as the art of the cinema. 'I told you. I want to better myself.'

'But – to take a full-time course you'd have to leave the office?'

'Yes.'

'Don't do that,' he implored. 'I'll see you have your lessons.'

Some weeks ago she would have said, 'Ta, ever so,' but now she said, very sweetly, 'Thank you so much, Sir James.'

He drove her back to Pimlico, thinking she was pathetic with her acting pretensions, her new carefully enunciated vowels, her *Peg's Paper* ambitions to be a film star.

But when she allowed him to hold her hand on the way home he was almost slaveringly grateful. Willy opened the car door for her, glittering with dangerous jealousy as she extracted herself skilfully from Sir James's farewell embrace.

'Thanks so much for the lift home,' she said.

Sir James pressed nearer, exuding the familiar scent of expensive cigars. Boots flapped her hands.

'Pooh, what a pong!' She drew back, smiling with that calm tolerance which was her deadliest weapon. 'Don't be a silly old Daddy, now. Goodbye.'

Willy might not have existed.

She ran off into the tall gloomy house, her exquisite legs

flashing, her neat round little bottom swinging provocatively beneath the tight, short, pale blue skirt.

Sir James took off his pearl grey Homburg, wiped his brow and leaned back in the car.

He had thought when Boots first entered his employment that she was a fast little piece, easy to catch. A few good dinners, one or two nice presents, and that would be that. But she had not turned out like that at all. She was like a virus, something you don't even notice when it enters the blood stream, and slowly pervades your whole system. He found himself making excuses to go through the main hall, just for a glance of the long slender legs and the curve of her young breasts beneath a sleeveless summer dress. The bare arms, so firm and tender, the quick glance up at him beneath the long, silky eyelashes, and the conspiratorial little smile galvanised his stout ageing body like an aphrodisiac. It did not help to know that practically every man in the office, including the impeccable Mr Brooker, was suffering, in varying degrees, in the same way.

He slumped back into the corner and nodded off as the Rolls purred along, weaving its way through the evening traffic. He did not wake up until it turned into the gates of Whitelands, a large low-built house, surrounded by lawns which ran down to moorings by the river.

'May I have a word with you, Sir James?'

He looked testily at his chauffeur, remembered the servicemen's band, and the well dressed, well set-up, well-spoken young man who had encountered him in the Strand. He hoped he did not want a rise.

'Yes?'

'I want to remind you that originally you considered giving me a start in the office. I took this job on because I was broke, but I think I've done it long enough. I think it's time I started looking round. I told Lady Peak that if you can't see your way to offering me something in the office, I'd look out for a more suitable job.'

Sir James glowered.

'I have nothing to offer in the office. I can get chauffeurs two a penny. Give in your notice if you want to – in fact it would be a very good time. Lady Peak is going to the South of

France for a few weeks. I can move into the Savoy and walk to work. I've enough worries without this sort of thing.' He turned towards the house.

'Oh, by the way,' Willy said casually, 'has Lady Peak met Miss Skinner?'

Sir James halted. Under the thick silver-grey hair the nape of his neck went crimson. He felt as if he was exploding. He looked over his shoulder at Willy's handsome face, the mocking red mouth smiling beneath the short, fair military moustache.

'You wouldn't dare!' he said.

'Try me!' said Willy impudently.

Helen found Hayman's Studio quite easily, a short walk from the Underground station. It was one of a long row of red brick buildings with large studio windows looking westwards over the busy arterial road and the playing fields of St Paul's School. The day had been too bright to last and already stormy purple clouds were beginning to blot out the sun.

Outside by the kerb stood a small, open tourer, very smart and well-kept and at the wheel sat a young man, reminiscent of the Latin lovers of Helen's schooldays – Valentino, Novarro, Rod La Roque. His black hair was brushed to a patent-leather shine, and long sideboards framed his fine, rather petulant face. He glanced indifferently at Helen.

At the door, her finger pressed on the door-bell stood a tall, lithe girl, elegant in a theatrical way, with her hair dressed *à la ballerina*. She was wearing a bright blue evening dress with a wide skirt that just cleared her slim, strong ankles and feet. Her shoulders were draped in a dark fur wrap. She was wearing blue satin shoes with diamanté-studded heels. Helen knew at once she was Matt's wife.

A single heavy raindrop splashed on the dry step, and the girl turned to the man in the car – surprisingly she was not a girl but a woman over thirty. The black hair was dyed, the strong, regular features heavily made up. She called to the man in the car. 'Buddy! Darling. Put the hood up. It's going to rain.'

The young man got reluctantly out of the car – he was in full

113

evening dress, beautifully fitted. Tail-coat, white waistcoat, and tie. Rather ineptly he began to struggle with the hood. The hinge on the pavement side stuck.

Helen went across, and said, 'Allow me. It's easier with two.' She had long experience with Cousin Millicent's old De Dion. In a moment the hood was up. He thanked her with an engaging smile and a seductive glance, and the woman on the step said warningly, 'Get back in, darling. Don't get wet.'

She glanced suspiciously at Helen, and asked, 'Did you want something?'

'I wanted to see Mr Wilson.'

'What about?'

'About? Oh, about some drawings at Peak's.'

'He's left Peaks.'

'Yes. There's an enquiry about some work. I'm Helen Redmaine, one of the senior artists.'

The sharp, dark eyes were intensely curious.

'Well, he's not in,' she said irritably. 'Or he knows it's me, and he's not answering. I'm his wife.'

'How do you do,' said Helen faintly.

'I can't wait any longer. Mr de Freece and I have an engagement up-river. At the Venetian Gondola.' It was a new expensive riverside dance club. Helen smiled, and said nothing.

The whole scene was like one of those weird and troubling dreams when one is surrounded by people who are demanding but totally unknown. Helen could imagine these two people in a spotlight swinging and stamping, and jerking their handsome heads in rhythm. She could not imagine Matt living with this woman. Talking with her over a breakfast table – making love to her.

'Well,' Mrs Wilson ran down the steps, 'if you see him, tell him I haven't received the usual. I can't help it if he's been fool enough to lose his job. I expect he's drunk or out with one of his little tarts. Tell him Betty was here.'

The heavy spots of rain were falling regularly now, smacking on the dry pavement. Betty Wilson gathered her befrilled skirts around her, got into the car, and in a few seconds it was lost to sight in the traffic.

Helen stared after them, the spattering rain flattening her

hair and making great damp splotches on her pink summer dress. She had imagined someone smaller, prettier, not this Queen of the Palais de Danse. Not this handsome, dominating woman. She could not relate her to Matt at all.

'Betty always loved to dance,' some office gossip had said. 'During the war, while he was away she was always dancing, and then after they separated, she became a professional.'

But Matt had shared his youth with this woman. As a boy he must have loved her. Helen had never thought of the gap between their ages before, and now it yawned ominously. Past loves should be past, not alive, domineering and greedy. The only thing she really knew about Matt was how much she loved him.

She loved his thin, tall whippy body. The clever grey eyes that sloped down at the corners. His sensitivity. The touch of weakness about him, revealed by the way he lost his temper to shield his edgy independence, his sharp tongue, and sudden laughter, and that one night together – his tenderness, touching her as though she was a delicate instrument that would respond to him as he wished, setting her alight with longing.

She shivered, she was getting very wet. She must find him – she must know what he thought of her. What she meant to him. Was she to have been just one of his little tarts – easy? Or just someone young and reckless, greedy for sexual experience for its own sake? Was that how he saw her? A wild virgin to be protected from herself? Had he found – when the morning came – that the memory of her bored him? Or did he really love her, as she was sure he did, and could not face the difference in their ages? Or was she just the victim of her own imagination – whistling in the dark, making it all up because she wanted him to love her?

She went down the area steps and knocked at the door marked CARETAKER, and presently a wheezy, elderly man smelling strongly of ale opened it, and gave her a bleary grin. Mr Wilson? Might be at the Court Tavern – often went there about now. Round the corner on the left, couldn't miss it.

As she went up the area steps there was a flicker of lightning and a heavier burst of rain from the threatening sky.

She opened the saloon bar nervously. She had never been in a public house before – there were not many women – it was

115

crowded with men on their way home. The air was heavy with cigarette smoke and the redolent smell of beer. A few faces glanced her way, a few grinned, one cheeky boy said, 'Looking for me, ducks?' and fell back before her imperious stare. Then she saw Matt.

He was alone, sitting with his elbows on the table, his chin resting on his folded hands, as she had often seen him sit over a drawing, thinking out the design. He looked up and saw her, and for a second she was sure it was all right. Then he rose politely and waited for her to come over. There was no welcome in his eyes. He looked tired and slightly exasperated.

'Hello, Helen,' he said, 'you shouldn't have come in here alone. Won't you sit down?'

She sat down gratefully, her knees seemed to have given away, the brief hope had gone, and she was drowning in fear. Boots's worldly wise predictions had seemed laughable at first, but not now. Helen, she said, had been brought up soft. 'I have always been protected by love and gentleness,' Helen thought. 'She's right. Life's not like that.'

'Is it raining?' He put out a hand as though to touch her hair, then drew back sharply, 'You're quite wet.'

She looked down at the shoulders of her pink cotton dress, and saw the damp patches, rubbed them vaguely.

'So I am. I hadn't noticed.'

'Can I get you a drink?'

She was cold. She was afraid her teeth would chatter.

'Yes, please, brandy.'

'Are you all right?'

'Yes,' she snapped fiercely. 'I just want a drink.'

His brows rose. For a moment she thought he was going to laugh and the lightning flash of hope revived and faded again. He went over to the bar, and came back with a glass and his own glass replenished.

'Soda?'

'No thank you.'

She gulped at the brandy, nearly choked, but its fire warmed her instantly. She said stiffly, 'I – I just wanted to know how things were with you.'

'Everything is fine.'

'We are all – in the studio – wondering why you left.'

116

'It's nice of you to be interested. Tell them I – I just felt I'd been there long enough.'

'It wasn't because of me?' she asked painfully. Her pale cheeks were suddenly hot.

'Why should it be?'

He would not let her through. There was no opening. Giving her no chance. She must find the strength and the pride to get up and go. She said painfully, 'I thought – after what happened, my being there might embarrass you?'

He said quite mildly, 'Don't be silly.'

There was a long silence. It was silly . . . and awful too.

'Just tell everyone that I'm fine, and it's no one's fault. They were a good team. I told Mr Meakin – I'm going freelance.'

He was waiting with a maddening, implacable politeness for her to go. Anger rose in her like a lava stream, and there was no pride, no dignity left, only raw fury.

'I came because I had to talk with you,' she burst out passionately. 'I thought it would be easy, but it's not.'

The clever, silver grey eyes were watching her, warning her.

'Then don't say it . . . it's better unsaid . . .'

He heard the sharp intake of her breath – audible, like a pupply yelp of pain and suddenly took her hand. He began to speak in a heavily paternal manner, like Mr Meakin, patting absentmindedly down her spine, or Sir James when he wanted something for nothing. She began to feel sick.

'Some things, Helen, are better forgotten. I know what's on your mind. That night at Frascati's? So let's talk about it. It was a wonderful night and we had a splendid time together and both got a little bit squiffy, and both of us felt rather romantic. But Helen, I honestly did not think you would take it seriously. I forgot that you're really very young. I should have been more – more restrained. But no real harm was done.'

She turned her head away, unable to look at him. Ashamed for him.

'I'm sorry. Everyone makes a fool of themselves at times. Especially when they're very young. You're a sweet little kid, and I should have had more sense, but I lost my head. I really am sorry. I wouldn't have upset you for the world. A few kisses, a few drinks – that's not meant to mean anything – if it were no one would have a good time. We did have a good time – and thank you. Now, let me get you a taxi and you run off and go out dancing with Boots, and forget all about it. You can forget I ever happened, and enjoy yourself with friends of your own age.'

She turned her head back slowly and met his eyes. She was white now, ablaze with hate. She knew a more experienced woman would have known how to handle it, or would never have got into it. Would have had the ability to charm and dissemble, to keep the *status quo* of good behaviour. Her anger burned in her throat and threatened to suffocate her.

'I *don't* believe you,' she said. 'I *don't* believe it's possible for you to talk like that and mean it. You're just trying to make me hate you, but you're not even kidding yourself. You know we are in love and have been since the first minute I went into your office. If you don't want me, or if you're afraid of what people will say, or that your wife will cut up rough, or Sir James will not employ you, then just say so, and I'll go away. But I'm not going to help you not to love me . . . if that's what you want, you must do it by yourself. And I am not going to stop loving you because I couldn't. I shall love you until the day I die.'

She rose, steadied herself on the corner of the table, turned stiffly, like an automaton, and went out.

It had started to rain. She walked to the wrong end of the street, and then stopped, not knowing why she was there. She turned and went back towards the main road. She passed the Court Tavern without glancing at it, the rain beating into her face. The nausea that rose within her was uncontrollable, and she vomitted into the gutter. A woman passing hesitated concernedly, then catching the sour smell of spirits hurried on. She was getting soaked, but she was unaware of it. The traffic was streaming past her westward – she wanted to go east. She must get across the road. She saw a gap in the teeming traffic, crossed to a refuge, started hazily for the other side, hardly able to see for the rain streaming down her face. She was unaware of everything except the conviction that she must get back towards the West End or the Strand, or

118

Victoria, the districts she knew in London, and then she would know how to get home. She was only halfway across when the central bound traffic was released. There was a shrieking of brakes and a taxi stopped, catching her thigh, so that she fell to the ground, grazing her knees, and started to crawl to the pavement.

'Gawd!' said the taxi driver, pulling in to the kerb. He jumped out and ran over to her. 'You all right, miss?'

She looked like a drowned girl, but said in her calm, upper-class voice, 'Quite all right, thank you. Are you free?'

'Well, yes . . .'

'Could you take me to 3, Becker Street, Pinlico, please?'

He helped her to her feet, and into the cab. Little pools of water ran on to the seat leather and the floor. She slumped back in the car. Twenty minutes later the man rang the bell at Becker Street, and when Mrs Murphy opened the door said, 'There's a young lady in the cab asked me to bring her here. She's passed out I think . . .'

Mrs Murphy ran across the pavement and found Helen, lying on the seat soaked through and unconscious.

'*Not* Miss Redmaine!' she exclaimed. 'It's *never* Miss Redmaine. What the divil's happened to her.'

The taxi driver began to explain, but she turned and ran into the house and upstairs to fetch Boots.

When Helen opened her eyes she was conscious of being very hot, tucked up to her chin in bed. The gas fire was roaring away and Boots was sitting on the bed, in her dressing-gown with her hair in rollers, staring at her. When she opened her eyes Boots seemed to breathe again.

'Gawd almighty, Nell, don't you ever do that to me again.'

'Turn the fire off,' gasped Helen, 'it's like an oven in here.'

'You were so cold I thought we'd never get you warm.' She turned off the fire. 'Mrs Murphy brought a drop of the hard stuff for you, but we couldn't get you to take it, so I thought to meself well, it's no use wastin' the good stuff, so I drank it up, sure I did.' She folded her arms across an imaginary apron, sounding so like Mrs Murphy that Helen gave a wavering smile. She felt safe, back here with Boots, but empty, worry-

119

ing about something she could not remember.

Boots put the kettle on, and came back to the bedside.

'So – he gave you the push-off?'

'Yes.'

'All men are swine,' said Boots.

'No. It was me. I was a fool.'

'Well, you're well rid of him.'

'No. But let's not talk about it.' She struggled up, and took a cup of tea. 'Did the taxi bring me home?'

'Yes. I paid him and Mrs Murphy took his number in case you wanted to sue him for bumping you.'

'No.' Again the wavering smile. 'That was my fault too.'

'Can you eat something now?'

Helen shook her head. 'No. I'll be all right in the morning. Don't you worry about me. I'm just tired. And there's something I can't remember . . .'

But, in the night Boots went down from her own room and quietly opened Helen's door and heard the slow, shuddering sobs. She lifted the bedclothes and slipped in beside her, putting her arms about her, and drawing her head down to her shoulder. 'What is it?'

'It's the years – I remembered – all the years I shall have to live without him.'

'There's other fish,' Boots, said. 'My mum used to come into my bed after Dad had given me a walloping. Never touched me other times. Never kissed me. But she never let me cry through the night. She said after three boys Dad couldn't remember I was a girl when he was drunk . . . that was why I copped it. I could never see that as a good reason myself . . .' She went on talking, rambling through anything that came into her head, holding Helen tightly against her, and as Helen's shuddering sobs subsided her own voice slurred and silenced, and they both fell asleep. In the dawn Boots wakened, carefully tucked Helen up, and went upstairs to her own bed. At eight-thirty Helen came upstairs to her room. She looked pale, and there were violet shadows beneath her eyes, and when she stirred her coffee the spoon rattled against the cup.

'You all right?' asked Boots.

'Yes.'

'Blimey last night I thought you were dead.'

Helen's smile wavered. 'I was.'

'Why don't you stay home – I'll tell them you've got 'flu.'

'No. I'd rather work.' She made an attempt to eat her breakfast cereal, then pushed it away. To Boots, raging within, she seemed fragile, her natural fine-drawn beauty withdrawing into itself. Her vitality draining away. Her grey-green eyes, usually alight with life and laughter were shadowed with pain.

'Thank you, Boots, for staying with me last night. You were right about – about it all.'

'Put it down to experience.'

'Yes. But – let's not talk about it anymore.'

'Right. We'd better get going.'

They went to catch the number eleven bus, rode as usual on top in the open summer air, and Boots talked until her voice trailed away into silence. Helen was not listening.

Peering over the half curtains screening the pub windows, Matt watched Helen cross the road, walk blindly through the rain, turn and go back to the main road, moving like a sleep walker, not appearing to know which way she was going.

He stood it until she turned along the main road out of sight and then concern for her destroyed his purpose. He left the pub and ran across the road and along past the studio, but could not see her. Ahead, at the corner of the crossroads he saw a small crowd of people staring across the street at a taxi which seemed to be half on the pavement. When he reached the corner the taxi had gone, the small crowd was dispersing. He buttonholed a man passing and asked him what had happened.

'Oh, some silly bitch crossed through the traffic and got knocked down.'

'Was she hurt?'

'I don't think so. She went off in the cab.'

'A girl in a pink dress. Without a coat?'

'Yeah – d'you know her?'

'Yes . . . well, thank you.'

He went back to the pub, feeling as if he had been wrung

121

out like a rag, and stayed there drinking for an hour before he went home. He tried to work on some layouts but could not. He knew why people took drugs. It was because they had reached the point of despair. To be able to take anything that would kill the despair for just a moment's blessed relief. At ten o'clock he telephoned Becker Street and asked to speak with Boots; when she came to the telephone he asked, tentatively, if Helen were all right.

'She is now,' snarled Boots, 'and no thanks to you, Mr Bloody Wilson. You've broken her heart – so damn well leave her alone!' And she banged down the receiver as though she was banging it on his head.

Matt hung up and leaned against the wall, shaking with bitter laughter. He had done it. Mission accomplished . . . only two casualties. Both with internal injuries. Internal bleeding which, so far as he was concerned, might never stop.

He had a big portrait easel which he had bought when he had first moved in after he had separated from Betty, thinking to start painting again, but somehow had never found the time or the heart to begin. He had needed money to provide for Betty, and the job at Peake's had been well-paid and exhausting. These last few weeks he had begun a preliminary sketch of Helen, hoping she would sit for him one day. He had thought of her as Primavera, the essence of spring and youth.

From memory he had sketched a seated figure. How often had he looked across the studio at Peak's and seen her sitting, talking to someone, head turned over her shoulder, cheek on hand, elbow on desk . . . and he had roughly brushed in a green dress, like the one she had worn at Frascati's, and the whitey-green flower in her hair.

He hauled the heavy easel about to face the wall. That was one portrait he would never finish.

He rang up an old drinking companion of his at the Arts Club, and they went out to dinner at the Café Royal and ended up at the Savage Club Bar, rather the worse for wear. But some opera tenor, a member, was singing beautifully of love, so he called a taxi and drove back to Hayman's and went to sleep eventually, weeping with no tears, but weeping inside as painfully as though he had torn his own heart out by the roots.

Chapter 6

Since her return from Featherstone Hall, Charlotte had only been able to see Willy when he was on duty, and even when they were alone in the car it was torment to slide back the glass panel and talk to him covertly, like a prison visitor, occasionally raising a trembling hand to caress the back of his strong, fair neck.

She had written to her friend, Roxana Cosimos, explaining that she would like to bring a friend with her to Juan. Roxana, sophisticated and accommodating, understood perfectly.

James did not care for the rich, raffish and cosmopolitan Roxana. 'An old whorehousekeeper,' he had called her, much to Charlotte's annoyance. She had worked hard at being Lady Peak but often found it boring, and had enjoyed her brief escapes back into Roxana's wider, more wicked world. But now she did not want to leave London, unless she could leave with Willy.

She had spent the day with her maid, packing. She had told the woman to take her holiday during her absence. She heard the rustle of the Rolls on the gravel drive beneath her balcony, and went out, looking down at the two men, Sir James, portly, silver-haired and hot – Willy, tall, slim and smart in his grey uniform.

She could not hear what they were saying, but guessed from Sir James's abrupt swivel turn and heightened colour, it was something to do with his deliberately forgotten promise. He had not wished to be reminded of it.

He marched angrily into the house. Willy looked up, saw her, smiled his frank, charming smile, white teeth aflash in the brown face. Boldly he held up a triumphant thumb and went to put the car away.

She kept on the black chiffon negligée she had been wearing, and when James came in she was lying on a long garden lounger out on the balcony. She smiled, raised her arms languidly and pulled him down to her for an unusually warm and welcoming kiss.

He responded briefly, taking off his jacket and undoing his tie, sinking into a comfortable chair, saying, 'Pour me a drink, Charlie, that's a good girl. By God, it's been hot in town.'

She rose at once saying, smiling, 'Have you forgotten we're going to the Elliot's for bridge?'

'Oh, God, I had! Must I really go?'

She packed two glasses with ice and let the Bourbon trickle down, topping them with a brief squirt of soda. James took his gratefully.

'Not if you don't want to, my darling.'

It was pleasant under the balcony awning, with the scent of the late roses rising from the garden. He leaned back and wiped his forehead. It had been an irritating day.

'It's been stifling in the office. I never had so many cancelled appointments. Some of these chaps seem to take a day off, or for that matter a week, whenever it suits their fancy.'

'Well, so could you,' she insisted. 'I've asked you to come down to the Riviera with me, to Roxana's.'

'Not with the Medway account in the balance.'

When that piece of business was secured, James had thought of a few days at Brighton. He liked Brighton. Fresh and blowy and full of fine hotels. He thought of having Boots all to himself for a long weekend. Quite long enough to be away from the office.

'You work too hard,' Charlotte insisted. 'Have you ever thought of having an assistant?'

'An assistant? What for? Brooker's the manager.'

'Yes, but a *personal* assistant, who could take over from you – just for a short while; so that you could take a break now and then? We had nice weekends once – when the firm was smaller!'

'Hmm.' He scowled at the carpet and said, 'What do you think of Hyde-Seymour?'

Her heart gave a terrible jolt.

'Hyde-Seymour? Oh, you mean *Williams*? Well, a very good chauffeur. Reliable, courteous, and considerate. And very efficient. He deals with the garage people splendidly.' Actually Willy was getting commission on all the spares he ordered, some of them quite unnecessary, but Charlotte was unaware of this. 'But then, of course,' she said indulgently, 'he's a gentleman. It's very hard on these youngsters who've been demobilised, used to command, used to taking big decisions, and now they can't get jobs. But he doesn't grumble.'

James had listened distractedly.

'Well the fact is, Charlie, when I met him – you know how, running that band of his for demobbed men, I – I, er, more or *less* said I'd think of him if a vacancy occurred in the office.'

Charlotte appeared to search her memory.

'Oh? Oh, yes! I remember – so you said. I thought it a bit rash at the time.'

'Well, you saying I ought to have a personal assistant made me remember. D'you think he'd be any good at public relations? Tactful and all that? Sharp?' Too bloody sharp, he thought to himself.

'Oh yes, I'm sure. But – we don't want to lose him as a chauffeur – I mean we've had no trouble at all since he came. On the other hand, if you did promise, I ought not to stand in the poor fellow's way. I admire young men with ambition. Yes. He has a delightful manner. I'm sure he would learn to handle that kind of work.'

'D'you think I'd be a fool to give him a chance?'

A flush of pleasure went over her entire body. Here was a gift to take to her beloved! She managed to say doubtfully, but admiringly, 'Oh, James, how generous! Are you sure, honey?'

'Well, I could give him a trial. Start him under Brooker. Then if he shapes up he could handle some of the small accounts, so, as you say, if I want to get away occasionally he could take over. It's too much for Brooker to do all my work, as well as his own.'

'When did you plan to start him?'

'I hadn't thought that far. Maybe right away.'

125

'D'you think that would be a good idea?'

'What d'you mean?'

'Well, your staff will know him – as a chauffeur.'

'When he comes for me the hall porter telephones up to my secretary. He rarely comes up into the office.'

'If there was a gap – say ten days, before he starts? It might not cause so much comment. Then your Mr Brooker can explain to the department heads that you intended to start him in the office, but had no opening, and that he volunteered to work as your chauffeur. To help you out and keep in touch. Kind of ease him in – then he can do the rest of the explaining himself.'

'He'll do that all right,' James said drily. He thought it over with some misgiving. Willy was intelligent and pushing and, it appeared, ruthless.

'Honey, I shall be away at Roxana's for four weeks, and then he will be hanging around with hardly anything to do. Just running you to the office. I shall need him until I go, for I've a lot of shopping to do. Why not give him a couple of weeks off, and let him start at the office afterwards? Then I'll get a new man as soon as I return.'

'You mean pay him *holiday* money?' Sir James said indignantly. The idea of paying Willy when he had blackmailed himself into the job was insufferable. But he could not tell Charlotte that.

'Well, don't forget he'll lose the garage flat at Ebor Place – that's the chauffeur's perk, and he'll have to find somewhere else to live.'

James agreed unenthusiastically. He would prefer not to employ Hyde-Seymour at all. Maybe he would get as sick of advertising as he had of chauffeuring. But he suspected not. Willy, he thought, was an opportunist, not a drifter. If he was dangerous – he was also pretty smart.

Charlotte said sympathetically, 'You work too hard. Why don't you have a little siesta here with me? We don't have to change for dinner till eight.'

He patted her hand. 'A good idea. And I'll speak to young Hyde-Seymour. But you go and play bridge without me, there's a good girl. I've brought some work home from the office to do after dinner.'

126

She kissed him and said he was a silly old Daddy and of course it didn't matter – she, of all people, understood just how hard he worked. He was grateful but a little surprised that she agreed to go alone to the Elliot's without any protest.

The minute the car left the grounds of Whitelands that evening she slid back the glass panel.

'It's OK,' she said. 'He's agreed. About you starting at the office.'

She had expected a rush of grateful thanks, but Willy only said over his shoulder, 'Ah! I thought he might. When do I start?'

'You leave this job at the end of next week, and take two weeks' holiday.'

'I can't afford a holiday.'

'He'll pay you your chauffeur's wages. Until you start at Peak's.' She caught the sardonic little twist of the red lips and added quickly, 'Dearest boy, you must let me help you.'

'How?'

'Well, your fares to the Riviera, and expenses. You'll be able to stay in Roxana's villa. She's very understanding. You must let me.'

He stopped the car, turned and took her hands, kissing them.

'Charlotte, you're so good to me.' He looked up smiling. 'How about when I get back? Where shall I live? The chauffeur's flat goes with the job.'

'We'll see about that when I get back.' Willy realised his error. He must not push her too hard. He took her eager hands.

'I'm sorry, Charlotte – it's just that I must make plans – and plans that will give us somewhere to meet.'

'Don't worry, my darling boy, let's just take this chance of being together. Roxana has the loveliest place, right on the ocean. I go to France next week. I'll stop off in Paris.' She gave him an envelope. 'There's the name of my hotel in here, and some money. If you get the night-train you'll be able to join me the morning after I arrive. We'll have to stay over in Paris and travel down to Roxana's together. You could spend ten days down there with me before you go back to take up your job.'

He stared at her with delight; it wasn't difficult to say haltingly, 'I can't thank you enough. You're too generous, Charlotte. I won't let you down. I promise you. I'll make good. You'll be proud of me.'

He really wanted to get into Peak's. To work in the office and learn the publicity business. It seemed to him a step to greater opportunities. Advertising was salesmanship, but on a larger scale. You had to have nerve, and think quickly. And you had to use other people's talents – people like Brooker and Matt Wilson. You had to have ideas and find people to help you build the ideas. It was not a matter of fast-talking on a doorstep, although he had done that for a time. Driving Sir James about he had seen and listened to some of the big advertising men – the advertising managers of the great national newspapers and of the advertising departments of manufacturing firms, and had been fascinated by their talk.

This was not a big deal for him, but it might open the way to one. So he kissed Charlotte gratefully and drove her to the Elliot's, promising to pick her up early, so that they could spend some time together on the return journey. The early storm had passed. He would drive back through the deep and scented beech woods.

He opened the envelope she had given him. A hundred pounds. He gave a little whistle of pleased surprise. Bless her old heart! He'd have to have some new clothes but he could get them in Paris. Not suits – one bought suits in London. Shirts, pyjamas – a new dressing-gown, swim wear. Charlotte would enjoy shopping for him.

He would have left Ebor Place by the time June came back from Scotland. Sooner or later she was bound to hear he was working for Peak's, but it would be better if she did not know his new address. Poor little Squirrel – but it was for her own good. Why were the women you did not really want so easy to get, and the ones that drove you crazy wanting them, as cold as mountain water? He put the money safely away in his wallet. He had to pick Charlotte up at ten o'clock. He had better get back to Whitelands for his dinner.

There was a strict ban against junior members of Peak's staff receiving telephone calls, except in cases of dire emergency, but Lily would put a call through if she liked you so this did not affect Boots. Her line was one of the busiest in the office. This particular morning Duncan rang as soon as she arrived. She sat down without taking off her hat, and said, 'Dunky?'

'It's tomorrow,' he said.

'What is?'

'Your screen test.'

'You're 'avin' me on!' She forgot her new and hardly acquired accent.

'I'm not. And don't talk like that. What have you paid all that money to May Rampton for? Tomorrow. Nine o'clock. It's only a 'B' picture they're casting. *Her Reckless Hour*. It may not even be made . . .'

'Then what the hell . . . ?'

'I've talked Rudi Strauss into seeing the rushes. He's off to Hollywood at any moment. Boots it's tomorrow or never.'

'Never?'

'Well, I could probably get you another test here but we want Strauss to see them, don't we? Before he goes?'

'How'll I get out there?'

'I'll come tonight and stay at Helen's, and then I'll drive you out here . . . you'll have to be here all day. They say nine, but God knows when they'll see you. Strauss has only come back to do some close-ups for the picture they've finished. He'll try to fit it into the day. But it's our only chance. No one knows when he'll be back from Hollywood.'

'I'll have to ask for the day off.'

'Yes.'

'I've got a dinner date – with a friend. And then to go to the Alhambra to hear Jack Hilton's band.'

'Oh, damn Jack Hilton and his band! For God's sake, Boots, I've been trying so hard to get this for you. Boots, this is your future!' He waxed grandiloquent. 'There's no future for you with any of these old men. We've talked, we've planned, and I've been so sure you'll make it. Boots, darling Boots – you have got the most wonderful unique and beautiful face and body, and you've learned so much, can't you see how important this is?'

Through the glass panel of the entrance door she saw Sir

James leave the lift. She twitched off her hat and threw it under the desk.

'All right,' she said, 'see you tonight.'

'I'll pick you at May's. Tell Nell I'll be staying the night at Becker Street.'

She found she was shaking. She had listened to Duncan but had never really believed it all. It had been deadly serious for him, but it had been make-believe for her. Part of Duncan, his charm, his absurdity, his flights of imagination. But now, suddenly, it was for real.

She loved him in a curious, inexplicable way, not wanting anything from him but his companionship. He was a fantasy brother, a joyous friend, affectionate yet full of guile – he was like the first friend one makes at infant school before baby-hood has quite gone, offering only pure trust and affection.

She loved his exuberance and their shared laughter. She treasured the sense of equality he gave her. He was really posh, not like Sir James and Tommy Medway, yet he never made her feel inferior. He was what her mother would call 'a real gent'.

Madame Rampton made her learn and recite poetry. Something about the rhythm being a discipline for sound, whatever the heck that might mean. There was one poem . . .

> Whence you came I cannot tell;
> Only – with your joy you start.
> Chime on chime from bell on bell
> In the cloisters of my heart!

It was like the ringing pleasure she felt when she was with Duncan.

He had a way of falling silent and just looking at her. As though there was something holy about being pretty. She could not let him down because he wanted nothing from her but her own success.

On her way to see Sir James she went in to the studio to see Helen. Outwardly Helen was all right. She had some authority in the studio and she worked hard. She was a little sharper, and her laughter did not come so readily. She went out with Boots in the evenings, and sometimes with men she met in the studio. She never mentioned Matt. But it seemed to Boots she looked quite different. Fragile. There were blue shadows round her eyes, and the smile had gone out of them. As she stood looking down at her work on the drawing board, she rubbed her nose critically, like Matt Wilson used to, and then realising what she was doing, thrust her hand deep into her pocket, and looked across to where Mr Meakin sat in Matt's place.

'Dunky's got me a test tomorrow.'

Helen started. 'Go on,' she said vaguely, 'that's great.'

'He wants to stay with you tonight, because he's driving me down to Greenstreet first thing tomorrow.'

'That's all right. I'll get the camp bed out.'

'I've got to ask the Old Man for the day off.'

'Ah, well, that's life. All the best, anyway.'

Sir James was busy and irritable, and when she told him what she wanted, glared at her indignantly. When she told him why, he laughed. He was under pressure from Medway. Charlotte had been away for two weeks already, and neither he, nor as far as he knew, Medway, were any nearer success in luring Boots into a yielding mood.

'Really, girlie,' he protested. 'I don't know how you can believe all this film stuff. It's the oldest trick in the world. They'll charge you ten pounds for the wonderful chance, and there'll be no film in the camera. On to the office couch if you're pretty. When you go back, the place will be closed up, and a whole crowd of silly girls crying in the street outside. It's the oldest gag in the business.'

Boots looked down her nose – and looked adorable.

'You think I'm stupid? Everyone knows that one. This is on the level. Greenstreet Studios near Ayling.'

His expression changed.

'That's John Goldman's place.' He knew the studio had made several successful films, and that Goldman was building a sound set out at Greenstreet. 'You won't get any change out of him. Is it the young one, Barry? You can forget him too. Old Goldman is as straight as a deacon, and they're Jewish. No future for you there.'

'I've met Barry Goldman. He's a friend of my friend. They were at school together. My friend works at the studio.'

'Who is this friend of yours?'

Boots panicked. Sir James knew everyone – he might even know Duncan's dreaded uncle, who did not know Duncan was working at Greenstreet. Her long lashes swept up indignantly.

'I don't ask who your friends are,' she said.

This was preposterous! She was the most exasperating little bitch he had ever met.

'Some casting chap, I suppose. He'll get you into a corner of his office, lock the door and have your skirts up over your head before you know where you are.'

Her indignation turned to anger. Colour flooded up her cheeks. She was outraged.

'I shall take the day off anyway,' she said, 'and if you sack me that's your own business. It's not the only job in London. I can always go back to Benjie's.'

She marched purposefully towards the door, but Sir James caught her wrist and drew her back. She looked cautiously into his imploring face and decided tears would help. She thought of the taste of green gooseberries, of her mother dying alone in hospital, or never seeing Duncan again, and tears suffused her eyes and clung to her long straight lashes. Madame May had been very impressed by her ability to weep on cue.

'Now, girlie,' he remonstrated, 'don't cry. You're being silly. I'll meet you this evening and we'll talk.'

'It's not silly to me.'

Her lithe and silken body, smelling of clean youth and Guerlain's L'Heure Bleu did not yield an inch. His importuning fingers creeping towards the tempting curve of her breasts were instantly rejected.

'Are you short of money, girlie? Here,' he opened his notecase and proferred ten pounds. 'Forget all this and get yourself something pretty.' She regarded the money dispassionately. 'Meet me tonight and we'll talk about it. I'll be at the Troc at six-thirty. There's a good child.'

The clear eyes were as hard as stones and her voice lifted into an imitation of Helen at her most aristocratic.

'Thank you, *no*. You must excuse me. I am meeting Mr Medway this evening, anyway.' She smoothed her dress down

132

over her hips. The skirt came just above her knees. She wore real silk stockings of a pale flesh colour, and just below the hem of her pleated skirt was a flash of pale blue garter trimmed with pink silk rosebuds. Sir James was painfully aroused. It was years since a woman had affected him like this. He was terrified that she might really walk out of the office and his life. He knew he was a fool. He told himself she was an ignorant, shallow child, on the make, a real little gold-digger, but it made no difference.

He mopped up her tears, insisted she take the ten pounds, and told her of course she could have the day off tomorrow, but just to be patient. The Medway contract would soon be signed. He had engaged a young man to take away some of the burden of management, then he would have more time, and she would see what he could do for her. How about her own little flat? In some smart new luxury block. Wouldn't she like a place of her own?

Boots said non-committally that it might be quite nice, and she would think about it, pocketed the money and allowed him to kiss her half-averted cheek, and then went back to her desk to put off Medway, who proved more difficult.

When she left the office she posted five pounds to her mother at a local post office in Hackney because if she sent it home her father would open it and appropriate the money. She had her hair done, washed and ironed her yellow dress, and when Duncan came about nine they went to a cheap local restaurant for a meal.

He talked about the test until she wilted. He hardly stopped to eat. He was pale with excitement and his eyes burned – it was terribly important to him and, he insisted, to her.

He explained there would be several other girls taking the test, and some of them would be very pretty, and some of them very gifted, and most of them would have had experience of extra or theatre work, but she must not let this put her off.

'You're kidding?' Boots did not know whether to laugh or cry, he was so serious.

No. Film acting was different to theatre work. It was how the camera saw you. Or rather how the director saw you through the camera. As though the camera was a third, big

133

eye. That's how it was – but now, of course, there was sound coming in.

'I could make a right muck up of that,' she said.

He would not hear of it. The Assistant Director would give them all a script of a short scene and let them run through it once before it was actually filmed. When the reels were developed they would sort out the best and show them to Strauss.

'Suppose they don't choose me?'

'They will. I *know* they will. They must!'

It was only a small part in the film – a receptionist, with a few words to say. Having done reception work should help her.

'When will you know?'

'As soon as Strauss has seen them.'

'How long'll that be?'

'It doesn't matter – so long as he *does* see them before they're filed. If he likes you, he'll remember. He's sailing this week. The film business is one long wait. You wait for everything. But when you're in front of the camera you've got to understand that *is* your audience. The one big eye – and behind it are thousands of eyes. Maybe all the film-goers in the world. You've got to remember that. A close up is taken right up to your face – you've only got to let feelings flicker across your face. Even when they're dramatic.' He had been working and planning for this all summer. 'You will try, won't you, Boots?' She nodded silently. 'There's so much opportunity today. They're beginning to take promising young people on contract now, and teach them. Don't let the director rile you. I'll help you all I can – just try to feel what kind of girl he's looking for. Remember, it's not a round eye – it's rectangular.' He made a frame with his forefingers and thumbs, and peered at her through it. 'That's what you're acting into. Understatement. That's the thing . . . your face will make all the statements you need, I'm sure.'

She put her hands over her ears.

'Don't go on. I can't *stand* any more!'

'But you'll try.'

'Of course I will. Now shut up about it, and let me eat.'

She understood more than she had before she had worked

134

with May Rampton . . . but it still seemed like a crazy dream. She knew nothing and she knew it. She was terrified of letting him down.

At Becker Street they looked down into the area window and saw Helen sitting at her drawing board, a green shaded light illuminating her work. She wore a blue overall, and her hair tied back from her face, hunched, concentrating on her work. Boots made to go down, but Duncan stopped her.

'No. She's working. There's nothing worse than being interrupted when you're really working.'

She was working, Boots knew, because she had nothing else to do, and she was lonely. Because tomorrow would dawn and Matt would not be at the office – nor anywhere. She wondered how much Helen had told Duncan. Probably nothing.

As she unlocked the door he said casually, as though answering her thoughts, 'She was pretty keen on the studio manager, wasn't she?'

'Matt Wilson? He's left.'

'Oh,' Duncan said, just as casually, 'I expect that's what she's got the mopes about. Mums was a bit worried – last weekend. Said she had a look of heartbreak about her . . . Mums is very romantic.'

'Weren't you worried?'

'She'll get over it,' Duncan said cheerfully.

'But Matt Wilson is married – and years older than Helen.'

'Well, your Sir James and Mr Medway are both married and old enough to be your father. I understand you were thinking of moving in with one or the other?'

'Did Helen say that?'

'She didn't believe it. Thought you were pulling her leg.'

He was holding her hand, and she broke away. 'That's different.'

'Better or worse?'

Boots did not reply.

'I suppose you think it's all right because they are rich?'

Boots turned away her head and began to cry. Instantly Duncan put his arms about her and rocked her comfortingly. He did not apologise, or grovel for her forgiveness like Sir James, or make promises like sweets to a child, like Medway.

He left the hurtful words with her, even while he comforted her, because he meant them.

'You oughtn't to say things like that to me.'

'We ought to be able to say anything to each other,' he said.

She was stiff with nerves, quaking inwardly. If only Dunky had wanted to come upstairs and sleep with her she would, at least, have understood. But his whole mind was tied up with that test tomorrow. As though she was not a girl but some part of a whole enthralling concept that he would one day put together.

He kissed her, lovingly, as he always did now, sometimes quite absentmindedly, and then went down to Helen's basement room. She lay awake and lonely for some time, watching the headlights of the taxicabs making swirling yellow lights across the ceiling, curving like threatening snakes when they hit the angles of the walls.

After Boots had left Sir James, he telephoned John Goldman whom he knew quite well. He adopted a friendly, man to man attitude. There was a nice little kid he knew, filmstruck, who would be taking a test at the studio tomorrow.

'Well, there are several of them,' said John Goldman, anticipating the usual request from a rich businessman who was interested in a poor but ambitious girl. 'Look James, I can't do anything. It's a test for a small part in a thing we're starting next year. I haven't even got the money for it yet. But its Rudi Strauss who'll decide the casting and I can tell you, I've no more influence on him than I have on the Almighty.'

'She's no experience. She hasn't got what it takes, and I want her let down lightly. You know how to do it, Goldman.'

'I'll look out for her. What's her name?'

'Boots Skinner. Lillian Skinner.'

'I'll see what I can do. The chances are I may not be there myself. But I shouldn't worry. Strauss is leaving for the States in the *Q.M.* and won't be back until the New Year. It's unlikely we'll sign anyone up at this point. We'll just keep the best takes on record, and he'll see them all when he gets back. *If* he comes back.'

'Can't you hold them back?'

136

'Well, let's say I won't push them.'

'I'd appreciate that.'

'No need to worry – if we make the film, we'll make new tests. These will stay buried.'

'I don't want the little thing's hopes raised unnecessarily.'

Sir James put down the receiver and looked uncomfortably at the picture of June on his desk. Boots had once said, 'She's not pretty, is she? But then she's rich, so someone will marry her.'

It was an uncomfortable thought – as though Boots could not imagine anyone wanting to marry her. If she came to him he would be very good to her. He would be generous. She would not regret it.

He telephoned a West End property agency and asked them to send him some details of a new apartment block on the other side of the Park. A two-bedroomed luxury flatlet. Well furnished. He was enquiring for a friend. Would they send them to the office, marked personal.

Sir James would have been astonished if he had seen Duncan's motor cycle leaving Becker Street just before dawn, heading north for the Greenstreet Studios.

Helen had made them coffee and waved them off with wishes of good luck but they were so strung up they scarcely exchanged a word. Boots in the sidecar was muffled up in a rug, a scarf tying a pink hairnet over the smoothly set waves of her hair.

The morning wind blew freshly on her cheeks. In the chill early light, the moon like a yellow coin was sinking behind the hills.

She heard birds singing. She felt as though it was a totally new beginning, or could be. A new life. And yet – it was not what she wanted. The trouble was she had not yet discovered *what* she really wanted. This held the thrill of adventure – and yet, it was still Duncan's adventure. What she really wanted was something of her own and she knew now that just being pretty was not enough.

Chapter 7

June spent an intolerable month with the Debereaux family in Scotland. The house was very beautiful, in wonderful country, and there were plenty of parties and dances. But she only wanted to get back to Willy. She felt she would die if she did not see him soon, and was certain that he must feel the same.

She wrote to him every day. He did not answer, which scoured a deeper anxiety into her loving heart, but then she told herself, he might be afraid his letters would arouse suspicion.

She spun dreams like a busy little spider – Mrs Debereaux would have been startled if she could have seen those webby visions filled with impassioned and explicit memories of pleasure.

So June pined and yearned and lost weight, which improved her looks very much, and September came to an end at last and with a sigh of relief all round, she packed her bags and departed for London.

The journey seemed endless – the slow local train to Glasgow and then the express to Euston. When she arrived at Euston in the early evening she was sure Willy would be waiting for her with the car. Maybe with Charlotte? She hoped not. She prayed he would be alone, and that he would have made enough time to take her to Regent's Park, where they might walk a little – and kiss, and make plans. And she could tell him *her* plans.

She had found out that, in Scotland, people could get married without the consent of their parents even if they were under age. She did not think that either her father or Charlotte would be angry for long. Much better to run off to Gretna Green and confess to them afterwards. Such a romantic thing to do. She was sure her father would make a place for Willy in the business, and that Charlotte would understand.

'*After all,*' she had written, '*I am a bit of a burden to her. She is very fond of society, and smart witty people and I'm not a bit like that. It's only when I am with you that I can talk or express my feelings at all. When I see you waiting at the station in your grey uniform, looking so handsome I shall feel like dying with joy. I shall run straight into your arms. The first thing we must fix is to meet in our little home above the garage and you will make me feel all the lovely thrills of belonging to you and the happiness that no one can imagine except your lover and wife, for ever and ever, your own little Squirrel.*'

At Euston she could not see the tall figure in the smart grey uniform.

'I can't think where the chauffeur is,' she said panic-stricken. 'I was told they'd meet me.'

'Will I get you a taxi then, miss?' asked the porter.

'Well – oh, there!' Her heart leaped at the sight of the familiar grey uniform, and then seemed to die within her, for the short, middle-aged man hurrying towards her was certainly not Willy.

'Miss Peak?' he asked in breathless apology. 'I'm really sorry, miss. The traffic was chronic, I thought I'd never get through.' He bent to take her hand luggage and met the incredulous questioning in her eyes, and apologised again. 'I'm so sorry, miss. I should have said. I'm Briggs – the new chauffeur. Are you all right, miss? You look so pale . . .'

'Oh – oh yes, I'm quite all right. It was so hot in the train.' They were following the porter, wheeling her luggage. 'Is Lady Peak back from France?'

'Yes, miss. Arrived on Friday. Very brown she is.'

Where was Willy? Why had he gone and where? In the car she pushed back the glass panel.

'Has Williams got another job?' She hoped the man could not hear her voice trembling.

'I don't rightly know, miss. Seems he left sudden like.'

'Have you the garage flat now?'

139

'Yes, miss.'

What had Willy done? Where was he? Had he met with an accident? How could she find him?

'He must have been a careless young monkey,' said Briggs. 'And extravagant. No end of stuff left in the place. Tinned food, clothes, bottles of beer, and wine. Madam said we could have it all when the wife took in the letters.'

'*Letters*?' She went white again. 'What do you mean?'

'Well, there were a lot of letters and bills, and he left no forwarding address. I didn't like to destroy them in case he turned up, but my missus wanted to get the place to rights. Madam said we was quite right to bring them to her.'

Charlotte had all her letters! When she got up into her room at Ebor Place, she washed her face, took off her travelling clothes, and lay down. Ruby came in to unpack for her, and she told her to leave it until later.

'Very well, miss. Did you have a good time in Scotland?'

'Very nice thank you, Ruby, but I am tired.'

'Right you are, miss. But her ladyship did say to tell you to go down to her boudoir as soon as you returned.'

'Oh,' June said faintly, 'is Lady Peak in?'

'Yes, miss. She just came in – just as you got upstairs.'

'I'll go straight down.'

She leapt up and pulled open the drawer where she kept all the expensive cosmetics which had been bought to turn her into a beautiful débutante. She kept the contraceptive diaphragm which the Wimpole Street specialist had provided with the necessary protective creams in an empty, pink and gilt box which had contained toilet soap. It was still there. She breathed again. Her cheeks went hot at the thought that Charlotte, after reading her letters, might also have searched her room. Had she told Sir James?

With a wild flare of absurd hope, she wondered if they would insist that Willy marry her – what a blissful solution! And why not? He was well-bred and well-spoken. The thought bore her up on wings of optimism. She changed into a new and pretty dress which she had bought on a trip to Edinburgh with Mrs Debereaux, the only dress she had ever bought without Charlotte's supervision.

It was a semi-evening dress in flame coloured chiffon over

140

taffeta, and when Ruby came up with the luggage, June got her to damp down her fluffy hair and press it into waves and curls.

'Why you do look pretty, miss! You've lost a lot of weight. What a lovely dress.'

'Really?' She did want to look nice. Tonight she wanted her father and Charlotte to love her and want her to be happy. 'You don't think it's too bright?'

'Not a bit of it. You ought to wear bright things. Cook and I allus say so.'

'Sure you're all right, miss? Not pining away from love?' Ruby went off into her up and down giggle, so that June had to laugh too.

'No. It was just that there was so much walking in Scotland.'

'You'd better get down, miss, her ladyship will be waiting.'

Charlotte too was already dressed for dinner in a striking black dress, with two large fronds of snow white ostrich plumes on one shoulder into which her maid was pinning a diamond brooch.

She dismissed her maid and sat down at her desk, nodding to a chair opposite. June sank into it. Her knees were trembling.

Charlotte took out a large envelope, and shook out all June's letters to Willy, looking at them as though they were too unpleasant to touch.

She was so angry that she could not bear to look at June.

She had returned from St Juan in a state of euphoria, drunk with pleasure after ten magic days with Willy at Roxana's. How handsome he was – how proud she had been to be seen with him, knowing all the women envied her. She did not grudge a penny of the money he spent, she loved to buy him expensive things; to stand by him at the Casino where he played as though money did not matter, and somehow, because they had both been so happy, he had won. She was possessed with that dangerous mixture of sexual passion and maternal pride which an older woman feels for a young lover. She had come home planning a whole new future for herself

141

and the beloved boy. Home to this bundle of filth brought in by the new chauffeur's wife among a smattering of tailoring and bookmakers' accounts – some twenty-one letters from June. She had paid his bills, and read the letters which left her in no doubt that June, that small, unattractive, pasty-faced child, too shy to raise her eyes to an eligible schoolboy, had been Willy's lover ever since he had worked at Ebor Place.

June's dark eyes held a placatory smile, hopeful and nervous, which faded instantly as she realised that far from loving her, Charlotte did not even like her. In fact she was looking at her with the undisguised venom of the classic stepmother from fairy tales.

'Well,' she said, 'you've made a pretty damn fool of yourself, haven't you, Junie?'

'Oh, *Charlotte*,' June babbled nervously. 'If only you understood . . .'

'I understand only too well. I spoke to Williams and he agreed it was better for him to leave at once. And I think it would be better if you too were to go away from Ebor Place for a time.'

'What do you mean?'

'You are only eighteen. Do you realise that if your father knew, he could make a charge against Williams?'

'You mean have him put in prison?' She was horrified. Willy – in prison! And it would be her fault.

'It could be possible.'

'But you haven't told Daddy?'

'No,' Charlotte's voice was edged. 'I have too much respect for your father to tell him his daughter has behaved like a common prostitute.' She watched June's petrified face, and added, 'But if you don't behave yourself I shall have to.'

'But Charlotte, it wasn't like that. Willy was so sweet to me. We love each other. He's not married, or anything – he *is* a gentleman. Why can't we get married? Daddy could help him get on . . . maybe start him at the office. It's what he originally intended, isn't it?'

'Yes. Your father is very impressed with him and he has actually started at the office.' June's eyes lit with premature

142

joy, and Charlotte continued remorselessly, 'But then neither he nor I knew of this terrible thing. Do you imagine your father would have taken him into the office had he known? I cannot understand Williams. It is a wonderful opportunity for him. He is penniless.' She took out a fine lawn handkerchief edged with four inches of lace, and carefully dabbed her eyes.'Oh Junie, I know you're only a silly child, but I can't *help* being angry. How *could* you? After all we've done? After all your father's hopes. Like some little servant girl. And this boy, Williams, will certainly be fired if Sir James should get to know.'

'Oh, don't tell him. *Please* Charlotte, *don't* tell him.'

'That is entirely up to you. I think it is best for you to go away.'

'Away? But where?' June's lower lip trembled like a baby's.

'You can have another year at school.'

'Oh *no!*' June was shaking with fear and dismay. 'I couldn't go back to school. I'm . . . well, I'm a woman now.'

Her pathetic attempt at dignity did not touch Charlotte.

'Nonsense – you're a silly little girl. A dirty minded little girl.'

'I'm not, I'm not!' June blazed at her defiantly. 'I'm grown up – and I'm in love with Willy.'

'Well, his future at the office is in your hands.' Her voice softened a little. She did not want to scare June into desperation. 'I don't mean an ordinary school. A finishing school. Abroad. In Switzerland.'

'Does Daddy know – about the school idea?'

'I had been speaking to him about it – before I knew of this awful business. I told him I did not think you were quite ready for your first season, and this would give you more confidence. He thinks it a good idea, if you are happy about it.'

'Charlotte,' June rose to her feet, 'I will go – but can I see Willy before I go? Just once – to explain? If he loves me, then he'll wait until I'm twenty-one. But if he doesn't – then I'll ask him to tell me honestly.'

'No!' Charlotte cried, then stopped. She *must* be kind – she *must* appear reasonable. 'Willy – that is, Mr Hyde-Seymour, is older than you are. I know he looks very young, but he is over thirty. There is no excuse for his conduct, although you certainly made yourself very cheap. You are out of your depth, Junie.'

June could not deny it.

'He has no intention of marrying you. He never had. But he is clever and your father needs to bring one or two young men into management training. Your daddy said he had fought bravely in the war and it was only right he should have his chance. Do you want to destroy him?'

'Oh, no. Oh, no, of course not.'

Charlotte rose and put an arm round June's shoulder, and June, beaten and bewildered, wept into the white ostrich fronds, which tickled her nose unbearably. 'Come, come, maybe I've been too tough on you. But you must see how naughty you've been. What a terrible risk you've taken . . . why you might have had a baby. Think of the disgrace . . . think of Daddy!'

'Oh no, that's impossible. Willy took care of me. He told me what to do.'

'Did he indeed!' The words seemed to be torn from her. 'I am horrified that you could be so – so shameless. A girl of your age – only seventeen. And your position as Sir James's daughter. We were planing such a wonderful début for you.'

'It will be like going to prison – going back to school.'

'Oh don't be so dramatic, June. Most girls would be over the moon. The school is on Lake Geneva, and it's terribly expensive. The Académie Florian. The girls are from the best European families. Now, are you going to be a good girl, and let me help you?'

June, facing the enormity of her behaviour, nodded dismally.

'Now – we'll forget all about this horrid little affair. You'll go to Switzerland as soon as possible. We'll have a grand time together buying you a lot of pretty clothes. And – if I have a good report from the headmistress – perhaps you'll come home for Christmas. How about that?' She sounded quite kind.

'Thank you, Charlotte. I will do my best.'

Ruby knocked and said Sir James had returned.

'Go down and see Daddy, dear, and don't let him see you've been crying.'

So June dried her eyes, powdered her nose and went down. But behind the quivering child's face was her father's daughter. A determined and possessive little woman who had been scared, bullied and wheedled, had been made to feel guilty, but who was by no means beaten and who owed no loyalty to Charlotte. She *would* go and see Willy before she went away. Sir James, sitting comfortably in the drawing room looked up and was pleasantly surprised to see how nice she looked in the flame coloured dress, how much slimmer, her cheeks pale, but her eyes bright and a sweet, timid smile of welcome on her lips.

'Daddy,' she said, and put her arms round his neck and kissed him.

When Charlotte went down to the drawing room she found, to her surprise, that June was sitting cosily on her father's knee.

'Ah, there you are, Charlie,' said James looking up. 'It's great to have our little girl back. Didn't realise how much I missed her. I'm not sure that I want her whisked off again.'

'We shall both miss her, of course, but this is a great opportunity for Junie, and she's just longing to go.'

Willy met Charlotte just after midnight on the balcony of the Café Royal.

She had the incriminating letters and immediately burst into loud, despairing and accusative tears. The waiters, who had seen many emotional scenes among the red banquettes and gilt framed mirrors, took no notice whatsoever.

It had taken a lot of talking and a bottle of champagne to bring Charlotte back to a frame of mind where she could at least listen to his explanations.

Willy managed to look suitably shamefaced and said, 'Darling, it's not easy for a chap – a young chap, when a girl keeps showing up at his rooms, practically demanding it. I'm no saint . . . and she was pathetic. I mean I'd only tried to be kind and friendly, but that was not what little June wanted. Charlotte, I could tell you tales about some of these well-brought up kids that would make your hair stand on end. She's full of the sentimental twaddle that she reads . . .'

'But sending her to Wimpole Street – to that woman doctor to be fixed up . . .?'

Willy drew himself up, and summoned the waiter, ordering more champagne. He topped up her glass, stony-faced, and said sternly, 'Perhaps we should not discuss it further. If you won't at least try to understand . . .'

'Oh I will, I will . . .' Her fingernails pressed sharply into his hands. 'It's just because I *want* to understand that I'm asking . . '

Willy looked down at the predatory hand pressing on his. He knew with a gambler's intuition, that his winning streak could not go on for long so it was better to play it for all he could while it lasted.

'I had to protect her – for your sake. And Sir James's. I mean with these unbalanced kids, you never know. Better be safe than sorry.' He kissed her bare arm and felt her shiver and knew that this time he had got away with it.

She was a little unsteady on her high heels when they rose to go. They taxied back to his new flat, where he reduced her to a whimpering subjection, pleading and demanding every stimulation he knew, until she was limp with sated desire. Reluctantly she gave him June's letters, which he immediately destroyed. He did not think he would have any more trouble with Charlotte. And he agreed with her – oh, how sincerely he agreed with her – that the Swiss finishing school for June was a first-rate idea.

When he went into Dominion House the next morning, he bounded up to the first floor, two steps at a time. He had gone in by the staff entrance before, but today, buoyed up by a new self-confidence he went straight through the main entrance and saw Boots sitting at the reception desk, apparently pasting cuttings into a large album. The green shaded desk light shone on the smooth, golden hair and the bright point of a diamanté clasp that held the waves back from her smooth broad forehead. She wore a long-sleeved jumper of fine beige coloured wool, and a pearl choker round her long slender neck. He felt the rush of fury and desire which the memory of their first violent encounter always roused.

146

Her limpid eyes gazed at him with polite enquiry, and she said, 'Good morning, sir. Can I help you?'

He leaned on the counter, removed his hat and smiled.

'You don't remember me, do you?'

Pause, upward glance, little frown.

'That night – when you'd been to Frascati's with . . .' The cutting book slammed shut before he could say Sir James's name. The charming expression vanished. Boots glared belligerently.

'You're that fresh chauffeur of the Old Man's. Got the day off?'

He straightened angrily.

'I work here now. In Mr Brooker's department.'

'In that case you should have gone in the staff door. This is for Sir James, clients, and Sir James's personal callers.'

'Oh, come on, kid,' he said. 'Don't put on an act. I'm sorry if I got off on the wrong foot last time. No hard feelings?'

'Foot? I should say so! As I remember, one minute you were helping me to put my shoe on, and the next you were halfway up my skirt!' There was a fraught and antagonistic silence. Willy felt like a fool. She had spoiled his morning. He could have hit her – he would have if he had dared. 'Get your elbow off this counter,' she said fiercely, 'Sir James doesn't like staff hanging about Reception.'

'Why – is he jealous?'

'If you've got a job here and you want to keep it, you'd better watch your mouth,' she snapped. Her voice had dropped and her accent slipped, and just as Mr Brooker appeared at the far end of the corridor she hissed, 'I know your sort, two-a penny stuck up snobs. Piss off, or I'll tell J.P.'

She went smoothly on with her work, with a bright smile of greeting to Mr Brooker, who beamed and said, 'Good morning, Lillian.'

'Good morning, sir.'

Mr Brooker turned to Willy and said cordially, 'Ah, good morning, Hyde-Seymour. You're bright and early. That's what I like. I'm just going over to Space to check some schedules there. Will you join me when you're ready?'

'Yes, sir, in one minute. I'll just hang my hat up.'

Willy went into the office he shared with two other juniors

and hung up his hat, fighting for self-control before he went to the Space Department where Mr Brooker was pouring over some new charts with the powerful and capable Miss Klein. He was all respectful attention. He was not going to be put down by a common little bit like Boots. But the thought of her nagged through the day like an aching tooth.

Boots had not heard from Duncan since the film test, which had been one of the most traumatic experiences of her life.

It had been a long, boring day, cooped up with a dozen girls, nearly all ravishingly pretty, half of them with stage experience and most of them with training. She was one of the last to be called.

Then she had been made up with pale yellow powder and a blackish purple lipstick, taken into a studio and on to a rough set. A page of script was thrust into her hand, and someone told her to sit down. There was a chair, and a table with a telephone on it. She sat down and a brilliant light went on. She peered into the busy gloom about the camera, a one-eyed idol regarding her indifferently as though she was an unappetising human sacrifice.

Then – in one of the row of chairs beside the camera she saw Rudi Strauss. The great man himself. There was no mistaking the monocle, the camel hair coat slung cloak-wise across his shoulders, the arrogant, breeched and booted legs, the black Borsolino pulled down rakishly over one eye.

Duncan, white and tense, was standing beside him. There seemed to be a variety of men of all ages who were all called Grip, because when anyone shouted 'Grip' one of them lunged forward and moved a piece of furniture, or a light, or a cable. There was one girl, taking notes, who was apparently called Continuity which, in her bewilderment, Boots thought rather a pretty name. There was a saturnine, bored young man in horn-rimmed spectacles who was looking at her, as indeed they all were, as though she was some kind of merchandise – maybe a succulent piece of lamb hung in a butcher's window. There was no chance of wheedling, charming or manipulating here. She felt exposed. Impersonalised. She hated them all.

She read the script. It was uninspiring.

Nanda comes through door R. Telephone rings, she answers it.

Nanda: Nanda here. Yes? What? Not Monty? Oh, God no!
And that was all.

The bored young man brightened.

'I see what Redmaine's on about,' he said critically. 'Lovely bones. Right. Let's have a high spot on her face. Right Miss . . . er . . .' He glanced at some notes. 'Skinner. *Cripes*! Training but no experience, right. I'll tell you how. Use the same lines all the time. Don't try and emote – you're not Garbo. Pitch your voice low . . . Right now . . . come on everyone, last one, we're nearly through, then you can all go home.' This last remark was greeted by an ironical cheer.

For an hour she walked through the door, answered the telephone, sitting down, standing up, kneeling on the floor, said the lines hopefully, sadly, gladly, laughingly, curiously, pitching her voice low, and obediently pushing the inflection about until she was dizzy. The great arcs flared and dimmed, frying her, and her exhaustion and temper edged, until she caught Duncan's eye, blew, and burst out, bright with temper, 'This is ridiculous. If you don't know if I can say it by now, you bloody never will!'

There had been an awful silence, then Strauss had said gravely, 'Little miss – Duncan has said you very much wish for this job. It is for him we saw you. In this business it is repeat and repeat and repeat. If not, no use. Again?'

'All right.' She did five more, recovered her nerve, blew the last one, and started to laugh, saying, 'I made a right Charlie of that little lot!'

Someone said she could go. The kleigs went off, and the studio lights on, and Strauss rose without a word and left the set like visiting royalty with a flutter of assistants round his heels, including Duncan. She went to have the muck taken off her face in make-up and then to the canteen where she found Duncan with the Assistant Director, who was not unsympathetic.

'He didn't say a thing,' Duncan said furiously. 'The miserable old kraut.'

'Well, he has a lot on his mind,' said the Assistant Director. 'He's after a contract with Metro.'

'Yeah. But he promised me he'd tell me what he thought.'

'Well, he will. Don't fuss, darling. He doesn't sail until Friday.'

Boots sat between them listening, still feeling she might just as well not be there. She could not recognise Duncan, her companion and friend, in this tense, furious boy.

'Well, she's great to photograph, like you said,' said the A.D. comfortingly, 'and her voice is all right.'

'She made a real muck-up of that last take!' Duncan looked at Boots accusingly. 'What made you blow like that?'

'I just decided I didn't want to be in films!' she snapped. 'What, get up at six, and do this all day? Not on your Nelly!'

'Children, children, don't worry. She looked the best. The others were just dolls. That nose! Those eyelashes. Right? No use worrying until he sees the rushes.'

'*If* he sees them.'

'Well, they'll get filed anyway.'

'They'll get buried,' said Duncan morosely.

'Was there film in the camera?' asked Boots. They both stared. 'Someone told me they often didn't put it in – you know, if they were just doing you a favour.'

'Oh, it was loaded all right. With Strauss watching they'd have to. He's got an elephant's memory. Look, kids, he may not see the rushes today – or before he leaves for Hollywood. But he could remember any time, and want them, and Christ, what a row there'd be if they weren't there. Don't fret . . ' He had kissed Boots, and patted her tired, childish face. 'You take like a dream. Dunky's right about that.'

They went out to the motor bike.

'D'you mind,' said Duncan, 'if I just run you to the station. I want to hang about just in case. He might just see them, and call me.'

'That's all right.'

'Oh, Helen's fixed up with Mums for you to come to Mill Cottage – in about three weeks! Can you make it?'

'Yes. I think so.'

They drove to the station. He did not dismount.

'When the train draws out – about a mile from Ayling Station, you'll cross a long viaduct, and if you sit on the right side of the train, you'll see Mill Cottage down by a waterfall.'

'That'll be nice,' said Boots.

The train came snaking in. 'I'm sorry, Dunky,' she said.

He clutched his curly head. 'It's just that I'm scared that I'm wrong about everything. About me as well. That I ought to give it up and do what everyone expects. Not because I want to – but because there's no other way.' They stared at each other helplessly. 'Well, I'll get by somehow. And you will too . . . I mean anyhow, I'm *sure* you will. Nell will fix a date with you.'

He kissed her goodbye absently, and turned away before the train came into the station.

The special feeling she had had of belonging to a bizarre and exciting world had gone. When they had talked about it over the travertine marble tops of Corner House tables, among the cigarette smoke and slopped coffee cups with the other dreamers from the theatre schools and ranks of extras, success had seemed real. It was something shining and glorious they had imagined – like Father Christmas and Happy Ever After. It was not like that at all.

Boots dutifully sat on the righthand side of the carriage, gazing blankly at the passing countryside. A woman opposite said to her companion, 'Oh look – *what* a pretty house,' and she remembered Duncan had told her to look out.

They were crossing a high viaduct over a valley winding from beechwoods golden with autumn, with a stream wandering through it. Far below, against the woods stood an old house of rosy brick, with a second, smaller building straddling the stream, with mill wheel and sluice, all set in a beautiful garden.

It was like a picture. Was it really Duncan and Helen's home? Was this where they spent the weekends when they were not in London? When they said, 'Must go to see Mums and Cousin Millicent at Ayling'?

They had always said they were hard up. To her, hard up was the mean house in the mean street where she and her brothers had been born. No hot water and an outside bog. The shabby rented rooms since she had left home. Pawning things to pay the rent. The distance between her and the Redmaines widened frighteningly. Before she had known them she had only been out for what she could get but at least she had known where she was.

*   *   *

151

Doggedly Willy refused to admit defeat. If Boots thought he was not interested she would come round. Women always did. If she was playing hard to get, he could wait.

He avoided the main entrance. If he passed her he gave her an indifferent nod, to which she returned a small, puzzled frown, as though trying to remember who he was, which was ridiculous. His impact on the office was effective. Mr Brooker took to him, Miss Klein, the spacebuyer, found him a dear boy, and not at all snooty, although obviously out of the top drawer. He took to advertising like a fish to water and set out to be liked. With his charm it was not difficult.

The first thing he discovered was that James Peak (Publicity) Ltd., the best-known advertising firm in London, was extremely old-fashioned. It had imposing offices and Sir James's talent for selling the idea of publicity was spellbinding, but the firm was operating much as it had in 1914. They produced nothing original in either design or ideas. Clients came to them, drawn by Sir James's persuasive personality, and then found their work was ordinary. Sir James would not pay for talent, nor would he delegate authority. They caught a lot but they lost a lot. They had two or three large accounts, of which Medway tiles was the most important, which were so large that the client and agency worked as one, and even when, as in the case of Tommy Medway, they would like to break away it would be so complicated that some major disaster would have to occur before they considered it. Sir James did not consider Medway's infatuation with Boots a major disaster, but the defection of Matthew Wilson certainly was.

Willy decided that advertising was the game for him – but not in his present set-up. He would stay a year or more at Peak's until he knew the business thoroughly and had made plenty of contacts, then he would move on, taking some clients with him. One day – before he was forty – he would start his own agency. He would collect some real talent and work on the new American group work-plan. He would need capital, of course, but if Sir James could start on his own, so could Willy.

Brooker liked and trusted him. He had given him a few small accounts to handle, and had let him sit on the campaign conferences. So he was very pleased with himself.

He left the office, his hat set at an angle, swinging his stick, and then saw Boots ahead of him, wearing a pale camelhair wrap coat, with a fluffy fox collar and a small brown felt hat trimmed with iridescent feathers curling round her cheeks. He fell into step behind her, forgetting his resolutions, admiring her strong, slender legs, noting how firmly her arched feet balanced on her high-heeled brown and fawn shoes. She might be as common as muck, but she certainly knew how to dress.

She could not afford to dress like that on her wages, and he wondered if either Sir James or Tommy Medway contributed to her wardrobe, and that the reason for his lack of success was his lack of money.

He caught up with her, falling into step beside her, and for once being perfectly natural. 'I say, look, Lillian, Boots – Miss Skinner – I am most frightfully sorry. I did behave like an absolute cad, and I do apologise.'

She stopped and smiled, and immediately responded.

'That's all right then,' she said, 'just so long as you don't try anything on again.'

'I wouldn't dare,' he said, laughing. 'Come and have a drink.'

He was triumphant. He had been right. She had *not* meant it. It was just an act, playing hard to get. He remembered that he had put her in the expensive category of women. Everything about her – from her manicured fingernails to the straight seams of her expensive silk stockings confirmed this. So he said, 'Let's go to the Waldorf.'

Boots considered. She had time to spare, and the warm and charming lounge at the Waldorf was preferable to Madame May's dusty studio.

'Righty-oh,' she said. 'Why not?'

They found a table, and he suggested champagne cocktails. She shook her head.

'No thanks. You do, if you want. I'll have a cup of coffee. I've only got half an hour before my lesson.'

'Lesson?'

'Speech lesson.'

He had forgotten. When he had tried to telephone after the

153

Frascati business, she had always been at lessons.

'I go to elocution lessons. With Madame Rampton. Haven't you noticed? I remember grammar now. I avoid clichés.' She giggled at this. 'I've stopped saying things like "Well it takes all sorts" and "Come orf it" and "Buzz orf".'

'You didn't say that to me. You trod on my hand.'

'No, well, I'd lost my rag – I mean my temper, hadn't I?' Her hands flew up to her mouth and she twinkled enchantingly. 'I've got to stop that, Madame Rampton says. Asking a question after every statement. It's London Cockney. Did you know? There I go again. And I'm getting this sound thing – ay-aye-eye-ee-oh-you. *Don't* tell me you haven't noticed?'

'I think you're super as you are.'

'That's what all the fellows say. I know different – different*ly*!'

'Well, what's it all in aid of?'

'I thought I had a chance in films – a friend thought so. I was photogenic, he said. But now you have to talk as well.' She looked lost for a moment. 'Now, I'm not so sure. I feel it's worthwhile, anyhow.' She glanced at her watch. 'I must go now.'

'Oh, go on,' he coaxed. 'You can skip one class.'

'Not if it's paid for.'

Boots recognised a great deal of herself in him. If he had tried the persuasive charm on her that he did on older women, she would have stretched wide one lovely eye, and asked if he saw any green in it.

She turned, caught a waiter's attention as expertly as any grand dame, and said, 'I'll have to hurry. Ma Rampton'll give me a real rollicking if I'm late.'

Up on the higher terrace, hiding behind a menu, June Peak watched them. She had been standing outside the office in the chill wind waiting for Willy to come out.

When she saw him, looking so handsome, somehow so powerful, as though he was already the important executive which she was sure he would be one day, she was choked with adoration.

Everything had been fixed for her to leave for Switzerland. She was to come back for the Christmas holidays. She had started to cross the road towards him when she saw his face light up with interest, and for a blissful moment thought it was for her – and then he had gone chasing down the road after a beautiful girl, swinging along with her pretty nose in the air like some sort of royalty, and had taken her arm and walked towards the Aldwych and into the Waldorf. June dived in after them. She found a distant table and ordered a dry Martini which sounded sophisticated, and hoped the waiter would think she was waiting for a friend.

When they left the Waldorf, she followed them round to Madame Rampton's studio in Endell Street. From a distance she watched Willy pleading with the pretty girl and saw her shake her head laughingly and go into the building. He strode off towards Shaftesbury Avenue in what appeared to be a temper. June hurried along after him, a scurrying little shadow in the October dusk.

When he took a taxi, she took one too, feeling like someone in a film. When he went into the apartment building she paid off her taxi and followed. The entrance hall was empty. But there was a list of tenants on the wall by the stairs.

Captain William Hyde-Seymour. Flat 4, 3rd Floor. She went up and pressed the bell. She heard him swear, the door was wrenched open, and he stood there, jacketless, tie in hand, staring at her furiously. He had thought it must be Charlotte, and his expression softened with relief.

'Why *Junie!*' he said. He was sorry for her. She was such a fool. 'What on earth brings you here?'

'I had to see you,' she said piteously. 'Charlotte is sending me away. You did hear that she was given my letters? By the new chauffeur?'

'Er – yes. I'm sorry, Squirrel. It was deuced careless of me. But with one thing and another, the new job, and moving here, I didn't go back to clear out.'

'Was she very angry with you?'

'Yes. Oh yes. Come in . . .' She followed him into the neat apartment, impersonal and convenient like a hotel room. 'She gave me a real ticking off.'

'Me too,' she said ruefully, and suddenly they laughed, confidingly, like naughty children. 'But at least she didn't tell Daddy.' He realised, with relief, that June did not know about Charlotte. He looked round quickly, picked up a packet

155

of Russian cigarettes and thrust them in his pocket.

'Thank Christ for that,' he said fervently. 'She's not a bad old sort, really.'

'But she did say she *would* – if I didn't go to Switzerland. I suppose she is right. In her way,' June went a little pink. 'It's true I'm only eighteen, and I am her responsibility. Until I'm twenty-one. I suppose I have been a naughty girl. But . . .' she burst out piteously, 'I do love you so, Willy. I had to come and tell you so before I go.'

'Of course,' he said understandingly. 'And you don't want to upset your father.'

'He's being very sweet to me. I'd go crazy if you were blamed for this, and it's just as much my fault as yours. That's why I had to see you. Just to make sure it's all the same. Charlotte said you didn't love me, but I know you do . . .'

'Of course I do, Squirrel,' he said, putting his arms round her. Today she almost looked pretty. Her soft dark eyes and full, sensuous mouth yearned for him, stirring him irresistibly. He was humiliated by Boots's indifference, and irritated with Charlotte who was becoming possessive and had put uncomfortable pressures on him since the halcyon ten days in the South of France. He could not bear scene-makers.

But tonight he was safe – Charlotte had to attend an important public dinner where Sir James was speaking on the importance of advertising in industry.

'Dear little Squirrel,' he said tenderly, 'I've missed you dreadfully.'

June threw herself into his arms. She was just what he needed. She was on fire for him – and one day Boots Skinner would be too, or his name was not Willy Hyde-Seymour. He was tired of middle-aged women.

He switched on a low light and drew the curtains, turned on the wireless and found some slow, sentimental music. He poured two glasses of brandy, and then he took June into his bed. Her shuddering abandonment at his touch brought solace to the wounds which Boots had so indifferently inflicted.

Chapter 8

The days of that summer seemed to Helen to stretch away for ever. She worked very hard. She got in touch with friends she had known at art school. She accepted invitations from men she met in the course of the day, representatives of studio supply firms, or executives from various clients. But – unlike Boots – she had no ulterior motive for seeking companions, except for her agonising need not to be alone. She was unaware of her inability to pretend, so these friendships did not prosper. A gravely polite interest is baffling to amorous young men. A few of them made her laugh, none of them quickened her heart beats by a second. She was looking for the mixture of tenderness and self mockery, the brilliance and the deep seriousness that she had found in Matt. They all seemed so very young.

She held her distress on a close rein. She and Boots were very close, sisters and friends.

Boots planned and schemed watchfully; she sought opportunity and the men who could provide it, convinced that she had been a mutt where Duncan was concerned. Telling herself, not very successfully, that he had been just another spoiled young man who knew nothing of the realities of life.

But to Helen the days stretched interminably, and every night was a terror of sleeplessness. She stayed in London at weekends, because she knew her mother would know at once that something was wrong. She parried her questions, and Cousin Millicent's probings over the telephone, making the excuse that she had urgent work to finish. When Mavis, not convinced by the calm, flat voice, said directly, 'Nell – is there anything wrong?' She said airily, 'Wrong? What should be wrong? You are an old worrier, Mums, I'm having a wonderful time.'

'I shall get used to it,' she told herself. 'Every day it will be a little better. Like when Dads was killed.' But she knew this was not true. 'I'm that stupid, awkward creature, a one man woman,' she said to Boots, who replied that was a dead loss in any girl's reckoning.

Sometimes she would have disturbing dreams of walking through pouring rain, searching the faces of all the men who passed, recognising in the distance the dear, familiar figure, hands thrust in pockets, lanky and lean, wide-brimmed hat at a rakish angle, eyes fixed on the pavement, but always when she drew near it was not Matt, but a stranger and she woke up with her pillow soaked with tears.

It was about this time that she realised Boots was 'Nannying' her. Watching her, worrying about her, fussing round her. At first it made her laugh, and then with faint exasperation, she began to resent it.

Boots was worried at her loss of weight. If they were not going out she would bring in something exotic to tempt her appetite. If they went out separately, she would appear at bedtime with cups of cocoa and sandwiches.

'No, thanks Boots. I had dinner.'

'Did you eat it all? Or did you send half of it away?'

'For God's *sake*, Boots, don't fuss.'

'Well, you're getting as skinny as a stick of celery. Did you enjoy yourself?'

'Boots, will you *stop* it.'

'Well, you don't look after yourself. And you don't seem to enjoy yourself, and you don't take to any of these chaps.'

'I had a nice time. I am not losing weight, and I always have a good meal.'

'You must sweat it off then. You're working too hard.'

'I enjoy work. And I'm doing good work.'

'I know, I know, Sir James's little genius! But what's your ma going to say when you go home?'

'Oh, Boots, mind your own business.'

Boots would glower, but would not desist.

They had always gone to work together on the number

158

eleven bus, unless Boots was going shopping early or to the hairdresser. But, now she always accompanied Helen, as though she was a child who had to be taken to school, and she developed a curious irrationality about the direction in which they went.

She would say at Charing Cross. 'Let's get off and change on to a bus that goes up the Aldwych, save us the walk. Get off outside the office.'

'It's only a five minute walk – I like to walk.'

Boots would suddenly express a desire to call at some shop in one of the small streets towards Drury Lane, so that they would change their route at the Strand, and go up Wellington Street. About the second week in September, Helen began to see a pattern in this behaviour. For some reason Boots wanted to avoid the Aldwych on certain days. But the pattern was irregular. So on one bright September morning, when Boots turned abruptly up Wellington Street, saying something about a button shop she had noticed, and she had lost a button from her camelhair coat, Helen took a few paces beside her, and then turned sharply back and saw Matt standing on the corner of Lancaster Place, looking directly at her. They stood motionless looking through the seething mass of traffic. She could not know that her face lit up with unconcealed longing and love, and that her arms rose and stretched out towards him with an encompassing joy. She felt as though she could fly across the road to him.

The great red wall of an omnibus came between them and when it had passed Matt was nowhere to be seen.

She ran down to the corner, looking frantically in every direction. For a sick and dizzy moment she thought it was an hallucination born of her own longing, and then she saw Boots's face and knew it was true.

She felt herself coming slowly alive, as though she had been cold for weeks, frozen, and that her pulses were beginning to beat, and the blood course through her veins again.

'Have you see him there before?' she said.

'Yes,' Boots said uncomfortably.

'How often?'

'Not often . . . maybe once a week. Maybe twice. I expect he has work around here. Well, he would have wouldn't he?'

159

Helen smiled. 'Why didn't you tell me?'

'Well, I knew you'd go rushing off after him again. You're so crazy. All the advertising offices and magazines are around here. Just because he makes early calls, and comes this way, it doesn't mean he wants to see you. I mean he could telephone . . . or just walk across. Maybe he doesn't want to run into you face to face, and he's watching so that when you've gone by he can feel free.'

'Don't be stupid!' She began to walk slowly up the long slope towards the office, but she walked differently now, with her pretty head poised in the old, assured way, and a smile on her lips.

'Nell,' said Boots desperately, 'don't start it all again. That night when you came back to Becker Street like a drowned rat I honestly thought you'd die.'

'I did die – I've been dead ever since. I've just come alive again.'

'But – he's no good for you, Nell. He's not serious. The way I look at it a classy girl like you is crazy to fall for a bloke like Matt Wilson. You could pick and choose. With him you didn't own yourself any longer – you only lived for him. And he made it pretty clear that he didn't want to play.'

'Have you ever spoken to him?'

'Once,' Boots replied reluctantly. 'That night, after the taxi driver brought you in, and I'd put you to bed. He telephoned. He only asked if you'd got home safely. I said yes, but no thanks to him and rang off. I've never spoken to him since.'

They had reached the entrance to Empire House. Helen stopped, and turned on Boots, blazingly angry, her gentle face on fire.

'Boots, don't you ever do anything like that again. You should have told me. Help is one thing, but you've no right to interfere. How do you know what I want? Or what Matt wants?'

'Oh, go to hell!' said Boots huffily, and ran into the hallway and up to the Ladies Staff Washroom on the right of the corridor. Helen followed her in.

'Does he come in the evenings?'

'I'm not telling you anything. He's poison to you.' They were both blazingly angry. 'You and Duncan are both the same, up in the air, high-handed, bloody naive fools, both of you. You imagined Matt was in love with you, and Duncan imagined I would make a film star, and it's all damned poppycock. After that evening at Frascati's all your precious Mr Wilson wanted was to get you off his back . . .'

Helen smacked her face.

Boots's face flamed – she hesitated for a second, staring, then struck back, hard and vicious, jerking Helen's head. There was a long moment, and then the door opened and Miss Prior, plump as a navy blue pigeon, came in carrying a clean towel wrapped round her celluloid soap box. Instinctively both girls bent over the bowls, turned on taps, splashed their hands.

'You're late,' Miss Prior accused, 'Sir James has just come in – he was roaring for you, Boots. Something to add to today's appointments, and old Meak's after you too Helen.'

'Jumping Jesus!' said Helen.

'Must spend a penny,' said Miss Prior and vanished within a cubicle. The two girls clapped their hands across their mouths, overcome by silent laughter though their eyes were full of tears.

'Sorry, mate,' said Boots. She peered into the mirror. 'Cor! Is it going purple?'

'I don't think so. Look at me! Wow.'

'Here, put some rouge on the other side.'

Helen did so. Regarded her usually untouched face. 'I look like a clown.'

'Well, we can't both say we ran into lamp posts.'

Miss Prior fussed out, busily washing her hands, looking at them suspiciously. 'What's the matter with you two?'

'Well, you'll not believe this,' said Helen, 'but I dropped my brooch, and we both went down to look for it, and looked up and banged into each other. Gosh it's made my eyes sting.'

'Oh? Oh, well . . . hurry up, anyway.' She bustled out. Sir James's voice could be heard roaring.

'Some people,' Boots said grimly, 'will believe anything.'

'Forgive me, Boots?'

'Oh, don't be soft.' She looked at Helen's eyes, alight again, her mouth smiling and said grumpily, 'If your best friend falls in the river, don't you try and save her?'

'Yes, but you don't stop her learning to swim.'

'*Smarty*! You Redmaines have always got an answer. Well, see if I pull you out again, Miss Clever.'

'You won't have to – not this time,' Helen said, and she turned and ran as swiftly as a gazelle out of the building.

Matt had not foreseen the sheer hunger for the sight of her which possessed him, even in the two weeks before he left Peak's.

The morning after the night at Frascati's he had wakened with the fairly familiar dry mouth and aching head of the morning after, and drinking liver salts and regarding his reflection in the shaving mirror had thought, as in the past seven years he often had, 'What the hell did I get up to last night?'

But this time it was different. This was nothing to be brushed away, or forgotten, placated with a gift, or flowers or the promise of a future date. This time he had fallen deeply and completely in love with a girl fifteen years younger than himself, a girl as unschooled in the ways of the world as a wild bird. She had flown into his arms driving him crazy. He could have brought her here and taken her and by God, that would have been forever – for him certainly, but at twenty-three what the hell would it have meant for her?

And he had been selfish enough and fool enough to let her unconcealed delight in him, her unabashed passionate response drag him down into the self indulgence of his desire.

But this was the cold light of morning, and he would have to extricate himself and give her a chance to escape. The minute he entered his office he knew it would be impossible if he stayed at Peak's. When he went in she was already there and the curly head went up, the bright eyes met his with such an unabashed welcome of love and greeting that his heart shrank with the pain of it. He loved her, he wanted to take this love and keep it and cherish it for the rest of his life, so he looked beyond her as though he had not noticed, conscious of the swift incredulous bewilderment in her eyes.

He gave his notice in, that morning. Sir James did not believe him. He thought it was a devious ploy to extract more money, and his two weeks notice developed into a long wrangle, Matt sticking to his purpose. Sir James employing every persuasion to make him stay. But it kept him out of the

162

studio and gave him a genuine reason to delegate everything he possibly could to Mr Meakin who was flattered and bewildered by this turn of events.

By the time he left he had brought avoiding Helen to a fine art. He had learned to ignore the appeal in her lovely eyes and the small, tremulous half-smile that greeted every careless glance.

But this hunger – just for the sight of her – could not be assuaged.

His early marriage had left deep scars. He was a man who liked women and whom most women liked instantly. But he had kept all his friendships since his separation from Betty on a casual level. Until now. And the only decent thing had been to escape.

That last, terrible time when she had come to find the truth, he had succeeded in hurting her unbearably, but not in killing the particular knowledge she had of him. He had only succeeded in rousing her anger, her scornful despair. He could see her passionate face now, her burning eyes, filled with contempt.

It was no use telling himself that it was finished. For him it never would be. He hoped it was for her.

His work took him to the Kingsway area. As the days lengthened he found himself lingering in the Strand opposite Wellington Street, lurking ridiculously in doorways to catch a glimpse of her as she went to work.

He could see the change in her – she walked soberly as though the spring of her youth had dried up, no longer darting and running with sheer exuberance. She listened gravely while Boots chattered by her side, obviously not hearing a word.

He had returned home late after a drunken afternoon, slept until eight, then worked through the night to finish a commission he had promised that day. The client was in Arundel Street, so he delivered the work early and then, as though hypnotised walked along the Strand to the corner of Lancaster Place, and stood waiting, watching the opposite side of the road. Once he caught a glimpse of himself in a shop mirror and was shocked at the grubby looking unshaven reflection – he fingered his chin grimly, amused, wondering what the devil she would think if she should see him. Then he saw her.

The two girls crossed Wellington Street, stopped on the corner of the Aldwych, apparently in argument, and then Boots took Helen's arm, pulling her laughingly up the slope towards Covent Garden. He relaxed. They were going away. Then suddenly Helen turned and ran back and was standing in the sunshine, looking across the traffic her arms outstretched to him, laughing at him and at the absurdity of it all . . . The surge of joy nearly destroyed him. A bus lumbered past inches from his face, hiding her, and he turned and ran along the Strand, darting through the tide of office workers, off the pavement, among the traffic, not pausing until he stopped, gasping for breath.

He thrust his hands into his pockets and walked slowly westward not knowing where he was going, or why. Time passed. Then a taxi drove slowly past, and stopped and, as he drew level, Helen stepped out. She just stood there, her hand on the door, white faced, waiting.

There was no escape for either of them now.

He put his arms about her and they stood oblivious of the crowd and the traffic, not kissing, just holding each other, until the taxi driver said, 'Excuse me, miss. Are you going to pay, or do you want me to wait?'

They turned and the man was startled by their radiant faces.

'Where to?' Helen asked.

'To my place,' Matt said and he gave the address.

Boots had followed Helen out of Dominion House in a panic and was just in time to see her stop a taxi on the westbound side. There was nothing she could do. She went back to the office. Sir James came in at nine and began telephoning appointments and arranging his day. When she returned to her desk, Mr Meakin appeared.

'What has happened to Miss Redmaine? It is half-past ten. Has she said anything to you?'

'Hasn't she come in?'

'She has not.'

'Well, she didn't feel so well last night. Look, when I get the appointment book filled in for Sir James, I'll ring home and see if Mrs Murphy knows what's happened.'

'I shall be greatly obliged.'

164

He stalked off, and the telephone on her desk rang.

'It's for you Boots,' said Lily, 'Helen.'

'Oh, yes,' Boots tried to sound cool, and then, 'Jeepers, Nell, where are you?'

'I'm with Matt. Tell Meakin I won't be in today. Tell him I'm sorry.'

'Nell, listen . . .'

'I'm OK, Boots . . . don't worry. We're mates, remember? Make it right with Meakin for me.'

'OK, but Nell . . .' But Helen had gone.

Boots hung up. A bilious attack? Something she ate? That sort of lie was easy enough. But, God, the look in Helen's eyes when she had seen Matt! It was as though she had seen a happiness Boots had never believed existed.

The studio smelled of dust and turpentine and the sun streamed in through the big window with golden dust motes floating in the bars of light. He opened the door and carried her in on to the divan bed, put her down and turned to draw the long blue curtains, shutting out the direct light, leaving the untidy room in a subaqueous bluish dusk. He lay down beside her and drew her into his arms.

'I'm so tired,' she said. 'It's only ten o'clock. It's morning but I'm so tired.'

'Then sleep . . . let us both sleep . . . we have the rest of our lives now.'

'It was all lies, wasn't it?' she whispered. 'I can't sleep yet. Was it because you were afraid?'

She felt his lips smile against her forehead.

'Of course. I knew you would not listen to reason.'

'I won't listen to commonsense and reason now. Not yet. Afterwards I will listen. Not now.' Her head was dropped back against his arm, her mouth just below his. She wore the pink cotton dress, and beneath the fine material her small breasts were outlined, the nipples erect. She was as open to him as a burgeoning flower. But he still held back.

'Helen, you know this is crazy.'

'Don't you believe I really love you? Don't you believe you love me – not even now?'

165

He touched her face, stroked her white throat, then the small, firm breasts. She sighed and shivered with delight.

'You're so young Helen. You're just a sprig of spring. You haven't had time to think . . . to look around at other men, to know what you want from life.'

She sighed and smiled, 'I want you, and I want you to want me, and I want us to love each other now. And if you get tired of me, well, that will just be my bad luck, but not so bad as not having you at all.' She sat up and undid the buttons of the pink dress, peeled it off over her head, then silk cami-knickers, then her stockings, and the small ribbon girdle with her suspenders, so the garments fell like flower petals about them and she sat naked, smiling down at him, her thin waist carved in beneath the fragile rib cage, her breasts and slender shoulders pearly in the blue half dusk of the curtained room.

All reason vanished. He drew her down to him and took her with an irresistible passion, so she cried out with shock and pain, and when he would have withdrawn, held him with a fierce, demanding triumph until the climax was reached, and she sank back, saying reproachfully, 'It hurt. I didn't know it would hurt.'

'It won't hurt any more,' he said, 'wait, wait and let me love you,' and presently he took her again, gently, beyond the pain of initiation into delight until flushed and sobbing, smiling, exhausted she fell asleep in his arms.

It was dark when she woke again. A distant church clock chimed. He switched on the electric lamp on the table. She stretched, shuddered, gave a long convulsive sigh, and wound her arms about him.

'You won't go away from me again?'

'Never again.'

'I was dying,' she said, 'I was really dying – the thought of living without you. Like space or eternity – vast and empty and unimaginable. I really was dying.'

'Yes. I know. . . I was too.'

Her eyes lit up, her mood changed mercurially to the enchanting mischief and arrogance that capitivated him.

'We should have met and married years ago – before you met what's her name.'

'That would have been about fourteen years ago. You would have been seven.'

He propped his long chin on his hands, looking down on her drowsy radiance.

'We *have* to talk, my love,' he said.

'Yes. I'll tell you how beautiful you are. You've got a beautiful mouth. A little weak.'

'I am,' he agreed gravely, 'very weak. Else what am I doing here in bed with you?'

'But I don't want a masterful dominating man. I want this one,' her finger ran down the side of his mouth but the touch sent his nerves tingling. 'So sweet and baffled,' she said.

'Nell, will you just shut up. We have to talk. Practically.'

'Oh, later . . . practical things will always wait until later . . .'

She was so endearingly certain that her battle had been won, that they had already come through to everlasting happiness that his heart ached for her innocent optimism.

'We *have* to come down to earth, Nell.'

'But not tonight, Matt. Tonight I only want to be with you. Not to think – or talk. I'm so hungry.'

'How long since you ate?'

'Not since breakfast.'

'You must be starving.' His face filled with concern. He pulled on a dressing gown and rose, paused looking down on her. She was defiantly herself again, glinting like mountain water, confidently pursuing her dreams.

'Come, my baby, my love, I'll take you out to dinner.'

He took her to a small local restaurant which served good Italian home cooking. She ate hungrily, and drank the rough red wine. The food seemed delicious, the simple restaurant a place of light and joy. She did not want to think of the future that could neither be planned nor shaped, but which they had to think of now. They could not marry. They should not have children. What should they do? What did he want to do?

'Tell me about you and that Betty,' she demanded, 'are you sure she's not hoping you'll come back one day?'

'Quite sure,' he said drily.

'Tell me about her.' He raised mocking brows, and she said, 'I find it difficult to believe any woman would want to let

167

you go. I'm very jealous.'

'Well,' he rubbed his nose, laughed ruefully, 'it wasn't all her fault. We were married on my embarkation leave, and I was a bungling young idiot and she, poor little devil, was frozen with distaste by the whole thing. She had never cared, she said, for that sort of thing. She and her mother seemed to think that to enjoy sex was a vulgar sort of thing. But in France I'd learned differently. I'd met women who were generous, particularly to chaps who might be blown to bits in a few days. When I came back I thought it would be different. I was wrong. We were two strangers without a thought or a desire in common.'

'What did she like?'

'Pretty clothes, smart cars, flirting, above all dancing.' He grinned. 'You can imagine what a disappointment I was there. I stayed until I could afford to leave her, and she took up dancing professionally. But she didn't like being deserted – that's what she called it. Though there was no other woman, and she knew where I was, and I was supporting her. But by leaving her I ruled out the possibility of divorce. I gave her a weapon against me.'

'I know what's she's like. I saw her. That night when I came to find you . . .' She hunched her shoulders, painfully, and he kissed her. She said, 'It's all right. I can talk about it now. She was very handsome. She was with a pretty young chap in evening dress. She said you'd be hearing from her solicitors.'

'Yes. I was behind with payments. I'd just left Peak's. I've managed an overdraft since – to tide me over until Sir James and Medway make up their minds.'

'But you're not broke.'

'I'm living on borrowed money. I don't like it. I have work, and I could get more, but until they decide I don't want to drum up work, or find another job. It will be a very big thing, if it works out.'

He was talking to her as though she was a colleague of his own age and she felt immensely proud.

'Waiting for it was a chance I was willing to take on my own. You see they both want me to work for them, either back at Peak's or with Medway's advertising department. When I know, I can offer you some security.'

168

Her eyes blazed. 'Who said anything about security?'

'Helen,' he said slowly, 'that first day when I saw you running up the Aldwych in your blue suit and emerald green beret, I couldn't get that song out of my mind . . . out of that opera by Handel:

> Where 'ere you walk,
> Cool gales shall fan the glade,
> Trees where you sit,
> Shall crowd into a shade . . .

He leaned across and took her face between his hands, turning her head so that the lights moved on the planes of high cheek-bones and small highbridged nose. He looked at her lovely, wilful mouth, the big eyes that could be so melting and so fiercely demanding, and sighed. 'What am I to do about you? Like the song, I don't want anything harsh to touch you. Not poverty, nor mean-mouthed gossip, not a word that might hurt you. You have taken me sailing into love as though nothing else mattered. You forget I am thirty-eight, and you are twenty-three, that I am not rich, or free and we may have to face many years of this . . .'

'You make it all seem so impossible,' she cried. 'My parents lived together for three years before they could marry. She was under age, and her parents forbade it – Uncle Royston cut Dad's money, so they were poor at first. But they didn't care, and they were happier than any two people ever could be and made us the happiest children in the world.'

Her words faltered at the expression in his eyes.

'Helen, don't compare our situation to your parents'. They were both young, and unmarried. He was an aristocrat, handsome and high-handed, could carry off anything. And a brilliant artist. Don't try to make me into some sort of Sir Lancelot.'

'I don't, I wouldn't – it's just that you lack vision, Matt.'

'And ambition?' he asked wrily.

'Yes, if you like – you said it.'

'For a long while I have had no need of either.'

'But you have *now*. Now we are together.'

He reached out his long, thin hand, and touched her cheek,

so she shivered with pleasure. 'We shall see.'

Her lips were trembling. 'I love you as you are. I only want you to love me. I don't need to be sheltered and protected. I want to work with you and live with you, and if I am hurt, then this is a price I am willing to pay.'

'And your family – your mother?'

'They will understand.'

'Then we must start to plan as best we can. Do you want to live with me?'

'Of course.'

The restaurant had emptied. The proprietor was turning up the chairs, and his wife tapping her desk meaningfully with her pencil. Matt rose, and paid the bill. For a moment Helen was beset with guilty doubts. Maybe he had liked his shiftless, lonely bachelor life? What right had she to barge into it?

Outside the moon was rising, a misty orange disc, not the blazing silver shield of that first night, walking back from the West End to Pimlico together. On that night anything had been possible.

'Matt,' she said, 'do you think that I ought not to have come looking for you?'

'Yes,' he said, and laughed, and drew her into his arms, with a tenderness that melted her fears. 'Of course. But you did, and now we've got each other. For better or worse. For richer or poorer, until death us do part. Forget that bit – you are free as air, my bird, to stay or fly away.'

'I'm not,' she said fiercely, 'nor are you. We belong to each other now.'

He knew that he would always be afraid for her, as she plunged impetuously into life. He had been safe in his bachelor cave. The easily mastered, uneventful job; the undemanding friends in pub and club; the anonymous, impermanent girls; the escapes of music and literature – a cave of quietism. No trouble, until she came crashing in. He laughed, and ruffled her hair. 'Let's go home, my baby.'

They went back to the studio and Helen stayed with him until morning. When she walked into the women's washroom at Peak's, Boots, perfecting her face for the day ahead, took one look at her and knew what had happened.

170

Chapter 9

Helen let herself into Number 4 Hayman's studio and set her basket down. There were signs that Matt had been in – his blue overall over his drawing stool, the grate cleaned and the fire laid. In the studio sink where they cleaned palettes and brushes there was a bunch of her favourite pale pink Korean chrysanthemums with a note, '*I love you, back soon. Matt.*'

He was working hard on the new campaign for Medway tiles, so that when Medway and Sir James came to an agreement they could show Sir James what they had in mind. Whatever was decided Matt's layouts and paintings would be used, and Medway was paying him an agreed fee, his first freelance earnings, in the interim. Nearly every night Helen came to the studio, made a meal, and when they had eaten they worked together. Everything she owned, except for a few clothes, was now at the studio, and her father's picture hung jewel-like upon the wall. Like a small window looking out on to the garden of her childhood.

The studio looked very workmanlike and a good deal cleaner. Their two drawing boards side by side. One end of the big room was their working area, the other their living room.

She lit the fire and then carried her basket of provisions through to the cupboard-like kitchen at the rear of the room. There was a small barred window, a chipped and shallow sink, and a gas cooker, a formidable object, burned black by previous tenants but still functioning.

She had seen her mother cooking often enough and in theory she knew what to do with the chicken she had bought.

Cut up four lemons and stuff them inside with butter and chopped parsley, butter the chicken all over, salt and pepper and add a sprinkle of paprika, put in a hot oven for twenty minutes, and then turn to a medium heat. But this cooker only seemed to have two heats – very high or very low.

She heard Matt's key in the door and flew to greet him. Every meeting was still their first, and every parting a desolation to be endured.

'What would be medium in this gas cooker?' she demanded. 'For a chicken?'

'What tender words of greeting,' he said smiling. 'I haven't the faintest idea. I never cooked anything in it.'

'Never cleaned it either,' she said disgustedly, 'nor any of the previous tenants!'

'What do you usually do?'

'I don't usually cook chickens – at home Mums does it. Or the daily help. But I have bought a chicken and we have to cook it.'

'Hmm.' The flamboyant sunset was vanishing behind heavy rain clouds. He switched on the light and drew the long dusty curtains. One of Helen's favourite games was to lie in bed and redecorate the studio in her imagination. She had even taken him to Liberty's and chosen the damask they could not possibly afford and ended up buying enormous Japanese paper lanterns, blue and white and rose, to hang over the light bulbs. They hid the dust and made the tall room glow at night.

'I should turn up the gas to full, leave it for fifteen minutes, put the chicken in, allow another fifteen minutes, then lower the gas halfway, and hope for the best.'

'Brilliant,' she said, 'why didn't I think of something like that?'

The flames were burning brightly, lighting up his preoccupied face. Apprehension, so new an experience for her, flared at once. 'What is it?' she asked. 'What has happened? Something horrid? Money?'

'No. I got Medway's first cheque this morning.' He took it out. 'A hundred pounds. Throw the chicken to the caretaker's dog, and I'll take you out to dinner.'

'No,' she squealed. 'We're going to be careful. Remember? We're going to pay off your overdraft and take an office near

172

Fleet Street. We're going to give the lie to Uncle Royston's idea that artists are always shiftless, spendthrift and impractical.'

'Let's take a trip to Paris, and I'll buy you a fine gold necklace threaded with beryl and lapis lazuli.'

'Lovely,' she kissed him, and said, 'but that's not it, is it? I mean the money? There's something else.'

'Go and put that blasted bird in, while I pour a drink,' he said. 'And I have got a surprise – something for me. Not for you.'

'A new hat? My God, you need one!'

'Get on with you!'

She went into the kitchen and put in the chicken, arranged the pink chrysanthemums and placed them on the high mantelpiece where they reflected a twin mass of pink blossom in a gilt-framed mirror. Matt had few possessions, but those he had were good, mostly old, and beautiful. But he was amazed at the way she could fill a room with charm and turn it into a home. He filled the sherry glasses and went to the portrait easel, draped in a dust cloth and turned to the wall. Her eyes lit with pleasure.

'You're going to start painting again?'

'I did start – '

'I wondered what it was.'

'You didn't peek?'

'No.'

He swung the heavy easel round, and pulled off the dust cover. The basic portrait was only just blocked in, but the figure was perfectly placed, the poise of the small imperious head tuned back to look out at the painter, instantly recognisable. 'You – as Primavera – in the green dress, with flowers and things. I started it – I thought it would be a bit of you to keep. But I couldn't go on without you!'

'You did this from memory?' she marvelled. 'How can you hold an idea like that in your mind and bring it alive.'

'Not quite,' he confessed, and took out a sketch book. Little brilliant sketches, done in the office. Looking up, laughing, meeting his glance with grave appeal. 'I've been drawing you ever since you walked into Peak's. Into my life.'

'I'm so glad, Matt.' She went to him, and he took her into

173

his arms, and they kissed with slow, sweet abandon. 'You've got the model permanently now. How long since you painted – like this. For yourself?'

'Since I married Betty.'

'I could hate her for that,' she said. 'To stop you doing what you do best. I knew what you could do the minute I saw that first sketch you did of me. It was the way Dad used to draw. Instantly. Picking up a piece of chalk, catching the object. Instant, so sure, wonderful. I can't do it. I have to think about what I am going to do. Why was Betty such a pig?'

'Oh, she wasn't. She just wanted nice things, and couldn't understand why they weren't all that important to me. Portrait painting did not seem a way to instant money. We spent a lot of money. After we separated I'd been with Peak's for some years – I'd got into the habit of commercial work. Of earning regularly. You know, that first monring when you came for the job, and told me so cheekily that I could do a lot better, I felt ashamed.'

They stood before the unfinished portrait thoughtfully, and she signed with pleasure. 'So you damn well should.'

'I'll finish it now. When I get time.' He drew up a chair and sat down, and she stood behind him, her hands moving over his shoulders and chest, up the spinal column, round his forehead, rubbing the tensions away until, with a sigh he relaxed, and his head leaned back against her breast.

'You're too good,' she said. 'You're too nice. You don't ever say anything beastly about anyone. Will you about me – when I'm not your girl any longer, but a bossy possessive wife?'

He swung round, the anxiety gone from his face, the look in his eyes sending her nerves singing. 'How long did you say that bird would take to cook?'

'An hour and a half,' she said faintly. 'Plenty of time.'

The smell of roasting permeated through the big room when they woke, and Helen shot up, clutching a gown.

'My God,' she said. 'The chicken!' She fled to the oven and opened the door. To her astonishment, the chicken appeared brown and crisp and perfect. 'Success, success!' she called.

'Come and open the wine while I mix the salad.'

He came in sleepily in his big cowled dressing-gown.

'We must write a receipt book – Chicken d'Amour, one and a quarter hours making love, allow fifteen minutes more for recovery, then serve bird with sprigs of watercress and kisses.'

When they had finished eating, she made coffee which they carried over to the drawing boards, and set up the work he had brought home. They switched on the wireless and a string quartet wove complicated patterns of music while they worked at their drawings.

'When will you start on my picture?' she asked.

'Weekends. Holidays.'

'This weekend I must go home. I haven't been for three weeks. I'm taking Boots down. Cheer her up a bit. If I can. She's changed since that screen test.'

'Was it a flop?'

'They don't know. It's just in the air. Dunky's sets his heart on something and he's absolutely sure it's coming off – just because he wants it so much.'

'He's not the only one,' he said drily.

'Why don't you come down to Ayling this weekend?'

He swung round slowly on his revolving stool, startled.

'Let me get this right? To your home? To meet your mother?'

'Why not?'

'How will you introduce me? "Mother, I would like you to meet the old geezer with whom I am having a passionate and totally unsuitable love affair"?'

'I haven't told her yet,' Helen said simply. 'We don't, Dunky and I – tell her things that might worry her. I'll just say we are friends. She'll fall for you. She loves distinguished men who work in the arts – especially when she knows you knew Dads and worked with him. Come on Saturday?'

'Saturday I can't. I'm going out to Medway's country place for lunch and a conference – Sir James will be there. They've got all the costing out now. Medway will decide whether he will go it alone or stay with Sir James. We have the programme worked out. If he decides to go on his own he will offer me the running of his advertising department.'

'You won't take it?' she protested.

175

He smiled slowly, and flicked her cheek. 'Let's wait and see what happens.'

'I don't want you to waste yourself working for people like Sir James and Medway.'

'It's a question of money now, sweetheart.'

'Oh, take no notice of me. Come down on Sunday. Come for lunch, please, Matt. Boots is coming. In the afternoon I'll take you over to Ayling Place to see the millstone as Duncan calls it. I want you both to see it so you'll understand what we have hanging over us.'

Her heritage – that she would never really get away from. It was there in her impatience, sense of privilege – her high-handed determination. It was in every expression, every movement of her finely-bred body – an innocent arrogance of which she was totally unaware.

She flickered with mischief. 'Mums and Cousin Millicent have been asking, ever so tactfully, what I do in London when I don't go home for the weekend.'

'And you tell them whopping great lies?'

'Well . . . whopping little ones,' she laughed, ignoring the gravity in his eyes. 'Oh, Matt, don't be so *pure*. She will have to know one day. You'll have to meet her. I want you to know each other first.'

'Tell me about her.'

'Well, she's nice, but timid – timid about Ayling and the Redmaine family and Uncle Royston. Dads got away from them and didn't care a damn anyway, and so long as he was there, neither did she. But now – she's not so sure. For Dunky's sake – and maybe for mine. She wants so much to do what is best for us.'

'She sounds a very responsible lady.'

'Meaning I'm not?' she flashed.

He laughed. 'Don't build castles – she may hate the sight of me.'

'I'm not building castles. I want you to meet her. You are the two people I love best in the world and I want you to be friends.'

He wanted to go. He wanted to see what kind of home produced his lovely wayward girl. It was agreed that he would go down to Ayling for the day on Sunday.

176

Helen and Boots went down on Saturday morning. Helen had arrived in a taxi to pick up Boots at about eight-thirty, having spent the night with Matt at the studio. Boots came down the steps at Becker Street in her elegant new autumn coat of pale camelhair, with a tie of stone marten. She was wearing an exquisite little black felt hat shaped like a helmet, stretched and moulded so finely it was like velvet. It dipped over one eye and was skewered by a diamanté arrow. Her shoes were fawn leather, high heeled with toe caps of black patent. Her stockings were of fine biscuit coloured silk. She stood on the steps and posed like a model.

'Will I do?'

'Stunning. It must have cost the earth.'

'I've got an account at Harrods now.'

Helen was silent. Boots fingered the pale fur framing her pretty face.

'For my birthday – from you know who.'

'I don't know – and I didn't know you had a birthday.'

'Last week. I was nineteen.'

'A useful birthday present.'

'Yes.' She looked defiantly at Helen in her old blue tweed suit and raincoat. 'I'm not right, am I?'

'Boots, you look heavenly, and you know it doesn't matter what you wear, you always look devastating.'

'I've never been in the country before,' said Boots. 'Or only when Duncan drove me out to the studio – for that ghastly test. All the girls there were glammed up to the eyebrows.'

She looked so disconsolate that Helen felt guilty. Helen always travelled third-class when she went to Ayling, but today she bought first-class tickets – but Boots was still conspicuous. She was too well-dressed, an illusion belonging to the world of fashion rather than reality. She crossed her beautiful long legs, and opened a magazine, gazing resentfully at the sketches and photographs of tweeds and knitted sweaters which she realised were the correct wear for a country weekend. Helen leaned back and closed her eyes and wondered how Matt was faring at the meeting with Sir James and Medway, and prayed that he would not give in.

The carriage emptied before Ayling. Boots slapped down the shiny magazine she had been reading, and was sitting

177

tense with unhappiness, staring blindly at the Buckinghamshire countryside sliding southward past the train. Helen sat up abruptly.

'Boots', she said helplessly, 'what on earth is the matter? You're not *really* worried about the clothes, are you?'

She had always believed in Boots's almost insolent confidence in her all-conquering desirability. Now she looked bleak, and so terribly young, like a thin child dressed up in her mother's clothes.

'I'm not going to fit in, am I?' she said fiercely. 'With your lot? I'm over-dressed, aren't I? They'll think I'm common. I shan't know what to say.'

Helen got up and sat beside her and gave her a warm and comforting hug. Boots rarely cried. If she cried her mascara would run and make her look a mess, and if she looked a mess she felt defenceless. She shrugged Helen away.

'Don't, Bootsy, darling, don't be sad. Mums and Cousin Millicent are great, really . . . and you look lovely. And if we go walking there's a heap of wellies and old boots and macs. You'll be fine.'

'It isn't that,' said Boots.

'Oh?' She had a flash of intuition. 'It's Duncan?'

'Why doesn't he telephone? I haven't heard a blasted word from him since that stinking test at Greenstreet. If I screwed it up he could tell me . . . He never stopped talking when he wanted me to do it, and now it's a flop he doesn't want to know. And anyhow, one way or another, why can't he tell me?'

'Perhaps he doesn't know. He's back at Oxford now. He might not have heard.'

'You mean he's *really* back? Not skiving off to Greenstreet every morning?' Her pale cheeks suddenly flushed, and she cried, 'Oh, *God*! Now he won't never speak to me. I swore not to say nothing to nobody.'

'You'd better tell me,' said Helen gravely.

'Well – he said it didn't really matter. That no one would know and that he wouldn't need all that college stuff if he was going to be a film director. Just so long as his uncle *thought* he was there, and didn't stop his money. So he used to go over to Greenstreet early mornings, spend the day there, and get back into college at night.'

178

Helen began to laugh. It was so simple and ingenious, and so typically Duncan when following his own purpose. Not to be distracted by a frivolous thing like education and the necessity of getting a degree.

'D'you mean he's been having us all on? He's not really been at Oxford? Not all the summer term?'

'Well, yes and no. He started – went up, you say – and then he worked this out. He sleeps there. It's only half an hour to Greenstreet on the bike. He said if he showed up in Hall, and saw his tutor, no one would know. He did a bit of reading at night, but he was at Greenstreet every day. I didn't know what it was all about. Do you mean it wasn't so awful? I mean, you're laughing.'

'Well,' said Helen, laughing again, 'it's so *Duncan*. Only Duncan would think of such an idiotic idea. I suppose it might be all right, if it comes off. But we thought it was just a holiday job he had at Easter and for the long vac. You mean he's still doing it?'

'So far as I know.'

'Well, if Uncle Royston finds out there'll be the hell of a rumpus.'

'You won't tell on him?'

'Oh, *no*! But he'll never get a degree that way. I'll have it out with him this weekend.'

'But if he knows I'm there, he might not come.' Boots was very serious. 'I reckon he wants to ditch me.'

Helen hugged her again.

'There's not a chap on earth would want to do that. He'll turn up, you'll see. Then I'll give him a load of sisterly advice.'

'Which he probably won't take.'

Lady Millicent was waiting for them at Ayling with her ancient car, wearing a large tweed Ulster and her usual floppy hat, and hung about with bags of brown paper carriers filled with knitting wools.

'This is my friend, Lillian Skinner, Cousin Millicent,' Helen introduced them. 'Boots, this is my mother's cousin, Lady Millicent Dermott.'

Boots held out her hand, and Cousin Millicent shook it heartily, gazing at her with awe.

'My God, Duncan said you were a beauty, and so you are,'

179

she exclaimed. 'Well, get in girls. And skip the Lady thing, my dear, and call me Cousin Millicent like the kids do. Are you the girl Duncan says is going into films? I hope so. Young people have such interesting lives nowadays. In my day life was so dull for a well-bred gel, but today there are so many chances. That girl Diana Manners acting in plays and films! But then she was very beautiful too, and I was always a plain dump.'

'Oh go on, Cousin Milly, you're lovely, and we all love you and you know it.'

Cousin Millicent sniffed scornfully. A porter, rewarded with sixpence, swung the starting handle and the old car sailed majestically out of the station yard.

Boots had never met anyone like Mavis Redmaine. A woman of over fifty who was still as beautiful as a girl in spite of greying hair and little wrinkles like stars at the corners of her lovely eyes. And so gravely polite and anxious to make her feel at home. She suddenly saw Helen and Duncan not just as her crazy but beloved friends but as people reared in loving kindness. She wanted to respond to this gentle courtesy but could find no words.

'Come in, my dear. Nell and Dunky have told me all about you and you're just as beautiful as they said. Duncan isn't back yet. He said he'd be back in time for dinner this evening.' She glanced apprehensively at Helen. 'Nell, you remember at the beginning of the summer – when you first went to Peak's? And Lady Peak wrote to say she would like us to go over to tea some time? Well – that sometime is this afternoon.'

'Oh Mums, *no!*'

'Oh *yes*. I thought she'd forgotten all about it, but she telephoned. I said we had a young house guest, so she said would I bring her too. You don't mind, do you?' Boots stared wildly at Helen who was trying not to laugh, and shook her head numbly. 'She really wants Duncan, I think. An extra man – she has this young stepdaughter. She seemed disappointed when I said he had not arrived home yet.'

'Clever old Dunky.'

'But you girls *must* come. She said they'd send the Rolls.' The lovely grey-green eyes crinkled with mischief. 'It's quite a lark, isn't it?'

'All right, Mums,' Helen said. 'We'll be martyrs, won't we Boots?'

'Bless you both.'

'And Mums, I've asked a friend to come on Sunday. For lunch. Matthew Wilson. He was my boss at Peak's but he's freelancing now. You'll like him. He was very kind to me when I started. Is that all right?'

'If he'll settle for roast beef and Yorkshire – of course!'

'Oh, he'd like anything I didn't cook,' Helen said thoughtlessly, and the startled expression on Lady Millicent's face brought her up short. 'I am doing some work for him at weekends, so I sometimes cook a meal for him,' she explained – a little too airily! 'I thought we might go over to see Ayling after lunch, tomorrow. It's lovely now the leaves are turning.'

'You're uncle will be there.'

Helen knew exactly what she was thinking. That both Boots and Matt would have to be explained to Lord Breterton. Such warnings always roused her stubborn resistance. Her friends were her friends. Duncan's too. It was none of Uncle Royston's business. She opened her mouth, and shut it. No disagreements, no rows about the Monster. Not this weekend.

She said, smiling, 'Oh Mums, the house is closed. No unfortunate tourists and visitors to marshall and lecture. He'll be out shooting for sure. We'll keep out of the Monster's way. Come on, Boots, I'll show you your room.'

Boots followed her obediently, up the cottage staircase, twisting between dark blue walls on which were hung bright pictures of the house and garden, the viaduct over the stream, black against the sunset, the mill-wheel by the house, the beech woods, Helen and Duncan, brown, barefoot children playing, Mavis in a big red shawl.

'My father did them,' Helen explained. 'Water-colours. Mums calls them the Mill Cottage pictures. She's been offered a lot of money for them but, of course, she won't sell.'

'Why not?'

'Well, they're part of Dads. She hasn't much of him. The house. The pictures. Us. We won't be around for ever.'

'She's very pretty,' said Boots. 'I should have thought she would have married again.'

Helen smiled. 'No. You only get what Mums had once. No one else would do. I know.' She saw the bleak expression come back into Boots's face, and said, 'I nearly gave the game away about Matt. Oh well, they'll have to know some time.'

'But what about this afternoon? At the Peak's place? It's awful, Nell. I mean, supposing the Old Man's there? He'll have a fit if he sees me. And so shall I. I'll bust myself laughing.'

'Me, too,' said Helen. 'but he won't be there. Matt was meeting him today at Tommy Medway's, and he's there for the weekend. It's a conference.'

The room was simple and plain and comfortable. None of the padded satin Boots associated with luxury. White walls, plain cool colours, straw mattings, a bedspread knitted in an intricate patchwork design; a smell of lavender. Boots sat down at the dressing table and took off her smart hat.

Helen opened the wardrobe saying, 'Hang your things here . . . there's plenty of room in the drawers if you want it . . .'

'Thanks.' Something in her voice made Helen turn to her. 'Sir James wants to take a flat for me,' Boots said in a small impersonal voice, 'on the other side of the Park.' The long lashes lifted and she stared defensively up at Helen. 'I might take him on.'

'Boots! You're not serious? You *couldn't*!'

'I'm thinking about it. He hasn't signed the lease yet. He says it's very nice. A service flat. Furnished. Ever so posh. There's a lift, and porters, a restaurant, so I wouldn't have to cook, and a swimming pool and squash courts in the basement. And a big bar where the tenants all meet and get to know each other. He says there are a whole lot of girls living there – with rich fellows. Show girls and models, all sorts.' The transparent eyes met Helen's appalled glance, and added, 'Girls like me.'

'What kind is that?'

'Someone who's got to make it with her looks before it's too late.'

'Oh *stuff*!' Helen could barely find her voice. The whole idea was hideous to her. 'You don't mean you're really going to accept? To be the mistress of that vulgar old man? You haven't *said* you would? You haven't agreed?'

'I haven't said I wouldn't.' Boots looked down at her

expensive shoes. 'You don't think I get this sort of outfit out of my wages, do you? I don't think Sir James is vulgar. I think he's silly, like most men, but that's all. And he's very generous. I'm not posh like you.'

'Boots – don't equivocate. He must think you're going to agree – if he's gone so far as to find a flat.'

'Oh, they all *think* that. I've been keeping the Old Man and Tommy on a string for a long time. Waiting to see which one comes up with the best offer. I didn't trouble about it when I first met you . . . I thought it was what most girls do. I knew I'd have to settle one day for some rich bloke, and I'd practically settled for Tommy until the Old Man fell for me. I had two options then, and old Sir James is easier to handle than Tommy. I thought you were crazy going to live with Matt. I still do. A chap ought to marry you – and if he doesn't, then he ought to see you right.'

'There's a little thing called falling in love. Have you any idea what it will be like, having to sleep with someone you *don't* love?'

'I can guess. But heaps of girls have to do it. Better than being married to someone like my dad. There's something I haven't told you about me. When I was fourteen my dad owed a chap some money – one of the heavy mob he hung around with. He was scared to go out of the house in case they roughed him up. But this chap was after me, so Dad sent me round to his place with a message – I was green then, and I didn't know what was on, until he told me my dad had said it would be all right.'

'You mean – he sold you?'

'Yes, you could say so. He wouldn't have to pay up if I'd given in. But when he realised I wasn't willing, the chap let me go and sent his mob round to teach my dad a lesson anyway, I left home next day, and I've never been back. I don't suppose I'll *like* living with either Tommy or the Old Man, but I reckon they'd both be soft touches.'

'Oh Boots . . . oh, how awful . . . You make me feel awful . . .' Loved, cared for, protected all her life it made her feel guilty. 'Boots, don't be like that. You make it all sound awful – beastly . . .'

'And so it is. My mum told me it was, and she was right. Make them pay for it she said.'

'No. Not if you love someone and they love you, like Matt and I. Then it's wonderful. It's just finding the right person – and I knew right away. The moment I saw Matt. Please, Boots, don't do it. What about Duncan? You're friends . . . and he's crazy about you . . . I thought you cared about him . . .'

'Well, think again,' Boots said harshly, 'and don't worry about me. And don't slop over me. I can look after myself.' Her voice had slipped back into a defiant, snarling London twang. 'You and Duncan, you were the first friends I ever had, and you've properly messed me about, haven't you? Once I thought I knew it all. Now I feel I don't know nothing. You with your Matt Wilson and Dunky with his dreams of me being a star. Duncan can't look after me. He's only a kid in spite of his big talk.'

'Boots, Duncan is in love with you.'

'Is he? He's in love with a picture on a screen. Well, I don't know any more. Not after that bloody test. I was just one of a dozen girls, and all of them knew more than me. And he was just a kid Rudi Strauss found useful because he could speak a bit of German. I haven't heard from him since and I don't suppose I shall. I've vanished with the rest of his dreams.'

'He's coming tonight.'

'We'll see.' Boots went to the mirror, carefully licked a fingertip and smoothed her fine dark brows, not glancing at Helen. 'My guess is he won't show up. I didn't come up to expectations, did I? If you ask me, there's no future for a girl with Dunky.'

Helen rose and went to the door. 'I'll get tidied for lunch. Bathroom's second on the right. I'll see you downstairs.'

'Don't worry about me, Nell,' Boots said, more gently, relenting. 'You're ma and Lady Millicent have been very kind, but if they'd be scared of your uncle finding out about Duncan working at Greenstreet, how d'you think they'd feel about him and me? D'you think they'd fancy me as the future Lady Breterton? Because that's on the cards for Dunky one day, whatever he may say about it. No, thanks, not for me. I know when I'm out of place. So I'll keep my options open, and Sir James is number one. OK?'

At luncheon, the conversation was about local happenings,

and a gentle probing on the part of Cousin Millicent as she tried to discover how Helen spent her spare time in London. Mavis asked about Duncan.

'I'm sure he doesn't eat enough,' she told Boots. 'And I worry about him.'

'You don't worry about me,' said Helen affectionately, trying to steer the conversation into safer channels.

'No, I *don't*, do I?' Mavis sounded puzzled. 'But then you're so sensible. You ring me up during the week. I know what you're up to.' Boots and Helen dared not look at each other.

'Nonsense, Mums,' Helen said briskly, a swift colour flushing up under her clear skin. 'Dunky's much more self-contained than I am.'

Her mother shook her head.

'I wish he wasn't so passionate about this film business,' she said to Boots. 'I can't tell you what a relief it was to me when he went back to Oxford after Easter. I was so afraid he'd leave. I don't know anything about films. You read such frightful things . . . that actor, Wallace Reid, dying of drugs. Helen was crazy about him when she was at school, and so were all the girls. Such a nice-looking young man – and then you read that. Anyway, Duncan is back at Oxford, and his Uncle Royston hasn't heard a word about this film thing, or so Millicent says . . .'

'Well, he certainly hadn't last time I saw him,' said Millicent, 'or there would have been some *Sturm and Drang*. So long as he's still paying Duncan's allowance, that's all right.'

Boots felt like a stranded whale, out of her element, bewildered, unable to keep afloat. She could not imagine being brought up by a mother like Mavis Redmaine, a mother who loved and worried about you. The only thing her mother had worried about was money. She was grateful when the conversation unexpectedly moved into her province. Cousin Millicent was beaming at her admiringly.

'You wear clothes beautifully,' she said, 'and that's a lovely dress. Such a subtle colour.'

'Thank's,' Boots said, and gave her enchanting smile. 'I think your jumpers are stunning. Do you really *make* them. Like Helen says?'

'Well, I design them,' explained Mavis, 'and we both make them – we have a couple of outside workers in the village. But the shop is closed during the winter season. When the big house opens, we open the shop.'

They had coffee in the conservatory where it was warm and sunny and filled with green plants in spite of the chill wind outside. Afterwards Boots was shown the workroom in the old mill barn, their stock of beautiful wools like rainbows, and the drawings of the garments which Mavis was designing for the spring. They showed her how they worked the pattern from the designs, with the difficult counting and tension measuring.

Boots was impressed. 'You ought to sell them in London. Not in the big stores. There are lots of nice shops round Bond Street. Like the one I got this dress from. I'll bet they'd sell them. And you making them . . . and Lady Millicent . . . it would be all snobby. People always pay through the nose for exclusive things! Why don't you make samples up? You'd make a lovely rep, Mrs Redmaine. Don't you think so, Helen?'

'You're probably right,' Helen said. 'You're always right about clothes. You must try it, Mums.'

Outside they heard the crunch of wheels on the gravel, and saw Sir James's grey Rolls glide to a silent halt at the front door.

'Oh, blow!' cried Mavis. 'I'd forgotten all about that beastly tea party. Just as Boots has had this lovely idea.'

They scuttled to their rooms to tidy up, and down again to the large imposing car, where they were sealed in, berugged and footwarmed against the faint chill of the autumn afternoon.

Cousin Millicent settled back, wrapped in her shapeless tweed cloak, her large shabby felt hat pulled down rather rakishly over her eyes and, folding her hands, said, 'Well, this is a bit uppitty, I must say.' And set both girls off into giggles.

'It's you whom Lady Peak wants to meet really, Helen,' explained her mother. 'You and Duncan. Sir James has a daughter to be launched.'

'Like a battleship?' asked Helen. 'He has a photo of her on his desk. A dumpling, gift-wrapped.'

Mavis gave her a reproving look. 'Don't be catty, darling. It's not like you.'

'I'm sorry, Mums, but it's a bit much. We have to put up with the Old Man all week, we don't want to meet his relations weekends. It's all this Hon. and Lady Millicent lark. Jumping Jesus, you ought to take Uncle Royston! He'd really impress her.'

So the Rolls cruised smoothly through the Buckinghamshire lanes and deposited them at the imposing frontage of Whitelands House.

Charlotte, dressed expensively for the country in a pleated skirt made from a tartan of doubtful lineage, a toning twin-set of finest cashmere, her beautiful pearls and elegant high-heeled shoes handmade by Pinet, came effusively forward, holding out her hand. Her visitors were standing wide-eyed and alert like a group of fallow deer pricking their ears at the approach of danger.

'My dear Mrs Redmaine, Lady Millicent . . . I am *so* sorry this meeting has been delayed. But really this summer has been so crowded. I was literally *so* worn out, that when my friend Roxana Cosimo asked me to go down to Juan for a break I couldn't resist – I really *couldn't* . . .'

'I do understand,' said Mavis. 'May I present my daughter Helen, who works at your husband's office, in the art department – and her friend Miss Skinner, who also works there.'

'Reception,' said Boots crisply.

'Boots – that is, Miss Skinner, also has a room in the same house as Helen. In Pimlico.'

Charlotte regarded the beautiful girl in the simple crêpe-de-chine dress and wondered if Willy knew her. The familiar jealous anxiety gripped her, but she said, smiling her hard bright smile, 'I am so sorry Sir James isn't here. He wanted to see you – but business, you know, intrudes even on our weekends.'

'It's quite a relief really,' said Helen. 'We do have him all week, you know.'

'Quite.' Charlotte's rock-hard social confidence was slightly shaken. She was not used to people who behaved naturally.

'How brave of you two young girls to go out to business. I

tell Junie she doesn't know how lucky she is. Do you like it?'
There was a doubtful pause, then Helen said, 'Well, I'm
learning a great deal.'

'Me too,' piped up Boots, and there was the tension of
rigidly controlled laughter between them. It was a relief to
everyone when June, also conventionally countryfied in a
tweed skirt and cashmere jumper, appeared at the door, her
nose rather pink and, though well-powdered, it was obvious
to everyone she had been weeping. Charlotte's eyes flashed
with exasperation.

She went to June with tender concern. 'Now then, Junie,'
she looked up at her visitors with apology, 'what shall I do
with this silly girl? She's going to a school in Switzerland until
Christmas – maybe until the end of the spring term . . . and
she was looking forward to it, learning to ski and everything,
and now, at the last minute, she's had an attack of
homesickness.'

'Think nothing of it,' said Cousin Millicent. 'When I went
to Cheltenham I cried for two whole days, and after that I
never wanted to go home. Such a relief to get away from
Royston.'

'You'll love it I'm sure,' said Mavis Redmaine, and her
smile was so sweet that June nearly started crying again.
Mavis really suffered for June – no one so young should be
allowed to look so unhappy. 'We used to go to Switzerland
when my husband was alive, and always had such lovely
times. Mountains are so pure, I think. I really understand the
Hindus thinking they are the abode of the gods.'

'Yes, well . . .' Charlotte said blankly. (What on earth was
the woman talking about?) She hoped that Junie was not
going to cry all over the visitors. 'Yes, well shall we go in?'
The tea table, set with silver and fine porcelain was laid near
the fire. 'I hope the room isn't too warm for you? I'm afraid I
like to be really cosy, and it is so cold by the river. As soon as
June goes, I shall close up here and stay in town for the
winter.'

The room was spectacularly furnished, like the house in
Ebor Place, with valuable pieces and *objets d'art*, the settees,
curtains and armchairs a riot of apple green chintz with a
pattern of rosy flowers. The carpet, a luscious spread of

matching green, was so glowingly untouched that everyone clung anxiously to their cups and saucers, terrified of marking it with the slightest drip of tea. 'Smelled of Harrods,' Cousin Millicent said afterwards. 'Everything did, did you notice? Harrods and Chypre. My God, I do like to be comfortable.'

Boots summed Charlotte up as a right old bitch. Hard as nails inside and soapily sweet out. She was unexpectedly sorry for Sir James. Poor old chump! She would have thought him too smart to be taken in by this one.

It was a difficult meal. Cousin Millicent's eyelids began to droop, and her lips to puff with small, silent snores. Mavis listened with her usual charming courtesy, but the girls could see her wilting under the strain. Charlotte spoke about June, who looked completely crushed while her stepmother went on about their ambitions for her, and how kind Mrs Debereaux was in offering to see her through her first season.

'I feel it will be such an advantage for Junie. In spite of her father's knighthood, I *am* an American, and I always think your old families, like yours Mrs Redmaine, manage this sort of thing so splendidly.'

'Not my family,' said Mavis with a touch of apology. 'I was at art school at June's age, so I don't really know. I was working for my diploma in the design school. That is where I met my husband. He was teaching there – in the painting school.'

'He was Lord Breterton's second son?'

'Yes. Royston is the eldest. The present incumbent . . .'

Helen started to laugh. 'Incumbent is for vicars, Mums, not peers.'

She hoped these explanations would do, but Charlotte pressed on.

'So – your son *could* be Lord Breterton one day?'

'Well, we all *hope* not, but it might happen. Duncan would be quite frightful at it.'

Charlotte laughed doubtfully. She did not believe Mavis thought this – she put it down to some kind of inverted snobbery.

She tried to extract just whom the Redmaine's knew of position and influence, but they did not seem to know anyone she had heard of, although they had many friends. Cousin

Millicent said she had been through a London season, and had not landed a husband, which was the whole purpose of the exercise, so her parents considered her a write-off. 'But I had a good time afterwards learning weaving crafts.' 'Now, let me get this straight,' smiled Charlotte, 'you are Lord Breterton's sister?' 'Cousin.' She was becoming restless. Helen and her mother glanced anxiously. Cousin Millicent was apt to take off if the conversation became dull or the food ran out. There was a scratching at the door, and a small, very beautiful Scottish collie was let in. It went straight to June and put its head in her lap. She rose and said hurriedly, 'It's time for her walk – if you'll excuse me . . .'

'But June,' Charlotte began to protest, but Helen said eagerly, 'Oh *may* we go too, Lady Peak? It would be lovely to have a walk before we go home . . . may we walk down to the river? How about you, Boots?'

Boots leapt up with alacrity, and the three girls were into their coats and out of the house in minutes. Helen – as though let out of prison – went racing off across the lawns towards the river, long-legged, swift as the wind, graceful as the handsome dog that ran and leapt beside her. June and Boots walked together, silently – June bursting with questions.

'She looks so happy,' she said enviously.

'Yes,' Boots said slowly, 'right now she's very happy.' She was silent, watching Helen's leaping figure, recharged with vitality and joy. Then she said sharply, 'If you don't want to go to Switzerland why don't you just say so?'

'I can't.' June's eyes filled with tears again. 'I *daren't*. She'd tell . . .' She stopped and glanced round as though she expected Charlotte to materialise out of the rhododendron shrubs. 'Well, I *can't*,' she went on lamely. 'Not now. Everything's booked. I suppose I'm just being silly.'

Boots was astounded. This was the Old Man's *daughter*. *Rolling in money*. There seemed no point in being rich if you couldn't do as you pleased.

'She's not your mother, is she?' June shook her head. 'Well, tell her to jump in the lake. And *don't* start crying again. It never helps – not unless it works. I'll bet it doesn't work with *her*.' The elegant little hat jerked significantly back towards the house. 'What have you been up to then – that she can tell about?'

'About me – and someone.'

'A fellow?'

'How did you guess?'

'I'm just a genius.'

'You know him.'

Boots frowned, puzzled, but June, in desperation, could not stop. There had been no one she had been able to talk to. Childishly, almost incoherently, she began to pour out all her jealousy and fears.

'I know you know him because when I got back from Scotland and Charlotte found out, and I didn't know where he was living, or his new telephone number, or *anything*, I waited outside Daddy's office, and you came out and then he came out and you walked off together.'

'It would help,' said Boots, 'if you told me who you're on about.'

'Willy,' said June, 'Willy Hyde-Seymour. He works for Daddy. It's no use pretending you don't know him. I followed you, and you went into the Waldorf and he had a drink and you had a cup of coffee, and then you went up Drury Lane and down another street, and you went inside the building, and he looked furious . . .'

'*Oh!*' exclaimed Boots, light breaking. '*That* one!' Her face was a study. 'You mean you follow our Willy about London to see what he's up to?'

'Not exactly.' June paused, recovering her breath, her pale cheeks flushing. 'It was just that day. To find out where he was living. When he was the chauffeur he used to live behind our house in the mews, and I could easily slip in there to see him. You see, we're in love. And Charlotte found out that we've . . . that I've . . . well, he left all my letters at the old place, and the new chauffeur gave them to Charlotte so she knew.'

'You mean, you've been having it off with him? You've been sleeping with him . . . ?'

'Oh yes. And it was *lovely* because we're so much in love. I told Charlotte this but she was horrified.'

'You're sure she's not mad about the boy herself?'

'Charlotte?' exclaimed June, astounded. 'Of course not.

191

He was the chauffeur. Besides, she's *old*.'

Boots felt as old as the hills. The poor little sod. And that awful Willy – like taking candy from a kid.

'Why are you telling me all this?'

'Well,' June said ingenuously, 'I wanted to be sure that you and he . . . I mean you are so pretty, and you do work at Peak's . . .'

'*No!*' said Boots positively.

'Oh.' June's face softened with relief, although she could not quite believe it. How could anyone resist Willy. 'It's just that he does like pretty girls, and well-dressed ones, and I never could see what he saw in me.'

'Why ever not?' Boots demanded. 'You're rich, you're young, and you're not bad-looking if you'd stop crying. You're a very good catch.' She put on her most upper crust voice, imitating Madame Rampton. 'Captain Hyde-Seymour of the Wandering Hands Brigade is extremely lucky.'

'D'you think so?' breathed June, unaware of any irony. Boots wanted to laugh at her and wanted to cry for her. 'D'you really think so?' Then despair engulfed her. 'But I shan't see him until Christmas. Perhaps not then. Do you think he'll forget me? I'll write every day . . .'

'Don't.'

'Don't write?'

'Not every day. Or – not at all. Willy Hyde-Seymour only values what he hasn't got. Maybe he can't help it. He's hard up and I know what it is to be good-looking and poor. If I were you . . .'

'Yes?'

'And I wanted him, which I don't, I'd treat him with obliv.'

'OBLIV?'

'Yep. Remember, you're everything that he really wants. Money, position, boss's daughter. Years younger. He's over thirty. Make him come to heel. Don't run after him. Make him run after you. Tell him about all the rich people you've got to know. Tell him about the expensive places you go to. Tell him what fun you're having. Don't say you miss him.'

'You really *mean* that!' June said incredulously.

'Of course I do. You try it. Keep him guessing. When you get back, don't go running after him. Unless . . .' a thought

192

struck her, 'you're not preggers, are you?'

'Of *course* not,' June said indignantly. 'He taught me to be very careful.'

'I'll bet he did. Yet, I don't know. It might be an idea – if you're really serious. You could really put the boot in. I mean your father couldn't refuse to let you marry him, and Willy-boy would lose his job if he wouldn't play. Then you *could* tell her ladyship to go fry an egg.'

'I couldn't. It would be awful . . . it would be like – like trapping him. And I love him.'

'Well, it was just an idea. It's your life. If you love him, I suppose you do, but there's no need to trust him, is there?'

Helen was coming back towards them, and Cousin Millicent was beckoning from the French windows. 'We seem to be going. Nice to have met you, Miss Peak.'

When Sir James got back to Whitelands, Charlotte told him about the Redmaines' visit, which had rather put her out. She was not sure that they could be any use to her socially, and she had an uncomfortable feeling that she could be no use whatever to them.

'A delightfully eccentric family,' she told him. 'They brought a girl from your office with them. Apparently a friend of the daughter's . . . a common Cockney girl. I am astounded that Mrs Redmaine should allow such a friendship. What was she called, June?'

'Boots Skinner,' said June, and Sir James choked into his whisky glass. 'I thought she was very beautiful, and very nice.'

Charlotte said, pityingly, that if June thought that it was high time she went to Switzerland and met some good class girls.

When June arrived at the Académie Florian she sent Willy a postcard of Mont Blanc, and told him she was having a wonderful time. All the boys she met were such superb dancers and one of them, Count Emil Defeavre, had invited her to his family skiing chalet – of course there was no snow yet, but they had a lovely party up on the mountain.

To her surprise she received a cautious but very sweet letter from Willy, saying he missed her, and was looking forward to seeing her again, adding that she had better destroy this letter in case some nosy schoolmarm came across it. She was to enjoy herself but not to forget him completely. June restrained the impulse to write five pages of joyous gratitude and covered this cautious missive with impassioned kisses. But she did not write again.

When the Mill Cottage contingent arrived home, there was a message on the telephone pad in the hall. It read, '*Mr Duncan telephoned and said he wasn't able to get home tonight, nor perhaps tomorrow. Sent his love to all.*'

'Very cryptic,' said Cousin Millicent, looking over Mavis's shoulder, 'and very much Duncan. He never seems to understand that his nearest and dearest would like, occasionally, to know what he's up to.'

'Usually no good when he's as cagey as that,' said Helen, glancing apprehensively at Boots, who met her eyes with the cool bright smile which parried questioning. Helen knew she was bitterly hurt. It was, after all, Duncan who had invited her to Mill Cottage.

Chapter 10

On Sunday, Helen startled the household by behaving most uncharacteristically. She was up early and first, and into the bathroom, emerging pink and fragrant, shaking Boots awake out of a restless sleep.

'Boots, be an angel and set my hair while it's damp.'

Boots struggled up, heavy-eyed, reaching for her dressing-gown. 'My hat, it's freezing!' she said, shivering.

'It'll warm up. I've just switched on the electric fire. Go on, Boots, I want to look fabulous.'

Boots drew up her knees and propped the perfect oval of her face on her hand.

'Why? You don't usually fuss. I mean, for heaven's sake you and Matt have been knocking each other up for over two months now, he must have seen all there is to see of you, so why . . .'

Helen blazed. 'That's a filthy thing to say.'

Boots reached for a comb from the side table, and began idly to pull it through her own hair – it sprang back out of the comb, smooth, shining regular waves, gold in the morning sunlight. Her lovely eyes were heavy with the bruised shadows of a restless night.

'So what?'

'So you're *not* like that! You've no right to make yourself sound cheap and beastly and dirty-minded. I know you don't approve of Matt and me. We don't like it.'

'I thought you said it was all wonderful,' Boots jeered.

'I mean we don't like not telling Mums, so don't you be a stinker, Boots Skinner.'

Boots coloured and said sulkily, 'What's so different about today, then?'

'Matt's coming to *my* home. To meet Mums and Cousin Millicent and Duncan. *My* people. I want everything to be perfect. I want them to like him and I want him to like them.'

'You sound as though you were getting married – properly.'

'Well, that's the way we feel. As though we are married. But it will make everything better if Mums likes him and he likes her.'

'You mean – she won't *mind* if you're not married?' Boots asked incredulously. 'A lady like her?'

'Of course she'll mind. Do you think *we* don't mind? Don't you think we want to scoot round to the Town Hall and make it legal? Or that I don't long to be married at the Minister in Ayling as our family always is? In a Honiton lace veil, and borrowing the family diamonds, and showing everyone how proud I am of Matt? Of course I do. But now – it seems impossible.' Her face was bright with anger, her clear eyes with unshed tears. 'I can't alter the laws of the country. But I'm not going to be one of those martyred women who nurse a broken heart throughout their lives then end up marrying the first free chap who asks them and despise the poor devil because he's not the man they really want. So don't be such a pip, Boots, and help me to make it a wonderful day.'

'So you're not going to tell them?'

'Not today. Not yet. One day.'

'Oh, *dear!*' thought Mavis Redmaine, watching her daughter rush into the garden to bring back scarlet berries, ivy and chrysanthemums to fill the vases, logs to stack up the downstairs fires, get the best sherry from the cellar, tear into the kitchen to drive Ada-from-the-village crazy with warnings that Mr Wilson preferred his beef underdone.

Her heart seemed too big for her breast – remembering the pain and joy of being in love for the first – and for her, the only time.

'She's as transparent as a pane of glass,' she thought, and wondered what kind of man it was who had filled her beloved child with this helpless passion, so that she was totally unable to disguise the suspense in her wild mermaid's eyes.

Long before the train was due she got the ancient car out and drove off to the station leaving Boots and Cousin Millicent to walk through the woods without her.

'It seems to me,' said Cousin Millicent, looping her straying grey hair away from her pince-nez, 'that young Nell's pretty sweet on this chap?'

Boots felt her cheeks colouring guiltily.

'What's he like?'

'Very nice.'

'And . . .?' Cousin Millicent's eyes seemed to pierce her brain.

She lost her head, and stammered, 'Well, he's a *bit* older than she is.'

'*Married*?'

Boots started, stared frantically, and said in a shocked voice, 'Oh *no*! Of course not! What made you *think* such a thing?'

'Well, she's known him since she started at Peak's and she's never mentioned him before. There must be something wrong . . .' She stared resignedly after the darting car. 'I wish she wouldn't grind my gears like that.' She shook her head under the floppy old hat, and her smile was kind in her leathery face. 'Well, trust Nell to chuck her hat over the windmill. Her mother was just the same.'

'But Lady Millicent,' said Boots lying valiantly, 'you really don't think Nell would do anything like that, I mean not after the way she's been brought up and everything . . .'

'Stuff and nonsense!' said Lady Millicent. 'It's always best to follow your heart. Look at Sandy and Mavis – happy as Larry, both of them. And look at Royston and his dear departed. Couple of sticks. No wonder they didn't have any kids. How would they have managed it? The mind boggles. Go and get a basket from the kitchen and we'll cut some grapes for luncheon.'

Boots did as she was asked, thinking all the time about that flat on the other side of the Park, and if she didn't take *that* up, what would she do then? She didn't want to be an office receptionist all her life. She had lost all confidence in Duncan's ambitions for her, although one way and another, that had been the most interesting thing that had happened to her. She liked the people she met with Duncan, and she liked the lessons with May Rampton . . . but without Duncan they seemed pointless. She couldn't see what use they would be.

She went up the ladder and, following Lady Millicent's instructions, cut two or three bunches of purple grapes and lowered them into the leaf-lined basket held up to receive them.

'You mustn't touch them,' Cousin Millicent explained. 'If you do it rubs the bloom off. Not that it matters, they get eaten anyway. Poets talk about girls like that, rubbing the bloom off and that kind of tosh. We all get chewed up by life in the end, the only thing is to enjoy oneself without hurting other people.'

Boots did not reply. Cousin Millicent tried again.

'Helen tells me,' she said, 'that you've got a crush on Duncan? Is it worrying you?'

'I don't know about a crush,' Boots said crossly, but the kind, faded eyes beneath the floppy old hat somehow melted her. The Redmaines were people you loved and rowed with honestly, but did not mess about with. 'He's a bit of a worrying person. I feel I've let him down.' Lady Millicent looked puzzled. 'By not turning out to be the new Garbo. Bones and angles, and being photogenic and responsive to directors. All that phooey he talks. He almost had me believing him.'

'I wouldn't give up hope,' Lady Millicent said firmly. 'He may very well be right. When his father went to art school instead of Oxford, Royston said he'd starve, and for a short while he nearly did – because Royston cut off his allowance. By the time he was killed he was making more money than old Royston was getting out of being a Baron. I sometimes think Royston can't forgive Sandy for being a success and catching a beauty like Mavis. He went on as though his death was a just punishment for profligacy instead of an unfortunate accident. Jealousy of course.'

'Would he – Lord Royston . . .'

'Breterton. His name is Royston Redmaine. It's all a bit confusing and absurd.'

'Would he really stop their money if Duncan went into the movies?'

'Oh, *yes*! He'd stop Duncan's. He stopped Helen's when she went to art school. He might even stop Mavis's. He's like that. I have a bit of money of my own, but we'd have a struggle to keep up Mill Cottage: without the shop – we only rent it on a weekly basis – he's our landlord there, of course.'

'Why, of course?'

'Well, he owns all the land round Ayling.'

Boots sighed. 'Fathers are all stinkers. My old man was the worst. I guess Lord Whats-his-name is pretty bad.'

'He might be more understanding if he *was* a father. Come on, come on child, cheer up. You've a lifetime to break your heart and many other people's.'

'Before I get chewed up?'

Lady Millicent went out of the hothouse carrying her trug of grapes. She supposed it all depended upon who did the chewing.

Helen left the car in the station approach and hurried through on to the platform although there were at least six minutes before the train was due.

It was nearly forty-eight hours since she had seen Matt and it seemed a lifetime. When she saw him her heart almost stopped with laughter and pride – he had so obviously made a special effort. He had had his hair cut. He wore a splendid new suit of a fine tweed, a blue and white spotted tie with his blue shirt, and a new wide brimmed felt hat with no grease stains round the band. She was as touched as though she had presented her with roses.

She said, a little shakily, 'I hope I get used to you soon – I don't think I could stand being apart from you.'

'Sweetheart . . .'

'A-ha,' she shook her head. 'Careful! The lady behind me is the local Bish's wife. In the HAT!'

He regarded the large lady in the improbable hat. 'I didn't know you had a cathedral.'

'The Minster. We're always baptised, married and buried there,' she saw the flicker of pain in his eyes. This business of not being married seemed to pop out and bump you like a Jack-in-the-Box. She hurried on, 'She's a friend of the Monster. Dines at Ayling Place. She'll go yapping to him about the strange artistic person I met at the train. "One of those

199

dubious friends of your late brother's, I suppose".' She looked down her nose.

He laughed, not very successfully.

'Let's go somewhere where we can kiss,' she said. 'I need it badly.'

She greeted the Bishop's wife distantly, and made no attempt to introduce Matt. 'Let her die of curiosity,' she said. Once they were out of the station, she seized his hand and they raced to the car. He regarded it with doubtful awe.

'Cousin Millicent's,' she explained.

'Good Lord. Does it go?'

'Of course,' she said indignantly.

'And you drive it?'

'We all do, more or less. Duncan has his motor bike. Can you start it for me?'

Matt braced himself and took the heavy starting handle. But the old car started sweetly and they drove across the market square and out of the town.

'That's the Minster.' She waved her hand towards the gothic spire and swerved towards the grass verge.

'Keep your eyes on the road.'

'I'm just telling you there are beautiful things in Ayling.'

'I know, I know.' He smiled down at her flushed face and the car swerved again. He put his hand on the wheel and righted it. 'Pull in here,' he said.

She did as he told her and waited. Matt did not take her in his arms. He pushed the new hat back from his forehead and stared before him into the beech woods. She felt scared again.

'Did you see our house – Mill Cottage – below as you crossed the viaduct? Dunky and I used to love watching the trains chugging across the sunset like toys. We used to make up stories about magic people who rode in them. We used to tell each other Dad would come back from France on one but . . . he didn't . . . Matt, my darling,' she faltered. He turned and looked at her. 'What is it, what has happened?'

He took a letter out of his pocket. 'This came today. It's from Betty's solicitor. She is going to divorce me.'

'You mean *this* year? You mean you will be free soon?'

'Yes. So it seems.'

'But aren't you glad?' she faltered, and then, high-handedly, 'We don't have to get married if you don't want to. It's not all that important to me.'

He reached out and pulled her into his arms, silencing her with kisses.

'You idiot child, of course I want it. But it's not as simple as that. It seems Betty has been having me watched for some while. Apparently she wants to marry her dancing partner. But she also wants alimony. As much as she can get. When you spoke to her that day . . .'

She put out a protesting hand. '*Don't* talk about that day.'

'I have to. You unwittingly gave her your name. She's naming you as co-respondent.'

Helen went white with relief and began to laugh, shakily. 'Is that all?'

'You'll get a letter, asking whether you intend to deny our association and defend the case.'

'So what do I do? Write back and say hurrah, yes, I'm guilty as hell, so please hurry up and get it over?'

He shook his head. 'Apparently she has all the evidence she needs. I understand the caretaker of the flats will be a witness. She can bankrupt me, but I don't think she wants that. I'm the golden goose. No – it's the scandal.'

'But you're not afraid of scandal, are you, Matt?' she said incredulously.

'What have I to be afraid of?' he said wrily. 'It is you, Nell. You and your family. I have no reputation to lose.'

'Who cares about reputation?' Her chin went up with Redmaine scorn, but Matt said gently, 'Your Uncle Royston certainly will, and you tell me he holds the family purse strings. How might that affect your mother and Duncan? You and I can struggle along together, but I am not rich enough to protect them against that. And your mother may be very hurt. All the rats of Fleet Street will be after you.'

She looked at him stubbornly, the colour rising like a flag in her cheeks, '"Lord Breterton's niece named? Love-nest in Hammersmith?" All that tosh? Gosh, how thrilling! Ayling will lap it up.' She paused, looked up, shrugged helplessly. 'Isn't it too late, anyway? To do anything about it?'

'I suppose there are ways and means. Betty might be bought off. Or we could defend the case and lie in our teeth.

Say it's a pack of lies, that you came occasionally for painting lessons. That the caretaker is a drunken old liar – we might win the case. But it would not set me free. You might persuade your uncle to pay.'

'Matt,' she was horrified, 'you don't really think I would ask him?'

He shook his head, and took her hands.

'No. Not for a minute. The way to get a divorce among your kind of people is for me to take a discreet and obliging lady to Brighton for a weekend, not for a young, well-born young lady to face up to public scandal.'

Her hands knotting into fists, banged against his chest.

'If we don't care, then who has a right to?' she said savagely.

'Oh, Christ, my little innocent, I'm only trying to make you see what is going to happen . . .'

'You are trying to say there is still a chance for me to run if I want to?'

'I suppose so. Yes. It's just possible. It is like some filthy mist engulfing you, and I can't stop it.'

'Are you blaming yourself? Why? You know it was me. You tried to run away – I wouldn't let you.'

'But Nell, you are so young. How could you be wise?'

'I asked you to love me. That's all. You did, and I'm not afraid of the consequences. Are you?'

'Yes,' he said soberly, 'of course. Every time I touch you I am afraid . . .'

'Oh, Matt, you must believe in me. I saw my parent's marriage, and I want mine to be the same. I don't care about scandal, or anything, and neither will Mums. But if you're going to be sad and guilty because you're older than me, and stupid people say beastly things, then I won't marry you.'

There was a long silence in which every sound in the fields and woods, every rustle and bird-call was magnified – and then he put his arms about her, and held her close.

'I just wanted to be sure you understood. So be it. I've taken you and I'm going to keep you and love you . . . we must learn to be happy sinners.' He kissed her again. Each wet eyelid, the eager young mouth. 'All right?'

'I am,' she said stoutly.

202

'Good.' He grinned. 'But I'm dreading this meeting with your mother.'

'She'll love you.'

He laughed. 'It might be easier if she hated my guts.'

He got out to crank the car, and Helen, snuffling happily into his handkerchief, started the engine. He marvelled at her changes of mood, flashing from sadness to gaiety like a kingfisher through patches of sunshine.

'Thank you for poshing up for the family,' she said, driving along the winding road between high banks held by the grey snakes of twisted beech roots. 'Oh, and tell me – what happened at the meeting yesterday?'

'Ah, I'd almost forgotten that.'

'Oh, Matt – It's much more important than worrying about what the *News of the World* will say about us.'

'Well, Medway had his costing man there and his advertising manager, and Sir James was there with a new boy called Hyde-Seymour – I didn't know him. Apparently the Old Man is bringing him along as a personal assistant. D'you know him?'

'A smooth bounder,' said Helen, nose in the air.

'Smooth and smart . . . he seems to have a good grasp of the business. Sir James's business.'

'Tell me what happened,' she said.

'I don't think Medway really wanted to renew the contract, but Sir James persuded him. The Old Man's a spell-binder when he gets going. In the end he persuaded him to renew *and* to double the allocation. But Medway stood out about the artwork. I'm to handle it – either freelance, or working for one or the other of them. I've to be in on every policy conference and have the last word in layout – and the copy-writers have to refer every scheme to me. I even have a say in the choice of media.'

'Jim-Jam didn't like that?'

'No. But that Hyde-Seymour boy understood. Peak's can't go on catching good accounts and losing them for want of ideas men, and young Hyde-Seymour knows this. I think Sir James has made a good choice there. I wish he'd been there earlier.'

'What difference does it make – you're not going back to Peak's.'

'This young Hyde-Seymour,' he said unexpectedly, 'he's very attractive. Has he ever made a pass at you?'

'You bet,' she said gleefully. 'Me and every other girl in the office – well, everyone passable or useful. I froze him off – like this,' she looked down her nose in icy disapproval. 'But you're not going back to Sir James?' she persisted. 'You *can't*!'

'I've got to think it over. Sir James fought hard to persuade me. He's paid me a penny-pinching salary for years and scotched every decent idea I've had, but now he needs me. And so does Medway. It's funny to have both of them bidding for my services.'

'But – you *won't* go back? Or work for Medway? You'll see about a studio – nearer Fleet Street?'

'I'll have to raise some money first. It is no use having a studio if I can't afford staff.'

'You'll have me.'

'But I shall have to pay you.'

'Why? You can feed me and keep me, but you needn't pay me.'

'Nell, if you work for me as a fully trained assistant, which you already are, you'll have to be paid. And we'd need another person. To answer the telephone, someone who can type a bit, won't mind delivering work and picking up stereos. You can't do that – you'd be wasted. And it's not just a studio – there's equipment. Lighting and heating, storage and filing. I'll need a car. I will wait until they both put their offers in writing – then we'll think again.'

'I won't change my opinion.'

He smiled thoughtfully. 'But it's not your decision.'

Her face fell. 'It is my responsibility, Nell. I must decide. Try to understand.' He changed course. 'I think Medway's a bit miffed with the Old Man. Is there something personally wrong between them?'

'Boots.'

'Is that still going on? I thought she dropped them both when she took up with Duncan. She is the flipping limit.'

'Well, you know Boots – she likes to keep her options open – she says. Who can blame her? I think Strauss let Duncan down over her film test. Put not your hope in famous directors.'

'Well, what did they expect? Duncan flies too high too soon.'

'And why not?' she demanded. 'We Redmaines *are* high-flyers. Dads was, Duncan's got his visions. He may fall on his nose more than most people, but he'll get to the top one day. And so will Boots if she sticks to him.'

'You're a good friend, Nell. Most of the girls think she's a gold-digger.'

'She's had to be. She's pulled herself up out of the sewers, and she's not going back. She's still only eighteen. We're mates – my mate, Nell Redmaine, she says. She means it too. Here we are.'

He saw a tall slender woman with faded red hair, wearing a rather old-fashioned dress of soft blue material, come out on to the porch to meet them.

'Is that your mother?'

'Yes.'

'She is very beautiful.'

'She was a famous beauty. People were always painting her. Dads did some beautiful pictures of her. They were often in the Academy.'

'I hate it that we can't just tell her everything.'

'Why upset her? She'll only worry – there's plenty of time for that. Today everything must be perfect. I so much want you to like each other. Let's not say anything to upset our happy day.'

'Mr Wilson,' said Mavis, offering him her hand, 'thank goodness you've come at last. Helen never stops talking about you, and we're all waiting to see if the reality is as impressive as she says.'

'It never is, I'm afraid.' He took off his hat, and kissed her hand. She was that sort of lady, and she smiled, pleased, accepting his homage, knowing it was sincere.

'Well, thank you for being so kind to her when she first went to Peak's.'

Lady Millicent came into the drawing room with Boots, who looked as though a light had been extinguished within her usually incandescent prettiness. Mavis introduced him to her cousin who shook his hand heartily, and said, 'My goodness, how like Sandy he is.'

Helen flushed, and looked at Matt, and then said in wonder, 'So he is. I hadn't noticed.'

'Oh, poor Mr Wilson,' said Mavis, 'take no notice of them. May I ask you to open the wine?'

It was a most enjoyable lunch. They left soon afterwards for Ayling Place, Helen driving with Matt beside her in the cramped little car, and Boots like a disconsolate bird of paradise, perched upon his knee. They hardly spoke, constrained by her obvious unhappiness.

Ayling Place, Helen told them, was officially closed for the winter, but of course the family could take friends at any time. Her mother had telephoned and been told that Uncle Royston, thank heaven, was out shooting, and as they drove along the winding country road they could hear an occasional shot and see the rooks rise from the woods.

'What does he do with all the things he kills?' asked Boots.

'Some are kept for the house, and he'll send us a bird or a rabbit, but he sells the rest at Ayling Market. The estate runs a big stall there. It's quite a good business. Doesn't cover what it costs him to rear the pheasants, but it all helps.'

They came to a triangular green with a scatter of cottages and a pleasant old black-and-white inn, a post box, a bus stop and a corner shop. There was an old stone butter-cross on the green and a large horse-chestnut tree, shedding its last leaves in an amber circle. Helen took a wider road from the green, passing a pretty cottage, with shuttered windows and an attractive swinging sign – *Mavis et Millicent.*

'That's Mum's wool shop,' she said, 'and that's Ayling – through those gates. The pride of the Redmaines and Duncan's nightmare.'

She stopped the car at the massive wrought iron gates hung between stone pillars topped with carved griffons supporting armorial shields. On either side were twin Lodge houses. Behind the gate a straight avenue of beech trees were shedding the last of their purple bronze leaves. In the distance on rising ground stood a great pink brick house, faced with grey stone turreted and castellated, its mullions catching the late sun in a hundred golden reflections.

'Good grief!' said Matt.

'Cripes!' said Boots, reverting to her native tongue. 'You

said it was an 'ouse, Nell. It's a bleedin' palace.'

Helen pressed her finger on the horn and a man came out of the Lodge, pulling on the jacket of his Sunday suit.

'Afternoon, Miss Redmaine. Didn't know as how you was coming.'

'Good afternoon, West. I've brought some friends to see the house.'

The man opened the gate and they drove on through the green, wooded park where black and white cattle grazed, and eventually through a stone archway into the stable yard, a fine square of cobbles surrounded by ancient stone built stables.

'Once there were thirty or more horses kept here,' Helen said. 'Now Uncle keeps two hunters. It's not good hunting country. Too hilly. Let's have a look round the gardens first while it's still sunny.'

She showed them the rose garden and the terraces above the trout stream.

'This is the same stream that goes through Mill Cottage garden, it runs down the valley . . . the great kitchen garden is through this gate here.'

They went through a wicket gate in the rose grown wall. The kitchen garden was huge, with meticulous beds of vegetables and large hothouses. A young woman came out of a small out-building as though expecting someone. Seeing Helen she hesitated. She was a charming, bosomy creature, very neatly dressed in navy blue, wearing a little blue churchgoing sort of hat. She had a full soft mouth, a skin like the roses and cream eighteenth-century poets wrote about, and big, soft grey eyes.

'Hello Rose, you're not working this afternoon?'

'No, Miss Redmaine – I just came up to check the lists for London tomorrow – the pot plants and hothouse stuff have to get to the station by six o'clock. I like to be sure it's all ready. Would you like to see?'

'Well, yes . . .' she glanced at the other two. Boots had scarcely spoken since they arrived. Never in her whole life had she even visualised such a place. 'These are friends of mine from London, Rose. Mr Wilson and Miss Skinner . . . this is Miss Granger, who runs the kitchen gardens for Uncle Royston.'

'It must be quite a business, Miss Granger,' Matt said politely.

'Well, yes it is,' she said, unlocking one of the big glasshouses. 'Especially the pot plants. We have to keep them indoors in case there is a frost before morning.'

The warmth of the steam heating enveloped them, close after the brisk autumn air and heavy with the smell of flowers. There were three long trolleys laden with exotic potted plants and ferns and dwarf chrysanthemums.

'It's very professional. Do they go up to Covent Garden?'

'Oh yes, sir. My dad's in charge, and His Lordship has spent no end on the glasshouses. The flower business has come on a treat. We can't compete with the continent for things like out-of-season lilac and gardenias, not yet, nor Parma violets, but we reckon to have the old vine houses put in order next year and force early vegetables.'

She went quite pink and looked so proud one would have thought it her own business.

'We're going to look over the house – we'll be about an hour. Can we give you a lift home, or do you want to get away?'

Rose blushed like her name flower, and said, 'Oh *no* thanks, Miss Redmaine – I've a little more office work to do, then I'll walk home across the park.'

As they went towards the house, Matt said appreciatively, 'Most delectable. Like peaches and cream!'

'Isn't she just? Her father is head gardener. They've lived and worked here for generations, before our lot came.'

'Your uncle seems a very competent business man.'

'Yes,' she said. 'He thinks we're shiftless because neither Dads nor Duncan have wanted to work for him. Heirs and second sons should put their shoulders to the wheel. To him Dads was letting the side down.'

She took them through the great house, through the hall which rose two storeys to a carved and gilded ceiling, and along the panelled gallery where the family portraits stared down at them. To Boots they were weird people in fancy dress. Some of them stared at her with the Redmaine's bosky eyes; occasionally there was a glimpse of Duncan's arrogance, impetuosity and mischief, and Helen's cool green gaze.

Matt was completely absorbed. Helen told him the history of the portraits, the names of the painters and they talked eagerly about the quality of the painting. Boots followed in silence, hating this strange rich world that she could not understand.

Up the grand staircase past the tapestries and through the State bedrooms where royalty had once slept.

'Not in our time,' Helen said. 'We were rich parvenus in the eighteenth century. Shipping. From Bristol.'

'Tea and slaves?' asked Matt.

Helen grinned. 'How did you guess? Yes. Then we went respectable and got the aristocracy bug – bought Ayling and a title. My great grandfather was a social climber – spent a lot of money on cards, race horses and expensive ladies. My grandfather and now Uncle Royston pulled the estate together again.'

'Throw backs to the old slave owners?'

'Maybe – but a lot of hard work and devotion as well. Uncle Royston is a monster, but I suppose it's because the place means more to him than people. He thinks Duncan should spend the vacs showing tourists round and save him the price of a guide. Mums says he married the wrong woman – he should have had a large family to bully – not just Duncan and me.'

They had stopped at a small but heavy oaken door in the corner of a room, leading to a turret.

'Do you want to go up on the leads?' asked Helen. 'It's a magnificent view, but it'll be cold now the sun's gone.'

'I'll stay down here and wait for you,' said Boots. 'I hate being blown about. Is it all right if I sit on one of these chairs, or are they just for show?'

'No, sit down,' Helen said uneasily, looking at her set white face. 'Are you all right, Boots?'

Boots gave a faint smile and wriggled out of her high heeled kid shoes. 'My feet are killing me,' she said.

'Oh, I'm sorry . . . I should have lent you some proper country shoes. Tramping round the gardens and all those galleries. Look, Matt and I won't be five minutes. Then we'll go home and have some tea before we catch the train to London.'

'Fine.'

Upstairs on the roof, Matt and Helen were alone under a racing evening sky, with grey clouds scurrying across the blue and gold gleams lighting the trout stream and the coppery beech woods and the tall grey tower of Ayling Minster away across the fields. The view, like the wind, was breathtaking. Alone under the sky they embraced and kissed.

The wind tugged back the hair from about her fine pure face. She searched his face anxiously.

'Well?' she demanded.

'It's overwhelming – but it's one thing we shan't have to worry about. I'd hate to be in Duncan's shoes. But I can understand your uncle's feelings about it. It is a beautiful place – and one can feel passionate about beautiful things.'

'I don't feel like that,' she said firmly. 'Not about things.'

'Are you sure? How about the picture of Mill Cottage – the one your father left you?'

'That's different.'

'Not really. Inherited, treasured, and loved. Something worth handing on.'

She signed. 'Yes. I suppose so,' she burrowed her nose into his lapel. 'I do wish you weren't *always* right – I'd hate to have to part with that. Like losing a bit of oneself.'

His arm about her, heads bent to the buffeting wind, they walked round the turret. From the north side it looked down on the stableyard and the big gate house leading to the drive.

A small estate car drove into the yard and stopped before the archway which led into the kitchen gardens. A tall soldierly gentleman dressed in conventional shooting attire got out. He was handsome, grey moustached, and only the slight stiffness as he unfolded his tall rather elegant height from the car gave away his years. He stretched, and sounded three toots on his horn. A man in gaiters appeared, pulling a trolley. He opened the boot and transferred several furry and feathered dead bodies onto the trolley and wheeled them away.

'Uncle Royston?' asked Matt.

'Oh, hell, yes,' wailed Helen.

'Ashamed of us?' teased Matt. 'Can't Boots and I escape down the back stairs, or hide under the royal bed?'

'Oh, don't be an idiot! It's just that he'll hum and haw and go over to Mill Cottage and quiz and bother Mums and Cousin Millicent. "Is there anything serious between Helen and this man? Has he any background? I am not keen, Mavis, on having another artist in the family".'

'And when he reads about the divorce?'

'Well, he will – and Mums will get into a fuss of anxiety, wondering if she's done the right thing by us. She worries that maybe Uncle Royston *is* right. And I just hate her to be upset . . . Oh, come on,' she said impatiently, 'let's go before he spots our car . . .'

'Nell, wait!' he said. 'Come and look . . .'

Helen went to his side. Rose Granger had come out of the kitchen garden and stood hidden beneath the archway. Lord Breterton waited until the man with the trolley of game was out of sight then, looking casually around him, he straightened his shoulders, pulled down his double peaked cap, and went beneath the arch, took Rose into his arms and kissed her soundly.

Helen stifled a small shriek. 'Well, I'm blowed!' she said. 'The old blighter! He's wilier than Sir James.'

It was like watching a scene in a silent film. They could not hear what was said. Lord Breterton emerged and presently Rose followed. He paused, as though he had just seen her, and raised his hat. Rose stood, flustered, they could imagine her creamy skin blushing confusedly. Lord Breterton opened the car door with an inviting but dignified gesture. Matt snorted with laughter. He turned to Helen and swept off his new hat.

'Ah, Miss Granger I believe,' he said. '*What* a surprise! May I give you a lift to the village?'

Helen dropped a shy curtsey. 'That's very kind of your lordship,' she said in Rose's soft Buckinghamshire drawl. 'But I'm used to walking.'

'Nonsense, my dear,' Matt said loftily. 'It's getting late.' He was getting into the part. 'We can't have you walking the lanes after dark. Your mother might be worried. Get in, my dear, get in. I'll have you home in no time.'

They both rushed to the parapet again and looked over. Rose was sitting in the front seat of the shooting brake. His

211

lordship folded himself behind the wheel and in a moment they had buzzed off under the entrance archway and out of sight. Matt and Helen fell into each other's arms, exploding with laughter.

'Oh, oh, the old seducer. Wait till I tell Mums,' cried Helen. She was alive with wicked glee. 'He didn't know I was here. He hasn't been in the house and if he came through the field lane he wouldn't see Cousin Millicent's car.'

'Will you expose him?'

'You bet!' she cried. 'You bet I will – if he says a word about us. Come along, let's get home. I'm longing to tell Mums.'

'And your Cousin Millicent will love it.'

'But maybe we shouldn't peach on him,' Helen said thoughtfully. 'Maybe we should keep it dark. A sort of heavy gun in case of attack. If he cuts up rough, we'll say quietly, "And *how* is Miss Rose Granger, Uncle Royston?"' She started to laugh again. 'D'you think he'll marry her?'

'He'd be a lucky chap if he did,' said Matt. 'He must be years older than she is. Much older than I am to you.'

'You're a boy compared to the Monster,' said Helen. She tucked her hand under his arm. 'Oh Matt, that's made my day. I always knew he must have an Achilles' Heel or Feet of Clay but I never, never thought of Rose Granger.'

When they reached Mill Cottage, Duncan had telephoned to say he would not be coming that weekend after all. He sent his love to the girls. Boots looked so wan and waif-like that Mavis was particularly gentle with her.

'I'm so sorry Duncan wasn't here,' she said. 'I'm hoping this means that he's doing some work. It's really necessary for him to work hard and get his degree.'

'Yes.'

'What did you think of Ayling?'

'It's very big.'

'Yes.' Mavis sighed. 'When I was your age it sometimes seemed to me like a great grey cloud hanging over us all. My husband said he did not want to inherit the past. He wanted to live in the present – "To be a man of my own time" he used to say. But I often wonder if you *can* get away from that kind of responsibility. So many people depending on you. But Royston's wife was still alive then, and there was always a hope that they might have a son . . . but now it does seem as though it will be Duncan who will inherit – and he ought to remember it. You see, it's *not* just him. There are so many people depending on the estate.'

'I suppose so,' Boots said woodenly.

Mavis's charming face was fraught with anxiety. She hesitated, and then said urgently, 'If you should see Duncan will you talk to him?'

'Me?' said Boots astounded. 'What can I do?'

'If you could just ask him to work at university, to get his degree, and then he will at least have that. Something concrete – an achievement, whatever he decides to do afterwards.'

'Dunky won't take no notice of anything I say.'

'No,' Mavis shook her head, 'or anybody else. He's his father all over. I don't want him to have that great place – but what's to become of it? Do you think he is serious about this film business?'

She made a helpless little gesture, puzzled and appealing. Boots thought she had always been taken care of and had never known what it was to fight and cheat and scheme to get what she wanted.

'I don't know no more than you,' she said. 'At first I believed him. It seemed we only had to work hard and it would all happen. But I told Helen today – and I don't know any more. But if I see him, I'll tell him what you said.'

'Thank you, my dear. You'd better get your things. It's getting towards your train time.'

'Thanks for having me,' said Boots. 'It's nice here. I've liked it very much. Especially this little house. It's like a fairy tale place.' She gave a small smile, very tightlipped. 'I'll go and get my things.'

Mavis watched her go into the house. The poor child.

Being in love with Duncan must be like being in love with quicksilver. She hoped he was not being a wretched cheat. She could not bear that. She would be very angry if she thought that.

Matt came out of the house and went slowly across to her. She looked up enquiringly, with her shy, mother-bird glance.

'Mrs Redmaine,' he said, 'you know I'm married?'

'I thought you might be.'

'Helen and I are lovers, but we will be married this year I hope. My wife has started divorce proceedings.'

'Oh! I'm glad – I mean I'm sorry.' She looked confused and relieved. 'I'm sorry if your marriage was unhappy, but I'm glad for Helen's sake – and yours. If you love her.'

'I do. Very much. My wife and I have been separated for many years, Mrs Redmaine. I am a good deal older than Helen. I'm thirty-eight. That is fifteen years.'

'But that won't matter – not if everything else is all right.'

'The rest is – a miracle.' He made an expressive gesture. 'I didn't think it would ever happen to me. I thought all that had passed me by. I can't let her go now.'

'No.' Mavis smiled, and added drily, 'Even if she'd let you. That Nell! She's so tenacious. I'll bet you didn't have a chance.'

He laughed. 'I did try. I left Peak's. I counted all the things against it. But – when she came to me – I couldn't give her up.'

'I think you'll be very happy.'

'But – there is more you should know. What's so rotten is that so much may hurt you. My wife is naming Helen as co-respondent. There will be publicity. We have been too reckless, but I did not think Betty would ever give me my freedom. It will not hurt Helen and me – but it might hurt you.'

She could imagine Royston's thundering anger, and said, 'If Nell is happy, we shall weather that. Thank you for telling me.'

'She did not want me to tell you today, she did not want to spoil our first meeting. But the day is nearly over now, and I'd rather you knew.'

'She meant to protect me, I suppose. They both do. They don't tell me things that they think will hurt me – but I always know there's something up. Nell can keep a secret, but her eyes can't. But I'm glad you were honest with me. Are you living together?'

'Yes,' he said uncompromisingly, and waited painfully for her reaction. But the beautiful tired eyes held no recrimination.

'She is so impetuous – they are difficult to refuse, these

impetuous Redmaines. Especially if you love them. Take care of her.'

'I swear. On my life.'

She made a small gesture, and a little hopeful smile, like a blessing, and gave him her hand.

On the way to the station Boots sat beside Cousin Millicent and Matt and Helen in the back, huddled up together under rugs. Cold came with the sunset, and the smell of later frost. The darkening sky was full of stars. He wrapped a rug about her and held her closely, and she lifted his hands over her breasts and her sweet chill lips to his.

'She did like you, I'm so happy.'

'I told her. About the divorce. I had to. She had guessed about us.'

'Oh,' she said in dismay, then, 'I'm glad really. Now she knows, I need not keep on Becker Street.' He held her closer. Her mother knew her well. She was so tenacious and yet transparently honest. She was like a gem stone which gleams changing colours from its many facets. He loved her so much that sometimes he felt that his bones were melting.

'I'll go back with Boots,' she said, 'and collect some things – and then I'll come tonight for keeps.'

Matt went straight on from Marylebone to Baron's Court and the girls took a taxi to Becker Street.

'Matt's wife is really divorcing him, and she's naming me,' Helen said shortly. 'He told me today – and he told Mums.'

'It'll be in all the papers,' said Boots.

'Boots, I'm not staying. I must be with Matt tonight. I'll take a few things and come back for the rest, and I'll give the Murphy's my notice next week.'

'You'll move in with him?'

'Why not? We'll be getting married this year. We already belong to each other. What's the point in being apart? Come down and help me.'

She packed a few clothes and toilet things, and when she fastened the bag she said, 'You don't think I'm deserting you, Boots?'

Boots shook her head. 'It's your life. I was dead against it

215

but now it seems to me it will work out. Things always do for you. That's what Duncan always said. One day, he said, I'd see – it would all come true. Looks like *he's* given up now, doesn't it?' She shrugged. 'No use crying over spilt milk.'

In the hall Helen put down her case and the two girls clung together.

'Don't you worry about me,' said Boots sturdily. 'I'll be all right. Thanks for the Saturday-to-Monday – only this was Saturday-to-Sunday. Your mother's very nice. And so is Lady Millicent. A real old toff, she is.' She gave a little grin. 'Ta-ta, then. See you at Peak's in the morning. Right?'

'Right,' said Helen.

She went out and Boots heard a taxi stop and then drive away. She looked round as though she had never seen the shabby hall before.

She thought of the flat on the other side of the Park. Small, cosy, with every comfort laid on. The rent looked after by someone else. All her money to spend or save as she wished.

'I don't want you living in that pig-sty in Becker Street,' Sir James had said. 'A pretty girl like you. Just come with me and look at it, that's all. Any time. I'm not rushing you. Just have a look, and then make up your mind.'

She was back where she had always been, alone, waiting her chance. Once it had seemed so simple. A rich man to look after her, and security. She did not want that now – Duncan had spoiled it for her. She found her door was unlocked, and opened it, a little scared, and switched on the light. Duncan was in her one armchair, fast asleep.

He looked tired and homeless and poignantly young. He was only a kid, after all, for all his fine talk. And there was Ayling Place, that great house – as his mother said, hanging over him like a great grey cloud. No one could just turn away and forget that sort of thing. That wasn't a dream. All those people who worked there. It was bricks and mortar, and land, and money, and tradition – responsibility and power.

Duncan woke up, saw her and sprang to his feet, his thin cheeks flushing, his eyes proud and defensive. He had wanted to bring her fame and glory, and now he felt like a stupid fool.

She had been full of rage, but now she said quietly, 'How did you get in, Dunky?'

'Your landlady let me in and said I could wait. I didn't come home because I couldn't talk to you there, not with the family around.' He squared his shoulders, and said curtly, 'Well, the whole thing is finished. Strauss has left for America without seeing the rushes. I went to his apartment today to see him, but he sent his valet to say he hadn't time. He had to catch the boat-train to Southampton. I went to Barry's and asked to see his father, and Mr Goldman did see me and said I ought to go back to my studies, that he didn't want me messing about at the studio, and he'd only let me do it because I was Barry's friend. Barry apologised when his old man had gone. He said his father told him that Sir James had asked him not to take you on, and that he was to tell me to lay off rich men's fancies. That they never had a thought of engaging you. They let me work there to please Strauss and auditioned you to keep me quiet. I must apologise for being such an utter, incredible ass.'

Boots pulled off her close-fitting hat and shook the smooth silken waves of her hair loose. Duncan could have wept at the unstudied grace of her movements, the soft curve of her mouth, the expressive indifference in her eyes. And as he watched her he knew he had been right. It was just that he did not know enough about anything, and men like Strauss and Mr Goldman and Sir James knew it all.

'Well,' she said, 'there's no need to get all worked up, Duncan. I expect he was right. I mean it's silly of you to waste your time when you should be working at university. It's silly for me to waste my time too. You made it seem great, but it isn't really. I've thought it over. Some of those girls have been extras for years, made up and on the set practically at dawn, and for what? Hanging about, waiting for two minutes action that likely as not ends up on the cutting room floor. No thanks. Not for me. I'd be bored stiff.'

'You don't want to go on?' He looked incredulous.

'I'm not going to. I want to be looked after, have fun, and be given pretty things and enjoy myself. I'm sick of spending nearly every evening at May Rampton's oohing and ahing and spouting Shakespeare and a lot of high-brow stuff I don't understand. It's best that you stay at college and learn about running that bloody great place at Ayling, and I'll look out for myself as I always have.'

217

She wished he would go. Then he said stiffly, 'I still think that if Strauss had really seen the rushes . . .'

'I don't want to hear what you think,' she said coldly. 'You're not stringing me along any more, Duncan Redmaine. No hard feelings, but just push off out of my life!'

He went out, white with anger, and at Paddington he spent all the money he had on him in the bar and stumbled into the last train back to Oxford.

Boots lit the gas fire, drew the curtains, poured herself a drink, and wept. But in the morning she was up as usual, bathed, made up her face, put on her new dress, her coat with the black fox collar and the smart little black hat, and set off to the office on top of a number eleven bus to face whatever life offered next.

Chapter 11

The autumn had set in wet and blowy, but inside the studio it was warm. Helen was sitting on the big divan wearing the green dress Boots had given her, her feet drawn up, one shoulder bare, a wreath of green leaves in her hair, bits of torn-up yellow and white paper, later to be transmuted into spring flowers, spilling out of her hands. Matt had fixed a spotlight so that the beam slanted across her. His face was closed and intent, utterly absorbed, his glance flickering between his model and the canvas.

Helen was not a good model. She tried to keep still, but her attention darted about, and at the moment, it darted towards the *City Advertiser*, lying on the low table beside her.

Matt stopped, and looked at her, his brush raised, then he rinsed it carefully, wiped it dry, put it down, and folded his arms.

'Well?'

She jumped guiltily, and said, 'Oh, darling, I'm sorry. Am I being awful?'

'You are.' He looked at the portrait on the easel, the pure, clear face emerging from the roughed-in background. 'But this is for me so there is no deadline. Better tell me what's on your mind.'

She swung her legs down, stretched, yawned, 'That's better.' A scatter of yellow and white paper fluttered across the floor. 'How much do models get? Whatever it is, it is slave labour. I don't know how they can bear it.'

She picked up the newspaper where she had marked off several items on the column advertising office properties for rent. 'Listen to this. '*Adjacent to Fetter Lane. Large studio office on 4th floor. Small outer or reception area. Good top light. Usual offices*".'

'You've been to see it?' But he knew she had.

Tenaciously she searched the property columns every day, marking out possibles, which nearly always turned out impossible, spending her lunchtime inspecting them. Matt took time off from his work, which he could not afford, to go with her, but he only did it because he knew her heart was set on it. But cheap offices were usually in old, dark buildings, with poor light and small, divided rooms. He was working freelance for Thomas Medway, who was still trying to get him on staff. So was Sir James.

But for Helen he would have signed up with Medway. She had asked him to wait for a month before committing himself. It caused a tension between them. Capital was the key. Bank managers were not sympathetic to freelance artists.

'Yes. I went yesterday. It's a bit high. Fourth floor.'

'No lift?'

'Matt . . . oh!' She caught his grin, and said reprovingly, 'Be serious.'

'Well, tell me all the good things first.'

'It's big and light and the position's good. It's a snip, really. An old man called Harry Grace had it for years and years.'

'The poster artist?' She nodded. 'I didn't think he was still working.'

'He's retired. But he's still got a long lease on it. Twenty years.'

'Now tell me the snags.'

'It wants money spent on it,' she paused. 'Well, decoration, general cleaning up.'

'If old Harry Grace had it, I'll bet it does, the scruffy old devil. How much?'

'Two hundred.'

'What?'

'We-ell – two-fifty. But we could beat them down. It's in such awful condition.'

'Just a little decoration.' His brows went up mockingly. 'How about key money?'

'No.' Again the pause, 'Well, a quarter's rent in advance.'

She watched his cool, abstracted expression, concentrated, calculating. They were always calculating. Calculating got in the way of all their ardour for each other, and the building of their lives together. Why couldn't he see that they would have to take risks and sweep all these small obstacles aside? Like her father had. It was as though his caution stood in their way, and she was sure it would be a splendid way . . . if only . . . *if only . . .*

'Matt,' she said, 'it is central. It is large and light – we could have a staff of six eventually. We could decorate it ourselves – weekends, and evenings . . .'

'And when do we sleep?' Again the faintly teasing irony.

'Promise me you'll come and see it tomorrow.'

He reached out, took her hands, pulled her across into his arms. She kneeled on the floor, between his knees. He took off the garland of ivy, and smoothed back her hair.

'I'm not going to paint the wreath, or the flowers in your hands until the spring . . . I want spring flowers . . . everything green and young . . .'

She reached up her arms and pulled his face down to hers.

'You will come tomorrow – to see the office?' she insisted.

'Oh, yes.' He would have to sacrifice two hours of his working time. 'Yes,' he said gravely, 'I'll come . . .'

'Shall I sit for another half-hour? I promise to sit still.'

'No,' he said. 'I have done enough for tonight.'

He met her next day at one o'clock outside a tall nineteenth-century house in one of the warrens of alleys and courts between Fetter Lane and Farringdon Street. It was raining and she wore a country mackintosh, and a big sou'wester, so that he could see her sweet, contradictory mouth, with its firm, decisive upper lip, and sweet tempting lower. He could see her imperious little nose. But not her eyes. It was as though she was hiding beneath the pulled down brim. The rain had flattened her hair into bronze curls against her pink cheeks.

It was an uninviting building built in yellow London brick. It was probably over a hundred years old and did not look as though it had seen a lick of paint in that time. It stood in a stone-paved court of similar buildings with a fine large plane tree flourishing triumphantly in the centre.

'Printer's Yard,' he exclaimed. 'I recognise it now. This was where Peak had his first office when I came down to London and your father did freelance work for him. Before the war.'

'It's an omen,' her eyes lit with pleasure. 'It was lucky for Peak and for Dads. It will be lucky for us. Oh, Matt, we must get it.'

'You look like Cousin Millicent in that hat!' he teased. Her eyes flashed impatience.

'Oh, don't joke. I can't *bear* it. I know it's right. I'll die if you don't like it.'

'You won't die,' he said, 'and it isn't a question of whether I like it. It's a question of whether I can afford it.'

She turned away, and opened the door. She could feel the edge of his obstinacy against her impetuous, over-riding will. A crack, a rift between them. The beginning of a real quarrel? She could not believe it.

They climbed the narrow staircase. The walls were polished with the grimy elbows of generations. There was the thud-thud of an old hand-press somewhere in the basement. The offices were filled with the small fry of Fleet Street. Obscure little magazines for even obscurer trades. Agents for office stationery, and artist's supplies. They stopped, panting, on the fourth attic floor and unlocked the old panelled door covered with messenger-boy graffiti and dirty blistered paint. But when they went through the tiny dark vestibule into the huge attic room beyond he knew she was right. It was what they wanted. But – two hundred and fifty a year? It was a shambles. It would take that and more to make it right.

It was filthy. Stacks of cuttings and old periodicals spilled out of the cupboards, milk bottles containing an evil green fungi stood by the gas ring next to a stained and cracked sink. There were patches of damp on the ceiling, and the skylight had a broken pane beneath which a bucket stood catching the falling drops. One or two useful but shabby bits of studio furniture had been left, as though the previous tenant had just walked out, tired of the whole thing.

But it was in easy walking distance of all his major contacts; it was large and light – or would be if the skylight was enlarged and repaired and the glass was cleaned. Helen stood with her sou'wester pushed back, glowing like a rose, smiling like a triumphant child, reading his approval.

'It will be great, Matt. You must admit it has potential.'

'That's about all!' he said drily.

She stamped her foot. 'Don't be a stick! You know it could be great.'

'I know,' he said gently, 'and you know, but does the bank manager know?'

'But you'll ask him?'

'And he'll listen, but he'll do his sums too.'

The triumph dropped away, she looked stonily out at the vista of slate roofs and the great grey dome of St Paul's rising over Ludgate railway bridge.

'I've only one account of real standing – the Medway campaign. Any bank manager in Fleet Street knows that money for art is slow in coming in. We may have to wait.'

'How long?' she demanded passionately, and saw his mouth tighten stubbornly, and swept on, unable to control her dismay. 'I'm just no good at waiting. I can't understand you . . . When Dads started he had no money – he had to borrow – he lived on credit for a whole year . . . to succeed you have to have more than talent. You have to have courage, and the will, and the belief in your star . . .'

He had not moved. Her voice petered out, she made a little gesture, but he did not respond. He did not look angry, only tired and drained.

'Matt – say something . . . Matt, *answer* me . . . tell me why!' She would have thrown her arms about him, but he held her away, his hands on her shoulders. She struggled free, distressed, flushed, childish, and screamed at him. 'Matt, don't *sulk*! I can't bear it! I can't stand it. *Say* something!'

'If I say something, then you must listen, Nell.'

'I'm listening – I always listen.'

He shook his head, with an amused anguish. 'I mean *really* listen. There is something that has to be put right between us. We have a ghost to lay.'

'What do you mean?' she faltered.

'I am not your father, Nell. You are in love with his image – Mill Cottage is like a shrine you all keep in his memory. Did you think I might fill his place? Did you think you had found a surrogate Dads who could put everything right? Or do you love me? Me, Matt Wilson. As I am?'

The blood drained from her face. 'It's not like that. It's not like that at all!'

'But it is. I knew your father. I was his apprentice. He was an aristocrat. He had enormous self-assurance, he was a spell-binder. I am not like that. I never shall be. Since my marriage broke down I have had no responsibility for anyone but myself. Now I am responsible for you . . . I cannot take on debts that I may not be able to pay. I cannot risk what we have, for what we might have. We *will* do this, Helen. We will work together, and be independent . . . but step by step. I will try to raise the money. But if I can't then I must take Medway's offer of a two-year contract.' He smiled into her stricken face. 'And at the end of that time you will only be twenty-five.'

She shook her head. 'This will have been snapped up by then. And I wanted it so much for us; so you could be free, now – and do the kind of work I know you can do . . . I am so disappointed.'

'I was afraid that one day you would say that to me.'

She sprang to him, arms tightly round him, rain-wet cheek against his face. 'No. No! Matt, my darling. I don't mean that. I am not disappointed in you . . . it's just that this place seemed so right. And I had so hoped . . . please, don't be angry.'

'With you? Never with you. With myself, yes. For the wasted years when I could have done so much more.'

She put her head down on his shoulder and they went down the stairs into the courtyard. The rain had nearly stopped. They went through the small courts and down the alley by the Cheshire Cheese into Fleet Street. 'D'you want some lunch?'

He shook his head. 'No. Medway telephoned this morning. He has decided to have a show house at the Home Exhibition next year, and wants to start working on the advance publicity. It will begin after Christmas. They've been manufacturing a new colour range of tiles – a little less aggressive.' It had been his suggestion – a long while ago, before Helen had joined Peak's. 'I have to see him today. And, while I'm in town I'll go back to the bank . . .' He stopped and kissed her. 'See you – back home tonight?'

'Yes.' She managed to smile.

He was hard at work over his drawing board, when she got in, and he looked up at once, meeting her questioning eyes. He shook his head. 'I'm afraid, no. I already carry a substantial overdraft . . . and I've no collateral.' His commitment to Betty was generous. Until the divorce case came before the courts and a final settlement made the bank manager had felt that no more money could be advanced.

She came to him, subdued and quiet, raised her face for his kiss, then took her basket of provisions into the kitchen.

He got down from his stool, and stood back looking at the rough drawing. The new colour chart for the tiles was pinned to the board beside it.

'We must have the Medway girl,' Tommy Medway had said enthusiastically. 'She's like our trade mark now. How about putting her chap in – a fiancé? You know, a decent young chap in a blazer . . . have them standing, looking up at the house . . .?'

'And then a wedding; and then a baby, and then back with the two compulsory brats?'

His irony was lost on Mr Medway.

'That's a great idea Matt . . . carry us through to 1935.'

Matt went to look at the original sketch he had made of Helen running up the Aldwych, long legs flying, emerald beret askew on her vibrant hair. Fleetness, youth and sheer beauty. Near it was Sandy Redmaine's masterpiece – the bright garden, the playing children, the flower-starred summer fields. Had his dryad been turned into a trademark? Had he imprisoned her with his caution? Clipped her wings?

She came out of the kitchen and he threw down his pencil and stripped off his overall.

'Don't take your coat off – let's go for a drink and a meal out . . .' His heart failed him at the relief in her eyes.

They enjoyed being out together, they fell in with friends and there was good talk and much laughter. And yet when they returned to the studio to their big divan and the comfort of love it was not quite the same – and they both knew it.

Sir James was not looking forward to Christmas. He had a

225

feeling of things crowding in upon him. Charlotte continually demanded his presence at society functions, but never seemed to have any time for him personally. Her bedroom door had been persistently locked against him. She was too tired, she said, and it was time he stopped making tiresome demands upon her for 'that sort of thing'. Her social life seemed to have acquired a new high, but did not give her any satisfaction. She was irritable, preoccupied and impatient. She had lost weight and it did not suit her. She began to wear frills and scarves of chiffon, and beads and chokers, and to read about cosmetic surgery in the magazines.

James had promoted young Hyde-Seymour. He was now his personal assistant and was proving a great help in many ways – and in others something of an irritation. A bit too keen. Always trying to take things out of his hands, to edge in on everything. James got the feeling that he was perpetually peering over his shoulder.

And June was coming home for Christmas and he would be expected to give her some time and attention.

Before she had left they had drawn closer. She had seemed grateful for his company, and for the first time he began to recognise her as someone he could love and spoil. It was a relationship in which he had not to prove anything, as comfortable as a pair of old slippers. He found the house at Ebor Place intolerable without her.

But Boots was driving him mad with her evasive uncertainty about the flat in Parkside Mansions. She said he was a darling old poppet, and took everything he gave her. But when he brought up the subject of the flat she said she would think about it, but she had so many dates, and she was still working at her elocution lessons, and when he tried to nail her down her face set into a beautiful, expressionless mask.

He knew she did not care for him. He was what the Yanks called a sugar-daddy – the pantaloon figure of popular films, but he could not draw back. To get Boots for himself would be to prove something to the snide Tommy Medway, who had not completely given up, and to cocky young bucks like Hyde-Seymour. But he must make Boots come to some decision, so it would be better if June came home for the holiday and then went straight back to Switzerland.

Mavis telephoned Helen at the office, and asked her if she was free for lunch. She was in Knightsbridge. Helen had been resisting the impulse to rush home to Mill Cottage and pour out her troubles to her mother. It seemed almost as though she had willed her to come up to town.

'Can you get up to Knightsbridge?' Mavis asked. 'Is it too far.'

'I can and I'll ask for extra time. But what are you doing in Knightsbridge? It's a bit expensive for the likes of us.'

'Well, you know what Boots said about selling our knitwear to some of the more exclusive shops? Millicent and I spent a morning ringing some of them up – Millicent was wonderful, pushing the Lady Millicent stuff, and I've got five appointments.'

'Good for you. You'll be needing an advertising campaign next.'

'It's a bit of a lark. We thought we'd have a go. Meet me at Harrods.'

'At one. You're just what I need.'

'Is something the matter, Nell?'

'No . . . no . . . I just want to talk.'

When she left the office, earlier than usual, she stopped to speak to Boots who was lunching on a large college bun. She offered Helen half.

'No, thanks. I'm meeting Mums. She's taken up your idea and is canvassing orders for *Mavis et Millicent*. Round Knightsbridge.'

Boots beamed. 'I'll bet she makes it.'

Sir James's number buzzed on the intercom. Boots put the last sugary morsel into her mouth, and dusted her fingers with a lace-edged handkerchief before answering the call.

'Yes, Sir James. At once.' She rose and picked up a pencil and the appointment book. 'Well, here I go. To a fate worse than death. He's on about that flat again.'

'Boots,' Helen was suddenly very serious, 'please don't laugh. If it's money, Matt and I could help a bit – '

'It's not. I don't want no help.'

'Oh, don't be so pigheaded. I just can't believe you'll go and live with that old man.'

'You don't have to. You're not me, and your life is

different. Don't poke your nose in. You Redmaines are all the same. Bossy. You think you can tell everyone what to do. What's right and what's wrong. It's on account of that bloody great house of your uncle's, I suppose. Soup for the poor, telling 'em not to have kids and to bring their girls up respectable. Well, no one is telling *me*! This is my life, and I'm in charge of it. Duncan's film-star rubbish, and you and your respectability. A fine one you are to talk about that!'

She walked jauntily off towards Sir James's office, her lovely slim strong ankles balancing on her high heels, slim hips swinging her short pleated skirt, the ceiling lights catching the glint of her hair as she passed beneath them. At the door she turned and stuck out her tongue like the brat she was, knocked and went in.

Helen turned away and nearly ran into Willy Hyde-Seymour, staring furiously along the corridor. He caught her wrist.

'Is she his mistress? Or going to be?' Helen stared, silently. He shook her. 'You're her best friend. You should know.'

Helen freed her hand, staring coldly up into the handsome brutal face and the angry blue eyes.

'I haven't the faintest idea,' she said, 'what you're talking about.'

Boots came out of Sir James's room about half an hour later. She felt the way she had seen gamblers look when they had either won or lost a large amount of money. Drained. She supposed she had won. because she had agreed to go and see the flat, but with no strings attached. He had been different today. Not pleading, nor hectoring, not pestering her or wanting to maul her. But it had been an ultimatum. He wanted a positive answer – or it was all off. He had looked tired and sounded irritable. Browned off? Fed up? She couldn't blame him. It had occurred to her that out of the office he must be quite a lonely man.

It was five o'clock. She took her towel and soap and went to the staff cloakroom and, although she was not meeting anyone, not Tommy Medway, nor Sir James, nor any of her lesser admirers, she could not go out of the office looking less than perfect. It was a habit – or perhaps a discipline. Not to look her best always would be like lowering a flag.

At the corner of the Aldwych, Willy Hyde-Seymour caught up with her and put his arm through her arm. Indifferently, she allowed it to rest there. She was used to him now.

'Off to your class?'

'Yes.'

'Can I walk along with you?'

'Suit yourself!'

They walked towards Endell Street in silence. He kept glancing at the firm young profile, withdrawn, miles away. 'How's it going? The lessons?' he asked tentatively.

'I'm giving them up . . .'

'That's the first sensible thing you've done in months.' She did not answer. 'Well, it's between Sir James and Medway, isn't it?' His hand closed on her arm, and brought her to a halt. 'Boots – don't play the innocent with me. I don't care which of those two old fools you string along. But why shut me out? We could have a wonderful time together. Whichever you pick needn't know.'

'That'd be cheating,' she said impatiently, pulling away. 'You know nothing about me.' She went on up the street. He caught up with her just as she was about to turn into Madame Rampton's doorway.

'I saw the agent's letter on his desk – what would Sir J. want with a little luxury flat on the other side of the Park? He's got a damn great house in Belgravia and another on the river.'

'He can take ten more if he wants, but that won't mean I'm going to move in with him. I haven't promised nothing so I'm *not* cheating.'

She was silhouetted against the dim light in the doorway, the steep stairway rising behind her. From above came the sound of a piano and the voice of a dancing teacher calling, 'one and two and three *and* . . .' and the thump of feet moving in unison. There was a smell about that staircase. Greasepaint and the dust of ages baking on heating pipes, reminding her of the Greenstreet Studios and Duncan, with his boy's hopes, and his abject sense of failure. She looked up thoughtfully. She did not want to end the classes. She would miss the lessons with the painted old woman as she missed Duncan.

How the old cow had worked at her. 'For God's sake, child,

229

don't be so blasted genteel. You sound like a Bond Street shop girl. Open your mouth, don't mince – O – *Gold*. You're saying "gewld!" *O, O, O* . . . Start again.'

Over and over and over until she had sagged with weariness and was sick with discouragement, so that when the faded blue eyes twinkled through the cigarette smoke and Madame said, 'Not so bad, not *so* bad, my lovely,' it was like praise from paradise.

Willy's importuning voice called her back.

'Meet me tonight. Come out with me, Boots. We'll go out on the town. Have some real fun. Go out to dinner, and on somewhere to dance. I'll go back to my place and change and bring the car and pick you up at Becker Street. About nine?'

She could see what attracted little June Peak. An impulsive, passionate, intensely physical man. A liar. Dangerous. Not to her. But the temptation to go out with a fellow who knew the score was irresistible.

She had dined in obscure, discreet restaurants, or dimly lit cocktail bars for too long, with old chaps looking at her as though she was a bit of rare fillet steak. Sick-making, she called it.

'Righty-oh,' she said. 'Don't mind if I do. Nine o'clock. Just what the doctor ordered!'

She ran up the stairs, leaving Willy gazing at her elegant silk clad legs until she disappeared round the turn of the stairway.

The bleak studio room was hot and stuffy but Madame Rampton was wearing a coat of Russian sable worn bald at the elbows and seat, thick woollen stockings, Russian boots and mittens. Her head was wrapped in a bright red shawl, and she wore very beautiful sapphire earrings – a mixture of grand dame and out-of-work pier-end fortune-teller.

Boots did not take off her coat and hat – tonight she looked bleak and beautiful, silvery and fragile as a piece of toffee paper.

'For God's sake shut the door, there's an appalling draught up that staircase!' Madame yelled. Boots shut the door and met the unblinking blue stare. Two blue stones ringed in black mascara. 'And what is the matter with you?' Madame enquired.

'I've come to say I'm not coming any more.'

'Think you've learned enough?'

'No – I won't ever do that.'

The old painted mask softened.

'Can't afford it?'

'Well, sort of. Not much point is there, now? I suppose Dunky told you about the screen test. Bloody flop.'

'Yes. Sit down, sit down, for heaven's sake, and take off your hat.' Madame dragged a crumpled packet of cigarettes from a pocket, lit one and yelled into the open office door, 'Beryl. Make some coffee, darling.'

The sound of typing stopped and a new secretary came in with two cups. There were always new secretaries. Young actresses 'resting', a student doing an evening job. Typing was required but no shorthand. She smiled sympathetically and went back to her work.

'And what has happened to my boy Duncan?' asked May Rampton.

'He got the push at Greenstreet. Strauss did not even look at the tests. Barry's father, Mr Goldman told him to go back to Oxford and not to be a fool.'

'Very sensible. *I* told him to finish at college before he started on this film lark. Duncan will survive. And how about you, chuck?'

'It was all just a big con trick. Old Strauss conning Dunky along because he was a bright boy and useful to him, because he could speak some German, and Duncan conning me.'

'He wasn't. He believed it all. Don't underestimate my boy Duncan.'

'Yes, well, it's all right for him,' snapped Boots. 'He's got a family, a home, free living when he's out of work and money behind him. Not a lot by his standards – but a hell of a lot by mine. I was the one taking chances.'

'Indeed!' May Rampton looked amused. 'How?'

'Supposing I had thrown up my job. Supposing I'd given up my gentleman friends. I nearly did. Who'd have looked after me? I couldn't have gone running home to Mummy!'

'You're working yourself into a fine old temper.'

'Well, all that stuff about me being a film star. He had me believing it. I must have needed my brains tested.'

'So you've been wasting your time here?'

231

'No, not with you, Madame. I've learned a lot about speaking proper – properly I mean. That's OK. I've learned the tricks – or a lot of them. The difference between the real posh and the phoney posh. Saying Saturday-to-Monday instead of weekend, and scent not perfume, and "How d'you do?" instead of "Pleased to meet you".' May Rampton gave a little hoot of laughter at the adept changes of accent. 'But I don't see the *point* of going on.'

'Duncan's mistake,' said Madame in her bell-like voice, 'was thinking of you dramatically. You're a soubrette.'

'Is it rude?'

The sunken blue eyes twinkled acknowledgement. '*There!* You see what I mean. I'll bet all your friends think you don't know you're funny? They think you're a dumb and dizzy blonde. It's a Cockney gift. Sharpened on adversity. A big-city thing – Liverpool, London, New York.'

'Come again. I'm not with you.'

'You come off it, Boots. D'you think I don't know when you're playing for a laugh? When things get tough get 'em laughing. That's how you work, isn't it? How often has it got you out of tight corners?'

Boots blushed. 'Since I was a kid at school,' she admitted. 'But I didn't know until just this minute that I was doing it deliberate like. But I do do it all the time. You know a lot about people, don't you?'

'I know when they're acting. It's my job. You've a gift for it. And you're a good mimic and getting better. You can see all sorts of variations. I'll bet you do a good impression of me.' Boots looked startled. 'That's all right.' The brilliant old eyes searched the lovely, young face before her and came to a decision. 'Moss Hartley's casting a musical. He asked me if I knew a girl, a good looker, able to speak lines. Second girl. I said yes. One of my students. Well?'

'Me?' She was open-mouthed with disbelief.

'Yes, you. Do you want to have a go?'

'Will they pay me?

'Oh yes. Five pounds a week. Maybe another pound if you speak lines. I'll want ten per cent of your first month's wages, agent's commission, but you won't get paid during rehearsals, so I'll wait for it. They're starting at Disbury Grand in February and they've got bookings for two months. They're touring the dorps.'

'The *what*?'

'The dorps. The North Country manufacturing towns.'

'What's second girl? Like in panto? Principal girl's friend? "Now boys and girls, remember it's May Day. And who but Prince Bertrando comes this way!" That sort of tosh?'

'Right. But in a musical she's usually funny. Leading ladies are romantic, unless they're naturally funny and can sing and dance well.'

'Like Binny Hale? And Gerty Lawrence? I thought you only trained legit?'

'I train anyone for anything on the stage if they've got a spark of talent and can pay the fees. You came to me for speech-training – remember?'

Boots nodded, realising just how much she had learned.

'Would I have to sing?'

'You can sing. I've heard you – you've had no training, but you can sing. Duncan tells me you're a fine ballroom dancer. Oh, for God's sake girl, Moss isn't looking for a *singer* or a *dancer*. He wants a good looker who can wear clothes, speak lines and feed the comic. You can do that naturally. I told him I had a girl. *Do* you want to try?'

'If you think I have a chance, yes.'

'You've a chance. I'll give you a card. Moss is auditioning tomorrow. I've told him about you. Don't let me down. So now – shall we have a lesson?'

'What's the name of the show?'

'*My One And Only.*'

'There's a good number in that. I went to the first night. "Picking Up a Broken Heart" . . . you hear it everywhere.'

'Yes. Well, we'll have a singing lesson. I'm not worried about the way you look – but Moss will want to hear you sing.'

She hauled herself up from her chair, hobbled across to the piano, the two disturbed Pekinese snuffling in her wake, and sat down at the piano. Boots started tentatively, a bit reedily, but at Madame's furious glare she found her real voice, a raw, clear boy's voice, dead on key and swinging on the beat.

At the end of the lesson Madame gave her the name of a dancing teacher in the building, and she floated off to Becker

233

Street, looking at the theatre lights along the Strand, and wondered if her name would ever shine out like that, laughed, felt a bit like crying, thought, 'I'm off again, worse than Dunky.'

All her Cockney optimism had flooded back. She was not trapped any more – not by any of them. Not Sir James, nor Medway, not even by darling Dunky. She had found another option.

But she owed this to Duncan. Without him she would never have thought of working with Madame Rampton. Never imagined she could do it, never discovered this hopeful rag of original talent.

She did not even think of Willy Hyde-Seymour until she got home, and then remembered rather crossly that she had promised to go out with him.

Mavis was waiting at Harrods, looking incredibly elegant, tall and chic in brown, with a long straight crocheted jacket of coppery flame designed by *Millicent et Mavis*. Great waves of gratitude welled up in Helen – gratitude that Mavis was her mother.

'You've been crying,' Mavis accused her.

'Oh, Mums,' Helen said, embracing her, 'how did you know I wanted to see you so much?'

'Actually I didn't,' Mavis said practically. 'I came up as Boots suggested to see if we could not get some orders from the smaller exclusive shops round Knightsbridge. I've been up and down Sloane Street and Brompton Road, and the doormen must be wondering if I'm a tart.'

'You are absurd!'

They took a taxi to a small, quiet restaurant that Mavis knew. Small alcoves surrounded the main floor with blue velvet curtains which could be drawn across the entrances.

'This was a very shocking place before the war,' Mavis told her. 'These alcoves were where the chaps took the girls, and *unimaginable* things went on behind the curtains. I never saw anything like that, only heard a few squeaks and giggles, so I think it was exaggerated. Sandy and I used to come in here when we had rows. You've had a row with Matt?'

'Not exactly.'

'Tell me . . .'

Helen told her. Almost all, and Mavis waited, and then said, 'What else?'

Helen coloured angrily.

'He said I was in love with Dads. With his image. His memory. He said that I fell for him because I saw him as a surrogate father. He said that Mill Cottage was a shrine we had set up to him.'

There was a long silence. She was stirring the little squares of gnocchi cooling greasily on her plate. She did not look up at her mother.

'Well,' Mavis said calmly, 'I suppose he's right. It is like that. What led up to this?'

The fierce green eyes flashed. 'I want him to be independent,' she said. 'I want him to start up on his own right away. I hate him working for men like Peak and Medway who vulgarise everything he does and haven't an original idea between them. I found a place that could have been made perfect, but it is in a bad state, and we would have had to borrow money. The bank wouldn't increase his overdraft. But raising money isn't a crime,' she said resentfully. 'You told me once – Sandy could always raise money, you said. For success you have to take chances. But Matt won't. He talks about security – I don't expect security. I've never asked him for it. I wanted him to realise his full talent, to be free to do so.' She was still pushing the gnocchi squares about in the congealed sauce. 'I really love him you know. But now it's not the same. It's as though we're not quite together. Physically it's great – but that's not everything, is it? It's only a part of being together.'

'Not the most important part,' Mavis said with a small smile, 'but you're young to discover that.'

'It's as though he thinks I feel this way because I always compare him to Dads. It's as though we're both trying too hard to make it work.'

'Matt won't give in you know,' said Mavis, unexpectedly. 'He's his own man, and pretty stubborn, I'd say. And he's quite right – about Sandy. And the shrine. I just wanted to keep it all as it had been for you and Duncan – I'd been so happy there I just wanted to keep it that way – but I can see

235

that it is a shrine – to my happiness, you know. And about money – your father could always raise money, Nell, because of Ayling. There it is, standing among all that land – hundreds and thousands of pounds of solid collateral.'

'I hadn't thought of that.'

'People don't. Your father was splendid and different, but like everyone else he was not perfect. Who is? It never occurred to me that you would not have understood that.'

'What d'you mean?'

'Well, you didn't know Sandy Redmaine. Only your beloved father. Everyone loved him. He demanded and accepted devotion. But he was arrogant, and often very selfish, and he wanted his own way: fiercely, like you do. Impatiently.'

'But you were happy?'

'Of course I was. Wildly happy. But often scared and sad too.'

'But he was very brave.'

'What is bravery to a man who does not know fear? He was reckless, he had made no provision for us – there was no danger, he said, nothing could possibly happen to him, and then he wangled a lift in a car going along a road often under fire because he wanted to spend the weekend in Paris and was killed. It was always what *he* wanted – immediately. He could not wait. He never considered any consequences.'

'Where there other women?' Helen said fearfully.

'I don't know. Women adored him. I never asked. There was so much he gave me I just took it all, and risked the rest. But never think he was perfect, Helen . . . Matt is quite right – with Matt you could build a partnership. That would never have been possible with Dads. I never planned with him. I never knew what money was earned, spent or saved, until he died – and then I knew. I was astounded at the money he had spent. I knew why Royston, in his clumsy way, tried to control him. Why he is afraid of this in Duncan. Don't think that we did not love each other, or that we were not happy, but don't think he was perfect, Helen, or that your sort of temperament could ever tolerate such a man.' There was a long pause, and then she said, 'If you're not going to eat that poor gnocchi have it taken away.'

Helen called the waiter, and asked him to heat up the gnocchi. She felt quite different. Older. She saw her way very clearly.

Mavis told her, amusingly, about her adventures that morning. Of the handful of orders she had been given. A good small beginning. They had to go slowly, she said, to be sure they could deliver on time. They would be able to employ their knitters throughout the year, if they could build up. It had been a brilliant idea of Boots's. 'Millicent and I would never have thought of it,' she added. 'I suppose Boots is like Dads in a way.'

'Yes – pirates,' said Helen, and they both laughed. Helen squeezed Mavis's hand, 'Thanks, Mums.' She picked up the bill. 'I'll take this. I'm a big girl now.'

Chapter 12

When Willy, impressively handsome in his white tie and tails, arrived in Becker Street, Boots looked radiantly beautiful. She wore the black taffeta dress, with the big hip bow which she had worn at Frascati's, with a new three-strand choker necklace of Ciro pearls. Her diamond watch, her diamond wrist initial and six diamanté slave bangles above the delirious curve of her right elbow. She looked like everything he admired and she smelled like a flower. To go out with a girl like this would turn every man's head with envy as they passed.

She took him up to the rosy cavern of her room, with its bright cushions and lampshades, souvenirs and dolls. It was shabby, Bohemian and cosy. A gas fire hissed heat out into the room, and there was a tray with cocktail glasses on it and a bowl of ice. Tinsel Christmas decorations hung round the mantelpiece and there were flowers, bottles of wine, boxes of chocolates and Karlsbad plums, boxes of silk stockings and pale kid gloves.

'Christmas loot,' she said.

'Where are all these from? You've got as much as the space buyer.'

'Oh, chaps who come in to see the Old Man.'

'The Redmaine girl's leaving, I hear. Gone to live with old Matt Wilson. I've always looked on her as an ice maiden. These virgin types are always the fastest. I wonder what her frightfully pukkah relatives will say?'

'Matt's divorce is going through. They're getting married then.'

238

'I'll bet!' Willy was scornful. 'Old Wilson knows his way around. I can't see him getting hooked again.' He faltered at the look in her eyes.

'I think,' she said, and her voice was a perfect imitation of the Redmaines at their iciest, 'we won't talk about my friends. You'd better get that straight. Or I'm not coming.'

'I'm sorry . . . I didn't mean . . .'

'So OK. So long as you understand. Have a drink?'

'Please.'

Expertly she measured and poured the gin and martini into the shaker, added ice and lemon, screwed it down and shook, poured it neatly into the glasses and handed him one.

'Where did you learn that?'

'When I worked at Benjie's nightclub.'

'What did you do there?'

'I was a hostess.' She met his eyes coolly and raised her glass. 'But don't get any fancy ideas. Happy Christmas.'

She tormented him. He wondered how she would react if he made violent love to her. He could not be sure with Boots. He did not know how to handle her, and it put him at an irritating disadvantage.

Smilingly he held out crossed fingers.

'Pax?' he said.

'OK.' She picked up a short jacket of soft, pearl grey squirrel. 'Shall we go?'

He held it for her to put on and he looked down at the smooth pale shoulders and the flat golden curls on the nape of her childish neck. She cuddled into her coat with a sensuous little movement, and he wondered jealously who had given it to her. Medway? The Old Man? Tonight he would take her somewhere special. He folded his arms about her and put his lips against her neck, but she simply waited until his arms dropped and he moved away.

'Why can't you love me?' he demanded. 'Or why don't you get angry and slap my face? Something. Anything. Just show me you feel *something* about me.'

Two small petulant lines showed between her brows.

'Oh do leave off, Willy! I thought we were going to have a good time?'

'I'm sorry,' he said, 'but you drive me crazy.'

239

She looked at him thoughtfully, then rose on tip-toe and touched his face with her cool, soft lips, but drew away before he could hold her. 'No, don't muck my lipstick about. And *behave*. Let's go, shall we?'

The car stood, sleek and shining at the kerbside. He was glad he had brought it – she looked impressed.

'Yours?'

'Yes.'

He opened the door and tucked a rug solicitously about her pale silken knees. When he got into the driving seat she was looking at the interior fittings approvingly.

'It must have cost a packet.'

'I had a run of good luck.'

'You don't use it to the office?'

'Not likely! And have Meakin and Brooker gossiping like a pair of old biddies. No fear.'

She laughed understandingly. 'When they saw my new winter coat with the fox collar the girls went on something chronic. I don't wear this one to the office . . . that would cause a panic.'

'And how did you get it?' he asked jealously.

'Father Christmas!' She laughed so infectiously he had to laugh too.

They had a good evening. They were young, splendid dancers, and Willy had money in his wallet. For the first time since he had come back from the Riviera he was really enjoying himself. He forgot about Charlotte.

They dined, and they danced tirelessly through the night, as the young did after the war. The alternating bands, swinging into view on their turntable, beat out the foxtrots, the onesteps and the Charlestons. Thrummed out the tangos; the leaders crooned the sentimental waltzes into a pool of shifting spotlights; couples danced entranced, cheek to cheek, or lip to lip in the smoky pool. It was a world they both knew, where they were both experts.

He drew up outside Number 3 Becker Street, and put his arm round her, as she knew he would. It was two o'clock in the morning, and this time, the time of parting, was the moment of truth for professional virgins. Helen had called her that once and she had been furious, although she knew it was true. This was the time when you found out about the man who had paid for the evening. She knew what Willy was. He pulled her against him and kissed her, and she felt his teeth bruising her lips and then a probing tongue, and an importuning hand sliding skilfully beneath her warm coat, dragging down a thin shoulder strap, seeking for her breasts.

'Lay off,' she said sharply, 'there's a copper.' He sat up sharply, and she pulled up her strap, jerked down the door handle, and would have got out if he hadn't gripped her arm, forcing her back again.

'For Christ's sake, Boots, be decent to me. Don't go. I won't let you. Stop kidding me along.'

'Who's kidding?'

'Let me come up with you. You know how I feel about you.'

'And you don't know how I feel about you. I'll tell you. Nothing. We've had a nice time and I enjoyed it. But you're just a chap I know, that's all.'

'I don't believe you. Tommy Medway and the Old Man don't hang about you for nothing. So what's wrong with me?'

She looked at him calmly, and said, 'You want something for nothing, Willy. I met plenty of your sort when I was working at Benjie's. The posh boys, we girls called them. Thought we should be honoured when they hired us. Always took it for granted we'd sleep with them. It's like I was vaccinated against your sort, Willy. I don't hold it against you, but don't push me. You've been halfway decent tonight. I needed some fun, and I've enjoyed it. Now open the door and let me go.'

'Don't think I'll forget it,' he threatened. His fair, handsome face was distorted with anger.

'What is there to remember?' She gave a little sigh, as though thinking it would be nice if there were. 'There's no need to get into a stew. I'll be leaving Peak's anyway.'

'It's true then? You *are* going to live with the Old Man?'

'Oh, for heaven's sake,' she said crossly. 'What's it matter to you what I do? It was a nice evening, so thanks for the buggy-ride. It really *was* ever so nice – until now. Night-night.'

She got out, he slammed the door and the car roared off

down the street. The winter sky was still black when he let himself into his flat just before dawn.

His room smelled of stale cigarettes and Chypre. The ashtray was piled high with half-smoked stubs of the yellow Russian cigarettes which Charlotte smoked incessantly.

For one furious, frightened moment he thought she was still in the flat and then he found her note. His time outside the office was never free from her. She would arrive at any hour without warning.

My darling boy,
Now that Christmas is nearly here life
becomes insufferable. The parties one
cannot avoid, the dreary buying of
presents for people one cares nothing
about. I had an hour free so I rushed
away from my prison, hoping for a
precious hour with you. I waited and
waited, as long as I could. Where are
you? My naughty suspicious mind is full
of jealousy. How can you be so cruel
to your own, Charlotte?

Willy dropped the note into the waste basket. Charlotte's long ivory and shagreen cigarette holder, with its tiny bandings of diamonds was on the bedside table. He picked it up and snapped it in two, and threw it across the room where it hit the wall and fell behind the bed.

He did not know whether it was Charlotte's neck or Boots Skinner's he had cracked, the way an angler breaks the neck of a trout when he has drawn it flapping from the stream.

Matt got out of the train at Baron's Court carrying a heavy portfolio – it was raining, and he had not been able to get a taxi. Medway had been delighted with his work and had made him a final offer. £1,000 a year for the first year, to be reconsidered every year of a five-year contract. It was the five years that he did not like – and he did not want to tell Helen.

The tension had passed – he and Helen seemed very close.

They had been frightened by the anger that had risen between them and had drawn back as though from a dangerous brink. The big beautiful dirty office in Printer's Court was still in their minds, although they did not speak of it.

When he let himself in the studio was as it always was at this time, the fire blazing, the dinner table laid, the smell of cooking, the brilliance of flowers – but something was different. He put down his portfolio, took off his wet coat and hat, looking round, searching . . . What was it? What had gone? Then he knew. Alexander Redmaine's picture was not there. The big shining picture of Mill Cottage garden, with the two small children playing eternally by the stream had gone.

Helen called from the kitchen, but she did not come out to meet him.

He went slowly to the kitchen door. She turned from the salad she was mixing, and smiled brightly, too brightly, and he could see her eyes were a little swollen, and that her lips were trembling.

'You sold it,' he said.

'Yes.' She took a cheque out of her apron pocket and put it on the table, 'One thousand pounds – from the Hellman Gallery. It's for us.'

He did not answer.

'Well, say something,' she shouted, 'at least *say* something.'

'You loved that picture. It was your last link with him. Helen, there was no need.'

'But there was. He would have sold it. And why not? All you said was true – I don't want you to be like him anymore. If you don't want the studio, then that's OK. But if you do, well, there you are – we don't have to borrow to start.' She began to cry helplessly, stubbing her eyes with her fists, trying to stem the tears, and he said, 'Oh God, darling, don't . . .' and took her in his arms until the tears ceased, and she leaned her brow upon his shoulder, rueful, half-laughing, 'What a goose I was, Matt . . . what an arrogant, stupid Redmaine goose . . .'

When Helen gave in her notice four weeks before Christmas

Sir James could not believe it. Damn it he was paying her six pounds a week now! Certainly she had a lot of work since Matt had left, but it was good experience for her. If he gave her more money now everyone in the studio would want a rise.

'I don't want a rise,' Helen said. 'I just want to leave.'

Sir James was deeply pained. He went on about the unreliability of women employees, the dishonesty of not telling him earlier. He had only given her the job out of respect for her father's memory, and this was how she repaid him.

'I *am* grateful. I have learned a great deal here. But I want to leave.'

'It was Matt Wilson who pressured me into taking you,' Sir James said accusingly. 'I should have known it was just because he'd taken a fancy to you.'

He received a frosty glance and began to bluster.

'You know nothing about the business yet. You haven't been working a year. You don't know your job yet.'

'Then why are you so cross because I'm leaving? It was you who gave me a senior position.'

Sir James leaned his head on his hand and his voice dropped sadly. Boots could do a fantastic impression of his more-in-sorrow-than-in-anger act, which was a feature of office get-togethers. Helen hoped she was not going to laugh.

'You've used the firm to get experience, and just when you're becoming useful to me you want to go. I suppose you will take all our ideas to a rival firm?'

Helen began to feel a slight compunction.

'Well, not exactly.' She caught the speculative glance in his rolling dark eyes and heard her mother saying, 'A wily old bugger, Dads used to say,' and hardened her heart.

'I'm sorry you feel like this Sir James, but I am giving a month's notice, and I will finish all my current work, I promise.'

'I suppose you're going to marry some society kid with no chin and lots of money.'

'No, I'm going to marry Matt Wilson.'

'He's married already!' Sir James said triumphantly.

'Yes, but his wife is divorcing him.'

He saw the lift of her brows and the quirk at the corner of her lips, controlling her laughter.

'Very well,' he said sulkily. 'You can go whenever you like.'

He made Helen think of a ruffled old pigeon with his silvery hair and pale grey suit.

'Oh, please don't be cross, Sir James,' she implored. 'You really do need Matt you know. Dear Mr Meakin is very reliable, but he's not an ideas man – and Matt and I have taken a perfectly splendid office just round the corner, off Fetter Lane – it will be very convenient – he'll have some marvellous ideas. If you want me to continue with the Friendly Liver Pills campaign then we'll be delighted to do it for you.'

Sir James began to laugh.

'You're just like your father. Blarney. There must be an Irish strain in the family. But perhaps young Hyde-Seymour is right. Perhaps it would pay us to use a high-class outside studio for our big accounts.'

'I'm absolutely sure it would.'

'Get the hell out of here,' he said good-naturedly, 'before I burst a blood vessel.'

She held out her hand and he shook it. For the first time Helen saw how attractive he could be. 'You really are the tops, Sir James,' she said, 'thanks for everything. I really have learned a great deal.'

Two weeks before Christmas, Peak's office had broken out in a rash of tinsel and coloured paper decorations. On the reception desk in the hall stood a small illuminated silver tree and a collecting box for the Advertising Benevolent Society. Hampers and parcels, cases of whisky and champagne arrived for Sir James, and similar gifts were despatched by him to important advertising directors and to his clients.

Miss Klein, the space buyer, was besieged with invitations to lunch, bouquets of flowers, and expensive chocolates. Mr Brooker and even Mr Meaker received the odd bottle of Scotch from the blockmakers' and printers' representatives.

Boots appeared in a new dress of holly berry red trimmed with touches of emerald green, and could have gone out every lunchtime if she had wished. Willy avoided the front reception. He did not speak to her.

The day before Chrismas Eve she went into the studio and put a small gift-wrapped parcel on Helen's drawing board. Helen looked up and smiled, and opened the box. It contained a single handkerchief of fine lawn, with a two inch border of real lace.

'Oh, Boots, it must have been frightfully expensive. It's lovely.'

'I like nice things. You don't have to give me nothing. I just wanted you to have it.'

'Are you going home for Christmas?'

'Not likely,' said Boots. 'I'll send my mother some dough and tell her to spend it before my old man gets his hands on it. I'll send him a card saying drop dead!'

Helen had a vision of Boots spending Christmas alone at Becker Street. Or in a plushy little flat. She said quickly, 'Won't you come down to Ayling with Matt and me?'

'Your mother telephoned and asked me.'

'She *did*?' Helen flushed with pleasure. Mavis had such a talent for doing the right and sensitive thing. 'That's all right, then?'

'I told her no. Well, from what I heard last time, I thought you'd be going over to the big house.'

'You thought Duncan would be home, didn't you?' said Helen. 'Well, he won't be. He's gone to Germany with Barry Goldman. To Berlin. They've got an introduction to Fritz Lang and to a lot of the studios over there, through Strauss, who has reappeared. They're being shown over U.F.A. and meeting all sorts of stars, like Veidt, and Lillian Harvey . . .'

Boots changed colour. 'You mean he's still skiving out of college and going over to Greenstreet?'

'Oh no. He's been at college and working hard. But he's not taking estate management as an extra subject. He's taking a technical course in cinematography at the tech. Of course, Uncle R. doesn't know. Nor Mums. Uncle R. would rage and Mums would worry. He hasn't given up, and you'll see, Boots, he'll make it one day. Not overnight, as he thought. But he will.'

Boots was crestfallen. She felt disloyal. She had thought it all nonsense. She'd thought herself a fool to be taken in. But he'd started again. What had May Rampton said? 'In our

246

business, never take no for an answer. Not if you want to be a real pro. Never think you can't do it – always have a go. If you can't make it this time, then start again.'

'Well, thanks for telling me about Dunky, Nell. And thanks for the invite, and tell your mum I'd love to come. *And*,' her eyes sparkled, 'I've got something to tell you. I'm going on the stage.' And she told her in an excited gabble about the part in *My One And Only*. 'I was scared out of my life at the audition, especially when this chap, Moss Hartley said he'd let me know. They say that when they don't want you. But he telephoned yesterday. He wasn't sure because I'd not had any experience . . . but he said he'd take a chance. He said if Madame said I could do it, he'd trust her. So it's fixed.' I can't let her down. If she says I can do it, I can.'

'Boots,' Helen hugged her rapturously, 'and you'll forget that business with Sir James. I mean . . .'

'I know what you mean,' Boots said gravely. 'I'm not sure. I've got to think about it.'

'About what? You'll be independent.'

'On a fiver a week!' The studio was empty because it was the lunch hour, so Boots lit a cigarette. 'A London flat of my own. A telephone, and a porter who takes messages if I'm not in. Food, light, gas, clothes. It's a thought.'

'Boots,' Helen was horrified, 'you can't do it.'

'I dunno. I'll have to find out.' Her eyes met Helen's aggressively. 'You never know your luck until you step in it. Lots of actresses – really famous ones, live with rich chaps. It'd make things a lot easier.' Her chin went up defiantly. 'Well? D'you still want me to come for Christmas?'

'Boots, of course. It's not for me to tell you what to do with your life. You told me not to live with Matt, but it didn't stop me.'

'Well, I was wrong.'

'Perhaps I am, too – perhaps you'll be blissfully happy with the Old Man as a standby.'

'Oh, shut up!' Boots felt embarrassed. Happiness had not been part of the option.

'When do you start?'

'The week after Christmas. Rehearsing. Then we start the tour at the end of January. I'll be taking extra lessons all the time. But – I've got to tell Sir James – that I'm going on tour, and he's not going to like it at all. Or . . . I don't think so.'

'Supposing you had to choose between – between the flat and show business. You'd choose show business, wouldn't you?'

'Of course,' she spoke without thinking. 'But,' she added a trifle defensively, 'I don't see why I shouldn't have the best of both worlds.'

Sir James left his taxi outside Parkview Mansions and found Boots sitting in one of the overstuffed pink brocade chairs in the walnut panelled entrance hall.

The floor was black and white marble with imitation Chinese rugs in which pink predominated. There were wall-lights with pink half-shades and crystal drops, and there was a large jardinière filled with pot plants. There was a reception office with pigeon holes for letters and hooks for keys, a telephone switchboard and a porter in attendance in a maroon and gold uniform, just like a superior hotel. But it did not look like a place people lived in.

Sir James went forward extending his hand affably, and greeted her with the smiling but distant affection he might have used to a favourite niece if he had had one.

'Boots, my dear child! Have I kept you waiting?'

'No. I was early.'

'I can't stay tonight . . . but I'll have time to show you the flat.' He went to the reception desk and collected a key.

The lift was made of gilded ironwork and was worked by a pale small boy in a maroon uniform, whose hair was slicked wetly back from his rather bulbous brow. Sir James did not touch her or try to kiss her. She wondered if he was regretting his decision. Or if he'd gone off her. It was a funny sort of set-up, really. She'd kept her promise and ended it with Medway as soon as the new contract had been signed.

As she stepped out of the lift she met the sharp eyes of the undersized lift-boy, who closed the gate with a clatter and gave her a knowing wink. She felt angry. The little blighter had summed them up all right, or thought he had – like that Willy Hyde-Seymour. She was surprised how much she resented it.

Sir James inserted a key into a polished oak door and opened it into a minute hall. When the door closed he put his arm round her and led her across into a doll-size living room overlooking the greenery of the Park. Like the hall, it was furnished with bright over-stuffed furniture, this time golden yellow. Pale panelled walls, shaded wall-lights, one or two reproductions on the walls, Kirchener and Baribal girls, ripe-lipped, sweet-bosomed, revealing glimpses of creamy flesh and high cherry-tipped breasts. There was a large cocktail cabinet, with inner illumination and lined with peach coloured engraved glass, fitted with glasses and cocktail shakers. The central heating made her feel as though she was in a slow oven.

'Well, what do you think?'

'It's too hot,' she said positively.

'That can be adjusted. Have a look round. I think you'll find it has everything you need.'

A bedroom larger than the lounge, a big double bed with a padded satin headboard draped with gold and cream satin. White and gold furniture. Plenty of mirrors. One surprisingly in the ceiling above the bed. A small but very adequate bathroom, walled in turquoise tiles with gilt fittings. More mirrors. Sir James stood at the door watching her.

'No kitchen?' she asked.

'Well, it's very small, through there – off the lounge. It's really only for snacks, tea and breakfast . . . but there's full room service and a good restaurant downstairs. And a club – for residents. Bar, dance floor, swimming pool. Everything you could want.'

'Expensive?'

He looked directly at her for the first time. 'That won't have to worry you, my dear.'

'For six months?' She sat down on the small plump sofa, and linked her long, lovely hands about her knees. She looked young and innocent. He sat down beside her.

'I thought by then we should both know whether we liked the arrangement.'

Boots was silent.

'You don't like it?'

'Well, look at it. I mean *look* at it! It's a tart's place, isn't it?'

'And you're *not* a tart?'

'No.'

'You've taken me for quite a bit since you came into the office. And Medway. And I'd guess other chaps.'

'That doesn't make me a tart.'

He rose, the familiar angry colour rising in his heavy features. He hated to look a fool, and he was afraid she was making a fool of him.

'Then what the devil does it make you? A cheap little gold-digger – a bloody little prick teaser . . .' She did not flinch. She had heard all this before.

'It makes me pretty rotten,' she agreed. 'You likewise. Ever since I left school chaps have been trying to get me into bed for nothing until they find it's no go – *then* they start to pay. We-ell, they pay for clothes, and treats, the odd bill, and a fiver here and there. So I let them. *I don't give nothing*, I reckon I'm worth more than that,' she looked round the pale yellow room, and drew in a big breath. 'I reckon I'm worth more than this too. Now I'm sure.'

There was an edgy silence. She saw the empurpled veins in his forehead and was slightly alarmed.

'You all right, Jim-Jams?'

He raised his head. 'Why do you think I went so far?'

'I dunno,' she said, without rancour. 'Maybe to put Tommy Medway's nose out of joint.' She knew she had hit the bullseye. Huffily he began to put on his overcoat and prepare to leave. She patted the place beside her, friendly as a pup, and he sat down sulkily and allowed her to hold his pudgy, well-manicured hand, trying to think why he had been so crazy to possess her. He patted her hand, and said slowly, 'I believe you're a good kid, really.'

'D'you mean good good, or just respectable?'

'Maybe both.'

'Well, thanks for that.'

'I asked for it, I guess.'

'Me too,' she agreed, nodding like a wise child, 'Chaps get the wrong idea about me, but it's my own fault. You know what Helen Redmaine called me? A professional virgin. I wasn't half mad, but I guess she's right.'

Sir James laughed, and said magniloquently, 'You can stay

250

on at the office if you'd like to. It will be all right with me.'
'No.' She knew he was trying to be generous. 'You
wouldn't really like that. And I'd never get away from
Medway.'
'Then what will you do?'
'I'm going on the stage. *My One And Only*. Moss Hartley's
second touring company.'
He looked horrified. 'A chorus girl.'
'No. I've got a small part. It's all Madame Rampton's idea.'
'It's a pretty rough life touring those one horse towns.
Every provincial yobo will be trying to make you.'
'Well, I'm used to that,' she said and looked at him with
great, serious eyes. He glanced away sheepishly. 'I've
changed,' she said. 'Just lately. Well, I've had one of those
things religious people get.'
He looked alarmed.
'Don't look like that, I'm not barmy. It's like being saved
. . . or converted . . . when you know you're on the right
track at last.'
'A revelation?'
'Yes. That's it. Well,' she was off, full of this new found joy,
'Madame Rampton, she's not like Duncan. He thought of me
– well, like through his *eyes*. Sort of, through a camera,
because that's what *he* wants to do. But old May Rampton,
she's a real pro. I tell you, she can do anything . . . *anything*.
She can act, and sing and dance . . . yes! The other day she
was telling me about this play, in the old days, you know when
they wore those powdered wigs, and she picks up a fan, and
starts gliding about the floor, fluttering it, and fluttering her
eyes, and singing a tune . . . and she must be a hundred, and
full of rheumatism but she makes you see someone lovely and
young, dancing like Cinderella in a panto.' She stopped for
breath. 'She's acted with all the famous people. She was
famous herself. And if *she* thinks I might do it, then I damn
well can, and I'm having a go. And it's *for me* to do it. Me –
myself. Not because someone else sees me as something. This
is different – like Helen Redmaine. And Matt . . . and
Duncan too, when he finds his way . . . and you . . . you *know*
about this advertising thing. How to sell things . . . it's something you've made yourself. Do you understand?'

251

'My Christ, yes!' said Sir James fervently. 'I do!'

'That Willy Hyde-Seymour,' she went on, 'he's like Duncan. Oh, they're not the same, because Duncan's nice, and poor Willy's a real stinker – but they both think they know it all. W.H.S. doesn't know a thing compared to you, and Dunky's only begun to learn. Old May, she says, it's only when you know how *little* you do know that you start to learn.'

Sir James nodded like a china mandarin. She was right about that pushy boy Hyde-Seymour. He realised that Willy had been one of the causes of his depression. He had good ideas and he took work off his shoulders, but there was that about him – his virile good looks perhaps – that made Sir James feel his years.

'What are they paying you?' he asked.

'Five pounds a week. Seven if I speak lines and if I'm given a song. No pay for rehearsals, but I've saved up enough for that.'

'You must let me help you . . .'

'No,' Boots said flatly, 'it wouldn't be right. Not now.'

'My dear little girl, I'd like to help you. Isn't there anything I can do?'

Boots hesitated.

'Well?'

'My new fur coat,' she said doubtfully. 'Remember you gave me ten pounds – in November – for my birthday? It wasn't my birthday, but I wanted ten pounds. Well, I put it down on this grey squirrel coat, it's really warm, and it makes me feel wonderful when I wear it. I haven't finished paying for it – eight bob a week, I'm paying. If you'd lend me the money, I'll pay you back, honest. I'll pay back the ten pounds too, seeing I was having you on about my birthday.'

He looked at her with astonishment. To him she had been the personification of modern girlhood. She was just a perky London kid, trained in the sharp awareness of hard living, with an odd, irrational honesty to people she trusted and no scruples about using people who tried to use her.

'Boots, will you be leaving soon?'

'Christmas Eve. Going down with Helen and Matt to her mum's in the country. We start rehearsals after the holiday.'

'Ah yes. How much do you owe now?'

She took out a small note book, flipped through the pages and said, 'Four pound ten,' in a very businesslike manner. He shook his head and laughed. She could have said ten or twenty or even thirty pounds, and he would not have known. 'Well, here you are . . .' he spread out his wallet, 'take what you need.' She carefully took five pounds and handed him back ten shillings.

'Thanks a million. I'll have to owe it to you until I've got my first week's salary. Where'll I send it?'

'Boots, you'll do me a favour by not sending it. How do you think I'm going to explain it to Peggy Prior? She does all my correspondence and banking. No, this you'll have to accept.' He took out a ten pound note and added it to the four pound ten. 'And this.' Boots looked at it unhappily.

'It looks like I'm kidding you along. I'm not – not now. You're a nice old guy, really!' She gave her bright, innocent stare. 'Well, I reckon most chaps could be – decent I mean – if they were not always trying to get up your skirts whether you want it or not. It'd make life a lot easier.' She rose and began to put on her gloves, smiled and said, 'I reckon your daughter's a lucky girl to have a dad like you.'

He was incredibly touched and flattered. He picked up his hat and his silver-topped cane, and gave a last look round.

'You're quite right. It is a tart's place. No place for a nice girl like you.'

He left the keys at the Reception, telling the porter that he had decided against the flat after all. He asked if he could give her a lift to Becker Street, and they sat in the taxi talking companionably, as they had never talked before.

'Well, thanks for everything,' Boots said as the taxi drew up outside Number 3, 'and a Happy Christmas.' And she kissed him on the cheek.

'Thank *you* my dear, he said and kissed her warmly in return.

June came home the week before Christmas. She was not quite sure how she would be received. There was a glittery restlessness about Charlotte which she found somewhat unnerving.

'I am not going to mention a word of that miserable business before you went away,' she said, fitting one of her thin, Russian cigarettes into an amber holder.

June said politely, 'That'll be best for everyone.'

The school had been recommended for giving confidence and poise and seemed to have succeeded. June had slimmed down. No spots now. The clear dark complexion glowed with health. Her eyes, always her best feature, smiled beneath heavy lids just faintly touched with blue cosmetic. The thick dark lashes needed no mascara. Her hair was shingled to a smooth dark cap, exposing small pretty ears, flat to her head, pearl studs gleaming against her skin. The beauticians in Geneva must be very good. They eyed each other warily. Charlotte's eyes narrowed like a cat whose territory is being invaded.

'Of course,' she said smoothly, 'I shall expect you to keep your promise.'

June's newly shaped brows rose in query.

'What promise was that?' she asked.

'That you would not see that young man . . . what's his name . . .'

'Willy Hyde-Seymour?'

There was something in the way she said it that both panicked and infuriated Charlotte. June too knew what it was to be in Willy's arms.

'The promise that you will not start that disgraceful affair again. I kept my promise, I did not tell your father. But, June, I certainly will, unless you behave.'

June smiled. She had a pretty, full lipped mouth with small white teeth, the two canines rather pointed, like a kitten's.

'So long as we understand each other.' Charlotte rose, looked in the mirror and patted her hair. 'What are you doing today?'

'Oh, nothing much. Not until after lunch. Then Daddy said I could take the car and finish my Christmas shopping. Will you be going out tonight?'

'Yes, we are going to the Debereaux'. You were invited, but of course, as we did not know when you'd arrive I couldn't give them any positive acceptance. I'm sure they would love to have you if I just telephoned Mrs Debereaux – '

'No, please,' June said quickly, 'please don't worry about me! I must go and finish unpacking. Give my love to Adelia and her mother.'

The door closed behind her. Charlotte sat down at her desk. A year ago she would have put up with anything just to know Mrs Debereaux and be invited to her parties. Now it was just another boring evening in this tiresomely crowded Christmas season when she would not be seeing Willy.

June had not told Charlotte she had arranged to pick her father up at the office. Willy would be at the office. She would not ask for him – but she was praying that they would meet.

Boots was at the reception desk, the lights shining on her golden hair. She smiled in instant recognition.

'Sir James said you were coming, Miss Peak. You're to go right in.'

June whispered, 'I did as you said. About – *you know*!'

'Didn't write?' Boots remembered instantly.

'Only once – said I was having a great time. *And* he answered.'

'Go on! What did I tell you.' She smiled, gleaming with mischief. 'Want to see him?'

'Oh, I couldn't. I mean I couldn't ask for him.'

'Oh, no. I'll get him. You'll see.' She plugged into the inter-office switchboard on her desk. 'Mr Hyde-Seymour? Is Sir James with you? Oh, if you see him will you tell him Miss Peak is here and is waiting in his office. Thank you!'

She jumped up. 'Come on. I bet that'll bring him running. I'll show you the way.'

She ushered June into Sir James' office, wished her good luck and a Happy Christmas, and went, leaving her alone. June went to the window and looked out over Kingsway.

There were no leaves on the plane trees now, only the pendulous seed bobbles like blackened Christmas decorations. The door behind her opened and she turned and saw Willy, and felt her knees go weak.

For a moment he did not recognise her – a tiny, elegant figure in a smooth black facecloth coat, lined and collared with white ermine. A cloche hat of silky white felt trimmed with black leather flowers. He could not believe it for a moment, and then he said quite sincerely, 'Why, *Squirrel*! I didn't recognise you. How absolutely tophole you look.'

'Thank you, Willy,' she said primly, but her dark eyes were brimming over with love. She was like a sea of honey to him – like the rays of the southern sun, like Balm in Gilhead. Limitless, comforting, unquestioning adoration. Between Boots's indifference and Charlotte's exacting demands he had been rubbed raw. He took an eager step towards her just as Sir James bustled in, having only just remembered he had planned to take her shopping.

'I'm so sorry, June, I really can't make it. I have to go to this do tonight with Charlotte, but I must see a chap at six for a pre-Christmas drink.'

'That's all right, Daddy, I know you're busy.' June put her hands through his arm and smiled up at him. Willy saw she had the Old Man on a string. 'You give me your list and I'll get everything.'

'That's my girl. I wish you were coming with us tonight.' And he really meant it. He was proud of this new edition of his daughter. She began to collect her shopping.

'Can I help you with your parcels, Miss Peak?' Willy asked eagerly.

'Oh, thanks awfully, but there's no need. Miss Skinner will ring down for the chauffeur.'

'It would be a pleasure. *If* you'll excuse me for a moment, sir.'

'That's quite all right, my boy,' said Sir James affably. He picked up the campaign charts Willy had put down on the desk. 'I'll run through these while I'm waiting.'

His arms full of parcels, Willy followed June to the car. Impetuously he picked up the affair where Charlotte had broken it three months before.

'Can you come to my place this evening, Squirrel darling?' He was delighted at the way the colour rose and faded in her smooth cheeks.

'Oh *Willy* – do you think we should? I promised Charlotte.'

'That sort of promise is meant to be broken. At eight?'

'So long as I'm back before they get home. About eleven?'

'I *swear*! I'll be waiting for you – eight o'clock? We'll have dinner. There are lots of very decent little places near me. Then we'll go back to the flat. Like old times.'

She nodded without speaking, shook her head warningly as the chauffeur came round to open the Rolls' door. They waited until the man went back to the driving seat.

'I've longed for you so,' said June. 'I hated being in Switzerland among all those snooty debs.'

He laughed. 'I'll bet there's not one as sweet as you. Eight o'clock then?' She turned the window down and he bent recklessly and kissed her, heard her breath catch, saw the warm colour bloom, and stood back, wishing Boots would come out and see them. He wished Charlotte could see them too – that would give *her* something to moan about. She was on, all the time, about going away together. *Now!* Just when he had worked his way in, and knew something about the business. Just when the Old Man had begun to trust him. He watched the big grey car move smoothly away and June turned and blew a kiss through the rear window.

June lay in Willy's bed satiated with love. Her watch told her it was nearly ten. She must go home.

She rose on her elbow and looked down upon him, handsome and heavy with sleep, his ruffled fair hair catching the light from the bedside lamp. She had waited so long for him, and it had been pleasure beyond all her daydreams. He had been tender, fierce and tireless, and she felt sore and exhausted and terribly happy. In Switzerland, listening to her virgin fellow pupils speculating on the men they had decided to marry, she had felt like laughing. They knew nothing of the pains and bliss of love.

Her bare arm slipped down between the bed and the wall, and her fingers touched a hard object on the carpet – thin like a pencil – and nearby another similar piece. She lifted them into the light. An expensive shagreen and ivory cigarette holder. Broken in two. Charlotte's cigarette holder which Sir James had given her for her last birthday.

Stunned, she rose slowly, and pulled on Willy's expensive dressing-gown over her pretty nakedness. Like the bed it smelled of a familiar perfume. Chypre. Charlotte always used it. A flame of fury went through her. A flame of hatred. The old – *bat!* Being so sanctimonious and all the time she had

257

been deceiving Daddy! She looked at Willy.

He was so lovely. She could understand any woman falling in love with him. But she could not forgive Charlotte's pretence of outraged virtue. After all, Charlotte was a *married* woman. Convent bred – June had very positive ideas about that.

Willy spoke suddenly in his sleep in a clear angry voice. 'Tell her anything you like, Lily, but get the old bitch off my back.'

June dropped the broken cigarette holder into her bag and got dressed, then on an after thought tipped up the waste basket and found Charlotte's desperate letter. She took that too.

She stooped, kissed Willy lingeringly, shook him awake.

'Darling I must go. I must get back before they return.'

So she kissed his sleepy, smiling mouth again. She was filled with a new sense of power. She was Sir James Peak's only daughter and he loved her. She could break his marriage if she wished. She was a rich girl, no longer timid, plain and dowdy, and she could marry anyone she wanted, and she wanted Willy Hyde-Seymour, with all his faults, more than anyone or anything in the world.

Chapter 13

Matt signed the lease for the office in Printer's Court, and stood out for a rent reduction because of the state of the place. They spent most of their weekends reading builders' estimates, and their evenings working on the Medway project for the Home Exhibition the following year. They were always dead tired and blissfully happy.

They decided to employ builders for structural alterations and repair, and to do all the decorating themselves. They invested in a typewriter, filing cabinets, and a draughty but sound secondhand Humber four-seater.

They went into two-way conferences about extra staff. They considered a messenger boy. But he would be hanging about half the day.

'An all purpose assistant,' said Helen, 'like an apprentice, is what we need. A bit of drawing and lettering, cleaning, tea-making, filing, typing, running round Fleet Street, telephone answering. Someone to be trusted with keys, post . . . someone reliable . . .'

'The Angel Gabriel,' suggested Matt. 'At least he'd have wings. Or someone worth a thousand pounds per annum. We can afford about a pound a week. Where do you expect to find this miracle?'

'There's Alfred,' Helen suggested tentatively.

'He's too good. His lettering is splendid, and he's underpaid at Peak's.'

'That's it. They give him all the dogsbodying. With us he'd have a bit of that, but also a chance at some decent work. He's always been very helpful to me.'

'Undying love.' She had the grace to blush.

'Well, I think he'd like to come. He'll never get promotion at Peak's, and he'd learn more working with you than he'll learn in a hundred years with Meakin.'

'Well, put it to him. He can only say no. We'll find three pounds a week. And Helen, tell him that if the firm grows he'll grow with it. Tell him we'll get a real dogsbody when we can afford it.'

'So long as he doesn't start writing me poetry again.'

But Alfred was delighted to come.

On the afternoon of Christmas Eve, Matt went to pick up Boots and Helen at Kingsway. At Peak's the office parties were in full fling. Each section of the firm held its own celebration with Sir James and the department heads circulating like heavenly bodies from office to office, becoming increasingly convivial as they proceeded. Matt found the girls in Space Buyer's party, very much the centre of attention.

'It will be deadly dull without you,' Lily, the switchboard girl, complained.

'You've brought a lot of glamour,' Peggy Prior conceded, a little over-dignified after her second glass of sherry. 'I think you would have done really well, Boots, if you had stuck to your shorthand and typewriting.'

'Absolutely imposs.,' Boots replied. 'It drove me nuts.'

'And what kind of work will you be doing in your new position?' asked the queenly Miss Klein.

'Theatre work. I'm going on the stage.'

'My dear child, you are very pretty, but do you have any talent?'

'Well. I've got the old face and decent legs, I can sing in tune, and I'm learning to dance, but what's more important I've actually got a job – so I reckon I've an even chance.'

No one questioned Helen. During the weeks before Christmas rumours, speculation, disbelief and disapproval circulated. Voices died at her approach. A few of the older women ignored her. She met it with the detached Redmaine stare and pretended she did not mind.

They said, 'She's got a nerve, living with a married man.'

They said, 'What! Helen Redmaine gone off the rails? I don't believe it. She's too much of a lady.' They said, 'Still waters run deep, you know.' Boots collected the best of the gossip and told Helen when they met at the ABC at lunchtime.

'Old Peggy Prior asked me if Matt's wife was taking steps, and I said yes, she was opening a dance salon.'

Their laughter helped Helen to face it all. She was happy because Boots had turned Sir James and Medway down, but Boots grumbled, 'I dunno, I haven't one well-off chap in tow. I haven't a guy who'll stand me the price of a dinner. I shall starve before the show opens, and it'll be your fault.'

She said it to make Helen laugh. She had not heard from Duncan. She and Helen needed each other these days.

But the office would miss them. For nearly a year now they had been the stars in that circumscribed world. Who would now Charleston down the corridors, flirt with all the men, hold the typists' room in thrall with her highly-spiced adventures, or mimic executives with devilish accuracy? Who would draw wicked caricatures of department heads, clients and even Sir James himself, which were fished out of waste baskets to be circulated with shrieks of laughter.

Willy Hyde-Seymour made a brief tour of the office, with hearty handshakes for the men, and a sprig of mistletoe for the girls. He did not kiss Boots, determined to match her indifference. Someone had brought a gramophone and she had climbed on to a desk with one of the junior copywriters, and was dancing with him, a vision of supple scarlet-clad body and flashing silken legs. Sir James too was halted by this exhibition, and the sight of Helen Redmaine, captured by Mr Meakin under the mistletoe, helpless with laughter. She saw Matt come in, and escaped to his side.

A Cage of Butterflies. Sir James remembered what Matt had said to him, months ago. Helen had been the rarest that year, but Boots had been the most spectacular, and already they had taken everything Peak's could teach them, and were flapping off to where the nectar was sweetest.

Sir James was relieved, now the scandal had broken in the newspapers, that Matt had left and Helen was leaving. The affair had been headlined that morning, '*LORD BRETERTON'S NIECE CITED IN ARTIST'S DIVORCE. SECRET*

LOVE NEST NEAR HAMMERSMITH', and he had used his considerable influence to keep the reporters away from the office.

Sir James and Willy wished the staff a Happy Christmas and went down to the Rolls, the new chauffeur carrying their gifts. Willy glowed – it was not so long since he had worn that grey uniform and carted baggage about, tipped his cap and opened doors, spread rugs, received orders. There was a whiff of Chypre inside the car, reminding him uncomfortably of Charlotte.

'Matt Wilson's a funny chap,' Sir James mused.

'How d'you mean?'

'Well, he fell for the Redmaine girl like a ton of bricks, Then he did not want to be involved, so he left. But now neither of them seems to mind what people think. Or if they do – they don't show it.'

'But won't her family kick up a row?' asked Willy. 'They're pretty top-drawer.'

'Old Breterton might. He made enough fuss when Sandy married Helen's mother. Not much anyone can do now. It'd be shutting the stable door after the horse has bolted, don't you think?'

Willy laughed dutifully, and the car put them down at the Savoy Grill, where Sir James's usual table had been booked for them.

'Sit down, my boy, sit down. Dry Martini to start with? I want to have a serious talk with you.' They gave their order, then Sir James said confidentially, 'You seem to have a good grasp of things at the office, W.H.S., and you get on with the clients. I have to go to the States on business, but I'm thinking of taking the wife and making it a holiday too. Brooker would be in charge, of course, but I'd want you to be a back-up. Have your own office and secretary, and take over the accounts I handle personally while I am away. D'you think you could do that?'

Willy's heart leaped. A month to get a few things running his way at the office. A month with Charlotte out of his hair to get his life re-organised. He assured Sir James that of course he could manage.

*   *   *

Matt, Helen and Boots arrived at Mill Cottage in the winter dusk. The sun had gone down in a stormy splendour behind the viaduct, and as they drove through the gateway the afterglow still touched the windows and the stream and coloured the wet slate roof like pigeon plumage. Helen sighed. It was still the most beautiful home in the world, but it was sad that Duncan would not be there.

Her mother and Cousin Millicent came rushing out to meet them as soon as the car stopped in the drive.

'Oh my dears,' cried Cousin Millicent, 'I do hope you've brought *all* the London papers – our local evening has given you a fair coverage, of course, being a local family. But nothing sensational.'

Mavis just hugged Nell, and looked at Matt and then hugged him, and they both hugged Boots and said they were delighted she had come.

'How about Uncle Royston?' Helen asked warily.

'Not a word,' said her mother. 'We're still waiting – the calm before the storm.'

The curtains were drawn, the open fire heaped with logs. Garlands of evergreen trimmed with holly, fantastically interwoven with threads of glitter and bright with clusters of red berries were hung from the oak beams.

'They're magical,' said Boots. 'Did you really make them?'

'They're so professional,' said Matt.

'Well, it's a bit like knitting, only more prickly,' said Cousin Millicent. 'We make them for here and the Minster and for the great hall at Ayling, and we sell quite a few for charity.' She was peering at the London *Evening News*, and she pushed her hair back and looked up over her glasses. 'You know your ex-wife has a remarkable flair for publicity, Matt.'

'Betty? She's not quite ex yet, Lady Millicent.'

'Bless the man, we *always* think of *Nell* as your wife now. But your ex – that is Betty – says here that she does not wish to speak of her divorce, it is too painful but she is busy making a new life. Her dance salon in Mayfair will be opening a series of tea-dances there with Ken Kenny and his Rainbow Boys, when she and Mr de Freece will be giving exhibition sessions. Tickets obtainable on request. Isn't that a perfectly splendid way of using divorce publicity?'

'Pity we can't do the same with the new studio,' said Helen wryly. 'But then we're the guilty parties. Funny, I don't feel guilty in the least.'

'The Redmaines *never* feel guilty,' said Cousin Millicent with dignity.

'We were so thrilled when Helen told us of your new job, Boots,' said Mavis earnestly. 'The stage is so much more satisfying than films, don't you think?'

'I hope so.' Boots's old, flashing, merry smile glittered. Mavis could hardly believe she was the sad waif of her previous visit. 'My one try at films was a floperoo! This is only a second touring company. Nothing very special. I'll be one up from a chorus girl – I've got some lines and one song.'

'Well, we shall *all* come to see you if it comes anywhere near. And, oh Matt, when you take the cases upstairs I have put you and Nell in the big blue guest room . . .' She met their questioning looks authoritatively.

'My own dears – when my parents wouldn't give consent to our marriage, we got engaged and I moved into Sandy's flat and they said he was a decadent aristocrat. His grandfather, the Lord Breterton of that time, said I was a jumped up little piece. Everyone said Sandy would never marry me, but of course I knew he would, and we were so happy that I was quite frightened that marriage wouldn't be as good. But it was, so I want you and Matt to think of Mill Cottage as your second home, and that there is always a room and a welcome for you here.'

'Oh, Mums,' Helen launched herself at Mavis with open arms, 'you are unique. You are the loveliest mother anyone could possibly have, isn't she Matt?'

Up in their airy blue-walled room where leaping firelight flickered on Helen's curling bronze hair, Matt remembered his own bleak northern home and his parents' joyless marriage, their bigoted fear of anything natural and generous. Always looking for a catch in it. Mavis trusted the world even when it hurt her, and trusted the people she loved. She had given Helen into his care and he could find no words to thank her, no way of repaying her except with the same love and trust she offered to him.

'You were lucky in your parents, Nell.'

'Yes, oh yes! I'm glad you knew Dads too, it makes it more complete.'

'Your mother is wonderful. She and Millicent – they're crazy, both of them, and so nice, and kind – and good.'

'Mums is a bit scared of how Uncle Royston is going to take it though. It is a wonder she hasn't heard. He doesn't usually hold his horses. The first blast of fury will come soon. I'm glad we're here with her to take it.'

'Perhaps he hasn't heard.'

'I'll bet he has. The local evening rag will have headlined it. If he hasn't seen that, then the Bish's wife will be ringing up. We shall see on Boxing Day.'

'What happens Boxing Day?'

'We always go to lunch at Ayling Place. But before lunch there is an annual cocktail party for the local bigwigs.'

'You and me?' exclaimed Matt. 'The black sheep? The scandal makers? We can't go!'

'Mums won't go without us. When she makes a stand she holds firm. He'll either tell us not to come, or he'll keep the row until we get there.'

'What would your mother prefer? That we should politely opt out. Or put our chins up and accept?'

'What do you think?'

'I think she will expect us to go.'

Their eyes met, half-smiling, and Helen said, 'I wonder about Rose Granger. D'you think we're the only people to know?'

He laughed, 'I should think it very doubtful.'

They changed for dinner and Helen put on a dress of knitted wool lace, warm and fragile, blue over lilac taffeta, so that the two colours blended like delphinium petals.

'They made it for me for Christmas, Mums and Cousin Millicent. I think I'll get married in it . . . hold on, I'll tie your tie, you're making a mess of it.' But when she did he held her so closely and they kissed for so long that when the dinner gong sounded the tie was still untied.

The telephone bell rang just after dinner. Katy popped her head in and said, 'It's Lord Breterton for you, ma'am.'

Mavis rose, paled and scurried into the hall. Helen and Cousin Millicent, without the slightest hesitation, rushed

265

after her. Matt looked at Boots.

'Do we maintain a well-bred indifference, or do we go and listen too?'

'You do what you like,' said Boots. 'I'm listening. My drama teacher says I mustn't miss out on the experience.' She darted out after them.

'Hello, Royston,' Mavis was saying tentatively. 'A Happy Christmas. I was going to ring anyway, to know if you still wanted us to come on Boxing Day.'

There was an expletive burst of sound from the receiver.

'Why not? Well, because of all the kerfuffle in the press about darling Helen and her young man, who is here with us, and whom we cannot possible leave behind.'

Another furious explosion.

'Yes, I know, Royston dear, the press are awful and never get things right. It was you I was thinking about.' A positive barrage of indignation rattled over the wire. 'Very well then. It's very charming of you. As you say, we must simply rise above it. We would love to come, of course. Yes, I *do* agree. The family must stick together. Oh, I also have a young friend of Helen's – Miss Skinner, an actress, a house guest . . . Well, thank you, we'll be with you about eleven. Goodbye, and a Happy Christmas to you, Roy . . .'

She put down the receiver and flopped into the nearest chair, utterly confounded.

'He says he is expecting us as usual on Boxing Day. That reporters are snotrags and muckshovellers and we must all come.'

'Well, I wonder what's got into him?' said Helen innocently.

'Rose Granger?' suggested Matt.

'*Who?*' said Mavis and Cousin Millicent together.

'The gardener's lovely daughter. The one who keeps the books at Ayling. Nell and I saw him kissing her in the stable yard – the first time I came here.'

'Beneath the archway,' said Helen. 'I took Matt up on to the roof to see the view. Do you think he's going to marry her?'

'Marry Rose Granger!' exclaimed Cousin Millicent. 'Old Royston! He'd never do anything so sensible. He hasn't got the nerve.'

266

'He only said that the usual crowd would be coming before luncheon for drinks, and that means the county, the hunt people and the Minster lot – oh dear, what a *frightful* barrage. But – but – just a moment . . .' She stood up. 'Why hasn't Katy brought in the evening papers.

She went to the kitchen and opened the door. Katy and her mother who had come over to help with the cooking were pouring over the local *Argus*.

'Katy? Is that the evening paper?'

Katy coloured up to her starched cap.

'I'm that sorry, ma'am, but it's all so exciting, all the family in the news like . . .' She folded the paper neatly and handed it to Mavis. 'Some of them in the village will look down their noses, but don't cast stones I say – our Miss Helen would never choose any but a real gentleman, but as for his lordship, who'd ha' thought it . . .' She gave a small shriek of delight. 'Though Mum here says he was a real terror with the girls when she was working at Ayling.'

'That'll do now, Katy,' said her mother sharply, and Mavis said they were ready for coffee and took the newspaper back to the drawing room.

The story of Betty Wilson's petition for divorce occupied a short column. There was a picture of Betty in a slinky satin dress, doing the tango, and another of Helen, looking about thirteen, on a scruffy pony. But the great local spread was headlined – '*LORD BRETERTON TO MARRY AT 60 – Lord Breterton announced yesterday that he is to marry Miss Rose Granger, 26, who works at Ayling Place as his estate secretary. Miss Granger is the daughter of Mr Joseph Granger, the head gardener, who has developed the market garden business for Lord Breterton.*'

'And we didn't guess,' said Cousin Millicent, disgusted at her own obtusity. 'That rose-coloured angora scarf he bought from us the other day. Present for the wife of a business friend, he said. All my eye and Betty Martin.'

'He was a bit shifty,' Mavis agreed. 'And then can't you remember that the Bish's wife went on about him giving Rose lifts home from work? She said it would get the girl talked about because of her position and her being so young, and Royston should have more regard for the proprieties.' They all began to laugh, then she said, 'Poor little Rose, I know just how she feels.'

'And poor Uncle Royston,' said Helen. 'He'll have an awful time with the county. All those hunting ladies who thought they'd land him!'

'*And* the Minster lot,' sniffed Cousin Millicent. 'All those church widows who have been after him for years. Their hopes dashed . . . hell hath no fury and all that.'

'Who says country life is dull?' said Matt. 'But Rose will make a luscious lady of the manor.'

Mavis glanced round at them like a general inspiring his forces before the attack. 'We must *all* go tomorrow. Everyone to the rescue . . . what a pity Duncan isn't here.'

'I say, Mums, have you thought,' Helen said excitedly, 'if Rose had a boy it would let Duncan off the hook . . .'

'Oh yes, how *lovely*!' Mavis's face lit up hopefully. 'Won't he be delighted. And I could stop worrying about him. It's been so wearying – I never could make up my mind whether I ought to make him get ready to be a lord or encourage his natural talents – like making motion pictures. We must pray for a new heir for Royston.'

'Poor little beggar,' said Cousin Millicent lugubriously.

'You must get Uncle Roy to commission a portrait of Rose, mustn't she, Matt?'

'She would certainly make a lovely portrait.'

'Matt's going to send my portrait to the R.A. this year and it will be hung on the line, and then he will get hundreds of commissions and we shall put a manager in Fetter Lane and live down here, Mums, and every so often one will be a masterpiece and be bought by a national collection.'

'She's still flying on dreams,' said Matt, 'just when I think I've got her feet on the ground.'

'Well, they sometimes come true,' Helen said. 'If one works hard enough at them.'

When the party from Mill Cottage arrived at Ayling Place on Boxing Day the drive was full of cars, and the great hall filled with people from all over the county agog with curiosity to see the future Lady Breterton, and shocked but thrilled to find that the now notorious Helen Redmaine was there, brazenly accompanied by 'that artist chap' from Hammersmith.

Mavis rallied her party. 'Stick your nose in the air and be damned to them, your father used to say, and it usually worked.'

Rose stood by Lord Breterton's side looking extremely pretty and scared to death, her parents, and her brother and sister grouped behind her, uncomfortably but solidly loyal. The room was full – not an invitation had been refused. She heard the butler announce, 'Lady Millicent Dermott, the Honourable Mrs Mavis Redmaine, Miss Helen Redmaine, Mr Matthew Wilson, Miss Boots Skinner,' and saw the heads switch round like a flock of sheep hearing a dog bark, she heard the voices subside as the Mill Cottage party swept across towards her, led by Mavis, tall, distinguished, smiling, bearing the grace and *élan* of her once great beauty, cutting a swathe through the local gentry like a scythe blade, her face alight, her arms outstretched in affectionate welcome, and nearly burst into tears of gratitude.

'Rose, my dear child, how lovely to welcome you into the family,' she kissed her on both cheeks. 'We are so delighted. I never dreamed our stuffy old Roy would have the courage to ask you.' She swung round to Rose's family, seizing Tom Granger's horny hand, enfolding the entire Granger family with the sheer charm of her well-wishing, her clear voice carrying across the now almost silent room. 'You must meet *my* family. You know Lady Millicent of course, and Nell. Duncan is away in Germany, this is Mr Wilson, Nell's fiancée – I expect you have all read that silly kerfuffle in the newspapers. The journalists have had a high old time with us all this week, but then they have so little to write about these days, poor dears, except depression, unemployment and that awful Mr Hitler . . . oh, and this lovely young lady is Miss Lillian Skinner, who is an actress and has just accepted a perfectly wonderful part in a musical comedy . . .'

She paused for breath and everyone began to talk at once.

'Thank you so much, Mavis, my dear,' said Lord Breterton and for the first time in his life he kissed his sister-in-law. Mavis blushed like a girl. Lord Breterton pulled himself together, greeted the rest of the party warmly, shook Matt's hand, squared his shoulders, beamed down at his fiancée, and

said, 'Well, my dear, we came through that all right. It wasn't
so bad, was it?'

Rose, pink with relief and gratitude, said in her soft Chiltern burr, 'Than-ank you, Mrs Redmaine, you saved my life,
for sure.'

And then the champagne was circulating and everyone was
wishing everyone a Happy Christmas.

Helen and Matt returned to London early next morning, and
spent the whole week, with the help of Alfred, decorating
their new office.

On New Year's Eve the new linoleum was down, the walls
painted white, the shelves filled with reference books, the
drawing boards in place, their stock housed in drawers and on
shelves, a secondhand typewriter and filing cabinet in the
outer office, and a plate screwed proudly to the shining white
door, Matt and Helen Wilson, Layout and Advertising
Advisers, Commercial Artists and Copywriters.

They were dead tired. Too tired to even feel triumphant in
the transformation of the grubby old attic premises. Matt said
wryly that he missed the Dickensian ambience. Then they
went to the Turk's Head, and bought Alfred a drink before
dropping him off at Charing Cross station, and driving home.

Hayman's Studio looked bare but lonely without their
working gear. They had a scratch dinner and a bottle of wine
before the blazing fire – only Matt's big easel with her half-
finished portrait, and his table of oil paints, brushes carefully
cleaned, tubes meticulously screwed tight made the room still
look like a studio. Helen's portrait was emerging against a
vague bosky woodland background. Slender, straight
backed, glancing over her shoulder, a dryad with ivy leaves
wreathing her hair, a scatter of spring flowers in her hands,
delicate head on the long stem of a neck turned over a raised
shoulder.

He had caught her exactly, eyes wide, wary, tempting, shy
. . . the way she was always poised between her varying
moods. He knew it was good. This, she told him imperiously,
was where his real work would be done. The office in Fetter
Lane was their factory.

'For the next few years the factory is where our time will be spent.'

'You'll take it to the Academy?'

'If I get it finished.'

'What are you going to call it? Primavera?'

'I thought – Portrait of the Artist's Wife.'

She glowed with pleasure. 'Oh, my darling – that's beautiful. A public statement that you love me.'

'Like being married at the Minster in the Honiton lace veil?' he smiled.

'Yes. Did Boots tell you I said that?' She laughed. 'How silly women are – why do they want everyone to know when they are happy? As though being happy isn't just enough. I never thought about *being* married before – just us together. But now it seems like a safe harbour, just in sight.' She sighed against his shoulder. 'Tomorrow it will be 1929. It's a bit scary – I want it to be a wonderful year for us. A new life. When I went away to boarding school Mums would take me to the station and I always said to her, "Will everything be all right when I'm away?" And she would answer, "Quite all right, darling". Then I'd say – "And you *will* be here when I get back." And she would say, in just the same quiet but absolutely certain manner, "Of *course* I will." Then she'd kiss me goodbye and the train would go out.' She paused, sighed, kissed him, 'I feel like that about you now. Everything will be all right so long as you are here with me.'

'It will be as right as I can make it.'

'Will there be another war?'

'What on earth made you say that?' He was startled.

'It can't happen, can it? Now Germany is disarmed. D'you know, Mum worries. About Duncan, I suppose. She has all Dads' letters from France, with those wonderful sketches and drawings he did. Some of them funny, some beautiful and some terrible. She wouldn't let us see those when we were little, but, of course, we found them. The wire with bits of men caught in it; the skeleton hands sticking out of the mud.' She gave a little shiver. 'It won't happen again will it?'

'It's past,' he said, 'no one is going to be mad enough to start that again.' He had seen things she had never seen, and heard things he hoped she would never hear. The mud, the

271

stench of chlorine, the awful reverberations of the guns.
'Come out of that witches' mood of foreboding.'

She flashed with laughter. 'Cousin Millicent says there is no point working up a sweat about something you can't do anything about, and with a bit of luck it will never happen anyway.'

'A very good philosophy.' He leaned across and switched on the wireless set just as the chimes rang out from St Paul's and the crowds circling the great cathedral burst into cheers and began to roar out 'Auld Lang Syne', as though the New Year really promised peace and prosperity and happiness and not just another chance.

During December, Boots took lessons of some kind every day. She paid for them by pawning her diamond and platinum watch, her diamond initial strap and her long string of good, cultured pearls. Sometimes she turned up at Printer's Court to help with the decorating, but was too exhausted to do more than make the tea. For both the girls the New Year was a gateway into something different. Apprehension, hope, filled them in alternate waves of anxiety and euphoria.

'It's like playing Russian Roulette,' said Boots. 'Could be great – could be disaster.'

The engagement to join the *My One And Only* company was confirmed and euphoria had ruled. But now here she was on New Year's Eve, huddled over her gas fire, every limb aching from a long and arduous dance work-out, the unknown waiting to engulf her.

She could have been in that plush little padded cell in Parkview Mansions, but she would have been alone there, because Sir James and Lady Peak were giving a large party at Ebor Place.

She could have telephoned some chap to take her out, but she was too tired. She could have gone over to see Helen and Matt but she did not want to play gooseberry and it was a long drag out to Hayman's Studios. She would just have to get used to being alone. On tour she would be alone in strange lodgings. She turned the radio on and a dance orchestra blared:

If you knew Susie, like I know Susie . . .
Oh, oh, oh what a gal.
There's something classy, about that lassy,
Oh, oh, holy Moses what a chassis . . .

She snapped down the switch. She wished tomorrow would come. She wished someone would telephone. If she went on like this she would be howling in a minute. And then the telephone did ring.

She was downstairs in the hall, whipping the receiver off, barely aware that she had moved – it was Duncan, from Germany, and it was like a rush of warm air through the cold, bleak hallway.

She said, elaborately casual, 'Oh, it's you!' He replied – in exactly the same voice, 'Yes. Hello. I just wanted to wish you a Happy New Year, and good luck on the stage. Mums told me.'

'Thanks.'

'And . . .' there was a long pause filled with faint ghost voices and ominous clicks and buzzes, and then he said, 'Oh, God, Boots, I've missed you like hell, and I just wanted to hear your voice, and say I'm sorry.'

'What for?'

'For being such a bloody, stupid idiot. All that stuff about getting you into films and getting Strauss to make you a star. I wasn't trying to con you, Boots. It did seem possible. I believed it.'

'Well,' she gave a hiccuping little sound, tears and the delight in hearing his voice mixing uncomfortably, 'you made me believe it too.'

'I don't suppose you'll want to see me now?'

The depression in his voice roused a fierce desire to protect him. Duncan was a purveyor of dreams – his self-confidence had been arrogant and absurd, but she needed it.

'You are crazy, Duncan. I'd have never thought of taking speech-training lessons if you hadn't made me, and if I hadn't Madame May would never have found me the job. And it's nothing – a third-rate touring company. It's just a lucky break.'

'But *you've* done it. *On your own*. And there was I prancing about fancying myself a big shot. And you've actually started. You're a professional now.'

'You're jealous,' she accused.

'And so why not?'

She began to laugh. 'But *you* started me! It's all thanks to you.'

But he was not to be comforted. 'I only saw how wonderfully you'd photograph. It took old May Rampton to see how funny you could be. And Mums – Mums says you make her laugh all the time. But I didn't see it, although *I* laughed. I didn't see that was a talent too. What sort of a bloody director should I make?'

'Oh, don't go on!' she snapped, losing patience. 'Who asked you to go to Germany? Strauss? He must have been impressed, or why would he bother?'

'Do you really think so?' They both had a weird feeling that all their lives they would be on this see-saw. One up, one down. The one who was up encouraging, comforting, the one who was down. Occasionally they would be level, on a wave of optimism.

'I wouldn't say so otherwise,' she snapped. 'So shut up about you. What about Germany? Is it interesting? Did you meet up with Strauss?'

'Yes. He has been great entertaining us. But that's not for me,' he said wryly. 'It's for Barry. His father is important to Strauss now that things are difficult in Germany. We went round UFA studios. It makes Greenstreet look like a church hall. The camera crews are fantastic. Makes me feel I know nothing. But Strauss did tell me he didn't see your tests. His wife Eleana has a contract in Hollywood, and he's hoping to get the chance of directing it. He can't promise me anything yet. He says I must finish at university and then come back to him.'

'Well, that's sensible. It's what your mother would like. And Madame May thinks so too.'

'I thought at least I'd get back into Greenstreet on the floor.' He said disconsolately. 'When do you start?'

'End of the month. Rehearsals start next week. At a place called Disbury – right up North. Will you come and see me when you get back?'

'Of course.'

'Duncan,' she said, 'please *don't* give up, love. I honestly couldn't bear it if you did. Like Nell says, you fly so high you're bound to crash sometimes. But don't give up.'

'Oh, darling Boots, I won't, I promise you. It's just that Berlin gets me down, when you see great directors like Strauss and know they're begging for jobs in Hollywood because their world has gone wrong, not because they've failed but because of politics.'

'Duncan – it was you who told me I had to believe in myself.'

'Yes. And you must. That's the really important thing.'

There was a long pause. She could hear voices and music.

'Where are you?'

'In a night club. With Barry. We thought it would be fun on New Year's Eve. It's awful – full of Brown Shirt Yobs and chaps dressed up as women.'

'You're kidding?'

'No, honest,' another long pause, then, 'I do love you, Boots, it wasn't all guff. I wish we were together and could really talk.'

'Me too.'

'I'll tell you soon. Happy New Year.'

'And to you. Goodbye.'

The line went dead. The rehearsal call was at nine the following morning. She must go to bed. The future did not haunt her with apprehension. She never doubted that somehow she would get by. It was Duncan and Helen – and their mother – who had brought new values into her life, and now Duncan seemed to need her as much as she needed him. It made her very happy.

At Ebor Place a red drugget had been stretched across the pavement below a striped awning leading up to the columns of the portico. It was the most important party Charlotte had ever given. But it did not give her any pleasure.

Roxana told her she was a fool to let an *affaire* get under her skin – Willy was charming, but not to be taken seriously. But she was obsessed with him. She was even jealous of his job. She had thought of it as something to keep him out of mischief

275

– she had been amazed by the drive of his ambition.

She went through the reception rooms at Ebor Place, the lights from the chandeliers glinting on the palettes embroidering her black georgette dress in the colours of a peacock's tail. Automatically she checked the banked flowers, the long buffet. The band would cost £100 at least. The caterers were the best in London. She had spent weeks organising all this. And now she was wondering how she could get through the evening without betraying herself.

In the study Sir James was seated happily in his big arm chair with June on his knee – they both smiled a welcome. June looked a picture.

She wore a dress of dark blue velvet. The smooth skin of her shoulders was framed delectably in a band of snow-white fur. She wore the treble link of pearls James had given her for Christmas.

Charlotte experienced a stab of exasperated jealousy. It was ridiculous to spend so much money on a schoolgirl. James was spoiling her and she was loving it. She seemed to become prettier every day, like a spring flower in the sun.

When James was home they were always talking and laughing together. June listened with interest when he spoke of the business. She teased him, telling him what a handsome old Daddy he was. It seemed to Charlotte as though June was taking her place.

On a sidetable stood a long florist's box which contained a dozen red roses and Willy's card, formally inscribed, wishing her success and happiness in the New Year. There was another small box, already opened, addressed to June.

'Did you have some flowers from Mr Hyde-Seymour too, June?'

'Yes,' June said, smiling proudly. 'Look . . .'

In the white fur, just above her left breast were two small pink orchids. Perfect and exquisite.

'Aren't they sweet? Don't they look lovely against my fur? Wasn't he an angel to think of me? I look really grown up now, orchids and pearls. Don't I, Daddy?'

Sir James looked up from his evening paper and laughed. He wore a velvet smoking jacket over his evening shirt. 'Yes, indeed,' he said teasingly. 'W.H.S. is a great ladies' man.

You've no idea the havoc he causes among the office girls – so you watch out, poppet. Are the roses from him too, Charlotte?'

'Oh? Oh yes. I don't know why you asked him tonight, James. After all, he's not in our crowd. He's only staff. We've never done it before. We don't want to set a precedent. Every little typist and messenger boy will begin to expect an invitation.'

'Well, you should be proud of your protégé. He's proving very useful and hard-working. Very anxious to learn – he's got a bit of class. When I go to New York I'm leaving W.H.S. in charge of all my personal work. I'm glad I listened to you. I'll go away with an easy mind.'

Fletcher wheeled in a trolley with cold food and a tureen of soup simmering on a heater.

'Shall I serve now, madam?'

'Just serve the soup – then we'll help ourselves.'

'Very good, madam.'

'And take these flowers to my room and ask Ruby to put them in water.'

'Yes, madam.'

She sat down as the door closed behind him and said, 'Come and eat, James. People will be arriving at nine and you've still to get in to your white tie – you know how mad it always makes you.'

'I'll do it for you, Daddy,' said June, taking her place. 'Mademoiselle taught us how.'

'I'm perfectly capable of tying your father's dress tie, Junie,' said Charlotte shortly. June, crestfallen, looked up at Sir James with appealing eyes.

'Now, don't you two quarrel over a tie,' he said, patting her hand reassuringly. 'Have you thought about this trip to New York, Charlie? I'd like you to come. We'd go out on one of the big Cunards – you know you enjoy an Atlantic crossing. We'll have at least a month in New York.'

She did not reply – stirring the cup of hot soup without attempting to taste it.

'We'll stay at the Plaza, and see all your friends and some shows, and you can go shopping down Fifth Avenue while I'm getting through my business appointments . . .'

'No,' said Charlotte, 'I really *can't* James. It will mean cancelling too many dates . . . and there's so much to see to here.'

'But Charlotte,' said June eagerly, '*I'll* be here – I'll look after *everything*. I really can. You go off with Daddy and enjoy yourself.'

Charlotte felt herself going white. Her spoon rattled against the soup plate, so that she let it drop and it chopped the finely scrolled gilt edge.

'Oh hell!' she exclaimed. 'Look what you've made me do! How can you take over the house? You'll be back in Switzerland.'

'But didn't Daddy tell you? Oh, Daddy, you *promised!*' June said reproachfully to Sir James. 'We think that I've had enough finishing. I'm not going back.'

Charlotte took out her cigarette case, extracting one of her Russian cigarettes and began to scrabble nervously in her handbag.

'Oh, I forgot! I've lost my holder. Ring the bell, will you, June, and tell Fletcher to go up and bring my amber one. Ruby will give it to him.' She pushed her plate away. 'I'm not hungry. Besides, we shall be eating at supper time. You don't mind if I smoke?'

June put down her fork. 'You mean your shagreen holder? The one Daddy gave you? I found it. I'd forgotten, I'm sorry.' She opened her own evening bag and took out the two pieces of slender green tube and held them out to Charlotte. 'I'm afraid it got broken somehow.'

Their glances met, locked, then Charlotte glanced away. She stretched out a hand for the broken pieces – it was trembling visibly.

'Shall I get it mended for you? I could take it along to Asprey's tomorrow.' June was smiling at her steadily. A year – six months ago she had been overawed by both her stepmother and Ebor Place. Now, tenacious and shrewd beneath her soft, new prettiness, she really resembled Sir James.

'Where did you find it, poppet?' asked Sir James.

'It was under the bed,' June said, and smiled again at Charlotte with pity – and contempt.

Charlotte rose abruptly. She had to get out of the room.

She felt she was stifling. 'You must forgive me, Jimmy dear. I've got so much on my mind with this party. You two just carry on and finish your dinner. I'll have some coffee sent to my room.'

'Well, don't overtire yourself, Charlie,' Sir James said kindly. 'Have a nice lie down. There's plenty of time before people start to arrive.' When she had gone he shook his head. 'I can't think what's got into her,' he said. 'She's all nerves. I can't understand why she won't decide to come. She has heaps of friends in New York.'

'I think she'll come, Daddy,' June said quietly. She rose and turned out the main lights, leaving the table lit by the rosy glow of the small red-shaded table lamps. 'There – now what will *you* have? Salmon? It is delicious. I must say it's awfully cosy here, just the two of us . . .'

Sir James patted her hand, and poured the wine, and was conscious again of being *comfortable*. That was it – comfortable.

Two hours later, pleasantly replete, wearing his superb evening suit, his tie beautifully fixed by June, he stood between his two women to receive their guests. Charlotte had apparently recovered, and was smiling brilliantly. Sir James was very proud of them both.

The night was cold but dry, most of the guests were well wrapped as they came through the main entrance door. Standing a few steps up the main staircase Charlotte saw Willy, his fair head hatless, with no overcoat, spring two at a time up the steps, crossing the hall, grasping Sir James's hand.

'I say, what a perfectly splendid house this is,' he grinned mischievously. 'I didn't see much of this part of it when I worked here. Lady Peak – how kind of you to ask me.'

Charlotte extended her hand and, smiling automatically, said, 'My husband has told me you have made a great success at the office. He says you're a real help to him.'

'That's terribly kind of you, sir,' Willy said ingenuously. He looked at her like a pleasant young stranger. It seemed impossible that only a few hours ago she had been lying naked in his arms.

'You know my daughter, June?' said Sir James. 'Of course, you met her in the office before Christmas.'

'Before that – I once drove her to the dentist.'

June giggled excitedly, and said, 'Hello. How awfully jolly that you could make it.' She looked as pretty as a kitten with a bow round its neck, his pink orchids nestling into her white fur.

Above, in the ballroom, the Rainbow Boys were playing a foxtrot, and he said eagerly, 'I say, Miss Peak, have you really to stay and welcome all these people? Can't you come and dance with me?'

'Run along, Junie,' Sir James said indulgently. 'There's no need for you young people to stay here. Get the party going. After all – it is New Year. We old ones will do the poodlefaking. You youngsters go and have a good time.'

'That's very good of you, sir,' said Willy. He caught June's willing hand and they went off to dance. Charlotte felt the smile would set permanently on her face and that the line of chattering, elegant, boring people would never come to an end.

Chapter 14

Charlotte woke up late after the New Year party at Ebor Place, with an appalling headache and a feeling of impending disaster. She was facing decisions which she did not want to make. She did not want to leave London – the thought of putting the Atlantic Ocean between Willy and herself was unendurable. She had to decide whether she could continue life as James's wife or give up the advantages of being Lady Peak. She had fantasised about a life with Willy which she knew was impossible, and last night he had shown her pretty plainly that he thought so too. Last night she had almost committed the unforgivable – she had nearly made a public scene.

He had danced with June nearly all evening, and had at last come to claim her, paying polite homage to his hostess. She stumbled in his arms, unable to follow his steps.

'Are you all right, Lady Peak,' he had asked solicitously Anger flamed through her. 'Willy – we have to talk.'

'People will notice if we leave the floor.'

'Then they will have to notice – I have to talk with you. I'm desperately unhappy. Shall I tell you why? Or shall I announce to the whole room why? And Sir James?'

His fair head was bent towards her politely; he recognised hysteria. He said courteously, 'All right, Charlotte. Let's talk.'

He followed her to the little study. There was a trolley of drinks there, and she went across and lifted the whisky bottle. The lip of the glass clattered ominously against the bottle mouth.

'Allow me,' Willy said courteously, and took the bottle from her to pour a drink.

'Willy, James is pressing me to go with him to the States. I don't know what to do.'

'Well, why don't you go? You'd have a great time. You've loads of friends there. I only wish I could go.'

She wanted to tell him she knew he was seeing June, but was afraid of the tensely controlled hysteria within her.

'It's becoming too much for me, darling,' she whispered dramatically. 'You know we must be together, for always, as, we planned when we were at Roxana's . . .'

He had left the door open and they could see late guests arriving. He looked straight past her.

'I say, there's old Medway and his wife. We must go and say hello. And I must ask her to dance . . .'

Her control broke down into melodrama. 'Willy, for God's sake listen *to me*. Meet me tomorrow. We'll have lunch. At the Mayfair. One o'clock.'

He gave a little edgy smile.

'That's a bit daring, isn't it, old thing? We might be seen.'

'Willy, if you don't come I don't know what I shall do. Kill myself, I think.'

He patted her arm gently. 'Don't talk such nonsense, Charlie.'

The band was playing a frantic Charleston. Her cheeks were tear-stained and streaks of mascara clownishly blurred her eyelids. He knew she was near to breaking point. 'Better go upstairs, darling, and make some repairs – before anyone notices.' He glanced round the hall, kissed her quickly on the side of her trembling mouth. 'Don't want to spoil your lovely party. Don't you worry about lunch tomorrow – I'll get my secretary to book the table. Looking forward to it.'

She bolted up the stairs – he thrust his hands into his pockets and, whistling to the band, went back into the ballroom in search of June.

Charlotte was at the Mayfair Hotel on time. She ordered a dry martini and waited, glancing every other minute at her diamond encrusted watch. One o'clock came and went. She checked with the *maître d'hotel* but he told her that no table had been booked in the name of Mr Hyde-Seymour. She

282

caught a glance of amused sympathy in the knowledgeable Italian eyes when he asked whether she would like a small table by herself.

There had been a mix-up, she said frantically, would they call her a taxi. He would be at the office. Should she go to the office, confront him there, and have a showdown with James? That would be crazy. She would ring him from the flat. She would make him understand. He had no right to treat her like this. He owed everything to her.

The key would not fit the lock. Frantically she tried to force it, but it was useless. She called the porter. The locks had been changed. Mr Hyde-Seymour had given him express intructions that no one was to be let in without his personal authority.

Charlotte walked back to Ebor Place through the cold January air. The caterers' van was outside – they were removing the last traces of the New Year party. She went upstairs to her room. She would go to New York with James. She might stay there, or she might go to the Riviera with Roxana. She began to weep, unable to face the truth, that from the beginning she had known that even if Willy were capable of love he certainly had never loved her, and that it could not possibly last.

Sir James and Charlotte sailed for New York on the *Aquitania* in the first week in February and June went to Southampton to see them off.

Willy had been at Waterloo, armed with a bouquet for Charlotte and varius last minute papers, letters and cablegrams for Sir James, the picture of efficiency and well-bred consideration. He had winked at June as the train drew out.

The stewards were striking the gongs and calling to the visitors to go ashore. Her stepmother's tired and tragic face unnerved her slightly. She had not meant to hurt anyone – she just wanted to marry Willy.

'You don't really think he'll marry you?' Charlotte blurted out, almost as though she read her thoughts.

'I *know* he will.'

Charlotte went white. 'So that's how it is?'

'How it is?' June repeated, puzzled, then laughed. 'Oh! No. But I wouldn't mind if it were. I just think I'm his best bet, that's all.'

'Would you have told your father – about Willy and me?'

'Oh yes, if you'd told on me.'

'I may still do that.'

'It doesn't matter now,' June said defiantly. 'Willy's important to Daddy too. In a different way so am I. He needs us both now.'

The visitors were disembarking; passengers were throwing streamers down as though to tie the great ship to the shore.

'You're so sure of yourself,' cried Charlotte. 'It's because you're young. I tell you he'll never make any woman happy.'

'But I'm not expecting happiness,' June explained. 'Willy wants success and he's got no money. I want him, and I've got some money – and I'm Daddy's daughter. If we both get what we want I think we'd have a fair chance.'

'He wanted me too,' Charlotte cried painfully.

June did not reply – Charlotte could not bear the pity in her eyes.

Sir James bustled up anxiously.

'Off you go, Junie. Or they'll have the gangway up. Goodbye my darling. I'll telephone you.'

She kissed him, promised to look after everything, and touched Charlotte's white cheeks with her lips in formal affection and bade them goodbye. The great ship was pushed and bullied by the tugs into midstream and she went to catch the boat train back to London.

She had just sat down to a solitary dinner in Sir James's small study when the telephone rang. It was Willy calling.

He was bursting to talk to someone about his first day in charge – or almost in charge – of the office. She invited him to dinner, consulted Fletcher about the wine, and went to her room to choose her prettiest dress.

Boots travelled up from Euston to Disbury on a bleak February day, meeting the rest of the cast of *My One And Only* already staking their claims to corner seats in a second-class carriage. All watchful and critical of the newcomer, jealous that she had lines, and a song and a few more pounds a week, and no known experience. They all suspected she was Moss Hartley's girl.

There was the leading comedian, Billy Batley, described in *The Stage* as 'YORKSHIRE'S BIGGEST LAUGH'. A neatly dressed little man with dyed red hair and a north-country accent, mechanically affable, greeting the chorus. 'Hello girlies, here's your Uncle Billy again!' There was quite a lot of kissing.

The juvenile lead was a good-looking boy called Maurice, with an affectedly posh accent, looking a little blue on the cold February morning without an overcoat. Boots made a place next to him and shared her fur coat over his knees, and her pack of sandwiches, which he wolfed into as though he was starving and, she thought, he probably was.

The leading lady was an experienced and pretty actress with a wary eye on Boots's ebullient youth.

Boots had known these people at rehearsals but now it was different, like suddenly belonging to an eccentric but united family whose jealousies were shelved for the sake of the show.

Saturday and Sunday they rehearsed in a school hall, Monday morning in the theatre. Monday night they opened first house at six-thirty.

At rehearsal the stage had seemed enormous, cold and dreary. But miraculously, tonight it came alive. The painted background *was* the blue Mediterranean, the stage, the terrace of the Hotel Grande Luxe, Nice, and she and the other girls rich, young guests skipping about in their petal hued chiffons, forgetting the goose pimples on their bare arms and the old theatre smell of grease paint and years of thickly settled dust.

This was different. This was it. She looked through the peephole at the bleak half empty Monday night first house and wanted to die.

'Hey,' said one of the girls. 'Pipe those two boys in the stalls! Don't look like locals to me.'

Boots looked again – Barry Goldman's thin, dark elegance, and beside him the familiar yellow polo neck, the arrogant tilt of the curly coppery head, the long stretched-out legs, the wary, watchful, highbred boyish face.

'Oh *Duncan!*' she squealed. 'He's come!'

'You know him?'

'He's my boyfriend.' She was incoherent with gratitude. He'd come all the way from Oxford. Oh, bless him, bless him, bless him, her idiot darling. The only person – apart from Madame May – who knew, *really* knew what it meant to want to do this mad thing.

She had the opening number. The orchestra at the Theatre Royal was strong on brass and for one awful moment Boots thought her voice would never reach above it. But Maurice said, 'Pitch it up at the top shelf, love.' The girls were already singing and tapping on stage. Billy Bradley was pushing her forward, saying, 'You're on kiddo, sock it to them,' and she sailed into the lights every inch of her determined to charm and cajole and bulldoze the audience with the vitality and effrontery with which she had met every challege of her young life.

The weeks Sir James spent in the United States were probably the happiest and certainly the most comfortable Willy had ever known.

Every Friday he picked up June, accompanied by Ruby, an ally totally to be trusted, and very tight lipped. At Whitelands they lived like any rich young married couple spending winter weekends in their country home, and they slept cosily together in June's pretty quilted satin bed.

At the office he was equally successful. Mr Brooker, a desk worker and costing expert, was happy to leave Sir James's country to Willy who was in his element in it. The cosseting of clients, the consultations with advertising chiefs and newspaper men were sheer joy to him. There was something of the same exhilaration he felt at the gambling tables.

He knew he was good at the job and that he would be better. He dreamed of being his own boss by the time he was forty; of a streamlined agency employing the best brains and talents he could afford. Specialise in a handful of very rich companies. Cut out all the small trading firms that spent little money and took up so much time.

He was suprised to receive no account from his garage, and was told by the proprietor that Miss Peak had told him to send on the bills to Ebor Place as usual. 'Apparently she is looking after the accounts while Sir James and Lady Peak are away.' He wondered what would happen when the rent fell due at the end of the month. It was paid. Charlotte had always reminded him of every penny of the money she lavished on him. June never mentioned it.

The girls he had amused himself with and the women he had exploited always wanted to talk about themselves. But June just made him comfortable, listened to his every word with wide-eyed interest, and when she made remarks they were pertinent and intelligent and fed him a great deal of information about Sir James's business tactics. And she was still blissfully eager and ecstatic when he made love to her. Dear little Squirrel! She certainly knew how to look after a chap.

It ended early in February. Drifts of snowdrops were breaking into blossom in the lawn outside the window, and Willy and June were sitting at breakfast before he drove into London. Porridge, grilled kidneys, bacon and sausages, fresh coffee, everything served impeccably by Ruby in her crisp pink cotton morning dress and starched cap and apron. June was sitting opposite him.

She said suddenly, 'Daddy telephoned – last week. He will be sailing tomorrow.'

Sometimes – in the Whitelands lotus land – Willy forgot that this was not his home; that he was not master of this fine house. He came to earth with a jolt.

'That means back to poverty now,' he joked bitterly. 'Why didn't you tell me?'

'I thought I wouldn't upset your last weekend here. He said he would either cable or telephone you at the office this morning.'

He threw down his paper. 'I'd better be moving then!'

'You go alone. Ruby and I will stay on and see everything is tidy here.'

He grinned. 'Remove the evidence, eh? Right, I'll have another cup of coffee. I'll be able to put my foot down, driving alone.'

A shadow crossed her face. She objected to unnecessary risks. But she would not plague him with pleadings about taking care and warnings about safety.

'I suppose,' he said, 'I ought to send your stepmother some flowers – to Southampton, when they dock.'

'She won't be there,' June said, pouring his coffee. 'She is not coming back to London.'

'You mean – *never*?'

'Daddy didn't say. He just said she was staying on with her friend Roxana Cosimo for the present, and then going with her to the South of France.'

'She's a terrible old bag – that Roxana.'

'And *very* rich.'

'Yeah,' Willy sighed, remembering the white villa above the blue sea and the ochre rocks, and the pool, and the smart, rich and famous people who crowded into Roxana's high-spending life. 'An old woman like that wouldn't have a friend in the world if she was poor. With her tongue – and that wig!' He laughed bitterly. 'But she's very, very rich, and all because some millionaire was sap enough to marry her years ago.'

'You know her quite well, then?' June handed him his coffee.

'Not really. I met her once. I can't remember when.'

'Charlotte stayed with her at Juan-les-Pins when I was in Scotland with Adelia Debereaux last year.'

'Oh yes?' he said indifferently.

June had guessed that he had been with Charlotte and that he knew she knew. But neither of them ever mentioned it. June never made an unpleasantness if it could be avoided. She knew all about Willy now. He was as transparent to her as a piece of glass. She could see the devious thoughts sliding through his handsome head like goldfish in a bowl. Often, like startled goldfish, they darted away so that he need not face up to them. Sometimes it puzzled her that in spite of this she loved him so much.

'Darling Squirrel,' he said, and pulled her up into his arms. 'Thank you for giving me such a wonderful time. It has been lovely. Like having a real home of my own. It's a pity it has to end.'

Her eyes filled with quite genuine tears. 'D'you mean you don't want to see me again?'

'Oh *no*! Of course not. But I shan't be able to come here like this. What would your father say? He thinks the world of you . . . and he's beginning to give me great opportunities. Of course I'll be able to take you out, and call occasionally. But we must be careful.'

'I'm sorry, Willy, but I think Daddy already knows about us.'

His mouth dropped. Suspicions shot through him. 'You didn't tell him?'

'Of course not.' She sounded so shocked that he should doubt her loyalty. 'But maybe Charlotte did.'

Willy went crimson, rose to his feet, crushing out his cigarette, walking excitedly about the room. 'The bitch,' he said. 'The bitch! She thinks if he chucks me out I'll go running back to her.'

'He won't give you the sack. Not if I ask him not to.'

He dropped back into his chair. 'What makes you think he knows about us?'

'Well, when he told me that Charlotte was leaving him, he said to remember that whatever I did, or decided to do, he wanted me to know that he loved me and would always stand by me. Why should he say that?' Then very quietly she said, 'Willy, I'm going to have a baby.'

In the silence that followed June thought he must hear her heart beating. He went white. It was like the sudden flick of a barbed whip.

'It isn't true!'

'Yes, I think it is.'

'But I fixed it for you. I sent you to that women in Wimpole Street – I thought you were taking care of that.'

'Sometimes,' her voice was barely a whisper, 'one forgets.'

'I told you never to take a chance . . .' he thrust his hands into his pockets. They were shaking with anger and frustration. Then on a gleam of hope, 'Maybe it's not too late. The woman in Wimpole Street . . . maybe . . .'

'No,' said June, and she looked him straight in the eyes and her voice was firm and clear. 'I won't. Last year, before I went to Switzerland I thought you loved me. My letters told you that – if you read them.'

'I do, Squirrel, really, but you must understand . . .'

'Yes, you love me in your way. Well, if you leave me now I'll still have something, won't I? My baby. Daddy will stand by me. I'm all he has now. But I don't think he *could* keep you on if we're not married.' She smiled tremulously and added, 'I think you should think about it, Willy. I'm really quite a catch.'

She made him feel ashamed and he never allowed himself to feel ashamed. And a bit of a fool. Yet there was something reassuring about being accepted for what he was, and what at bottom he knew himself to be and yet still be lapped in love.

'I've got no money, and you're used to all this . . .'

'I'll still have all this.'

'Squirrel, I've *got* to think and I've got to face your father. He's put a lot of trust in me . . . you can imagine how I feel . . . just give me a little time . . .'

She knew that he could bolt. She knew how he could tire of anything – and walk away from it. But she also knew, because now she was using her brains and not her heart in her battle for Willy, that it would destroy him to walk away from Peak's Publicity. That the advertising game was his element and no better chance could be offered to him. He would be Sir James's son-in-law. The father of his grandchild. His stake in the future. Who better to take charge when the Old Man retired?

'He'll be back next Saturday. I shall go down to meet him at Southampton. I was hoping you'd come with me. So we could be together.' She paused. 'But if you're leaving me then I must know – before he comes home – before I see him again.'

He stood by the window looking out across the terrace, and the lawns spreading to the river, the black cedars sweeping down like great birds' wings. The white boathouse housing the sea-going cruiser which no one had ever used until he came. All this. He turned slowly and looked at June.

She was sitting examining the highly polished nails of her plump little hands. Capable and solid, and her mouth in repose was like her father's, only soft and sweet with youth where Sir James's lips were thick and sensual. But it could shut with the same self-will and determination.

She was not Boots Skinner, fine and quicksilver, elegant and London-sharp, with eyes like clear sea-water and a perfect mouth that twitched with mockery and mischief. He knew that if Boots had let him make love to her, if she had only once showed by a gleam that she wanted him as he wanted her, he would not have given a damn about anything else. The job, Sir James, June and her pregnancy – that he would have told Charlotte to go to hell months ago. But she did not care – she did not want him. She never had.

'Squirrel,' he said shakily, and kissed June with an unusual tenderness and regret. She was a nice little thing, and a temptation to him. But she was not the one who haunted the times between sleeping and waking, when real longing stirred his body, and the half-dreams and unbidden lusts were agonising and empty with loss.

June watched him drive away, her hands clamped over her trembling lips. Had she brought it off? Had she overplayed her hand. Was it a real pregnancy?

Supposing it was just one of those alarms that did not happen. A girl had been through that at the school in Switzerland; and then it had been all right after all, and everyone pretended it hadn't happened. Don't let it be like that God, she prayed. Let it be a real baby. I want it – and Daddy needs it like he needs me. With a child she could hold both Willy and her father for ever. Willy would struggle. He might even escape – but not for long. Not if she was the one who was not deceived, but who would always forgive him, always comfort and care for him, then he would come back to her like a child looking for a long-lost mother, which she supposed, in a way, she really was.

When Sir James rang through to the office from New York he told Willy that he would be sailing the following day and would dock at Southampton on the Saturday.

'Yes,' Willy said, dry-mouthed, 'so Miss Peak told me.'

'I thought,' Sir James said affably, 'you were on first name terms.'

'Of yes, of course. June.'

'She told me you had been seeing her.' No outburst of accusation, rage or offended paternalism. 'Well, I'm glad she is having a good time. More than I have been in this bloody town. Can't get a drink without paying through the nose for it and then it could be liquid poison. I'm too old to crawl around speakeasies.'

Willy started to breathe again. This, then, was how it was to be played. The wily old devil. Sir James spoke of a few business matters and said he would see Willy at the office the following Monday. Willy said impulsively, 'I thought I might drive June down to meet you, sir?'

Sir James paused before he spoke.

'If,' he said slowly, 'that is what my Junie wants. Well, arrange it between you. Stay the weekend at Whitelands. June said she's opened it up. Give us a chance to talk. Don't drive yourself. Take the Rolls. Look forward to it.'

Willy put the receiver down. Pulling down his own coffin lid. Why in hell was he thinking in these terms of traps and death? June did not telephone him during that day, and when he went back to his flat there were no messages.

She was already in bed – listening to the Savoy bands she said, when he finally telephoned. He could imagine her, soft fleshed with sleepy dark eyes, wearing one of the beautiful satin negligees she loved, trimmed with marabout, ostrich fronds or rich dark lace. He longed to be with her in all that silken, scented softness.

'Your father telephoned. I asked if I might come with you to meet him on Saturday, and he said yes, and to take the Rolls.'

He heard her small, satisfied sigh.

'That will be lovely.'

'He asked me to stop over at Whitelands until Monday.'

'Oh goody. Then we'll get everything arranged?'

'It is, isn't it? Arranged. Everything? It's settled? That we get married? I mean – we have no choice.'

'You have a choice, Willy.'

'Oh, come, Squirrel. You know I couldn't leave you in the lurch.' But you could, she thought, and smiled a bitter and tender smile. It was the oddest proposal of marriage.

'It's OK then? Settled? Are you happy now, Squirrel?'

'Very, very happy, Willy darling.'

He put down the receiver and it seemed to clang like a prison gate. That was it then. The boys at the Weirside Inn would bust themselves laughing. He'd made a great deal out of making little Squirrel an honest woman; more than ever Jimmy would out of his shady inn.

He poured himself a drink, and started to go through the pile of newspapers he had brought from the office, checking the advertisements inserted by Peak's, examining and criticising the work of other agencies, and came upon a copy of *The Stage*. There was a notice on the front page.

The first touring company of MOSS HARTLEY'S successful production of MY ONE AND ONLY has been booked for a tour of the South Coast resorts. Boots Skinner, the young soubrette who has scored such a success on the northern tour, is joining the first touring company replacing Miss Lucy Lyle who has engagements elsewhere. This talented newcomer can be seen at the Queens Croydon, where the second company which has been touring in the North, has been booked for one week.

It was just after ten. The show at Croydon would be nearly over – he would have no time to drive out there. But he got out his car and drove over to Becker Street. Mrs Murphy a crisp little Irish woman, with grizzled grey hair, opened the door on a chain and peered out at him.

'If it's Miss Skinner you're wantin', she's not back from the theayter yet.'

'What time does she usually get back?'

'Sure and I wouldn't know. She's likely to go out to supper before she comes home. She often does. With all these chaps buzzing about her, she's out to all hours. It's no use you waitin' at all. Shall I tell her your name?'

'No, thank you.'

Who the devil was she playing about with now? No use going out to Croydon. He stopped at the nearest pub, and sat there drinking until closing time, bought a bottle of whisky to take in to the car, drove back to Becker Street and parked where he could see the door of Number 3, smoking one cigarette from the stump of the last, and taking an occasional nip from the bottle. It was a raw cold night. Even his fine warm overcoat and lined gloves could not keep out the cold. He was grateful for the bottle of whisky.

He had to find out who it was she was with. Some new fellow he did not know? Someone rich with a splendid car and money to burn? She had finished with the Old Man and Tommy Medway – Medway had bored him about it through a long business lunch. Or was it one of her theatre trash?

He supposed this crazy hunger for her *was* love. He had to make a choice tonight, and he knew if she gave him half a chance, what the choice would be. He sat there grimly, watching the door for her return.

After the show Boots changed to go home. Duncan came to pick her up – it was the last night of her last week with the Northern Touring Company.

The girls had been very nice about her new job. It was sheer luck that the part in the First Touring Company had become vacant. She felt a bit sad at leaving. It was her first experience of the extraordinary closeness of theatrical companies, the sharp rivalries and passionate friendships. She had learned a great deal, and she felt a bit down at having to leave them all. There was a bottle of sherry and a cake in the dressing room between houses, and promises to keep in touch, wondering if they would ever meet again.

The theatre emptied. The girls went out, one by one, bidding her goodbye and good luck, and then Duncan appeared, his arms full of spring flowers, wearing a new and splendid camelhair jacket over a new and well-cut suit. He heaped the flowers into her lap and beamed. 'How come?' she questioned.

He preened slightly.

'Well, it was the Old Monster. Uncle Royston. He wrote saying he was delighted to hear of my progress this term and that he had decided to increase my allowance. He said he was glad that I was really preparing myself for taking a responsible position in life, in the event that I should one day inherit Ayling.'

'And will you?' Boots asked, horrified. The great grey house with its hundreds of rooms and acres of farmland terrified her.

'No, of course not, silly.' He kissed her gently. 'Don't look so scared. No – I am working hard, because if I can get university finished in July, then Barry says the new sound studio will be opening this autumn in Greenstreet, and he'll work there, and he'll tell his old man he wants me back with him. And guess what?'

'Go on,' she was closing her make-up box, looking round to be sure she had everything.

'Strauss is back.'

She swung round, eyes wide and bright. 'In England?'

'For a few days. He's on his way back to Germany to settle up his affairs. Eleana's got a five-year contract with Metro and they signed him up to direct her first picture. He's a big shot again. In January it was scary – nothing for him in Europe – no reputation in America. Written off as a has-been. That's Hollywood for you.'

'If he wants you to go out there – will you go?'

'Of course. It would be a chance in a lifetime. Boots, he *saw* your tests . . . Barry said he came marching into the studio and demanded to see them, and they had to scurry round finding them, and when Strauss saw them he was delighted. He said you photographed perfectly. He said the last take, the one you fluffed, remember? The telephone business? Was a Lulu. I thought you'd screwed it up. But when they found your pictures, the card actually *said, "Natural comedienne, eminently photogenic."* Strauss said to tell you that he'll remember if anything comes up. Boots – you could come too . . . To Hollywood!'

'Not *yet*, Duncan.'

She saw dismay in his eyes. He always rushed precipitously towards the future while she went carefully, testing the heat. She thought primly to herself that she was really years older than him, not two years younger. 'I'm not ready yet. I've so much more to learn. You've got to wait, Dunky darling.'

'Oh no,' he said, distraught. '*I* must go, Boots. If he asks me. Hollywood is where everything is happening. They're running ahead with sound technique. They've got the best brains in Europe over there at the moment.' He sat down, and drew her back to her chair, and they sat opposite each other, their faces inches apart, talking, as they so often did. 'Thrashing it out' they called it. 'I am pretty sure he'll want me. I was very useful to him. His English is pretty shaky, and my German is good now. It's one thing, Boots, just translating – but it was more than that. I understood his ideas, what he wanted, and I could make the actors, and the crew understand. If you don't come, we may be apart for years.'

'Well, then,' she said slowly, 'we'll really know what we mean to each other, won't we?'

They were like children, clinging together for comfort. She put her hands into his, bowed her forehead against his.

'It's a funny sort of thing between us, isn't it Duncan?' she said. 'Yet we love each other, don't we?'

'Yes. We do. But you won't throw everything up and come with me and I wouldn't want you to. Not if you didn't want to. It would be letting yourself down.'

'Are we too selfish?'

'Aren't people who can do things well always selfish?'

'No. Helen and Matt are both clever and ambitious – but they would die if they were separated. Yet we do love each other.'

'People are different – love isn't always the same. Don't cry, Boots! I've not gone yet. Will you marry me, Boots?'

'This is crazy!' she said angrily. '*We* don't have to get married, now, or ever for that matter. *We* can do what we want to! We're artistes, Madame May says.'

He laughed at her vehemence.

'We could get engaged.' He grinned, and her exasperation died. 'It'd keep the chaps from pestering you.'

'And the girls from pestering you?' she said suspiciously. 'Do they?'

'You bet,' he said and added, 'It's not just my irresistible charm, sweetheart. At Oxford, people know I might be Lord Breterton one day. And at Greenstreet Studios, even a dogsbody who has the ear of the director could be useful. But, yes, they do.'

She had never thought of this before.

'They'd better not let me catch them.' She frowned and they both began to laugh.

'If I go in the autumn, I'll be making trips back. And you could come out – between engagements. Maybe there'll be a passenger flight to New York soon, like there is to Paris. You could come out to Hollywood and meet all the stars . . .'

'Oh, Dunky, for heaven's sake! We must be serious.' She

put her hand over his smiling lips, and he kissed the inside of her palm, and she snatched it away. 'We've got to be serious. We've got to work hard and not *mind* being apart. We could get married, and I could turn down this part, and spend my time ironing your socks. Or I could work, and you stay at Ayling and try to turn me into a second-hand lady.'

'It wouldn't work.' He was serious now. 'But if we are apart – there will be other people.'

'But will they matter, if we really need each other?'

'If you needed me, I'd come from the ends of the earth.'

'Me too.'

They dropped their armour of frivolity.

'It's not what we always *want* to do,' she said painfully. 'it's what we *can* do, and doing it *well, and sticking to it.* We have got to take what is offered and fit our lives round it. Am I talking tommy-rot?'

'No. But one day, Boots, they'll have to fit work round us. I'm sure of that.'

Her eyes glowed.

'But we will be engaged – it'll be a pact between us.'

She loved him when he talked nonsense, but she loved his single-minded ambition even more.

She sighed – they would never be quite happy apart, but they would never be quite happy unless they could grow separately to their individual heights. 'I'm so hungry,' she sighed, 'can we go and eat.'

They had supper in one of the more expensive Soho restaurants, on the strength of Lord Breterton's unexpected change of heart.

Over the *Crêpes Suzette*, Duncan said, 'I was a bit puzzled by Uncle Royston's letter. Saying *'in the event that I should inherit Ayling'*. He's always thought of it as a certainty before.'

'Ah,' said Boots, with a flash of comprehension, 'maybe because he's going to marry that girl.'

'You mean – she might be having a baby?'

'Well, she could . . .'

'Oh, *Boots*! Let's drink to that.'

In Becker Street Willy, hungry, cold, and rather drunk stayed on in a haze of sullen anger. He would wait, he would have it out with her, and he did not care who brought her home – not if it was Sir James himself, and it meant his job, or June or anything on earth.

It struck two o'clock from Big Ben in the silence of the black March morning, when he heard the sound of a motor bicycle turning into Becker Street, a sidecar combination which came to a halt outside Number 3. He watched stupefied as a tall, graceful boy dismounted and lifted Boots out of the sidecar, unwinding a long college scarf from his face to kiss her. Something seemed to explode inside him.

'It's that damned young clown Redmaine,' he said and jerked open the car door, and went across the pavement towards them, his powerful shoulders hunched like an angry fighting bull, shouting belligerently, 'Hey – you there, you – boy, I want a word with you . . .'

Boots and Duncan stopped in their tracks, heads turned, wary as two young deer. Willy stood and raged at them. He did not know what he said. She had provoked him, she had teased him, she had made him look a fool. What had he done to her to be treated like this? She was a cheat, a liar, a prick teaser, a cheap little gold-digger, getting into bed with any rich old fool for the sake of a new dress . . .

Duncan said in his clear, authoritative Redmaine voice, 'Who the devil is this, darling? Someone you know?'

Willy hit out at him, catching the side of his face, so that he grabbed at the area railings, but as Willy lunged forward Duncan stuck his foot out neatly, between his ankles bringing him crashing to the damp pavement, sliding along towards the gutter.

'That's neat!' said Boots.

'Learned it at school,' said Duncan. 'I can't fight. Trip 'em up and scoot for it. Had we better do that now?'

She shook her head. Willy had dragged himself unsteadily to his feet, and he stood rocking, burying his face in his hands, his big shoulders heaving with sobs. Boots went up to him, and tapped his shoulder.

'Don't' she said, 'I'm sorry.'

He did not reply.

'Duncan and I are engaged,' Boots said.

Willy raised a white, shamed, furious face.

298

'Hoping to be Lady Breterton one day, you little whore?'
Duncan came to her side, mopping at a thin trickle of blood.

'What on earth did you do to him?' he asked her wonderingly.

'Nothing. Nothing at all. I'm just something he couldn't have.'

'It has broken his heart, poor devil,' said Duncan.

'No,' she answered, *not* his heart.' She tapped Willy again, and asked kindly, 'Will you be all right, Mr Hyde-Seymour? To drive home? Would you like us to call a taxi?'

He thrust her hand away and went back to his car, slammed the door, and drove away.

Boots touched Duncan's face. 'That needs bathing. You'd better come up.'

There was a purpling bruise and a thin cut above his eyebrow. She bathed it gently with cold water, and put on a plaster. He caught her hand. 'Can I stay, Boots?'

'Yes.' He looked tired, and very young. 'You'd better get into bed. It's cold. I'll light the gas.' She lit the gas fire, and the gas ring, and put on a kettle, saying stiffly over her shoulder, 'Go on, I won't look.'

When he was in bed she put the hot bottle in by his feet, undressed in the dark, and slid in beside him: and his thin muscular arms came out and round her.

'When I said we did not have to get married, I didn't mean I wasn't ever so glad you asked,' she said primly.

He rubbed a long chin into her shoulder. 'We will – one day.' There was a silence. 'I'm not very good at this,' he said, slowly. 'Sex – I've no experience.'

'You mean – you've never done it before?'

'Yes, that's what I mean.'

'Nor me,' she said, then, 'though no one believed it.'

'I did,' he said, 'I always guessed . . . Funny, I was the one person it made no difference to – just so long as we're together. I suppose I just love you.'

'Me, too,' she murmured. His cheek rested on her smooth hair, and in the darkness she gave the faintest little snore. She was asleep. He smiled, and pulled the bedclothes up around her bare shoulders, and lay back on the pillow. Tomorrow was Sunday . . . no need to get back to Oxford until Hall. A long free day – and the rest of their lives to find out everything about each other, particularly love. His arms slackened, and in five minutes he too had fallen asleep within the enclosed and gentle warmth of the narrow bed.

Sir James docked at Southampton on a clear blowy day, very glad to be home. Businesswise the trip had been successful – he had captured two American accounts; one, a tyre company, was to have a large allocation when they began to market in Britain. But he was tired.

The business with Charlotte had been appalling. In New York she had been walking a tightrope of emotional tension, and the separation had been a relief to both of them. He would make a settlement on her. It did not matter to him if she wanted to retain the title. They could arrange a divorce if she wanted it. He would never marry again.

Below on the docks people were waiting to greet passengers. He saw June standing with Willy Hyde-Seymour. She looked sleek as a plump little pussy cat in her dark mink coat and pretty green velvet hat. They were talking earnestly, and then she smiled, put a gloved hand up to Willy's lapel and pulled him down to kiss. Sir James was not surprised, but he was totally unprepared for the stab of possessive jealousy.

They were waiting for him when he cleared customs.

'Daddy,' she said. 'I'm so glad you're back. Welcome home!'

'Glad to see you back, sir,' said Willy.

'Everything all right at the office?'

Sir James grinned inwardly – Hyde-Seymour had always been a bit of a card. Coming up to him in the Strand that day and asking for a job. Well, perhaps it had paid off for all of them.

'Daddy,' said June, 'we've something to tell you.'

'I can guess,' said Sir James. He looked thoughtfully at Willy. 'You're engaged?'

'Look!' June took off her glove and waggled a very presentable diamond. That must have put Hyde-Seymour back a bit. 'You're not cross?' she faltered.

300

He put his arm round her. 'With you, Junie? *Never*. Well, let's get home and talk about it, shall we? You're staying the weekend, Willy?'

It was the first time he had used his Christian name.

'Thank you, sir.'

'And when had you planned to get married?'

'As soon as possible,' June said unguardedly, and blushed crimson. Willy did not meet Sir James's eyes. 'Not a big splash, Daddy,' June added. 'Just us, and at Maidenhead. Not in London.'

'Ah,' said Sir James. 'Whatever my girlie wants.' He pinched her cheek lovingly, delighted when she glowed her gratitude.

He knew where he was now. He had to secure June's future and the future of her baby. He could not guarantee her happiness, but he could guarantee her well-being. And if he kept Willy on a silken rein, it would be a very, very strong one.

On the long smooth run back to Whitelands he listened indulgently while she chatted about Whitelands and the alterations she planned to make, and how nice it would be to live there, because she had always hated Ebor Place and had been miserable there. Of course they would all live together. Occasionally the two men spoke about the business. Plans began to form as, awkwardly, with some reticence, they began to be a family. No one mentioned Charlotte.

Chapter 15

EPILOGUE
In March that year Lord Breterton married Miss Rose
Granger at the Minster at Ayling. The bride wore the Honiton lace. There was a full choral service and a large reception
at Ayling Place, all the family bidden, and all the county.

June Peak and Willy Hyde-Seymour married at Easter, a
quiet wedding in the local church. Willy was taken on to the
Board and as a wedding present was given the Medway
account to handle. Sir James spent more time at Whitelands,
and did not go into the office every day. Charlotte did not
return to England. She divided her time between New York
and a sea-front apartment at Cannes, where she was seen in
the Casino most evenings, accompanied by a variety of good-
looking young men and a white Pekinese.

Matt's divorce came through in the summer and as soon as
the decree was made valid, he and Helen got married at
Hammersmith Register Office, all the family including Lord
and Lady Breterton were there, Rose was visibly pregnant
and her husband hovered about her with protective anxiety.

'Everyone is getting married but us,' said Boots to Duncan.
She was on tour and he was back at Greenstreet, working as
Barry's assistant on the new sound stage under an American
director. They met when they could, which was rarely, so that
every minute together was terribly important to them. They
were learning a great deal about their work and about themselves. Then, Strauss sent for him, asking him to come out to
Hollywood in September as his personal assistant. He
borrowed the fare, bought two new Saville Row suits, and

sailed on a banana boat two weeks later. They all went to Waterloo to see him off, he looked white and young and incredibly elated and he and Boots held hands until the train went out. Cousin Millicent wept beneath her old felt hat, and Mavis said, '*Children!* They take a little bit away from you every time they go away.'

'I'm glad I haven't got any then,' said Boots, 'I need all my spare parts right now.'

That year the unemployment figures began to rise, and there was a general election. Helen voted for the first time at twenty-four, so did Cousin Millicent at sixty-five and Mavis at fifty. Boots was too young, but in any case she was not interested. Moss Hartley had offered her a part in a new musical comedy which he was bringing over from New York in 1930, and second boy in the spectacular pantomime he was producing in Birmingham.

Duncan said he would be home for Christmas. He said everyone in America had gone mad on stock exchange gambling, and that the market rose every day, but money was the one thing Duncan did not gamble with. He also said that all the studios wanted to make musicals. 'They're dragging out every old comic opera from the past fifty years – anything goes so long as it sings and dances.'

At the end of her south-coast tour Boots took a few weeks off before the pantomime rehearsals began. Resting she called it, but she took singing lessons, dancing classes, and worked with May Rampton every day. She also spent time being measured and fitted for her pantomime costumes. She moved into a large flat in an old apartment building in St Martin's Lane right in the heart of theatreland.

'You must come and see it,' she told Helen. 'Three rooms, one as big as a church hall – room for two grand pianos. Opposite the Colosseum.'

When Boots was in London the two girls met nearly every day for lunch, in the marble splendour of the Strand Corner House, meeting among the luscious fruit and flower displays and the elaborate French pastry and confectionery counters on the ground floor. They always went up to the first floor where the orchestra played. It was a sentimental journey – remembering that first year when they had walked arm-in-arm together from Peak's on pay day, to a weekly treat of buttered toast and tea and cream cakes, then off up to the West End to the cinema, half-crown seats, or shopping along Berwick Street with the Jewish shopkeepers trying to lure them inside to see their stock.

They remembered the fun, the dreams and schemes, the frustrations, the poverty, and falling in love. Their lives had changed so much it seemed a lifetime away.

'D'you remember what a luxury it was for us that first barmy year at Peak's? All we could afford.'

'Oh, come off it, Boots,' said Helen, 'you were always being taken to posh places by your hoards of chaps. The Savoy, Ciro's, The Embassy, The Ritz – places the rest of the girls never sniffed at.'

'Yeah, right,' said Boots illogically, 'but I didn't pay, did I? Here we always split the bill – except when Duncan was with us. He's the only man I ever paid a bill for.'

'Aren't you longing to see him again?'

'Aren't we all? D'you think he'll have changed?'

'Yes. We've all changed.'

Boots sat down and drew off her gloves, and regarded Helen gravely. 'You don't change, Nell. Neither does Matt.'

But Helen had changed. Smoothed out. No high tension. Older – beautiful, with some of her mother's serene acceptance of that beauty. Better dressed, casually in grey corduroy velvet and a shawl scarf of fine lacy turquoise wool from *Mavis et Millicent*.

The band finished playing a waltz medley and then the leader looked across at Boots, smiled, bowed, and began to play her song from *My One And Only*. 'Picking Up A Broken Heart'. Boots kissed her hand to him, preening visibly, enjoying her celebrity, the recognition, the turning of heads in her direction, exuding charm and confidence as though she was already on top of the ladder, not tentatively on the first shaky rungs with so much still to learn. She was dressed in cream and tan, a close-fitting cream felt hat trimmed with autumn leaves and a shining mink jacket. No one would have thought that she had spent the whole morning sweating out an exhausting routine for the pantomime.

'In high heels too,' she said. 'My God, have you ever tried a

304

dance routine in high heels?'

'You'll look great in tights,' said Helen, giggling.

'All right Mrs Wilson. How is the firm going?'

'The studio? OK. We just about broke even this year, but we're starting the New Year with more contracts.'

'And how is marriage?'

'Lovely. Like a safe harbour.'

'I don't think I'd like that. I don't think I like things too safe.'

'Well, you've got the right man,' teased Helen, 'with Dunky things will never be safe.'

'I couldn't work in an office again. I like being on the move. I think I'd be bored with marriage.'

'Even to Dunky?'

'If I had to just be a wife. Run a house. Wait for him to come home.' She wore a beautiful new ring on her engagement finger. A huge aquamarine set in diamonds.

'Have you heard from him?'

'Every week. He'll ring tonight. Strauss insisted that the studio put him on contract. He's getting real money.' She wriggled the ring under Helen's nose. 'This came too. With a cable,' she fished a crumpled form out of her bag, and passed it to Helen. It read, *'Just to make everything official. Straight from Tiffany's. I Love You. Duncan.'* Her own hand only boasted a plain gold wedding ring – Matt had not been able to afford an engagement ring yet. First things first.

'He's staying for Christmas and the Breterton christening. Are you coming to Mill Cottage for Christmas?' Helen asked.

'For Christmas and the christening. I had a card – Lord and Lady Breterton request the pleasure of your company at the christening of their son, Alexander Royston, and so on.' Boots giggled, 'I didn't half show off about it. Pinned it to the dressing room mirror when it came. I open with the panto on Boxing Day, so I'll have to leave for Birmingham at the crack of dawn. Duncan will drive me up there. I'm going to book seats for all of you . . . Duncan will go back after New Year, then I'm going to join him.'

'Will you be staying – with him in America?'

'No. I'll go as soon as the panto is finished, and before rehearsals start for the new show. It's West End, Helen!' Her

305

eyes opened wide, scared and excited, 'Do you think I'll make it? Moss thinks so. Madame May thinks so. Duncan thinks so. But I'm not sure. It's not the lead, but it's a good part. I think it's too soon. I don't think I'm smooth enough. That's why I'm going to New York. The original cast is playing there, and I want to see how they do it.'

'Not to see Duncan?'

Boots flushed, 'Of course.'

'But if Duncan wasn't there – you'd still go – to see that show?'

'Yes.'

'You'll have a funny sort of marriage.'

'We're funny sort of people.'

'But doesn't it hurt?' Helen could not understand. She could not bear to be away from Matt.

'Yes – but our life is like that. I wouldn't marry anyone else – neither would he.' She looked so grave that Helen burst out laughing. 'You *are* ridiculous!'

Boots brightened. 'Well, then maybe we will get married – maybe when we're thirty . . . it doesn't make any difference.'

'How long will you be away for?'

'About six weeks. New York first – lots of people he wants me to meet, and then we'll go to Hollywood together before I come back. We'll stay with Strauss and Eleana. They've got a house at a place called Pacific Palisades. Here . . .'

She fished in her handbag and produced a photograph of a white hacienda-type house grown about with creepers, with a swimming pool set in a sunny terrace.

'It's like a clip out of *Picturegoer*, isn't it? Duncan has fixed up for me to have a film test there, so that Strauss has a new record of me if anything turns up. Musicals are all the go – and English girls. It'll be a real test, not like those blinking Green-street ones which Mr Goldman buried. That was a mean thing for Sir James to do. But I suppose he really thought I was no good. I thought so myself then. Funny how things turn out. One afternoon someone suggests you try something, and everything changes like magic. It was a funny old time at Peak's. Everything seemed to happen to us, didn't it?'

'Matt used to call it a cage of butterflies . . . he said it was seething with flappers all trying to get some chap or some job or something. I suppose – cut a slice of life for themselves. Well, we were lucky.'

'*How* lucky!' Boots said. 'You don't ever go there now? To see people? I never do.'

'No. But Matt's there almost every week. On business. He hears all the news. Matt and I ran into the Old Man's daughter,' Helen continued. 'June. You remember – the little dark girl? When we trooped over to Whitelands to tea? She was at the Academy private view when Matt's picture of me was hung. She married Willy Hyde-Seymour about Easter. She was pregnant when I saw her – I read that she has had a baby boy.' It was like hearing about people in a distant land.

'It seems years away. All of it. I seem to be centuries older. But then I never hear anything when I'm touring. Oh my golly!' Boots clapped her hands across her mouth. 'I remember telling her one likely way of catching him would be to get herself pregnant. You *don't* suppose?'

'Well,' Helen began to giggle, 'if she did it seems to have worked out all right.'

'Well, I didn't think she would take me seriously! I mean, for crying out loud, Willy Hyde-Seymour! God's gift to rich old ladies and the flappers' menace!'

'Willy is Managing Director now.'

'Still chasing the girls? W.H.S. I mean?'

'Well, not in the office. Remember Sir James's? No attachments between staff.'

'He didn't stick to it himself,' Boots laughed, remembering. 'Poor old Jim-Jams. It was a funny old time. We seemed to be wasting it. And yet we learned a lot – and you met Matt, and I met Dunky and Madame May. We all found out where we wanted to go.'

'And you and I met,' said Helen. 'Maybe that was the most important meeting of all.'

They were silent, and then Boots looked up and met Helen's eyes, and suddenly the tears rose, and their lips trembled. Boots, who always hid behind mockery, produced an ultra-smart, clipped Noel Coward drawing-room comedy voice, and said, 'One doesn't want to sound too frightfully, sick-makingly sentimental old thing, but if I could have chosen a sister, it would have been you.'

307

They laughed, shakily, realising the value of their friendship. Sisters and friends.

Helen picked up the bill and they had the usual wrangle as to who should pay, then as always split it meticulously, paid and went out into cold winter afternoon. A grey sky threatened rain.

Boots huddled her mink coat round her.

Helen stroked the shining fur.

'It's beautiful,' she said admiringly.

'It'll take me two years to pay for it. Oh, did I tell you my old man died. Dock accident.'

'I'm sorry.'

'Can't say I am. Mum did all the correct weeping at the time but she already looks twenty years younger. I can go and see her whenever I want to. The house looks a treat, and she goes down to see her grandchildren in Portsmouth. You'd have thought she'd had enough of kids.' She was searching the traffic for a free taxi. Over her shoulder, she said abruptly. 'I suppose you'll want to start a family?'

'Yes. As soon as we can. How about you?'

'No – I don't think we want it. There's too much we both want to do, and we want to be the best. Both of us, Duncan too. You can't do everything and do it well.'

'It takes all sorts . . .' Helen mocked.

'Hey, there's a taxi,' Boots put two fingers in her mouth and whistled like an errand boy. 'Can I give you a lift? I'm going up to Wardour Street for some fittings.'

'No, thanks. I'm going back to the office. We're very busy, thank heavens.' They stood smiling. Helen thought that meeting in Peak's reception hall nearly two years ago was probably the most important thing that had ever happened to either of them.

'See you at Christmas,' she said. 'I'll give you a ring. We're driving down the day before.'

'Maybe we'll do the same,' said Boots.

They stood for a moment, hand-in-hand, and then Boots was in her taxi driving up to Wardour Street for a three-hour costume fitting, with her limbs still aching from the morning's dance work-out. She would go home to the new flat, for a bath and a rest, a bowl of soup and a sandwich, and then precisely on time Duncan would telephone, and they would try to get the week's work, gossip, progress, worry and triumphs into ten expensive minutes. At ten the popular leading man she would be playing with next year was taking her out to supper. Moss Hartley said it was good to be seen about. He was not keen about her getting married. Most of her fans, he said, were very young men, who wanted their dream girl single.

Crazy but worth it. She and Duncan were going to be stars one day, and stars had little time to do anything but work, and shine brilliantly for their adorers. But it would be heavenly being together at Mill Cottage for Christmas.

Helen climbed the stairs up to the fourth floor in the old building off Fetter Lane. The staircase walls had been repainted, and the broken wooden stairs covered with linoleum. The firm of Matt & Helen Wilson were still in the big white attic, but after Christmas were taking over the floor below as well, and a typist and another full-time artist. Helen and Matt worked side by side, so she could still look up, as she had done at Peak's and see him in his blue overall, bent over the drawing board.

The portrait of her, with the flowers in her hair and wearing the green dress had attracted a great deal of attention at the Academy, and had brought him several commissions. He was doing more fine art work, making a name with his large and beautiful posters that shone on billboards along the gloomy underground stations. They planned that one day they would do that kind of work, of selling out the firm and going to live at the Wheel House at Ayling in Mavis's garden . . . but that was still a dream.

When she went in his face lit up, and he stretched out his hand, and he drew her to his side.

'Had a nice lunch?'

'Yes,' she began to take off her outdoor clothes, and pull on an overall. 'Yes. Boots was in great form. She'll make a smashing principal boy. She and Dunky are flying high. She's so sophisticated – and so young . . .'

'And you're so old?' he laughed at her.

'Yes. I'm in my twenty-fifth year. Duncan's bought her an engagement ring from Tiffany's as big as the Rock of Gibraltar. Out of his first real money.'

'And you haven't a ring at all . . . would you like one?'

'Oh, Matt, what do I care? What I'm really thinking of is a baby . . .'

'Ah,' he said, and pulled her down into his arms. 'I thought that somehow you were getting round to that . . .'

For the first time the festive season at Ayling Place would really be festive, with the treasured baby heir – a trifle premature according to village gossips – being christened on the 27th December. Mavis brought her pink and white Christmas roses indoors to decorate the Lady Chapel at the Minster especially for the baby who had brought new life to his father, who had a lovely, sensible, simple mother, and who had let Duncan off the hook of inheritance. She hoped the baby would be a sound county fellow, and not a 'sport' off the main Redmaine stem, like Sandy and Duncan, and grow up to take pleasure in the great grey mansion and being born into privileged landed society.

It was Christmas Eve and she was expecting the family before nightfall. She was longing to have them around her again. She was only in her fifties but already knew the anxious hope that they would always come home as a pleasure and not a duty, and never find her a burden or a bore.

One did not, of course, ever speak to them about this. It would be unfair to do so, for it was something that did not occur to the young. But Matt knew, and sometimes smiled at her as though they shared a small sad secret.

She saw him and Helen very often unlike the other two, so deeply involved with each other and their wildly unpredictable lives. Duncan was feeling his power, grasping all the possibilities of his chosen world.

Soon he and Boots would blow into Mill Cottage, bringing with them the laughter, ambitions, gossip, fantasies and the hard discipline of their extraordinary shifting life.

And Helen and Matt? It was curious how much more she worried about Helen and Matt who seemed to have come to safe harbour. Yet a mutual love as intense as theirs was at best a fragile thing. She knew just how easily it could be destroyed. For all their fantasies, there was a steel core in both Boots and

Duncan. They would survive and triumph or die.

'We want some blossom for this one,' Cousin Millicent looked up. 'It's for the christening table at Ayling. There's some winter jasmine out on the south wall . . . I'll go and get some.'

She rose jerkily, leaning on the table to rest her arthritic hip.

'I'll go, you keep your old bones toasted – maybe the children will be here for tea.'

'Old bones indeed,' Millicent said indignantly, but she sat down again quite gratefully. It was fine out-of-doors but bitterly cold.

The December sunset blazed across the western sky and the viaduct was silhouetted blackly against it, marching with Roman precision across the valley. A train whistled, running above the great arches like a toy. She remembered how she used to wait for Sandy to come home long ago, and how she and the two children would take the pony-cart and drive to meet him. Was Mill Cottage really a shrine? A shrine to a real if brief happiness.

Well, she had had what all loving, romantic women long for, the beloved man and his children, the family to cherish, the home to make. Helen and Matt needed children, as she and Sandy had needed them.

But life did not end there. Wars happened, men were killed, children grew up, shared their loves with strangers and went away. Happiness was not 'for ever after'. It gleamed like this stormy winter sky, until it filled the world with light, then slipped away behind dark mysterious clouds. One must never allow the bright patches to slip by unnoticed.

The sound of cars being driven along the main road made the rooks rise in the beech woods. Mavis shaded her eyes expectantly, and sure enough a dashing white sports car turned into the gate – begged or borrowed, emanating show business, followed more sedately by Matt's sober Humber. Duncan, of course, showing off, dashing cap, dark glasses, wildly waving gauntlet glove. Boots with a green hat, red lipstick and the tip of her pert and perfect nose practically engulfed in fox fur.

Mavis began to laugh as she went forward and Cousin

Millicent, forgetting her rheumatism, came out of the house, her wild hair covered with glitter powder and her cardigan stuck about with twigs and holly leaves, and then they were all kissing and hugging and asking questions without waiting for the answers and trooping into the warm welcoming house, a family, a clan, close for the brief and ancient season.

The brilliant winter light illuminated every window pane. Too soon it would be Twelfth Night and the house would be quiet again, and she and Millicent would take down the garlands and Christmas would be over for another year.